END OF
THE LEGEND

ABISH KEKILBAEV

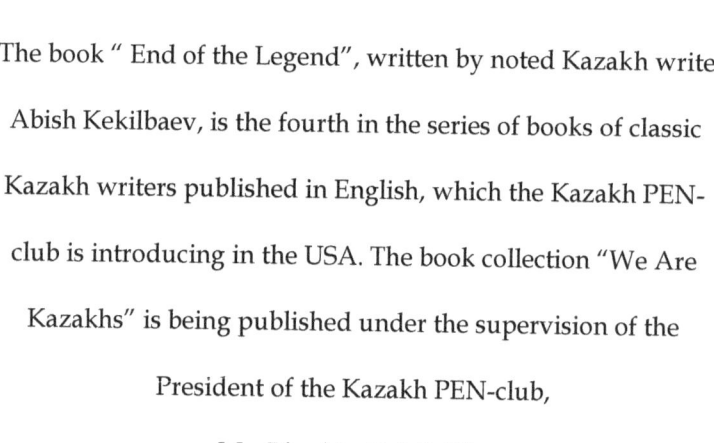

The book " End of the Legend", written by noted Kazakh writer
Abish Kekilbaev, is the fourth in the series of books of classic
Kazakh writers published in English, which the Kazakh PEN-
club is introducing in the USA. The book collection "We Are
Kazakhs" is being published under the supervision of the
President of the Kazakh PEN-club,

Mr. Bigeldy Gabdullin

END OF
THE LEGEND

ABISH KEKILBAEV

Translated from Russian by

Marina Vladi Kartseva and I. K.

KAZAKH PEN-CLUB
КАЗАҚ ПЕН-КЛУБЫ

"We are Kazakhs"

Classic Books of Kazakh writers in English

© 2016, Metropolitan Classics

135 Ocean Pkwy, Suite 1U

Brooklyn, New York 11612

End of the Legend •Abish Kekilbaev

ACKNOWLEDGEMENTS

The Publishers want to thank the Kazakh PEN-club for their permanent support and attention in this project. Initially, it was but an ambitious idea of the Kazakh PEN-club President Mr. Gabdullin, creating an environment for the best works of classic Kazakh writers to be exposed to the global literary stage, by way of their translation into the English language. Step by step, due to the tireless efforts of Mr. Gabdullin, the project received the financial and logistical support needed from influential Kazakh state organizations and private companies. The translation of this book was possible due to the generous support of the Akimat (Government) of Almaty region of Kazakhstan and The Trust for Support of Cultural Projects Samruk Kazyna.

End of the Legend •Abish Kekilbaev

Yesterday is merely fleeting, evanescence.

For when Today tires, it is transfigured into Yesterday.

CRIMSON APPLE

1

The countless swirls of the depressions in the sand, imprinted by the hooves of the cavalry marching amid the dunes, wind-swept in an instant, smoothed over by showers of cascading sands. The lead brigade of the Guard, each mounted on lean, beige-black galloping steeds – forged ahead on the steep, precipitous dunes - spanning the length of arrow's arc. The grand, greying desert – indifferent to everything, transpiring in the dust and frailty of being, swiftly brushed from her deathly-ashen mask, even the slightest trace of pettiness that may have disturbed her unyielding, everlasting countenance.

From the very inception of the conquering of the Great Sands, the Lord has attempted to safeguard the serenity of his soul from the malevolent alienation of the desert, though try as he may, he could not rid himself of the ever-present sensation of her intent and probing gaze. Seated, he intermittently swayed in his regal, shimmering gilded Khan's carriage, sullenly straining his attention to the sounds drifting in from outside - the movement of the cavalry, the neighing and snorting of the horses, tortured by the sweltering heat and the dust of the desert. Barely succeeding in traversing the trail, the horses continued slipping on the steep slopes, sinking up to their fetlocks in the powdery sands, attempting to overcome the sabulous swells, as though they were swimming through the ocean's elements. Sometimes, the Lord, unable to contain himself, would abruptly tug the netted curtain to the side – seeing the very same dusty, distressing, unsightly path that he knew was to be the only outcome for his mounted troops, exhausted by the desert.

And yet, it was early springtime. But, in the waterless desert, where snow makes no appearance in the wintertime, spring painted quite a disheartening picture. The *saxaul* and *zhuzgen* thickets, still untouched by the life-bearing coating of greenery, stood pallid, lifeless. It was as though the rolling, rippling dunes had chilled everything solid over the winter – showing no signs of retreat, overwhelmed by this weighty stupor, too exhausted and powerless to liven up, to wake and rise to greet the light, spring warmth and life. For five days, the tireless sandy hurricane raged on, dubbed in these parts - the "turtle's storm". Just recently, a storm had torn through the desert, scorching everything upon it - like the breath of a furnace – red, singed by the blaze. It was as if some unknown monstrosity's force had collapsed upon the earth, shaking off, unloading all that was existent within her, into one gigantic crucible, for it to then be purified by the searing winds, and launched up towards the sky, the remnant ashes and dust. And the cavalrymen – the warriors of this vast and endless mounted army, in which one rider could barely discern the form of the other beside him, and with the determination and drive of those destined for doom – they marched, pressing forth, to come upon this blistering tempest, and finally – converge with the blazing fury – face-to-face, chest-to-chest. It was as if the existent world had been lifted up on racks, and the harbinger of impending doom, the sky and earth, commingled in the fatal dust and ashes. Amidst the infernal wail and whistle, the horses and men – muted, the dust – the whirl-winds of this hellish sandstorm swept the land, as if in a mad and savage folly. It was inconceivable that this startled world could somehow regain any semblance of tranquility. His fate was all but one – disperse and distract himself in the ensuing, universal chaos. The vicious wind shakes and rattles the journey-tried, veteran Khan's carriage, swaying her, as though preparing to rip her from her earthen foundation and propel her skyward into the furthest reaches of the raging blizzard, this abyss of gloom. The horses, drained of strength, the people – blinded by the dust, barely survived the winds. And yet, perceiving this in its entirety, the unwavering Lord made no attempts to halt the procession of the cavalry, already under way. For there was not much sense to stopping for rest amidst the denuded desert, which provided no shelter from the raging, dusty storm.

Quite the contrary – upon halting, the wind would be capable of sweeping off the dunes, with loose and crumbling sands, the wagons, all brimming with bales. Or possibly, engulf with the sands, the weakened men, the animals – as had occurred in incidents past, on more than one occasion – a suitably horrifying disaster, resulting in entire caravans vanishing under the gargantuan dunes, without so much as a trace.

This situation was the first in his experience, in which the Master had commenced the journey while in the season of the "Turtle's Storm", coupled with the arrival of the frosts of fall. This time, he had decided upon returning to his native lands in time for the approaching spring season, and his will would not be tested by any imaginable obstacle.

He did not tolerate any form of insolence, and at the very first hint of disagreement with his wishes, he proved unfaltering, wildly gnashing his teeth. Even to the elements of the sand-fueled storms, raging but once a year, in springtime, the Master was unable to yield – quite the opposite: his power and strength were capable of overturning the entire world, and were greater in might than the desert's storms.

And he was flooded with a heavy, churning fury, upon having observed the unbridled self-will of the elements, which could not be sliced by sable, nor pierced by spear. The Lord remained harsh and unapproachable, paying no mind to his generals, who would appear before the Khan's carriage – visibly distressed, with pleading looks upon their faces. It seemed as though he neither saw, nor heard the surrounding deathly wind-dance of the billowing storm, in its horrendous entirety.

After five days of the terrifying storm, which in these parts, since the olden days, has been called "Beskonak", in memory of the five fallen journeymen, an abrupt, utter calm pervaded the air. It was like a shaman-*bahsi* after a frantic trance state – when all of the djinn finally release his body, nature immersed herself into a meek quietude. The parched land, from which the sands were blown, revealed her features: the bottomless fissures and fractures, a pitted, unforgiving landscape. Seemingly, from out of these crevices, emerged an infinitely long bale of turtles – and many of them, having been flipped over by the winds, lay there, sprawled on their backs, helplessly jerking their small dark, crooked, leathery limbs…

That very day, when the storm had subsided, the army arrived at the massive dunes. The men's eyes were met with staggeringly tall swells of sand-dunes, with toppled edges, and they appeared almost like the unearthed remnants of monstrous lizard-giants. Now, the troops were moving, occasionally slowed by their sinking into the ashen sands, fighting their way through the dunes. And if yesterday people had still not known, how to save themselves from the blazing, deafening tempestuous winds, then today they were weighed down by the blind silence and stillness of the desert. And underneath it all, fearing the thought, that the desert could turn even you into that very same silent nonexistence – lacking in movement or time, that whispers of native lips, without the rustling of foliage – the human heart cringes from the sheer distress of it, squeezing itself into a dense fist-sized, little ball of trembling, terrified flesh.

Desperately striving to crawl out from the lifeless, deadly quick sands onto living, earthen solidity, the cavalry prevailed over the crumbling mounds, those toppling sand-dunes that lay before them. Restless and hopeful, the troops would peer into the distance – but ahead, however hard one may have looked, stretched out only the furrowed, sand-laden wrinkles of the desert.

The granuled drafts had painted, imprinted upon the sands exquisite messages in a mysterious, zephyrous tongue - prophesying or invoking, yet for no one to decipher its hidden portents, however laboriously the inquisitive mind of a wise sage may try. As though that which could be uncovered in these unreadable communiqués would divulge the entirety of that truth, everything we call life – that very same incomprehensible oracle in a nonsensical tongue, written today by the wanderer-wind in the restless, sabulous pages of the book that is the desert. And tomorrow, that very same wind will smooth them over with an even dusting of sand. In exactly the same way, yesterday's tempest, omnipotently raging throughout the whole world of the sands – today, having transformed into a deathly silence within an hour, departed into the non-existence of oblivion. And thus, these quick sands, whose name – Ephemera, erase everything that had accompanied this transitory human commotion.

For four consecutive years, the Lord had led these military expeditions. Many lands had been imprinted by the hooves of a hundred thousand battle-ready steeds. Is it really possible that these traces of martial accomplishments, these incredible feats, will not be noted by the sands on the wind of the desert? Then what will remain for others – the ones who had not arrived here, for ages away from the mortal living, even if his memory, straining to remember all that is both minute and majestic – that he had brought into existence – something crumbling, and fleeting, as well, – like the sands of the wind-swept dunes? It turns out, that betwixt the soaring skies and the endless earth there is absolutely nothing for man, aside from his own painful, pitiful, purposeless existence. And this means, that here, on earth, everything for man is transient, of perpetual impermanence.

And so it is, without a doubt. In his past, he had been forced to overcome many trials and tribulations, many degradations, humiliations. And in these very sands, he himself wandered – a fugitive, his wife beside him, and his child in his arms. And what of it? Are they not these very same ashen sands, presently perceived through the window of his luxuriant, gilded Khan's wagon – which had suffocated him to death, scorching his heels? Was it not here, that those horrifying days, where he – with his lips cracking and splitting from thirst, his throat beyond parched, that he tossed about in search of some kind of brush, to shelter himself with, madly clawing at the sands with his fingers, until it could supply even the smallest drop of moisture? Back then, it had seemed to him that he would never escape from this desert-prison, and never again know the taste of plain, cold water. But who on this earth could possibly know this, besides him? Even his memory, as seldom as ever, grants him access to those days, and he remembers those daring days as if purely by chance, always – for some reason, in those distinct minutes of the soul's dis-ease and hopeless melancholy... Past humiliations erased by today's magnificence, former suffering left behind by the ultimate prosperity of today. But will every present day really be forgotten, as were those days of the past? Then why do people, in this state of sheer madness, grab and clutch at the days of tomorrow? What is it, really – this Tomorrow? This invisible destroyer, a ghostly angel of death with adamantine sword in hand, slaying everyone in his path with his treacherous impermanence? If Tomorrow – the sword of the angel of death seeks retribution – then why do we need Today – with the sword hanging overhead?

Where does the grandness lie, and where is the deathlessness of Today, if even he is to be met with weariness, doom and death's state of disrepair? Where is that valiant foe – who yesterday fought against me with the courage of a lion – could it really be this sweltering skull, these very same eyes upon which heaped the endless sands, who slashed him down to earth – could it really be my own lawless sword? No, for before my sword had had the chance, his life had been taken by the pathetic feebleness of his own puny destiny. For this reason, Tomorrow died of his own strength, spent. And this is why Today, weakest at the very end, had re-formed into Tomorrow. But, there does exist strength which recognizes not the power over it, which has the capability to triumph over Today and Yesterday and the unseen treachery of Tomorrow. The name of this power – Eternity... Though to make a deal with Eternity, requires relentless and unbridled strength. For Death will take the weak today, decides the average man's fate tomorrow - but only the one who truly possesses unbridled strength, and serves nothing and no one, will triumph over immortality, and attain – Eternity.

Today – is the prison that stands between fear and hope. Today – and only Today – the singular destiny of that majority that must abide ordinary mortality – whose wretched, pathetic existence can be likened to traversing the seas of life in merely a frail, tiny boat – ready to tip over at any given moment. And only in this despicable condition of fear are they able to obey, giving in to the will of the mighty, to bring about some kind of good. For without this firm grip, bearing its talons, this entire motley assortment would not be capable of triumphing over any matter. Indeed, without the iron will of the mighty, grabbing in one hand – horror, and the other – hope, seizing the weak and beat out of the myriads of the wretched – that strength and might. In this way, of those enslaved by Today – a Weapon is fashioned, one capable of conquering this treacherous Tomorrow.

Within his generals, he uncompromisingly instills: "No matter what kind of misfortune might befall thee, never say, that you have come to a dead-end, with no way out. One must always have many techniques and cunning strategies, to outmaneuver any type of trap."

What is written in the holy book?

One day, arriving at the abode of a wise-man Sulaiman, a certain ant arrived, who asked: "Can you foresee, oh mighty king, why the all-virtuous Creator had given you even the power to command the wind?" Startled by this unforeseen query, the Sulaiman was flustered, and could produce no response. "With this, the Creator has given you a hint, that one day – you and your entire kingdom will cease to exist - crumbling to dust, to be scattered in the winds." The Sulaiman, clearly distressed by this, had now changed his expression. "This is what they mean, majesty, when they say: via the lips of the worthless and pitiful, Allah preaches the truth to the mighty," – and, having uttered this, the ant scuttled off on his way. And if joy were to leave the very Sulaiman, what would the rest of the people have to hope for? Despite this, having spent his happiness, his life, the Sulaiman had certainly not spent his glory. So, should we not deduce from this, that happiness - with the destiny of your days on this earth being brief, much like glory – is the property of that boundless Eternity?

So, who was it that delivered, to this very day, the antiquated glory of the Sulaiman, if not for those very same *dekhan*, those age-old laborers, those busy-body ants? Then, unbelievably, the more insignificant that nameless, endless, tribe of heralds of Allah may be, the louder and more fastidiously they carry the praise and glory of the mighty in this world of ours. These running messengers, on whose backs this glory sails – are man's utterances. And while cautiously on the lips of the wise, with whom the truth has only yet begun to prepare to mount the saddle, the shrieking exclamations on the lips of this hasty chatterbox are already skipping along hills and valleys, his coat-tails swinging left and right, each time arriving everywhere, always having to be first.

This frantic chatterbox will gladly, readily involve himself in festivities of inflated meaninglessness. He'll sit in the seat of honor, occupying it of his own accord, of course, and will be guaranteed to be the first in line to devour the most delectable foodstuffs available, the fattest little morsels served at the *dastarkhan*.

To amaze and catch the eye of a lesser person can be accomplished by many means. Awe-struck, such a person is quite incapable of discerning that which is noble from that which is foolish. For example, along the road, strolls what is unmistakably an elephant, compressing the earth with his portly trunk-like legs, while transporting on his back cargo of gold and other precious items from the treasure reserves of various wealthy countries. The beady, little eyes of this little critter, seeing the elephant first, lack the discernment to identify whether this animal in front of them is indeed good, or bad, and also – what to expect of it – harm or benefit? And faced with this massive, almost mountainous creature, with this absurdly elongated makeshift snout-nose, slithering about all snake-like, the Philistine experiences neither fear, nor disgust – and only gawks in amazement with his beady, little eyes, while clicking his tongue in further emphasis.

The beady little eyes, wait, expectantly, for you – the Lord, to produce nothing short of a mammoth, elephant-like, deed, so that he – insignificant little person that he is, could in his dumbfounded state – ogle, and yet, somehow, it is of no relevance to him whatsoever – be you benevolent, or the contrary. Besides, your measly little crumbs will not bring satisfaction to these inhabitants, but, if, in their little eyes, you end up committing even the most trivial, trifling offense – oh, well then! How they will set about exploiting and abusing you, until there is absolutely nothing left of you at all. Lest you give someone a bloody nose, oh – they will do nothing short of bombard every accessible part of you with endless accusations of every crime that has ever been known to man, but – if you happen to drown half of man-kind in a sea

of blood – they will express no semblance of judgment, rather an over-arching sense of astonishment, which will lead them to inquire –
"And… how is it, that he accomplished this?"

And so, whilst you live and reign on – make sure to astonish all those, who surround you. Horrify and amaze, so that their eyes may crawl up to their hair-lines – and then – those who had been unceasingly astonished throughout the duration of your lifetime, will never fail to be amazed by your deeds, even long after your death. It is essential to leave behind demonstrations of your might and glory, and then – for every instance your name is mentioned, those discussing you will go about vigorously nodding their heads and uttering emphatically – "Oh…and how we remember him! That was exactly how it had been."

For this does not come easy to every Ruler, but – you have risen to the very top of might and power, having bent to your will and solemnly trodden on all of the neighboring lords, with all of their myriad treasures, having pulled together every single one of the banners of the military world. Just remain in power, don't grow weary ahead of time… And never cease, don't you dare pause for the sake of enjoying your accomplishments! Do not risk showing any sign of weakness, not even once – or prepare for this chaotic, misleading, deceitful world to turn its back on you – like a helpless wandering grandmother – always willing to betray you for someone stronger, more lucky, and exceedingly more experienced than you…

Was it not you yourself who has accomplished your present glory, having picked apart the weaknesses of all of your foes, ruthlessly slamming them down with all of your might? And so, you must never permit anyone to uncover your weaknesses. Let them only be known of by the Almighty, for it could not be for the simple, unassuming mortals to ever uncover.

But what if the Almighty should ever decide to collect his due penalties for all of this... Then, what would this be? Lately, in the course of his return trips from battle, he had never allowed himself to entertain such thoughts – terrifying, somber, heavy thoughts. All according thoughts were securely safeguarded in his deepest, innermost hiding-spots of his heart – it was as though all of these worthless things were the treasures in his chest, under no circumstances subject to inspection, so as no one may discover them, or be given an opportunity to prey upon them. He kept all of these merciless, treasured thoughts distant – even from himself, away from his unwise emotions, and his ruthless reason. He made do with what he knew, keeping these treasured thoughts always within him, but buried deeply in an impenetrable place…So then why is it that specifically today, his heart had decided upon drowning itself in its own blood? Why is it that he – like an aging, mangy camel, rejected by his herd – is suddenly choked up by this hiccup of his oppressive, sticky nearly forgotten past, if it is not something he now has to chew? Why has he chosen to stir up this fossil, this stale, hoary veteran – though fear-pressed by death, the unfathomable – remains somberly safeguarded, thoughts long ago visited, and revisited – resting in their cabinets neatly – categorized, labeled, filed away…even weighed, down to the very last grain? And if one does possess such an accursed, enigmatic secret, then make sure to maintain her, like the Sword of Damascus, do not swing it about aimlessly, otherwise it may slip from your grasp, thus becoming your enemy's plunder – and then, accordingly, will be the very same weapon to lop off your head.

He would not allow himself to alter his own decisions – better to measure it forty times rather than simply proceeding. The present condition of his soul, on this very day, was unpleasant – and troubled him greatly. In present expeditions, however grueling and punishing they may have been, he had never experienced such inner turmoil. Or perhaps, the reason behind all of this – the Beskonak, this fierce dust-storm, flying in at exactly mid-season, right on the brink of winter's expiration and the torturous birth of splendid spring? And yet, there are no reasons for this disturbance – for the four year-long expedition had seen its fair share of conquests and triumphs, more than a few lands subdued, several thrones overthrown, subjected to their rule…He had conquered two longstanding, bitter rivals, who due to the remote distances of their territory's borders, quite openly and brazenly declared their recalcitrance to his rule. In having subdued them, he simultaneously aligned with his own mighty rule several other minor kingdoms.

In the past, when the overturned foreign crowns would roll at his feet, the Lord would experience a tremendous elevation of emotions, and in his own eyes, as in a fairytale – fantastically, he would shoot up sky-ward, soaring above the whole world. And yet now, he had already forfeited these feelings, so that nothing could trouble him. Or perhaps, he had not detected it – inconspicuously, stealthily – sneaking up on him – old age, that insurmountable creature – which cannot be deceived by even the most cunning of military maneuvers, or conquered by the most formidable of armies? Old age lets loose her ferocious dogs, savagely salivating, and sics them on you – she does not position herself in front of you, like an adversary's castle, which can be wrathfully taken by storm, or seized – no. She simply pitches the invisible tents of her blockade under you very nose, and you, all the while, still refuse to abandon your dedicated attempts to storm her - launches her very own squadron of warriors, already condemned. She grips and seizes your castle gradually, silently, taking her sweet time, and with the indestructible persistence of your other ant-foe, shreds your confidence, satisfied, watching it turn to dust, as she picks your composure to bits.

At present, she readily informs - that future expeditions (in the course of which he had disappeared sometimes for years on end), are now rendered exceedingly more difficult for him.

Upon clearly having revealed this thought to himself – he suddenly felt it pierce his very heart, like a penetrating, icy spear.

And yet, from the very start, as soon as he had ascended to the throne, he had opted to dedicate his life not to this gold throne, but to spend it in the warrior's saddle – conquering and vanquishing his long-standing foes.

And until this very day, that was precisely how it had come to pass. Many lands he has conquered. All of the lands surrounding the Khan's massive expanse had been dominated, brought under his rule. Only one majestic Eastern empire would evade his rule. Relying on its vast numbers, comparable only to that of the swarming ant-colony, this land fails to fear him – the conqueror of half of the world, refusing to submit to his rule, unlike all of the others.

Today, the magnificent army, known to have struck terror and panic in the hearts of many an adversary, find themselves precisely at the zenith of their combat-readiness, strength and glory. And his last thought as Lord is – to march east, while the troops still retain their tremendous, tirelessly accumulated, extensive combat force. All he requires is but a two-month breather, and then – time to strike.

Realizing that he must preserve the order and well-being of his recently conquered lands, the Lord had given the order to entirely, and without any exception, annihilate the local forces. This way, there will be no need to retain his power by means of force, bearing in mind the further possibility of having to suppress any potential uprisings.

End of the Legend •Abish Kekilbaev

In the process of investigating his own forces, the Lord had made the decision to replenish their numbers by employing mercenaries from his recent territorial acquisitions. And so the troops were not to be diminished in numbers, but on the contrary – rapidly growing. Thousands upon thousands of stallions progressed, toppling the massive dunes with their hooves, thousands upon thousands of steel blades shining in the sun's scorching rays, thousands of warriors – both mounted and on foot, an endless dark mass pouring through the dunes. Observing this infinite swell of forces, one might think that this battle-ready mob was not on their return journey, but instead – just commencing their expedition. The troops seemed fresh-faced and lively, as though they had just been enveloped in a woman's embrace. The warriors' banners and crescents of personal prowess on the blades of the centurions who had distinguished themselves in battle, flapped proudly, dancing in the intermittent gusts of wind.

One could easily have deduced that this mass of fighters was returning from a successful mission by observing the densely loaded caravans, stuffed with plunder, and largely in part due to high number of shackled slaves and numerous prisoners of war.

The Lord had intended to arrive in his capitol city, with the entirety of his forces – incalculable, like a swarm of mosquitoes. Let the people see with their own eyes the glory of their Lord, to whom heads bowed down – by all of the citizens of the lands spanning the three corners of the earth. May the hearts of these people be gripped with fear in the face of his might, and then – be filled with pride of their involvement with such a formidable force and monumental glory…

Suddenly he saw, near the hazy, distorted horizon, above the pale outline of the sandy desert, a slender, ghostly pole appear – its sharp, defined outline piercing the cerulean spring skies. It was perfectly straight and slim, bluer than the skies themselves, an unbelievably tall, needle-like pole – something never before seen in his lands. At first, the Lord assumed that this was an apparition, a divinely inspired mirage – sent from above as a sign and portent of something, and his initial instinct was to send out one of his scouts, who might be able to figure out the meaning behind this apparition. Despite this, due largely to the fact that, as time ticked by, and as they drew closer and closer to the city, the blue pole suspended above the strip of white sand become exceedingly more pronounced, darkened and appeared much more tangible – the Lord decided to hold off on this urge for a bit.

The desert, with its gargantuan, looming sand dunes, was finally behind them, and were now being replaced with the small sandy rings of the yellow sand mounds. As the troops forged on, they were gradually met with rows of dunes, lightly blanketed by brush – at first – sparse and fragile in appearance, and further on, as the closed in on the city, it appeared progressively denser, more abundant – eventually clumping up into entire little separate islands of greenery.

Once the sandy ridges of the dunes were left behind them entirely, an immense vista opened up in front of them, and the sky seemed to ascend – the earth unraveled and stretched out before them, and even the landscape seemed to reach as far as the eye could see.

In addition to the newly unfolded skyline, which – almost cat-like, pounced back to the faraway mountains, the azure pole somehow appeared much further away now, even more enigmatic and alien than before.

Circumventing the impenetrable brush of zhuzgen, saxaul, and sagebrush – the Khan's numerous hordes climbed out onto the sloped soil mounds. Having finally surpassed these, the lead unit finally clambered out onto dark, level earth. Far beyond the outskirts of the city, in a washed-out, monochrome haze, loomed the tooth-like, jagged protrusions of distant mountains.

And not too far from there, it became possible to distinguish, up ahead in the expansive basin, which practically kissed the mountains, the numerous shadowy, opaque little boxes of the city's dwellings – both large and small. The azure pole, which was in reality a pale blue tower, surveyed the whole city from up above, alienated in its solitude, enveloped by the gentle, foggy haze of the cloud that had surrounded it.

And at this very moment, in the midst of a blue-green backdrop, sprawled out a multi-colored kaleidoscopic spectacle of the Great City of steel, opening its hospitable arms to the dust-covered troops, bestowing an air of festivity to the atmosphere with its majestic spires and minarets, practically gliding along the currents of the scorching, molten air. And in the very center of this soldier-welcoming city, that sky-blue linear structure, resembling a pole, had in fact turned out to be an astonishingly beautiful new tower. With its almost feminine silhouette, adorned with a pale blue finish, slender and indescribably tender façade, the tower evoked the image of a young, beautiful maiden, clothed in a pale blue silk gown pining for her beloved, who had set out upon his chosen path, to harsh and unforgiving martial toils – and finally, upon his return – she greets him, running towards him, cheerfully waving her hands. The more closely she drew near, the more vividly the colors of the tower would spill over and intermingle in the bright and playful rays of sunlight.

Once the brigade of troops finally lurched over the final mound of the desert, descending into the hospitable valley below, every bit of her earth was flooded with generous life-giving sunlight. The entire area surrounding the city was darkened by swarms of people working in the fields. The whole fertile valley was overtaken by the toils of springtime harvesting, blackened interchanging rows of freshly hand-tilled and ploughed earth. Many were plowing – some were handling horses, and those peasants who were handling the oxen, were busy stripping and chopping up the top layer of soil, hardened by the winter, the earth's bare back, which had been salted by floods created by the dissolving snows. With the joie de vivre of their springtime toils, the people earnestly celebrated the return of their triumphant battalion.

The archers lead the way, their taught bow-strings tucked into their quivers; behind them, lance-bearers and spearmen, walked with their pointed weapons glistening, looking as though they were menacing the very sky itself. Even further behind them, trudging along in a long, disorganized mass, was the caravan of slaves and prisoners of war, shackled in iron chains. Closing in on the caravan of slaves were the captive young women and girls, who had been grabbed from various tribes and peoples.

Only at the very end of the troops' caravan, tightly surrounded by a horde of personal guards consisting of ten thousand mounted *nukers*, trailed by the thundering war-melodies emanating in all directions, the magnificent, luxurious marquee of the Khan's carriage slowly drifting in on enormous wheels.

Making sure to maintain proper formation, both the left and right wings, the hand-picked units numbering well into the thousands, marched behind the lead centurions which comprised the Khan's bodyguards. And, in addition to the hundreds of henchmen encircling the Khan, was the Khan's cavalry, which, maintaining its perfect square formation, marched right up to the main city gates.

Surrounding the main road, were fields that stretched out on both sides, prepared for the cultivation of watermelon and cotton; the smooth hills extending upwards were blanketed by vineyards and fruit-bearing gardens behind fences fashioned out of clay. The fruit trees' had just begun to unfurl their blossoms, which adorned the whole valley in a delicate white-pink netting. Sprawled out underneath this canopy of fruit trees, were the long, narrow streets of the outskirts of the city; houses and little shacks, cordoned off by intricately hand-molded quaint clay fencing. Further still, on the wide streets of the city center, on either side, crammed tightly together, were small shops containing Chinese silks, various goods made of gold and silver from the farthest reaches of the globe, fanciful items, embroideries, leather and wool, little shops filled with small trinkets and all sorts of cheap knick-knacks. Wide counters, lined with numerous foodstuffs, heaping mounds of raisins and dried apricots, grills that expelled plumes of smoke as they prepared kebabs on saxaul branches, pans that fried *samsi* as they sizzled and popped in scalding butter, pots steaming with enticingly aromatic pilaf.

The blossoming billows of the gardens unexpectedly ended, and yet encounters with larger groups of city people became a more frequent occurrence, as well as the intricate, quaint clay fences, molded side-by-side, as though battling one another, perfected in their extraordinarily precise curvature.

Once the lead centurion had by-passed the gate and penetrated the city, like a clear current of small brook that splashes into the murky waters of a lake – from a tall burial mound right in the heart of the city, from the Khan's palace, surrounded by deep, water-filled moat – sounded the drawn-out, reverberating blast of the *karnay*. And at once, in response to this signal, all of the karnay-bearing men blasted their horns, at which point all of the drummers, carrying a *dauilpaz* and belonging to the main corps, who had been individually awarded Turkish crescents mounted on long spears, proceeded to pound on their drums, in recognition of their impeccable victory... The booming rumble of the hooves of thousands of horses upon the beaten, hardened earthen road, combined with the deafening roar of battle-music and the pounding of drums caused the ground to hum and shake violently. The domes that crowned each mosque, and the towers atop each minaret, towered over the city, giving the impression of battle-ready *argamaks* raised up on their hind legs, ready to heave themselves into battle in the midst of this barbaric, rhythmic resonance.

Stunned by this invisible, yet exceedingly palpable manifestation of might, the townsfolk gazed upon this spectacle – horrified, eyes widening at the sight of the rigid, glistening spears of

End of the Legend •Abish Kekilbaev

the foot soldiers, the menacing mounted cavalrymen; they watched from the tops of the *duvals*, from their windows and open doors, through all of the cracks and cavities – at this indescribable parade of the Lord's military force.

Yet something else had transfixed his attention entirely – the shining blue minaret – which, proudly and provocatively, raised its majestic dome to greet the bottomless skies.

2

Upon returning from his latest expedition, victorious, the Lord had decided to mark the occasion with festivities, for an entire two months. Once the feasting was finally over, the spacious town square was emptied. The townspeople returned to their daily routines, having relished in the prolonged and carefree revelry, feeling satisfied – with their bellies stuffed, feeling fully rested.

The Lord seemed to be the only one who remained bound by the clutches of exhaustion. The very next day, following the festivities, he moved into his isolated castle, located right outside of town, atop a hill, enclosed on all sides by dense gardens that provided a haven of shade, allowing temperatures to remain cool. In terms of luxury and extravagance, this particular palace of the Khan was in no way inferior to his other residences, but it was only here that he refused to hold any official meetings or receive any visitors. The garden that colonized the mound, had become quite overgrown – wild, almost – for the gardener was not permitted to concern himself with it – and so it grew and grew, reaching, wrapping, unfurling – like in all of the surrounding forests, freely and as nature intended. The peacocks, roe deer, and pheasants dwelling within its lush foliage – and were themselves wild, immediately scattering upon the arrival of any human.

It was in this palace that he would forget about all of his official obligations, instead of sitting on his throne – glowering, unapproachable. It was here that he enjoyed his isolation, and was peaceful, loving more than anything to stroll about in his enormous garden, in solitude, which he reached by crossing the drawbridge which towered over a moat filled with water, surrounding the entire castle. And not a single person was near - no attendants, no one to accompany him. The Lord could spend whole days by himself, wandering about the garden – a place where the guards would permit only immediate family members of the Khan entrance, and only with the Khan's approval at that. Occasionally, he would grab one of his grandsons, with whom he would spend the entire day in the garden, and come evening time, he would sit them in a coach, and would send them back to the residence of his *Baybishe*, his eldest wife.

Today, he decided against calling upon his grandsons. Baybishe had asked the Khan, through one of the castle guards, to permit her entrance to discuss one matter with him, but the Lord would not receive her, postponing the conversation until another, indeterminate, time. The lengthy, multiple year-long expeditions followed by the two month *toy* upon returning had worn him down, and weary now, he had no desire to see anyone else.

He had the urge to ball himself up in a secluded corner of the garden, a small spring erupted from in between the boulders, pouring out the most pristine, virgin waters in the form of a chattering brook. And it was only here, right by this brook, whose days spanned more than a millennia – that he no longer felt himself a Khan, nor a Lord. His orders were nothing to this spring – so cheerful, transparent; nothing to the roosters – merrily flitting about, chirping, nor to the broad-eyed dragonflies, who captivatingly twirled about, performing perfect aerial pirouettes above the pristine, reflective waters.

When he would depart for the spring, the guards that were stationed along the entire perimeter of the garden, would swiftly disperse, like mice, without so much as a sound. It was entirely unacceptable for a single guard or servant of the palace to make themselves visible to him.

Long hours he would spend in the company of his maiden spring. It was precisely here, that the Lord, in solitude, untroubled, was able to harness within himself enough spiritual strength and resolve for their next extensive expedition. It was precisely here, in this heavenly meadow, beside the spring, influenced by the spellbindingly sweet melody of the babbling brook, that the fates of many royal personages and allied families of nobility were decided. Each time he reached this place, he felt a surge of renewed strength and additional thoughts, as though they had been birthed in the very depths of the spring itself, and carried up with the crisp transparent, swirling waters. The flow of water would always originate but from one particular, modestly-sized stream

– unlike his thoughts, which were scattered in every which way. And so today – the Lord had wanted to think over the structure of his grand, newly-formed general's proposition, but instead, for some reason entirely unbeknownst to him, strange thoughts about some preposterous red apple kept infiltrating his mind. This invasive crimson apple at first glance appeared flawless, but upon closer inspection, the Lord had remembered noting a slight incision on one of its sides during his mealtime the day prior. This tiny nick, which was inflicted upon this fruit out of nowhere, roused a certain degree of suspicion within him, so he had decided not touch it. But today, yet again, the servant girl carried out the very same apple on a golden tray.

As though the Khan's majestic gardens weren't replete with plenty of other wondrous fruits, so why was this particular apple, with the incision on its side, served to him a second time, amongst other fruits? He proceeded to break it in two, and discovered within it a writhing worm. "No, I shall not show any emotion to my servants" – the Lord thought, decidedly. "I will pretend that I did not notice a thing." He then placed the two halves of the apple back onto the tray.

The servant girl removed the tray and the Khan, quite irritated with this internal disorder, nevertheless held back, trying to contain himself from any outbursts brought on by his sudden internal raging upsurge. He pretended to forgive the servant's negligence.

However, his all-seeing and utterly penetrating gaze, did consciously note, that the neither the face, nor the behavior of the servant girl seemed to betray any sign of confusion, nor any sense of timidity in regards to her negligence – on the contrary, could it really have been that he noticed her biting upon her slender, lower lip just enough to conceive a slight smile? But has it not always been this way that all servant girls, displayed their friendliness, zeal, diligence and modesty in this exact way – by biting their lips and smiling curtly? So, we must conclude that the servant girl finds herself, in no way, to blame? Or perhaps, as a result of her duties in maintaining the entirety of the palace, in replacing meals, taking care of all of the tableware, the poor, timid girl truly did not notice a thing? After all, not just the servant girl – but all of his highly praised generals, viziers, even his very own children bow down to him in an incredibly habitual fashion, not even daring to lift up their eyes at him? So then, what can we say of this lowly servant girl? Not for lack of having observed the mood of the Lord – probably can't even think of herself, or even feel her own legs underneath her feet, let alone master her own nerves.

Sometimes, the Lord was bothered by the feeble-minded plebeians that constituted his surroundings, unable to perform the simplest comprehensive tasks or rudimentary problem solving. However, later-having peacefully contemplated this, he came to understand their condition. How freeing it must be for him, the ruler, to hot have to answer to a single soul but God, to solve everything with no one to please, without any fear of making mistakes – but this was not a feasible option for his servants. They are bound to detect the Lord's glances, determine his wishes by reading his facial expressions and lastly, they may make mistakes only out of sheer fear of embarrassing themselves in his presence. In secluded conversations with close, trusted parties he wholeheartedly encouraged his companions to speak freely, without intercepting or interrupting them, preferring to remain dispassionate, immersed in silence, as though redirecting his focus entirely to what he was hearing. He would allow them to express themselves fully, till the very end. He even refrained from any head nodding, prompting or encouragement, or expression of discontent or disapproval of any kind on his behalf. This particular behavior, exhibited by the Lord in conversations, was in no way accidental – in fact, more than anything else, it encouraged his subjects to speak intensely on the matters at hand, without wavering, without omitting a single shred of evidence. Every ruler must create an atmosphere in which his most trusted subjects could speak freely to him, much like in a confessional, in order to ensure that no one is plotting against him. It was impossible for anyone living in the world subjected to his rule to keep any plots or secrets from him, and only he is the true omnipotent keeper of all of the kingdoms' secrets. For all of the simple mortals, predestined by fate – not out to fear, but their conscience – to serve him, sacrifice for him even their lives if need be, their blood, what would be the point of keeping any secrets from him? For he, the Lord, is obligated to, genuinely and in all senses, know exactly what each and every person within his entire kingdom is thinking and doing. The ruler should especially concern himself with uncovering that which remains hidden inside the minds and hearts of the courtiers, those individuals who most closely surround him. It can be likened to a reasonable person not having the desire to suddenly mount a violent, impulsive stallion with entirely unfamiliar behaviors – so, too one must not put himself in a situation that permits closeness to the types of people, who may be either secretively withholding their true intentions, or those who are entirely clueless as to what they desire out of life. Also, one must not forget, that so long as a secret is in your hands – and your hands only, it becomes your weapon, but – allow it to slip into the hands of even one other person, potentially an enemy – the weapon is now in theirs. Therefore, it had always been his aim to disarm the close circle of individuals surrounding him, having seized their right to withhold any and all secrets, of which he was unaware. In having revealed some type of secret, and having made it public, the Lord effectively tied those who served him to the belt on the back of his saddle.

Having allowed the guilty party an opportunity to explain himself, he would sometimes play the role of a simpleton – asking incredibly naïve questions, and the individual, unaware of Khan's superior cunning, in his mind would foolishly scoff at him, and seeing an opportunity to easily win over his favor, would unload – in tremendous detail – the very same information that just recently, he would never have considered releasing.

In this manner – having first forced the party to spill their guts, he would uncover the actuality, deducing the truth from the tiniest of details, brought forth by the raving utterances of the self-assured plebeian. Not anticipating such a turn of events, the poor plebeian, presently terrified beyond belief, and drenched in a cold sweat - would immediately fall mute. Following this kind of a lesson, the party belonging to the Khan's intimate circle – now humbled, obedient and reliable, much like a camel yearling, whose nose was pierced straight through the middle by his owners, so as he may be led around by a rope, forced to trail behind them.

And so, indeed within this lies the supremacy and might of the Lord, whose role it is to know the secrets of those who serve him, and never to claim any one of them as his "own". And not since the very beginning of time has there been an occurrence of a servant pressing his master for secrets.

Additionally, the veritable master should not only be impenetrable in regards to maintaining his secrets, but also impermeable to meaningless chit-chat and petty rumors. If the Lord were to stoop to taking heed to someone's rumors, then his gold crown should be ripped from his very head, and offered up as a spittoon to the dripping, salivating lips of the gossip-bearer.

He would avoid close contact with individuals who tried to approach him with complaints of others. And the limited few that had attempted such things, approaching him with tall-tales of "such-and-such did this and that" met their well-deserved end – ordered to hanging by the noose. Ever since, not a soul has dared to come forward to him with gossip stemming from questionable sources. If he does not directly ask so himself, not a single courtier or even child of his would venture to say a single word regarding anyone else. Incidents within the court or living quarters were not to be reported by the high-ranking officials, noblemen of the court or servants directly, but instead, through a series of specially authorized networks, such as highly respectable magi, fortune tellers or clairvoyants. If the news to be told was unpleasant in nature, then the sources would expound the information in the conventional format – through a series of intimations and parables. And if he required information in greater depth or detail, without the murkiness of parables or suggestions, he would call forth his most trusted seers and magi, asking them to interpret the given information. But, even these sources do not give explanation in a concise and comprehensible form, choosing rather to present ambiguous versions of the information, so that the analysis and comprehension of the wisdom embedded within the words of the magi would ultimately be left up to the Lord himself. And on the basis of his own personal conclusions, he would – solely, decide upon which verdict to dole out and the degree of the punishment that was to be inflicted upon the guilty party. However, dispensing justice – separating the wheat kernels of truth from the chaff of conjecture, while instating the proper decision – was no simple task, not even for a *Lord*. For the Lord, it was a matter of honor and prestige – a symbol of the embodiment of his reign, in its totality, as Khan, necessitating a verdict that was, in the eyes of his subjects, an entirely just, fitting and proper punishment given the crime.

"Whatsoever might befall you – never say that you have been trapped, with no way out," stated his military discipline. Staying true to this, even in matters of justice, he would under no circumstances, bind his two hands together, always searching and finding a way out of any judicial intrigue or treachery. He knew that any plot or slander could be always be hung over someone else's head, but yet he also understood that for a mighty warrior – as a result of whom many thousands had drowned in their own blood and many more had been sent into the field of battle, it is of incredible importance that the Khan display nothing short of the utmost meticulousness in his investigative process, while maintaining fairness and objectivity in carrying out his sentencing upon another person. A fantastic absurdity reigns supreme on this earth: however tall a person's glory may grow – when you sends thousands of warriors to their violent deaths, the same men who were born and lovingly reared by their mothers – that same glory may plummet just as remarkably low, if you let slip an apparent injustice towards so much as one ragged beggar – the son of one of these mothers. But if you were to, whilst solemnly seated on your throne, perform any good deed for that very same filthy beggar, the crowds will cheer, singing your praises to the very heavens, proclaiming you as their mighty champion, defender of weak and wretched.

Of this he became definitively certain many years ago, while on an expedition to the southern borders.

Back then, following a several month-long grueling crossing, the army finally set foot on the territory of the capital city of an enemy's kingdom. The path was blocked by a river, its water flowing down from the mountains, thundering as it rolled and spilled over the rocky barriers, forming mighty rapids, strong currents that were enveloped in white foam. On the opposite shore, spanning the entire width of the mountain-enclosed valley, preceding the capitol of this southern kingdom – peaceful farmland, which unfolded in front of them, lined with many bustling, barefoot peasants. A wide horseshoe of tall mountains encircled the city, the foot of which was covered in a colorful assortment of mixed forestry. The gusts of wind, which made their way down the mountainsides, and drifted across the river, carried with them the enticing aromas of abundant valley – the sweet smell of the fruits born of a garden's labor.

Amid this heavenly valley, the massive army erected their temporary camps. Without warning, and all at once, the karnays started to wail, followed by the resonating booms of the drums beating. Right away, it seemed as though the mountains – almost instantly spurred from a dream, and the *tugay* in the surrounding valley were bursting with noise – the snapping of branches, the pounding of thousands of animal feet, belonging to various wild deer, frightened by the unthinkable noise and the endless echoes that reverberated across the mountains, leapt out of the woods in huge herds, lunging themselves in the direction of the wide open steppes. Closing in on them from behind, flew whistling, red-hot arrows, which – in the blink of an eye – reached the animals, maddened with fear. One after the other collapsed on the ground, tumbling and flipping over, thrashing on the ground, and finally falling, fatally silenced. The countless *tumeni* swiftly, recklessly – and without much difficulty, secured for themselves a fantastic bounty of fresh game.

The barefoot peasants, equally terrified, madly sprinted from the fields, abandoning their ploughs and hoes, their bags filled with seeds. But not a single warrior's arrow followed suit.

It would be a while before the snapping of branches and the sounds of the various animals dashing through the forest would subside – these were the larger predators, who fled from the invisible formidable foe, clawing and thrusting their way up the steep mountain range, in search of protective shelter on the opposite side.

The soldiers of the countless regiments chopped down brushwood, dragged logs to the tops of the mounds, which surrounded the massive city, and proceeded to light their bonfires. And as soon as the darkness of night was upon them, the majestic valley reminiscent of a horseshoe began to glow, as though illuminated by a limitless swarm of heavenly stars that had descended upon the earth. To the inhabitants of the city, it appeared as though the entire horizon lining the night sky was ablaze.

Once morning had arrived, the city had to face the reality that the nighttime vision was, in fact, not a horrifying dream: the countless terrifying troops, unperturbed, stood firmly in place, the peaceful bonfires still smoking in the heart of their camp. And so it continued, for the duration of the entire day, and come evening – yet again, the mounds were flooded with the ominous flames of warning. Once more, the region residing between heaven and earth was engulfed by the hellish blazes of the bonfires.

The tranquility of the inhabitants of this capital city, so as endure tolerating their neighbors – the dreadful, infinitely vast army – whose bonfires somehow seemed more incalculable in number than all of the stars shimmering in the sky – had been able to hold out and withstand their condition of being besieged no more than two days. On the morning of the third day, from all corners of the city – emerged enormous rows of refugees who flocked to the enemy's camp, deciding to give themselves up in hopes of winning over the mercy of the conqueror, praying this might be enough to dissuade his need for battle.

The Ruler passed orders banning the entry of refugees into the soldier's camps, instead choosing to, in the meantime, under the watchful eye of the guards, herd them to an area on the brink of a long, narrow cape, stretching alongside the river's bend. He had concluded, in his own mind, that if the enemy were to decide to send out their battle elephants, that he would send out these cowardly *kafirs* first – to

End of the Legend •Abish Kekılbaev

act as a live barrier against his men, so that the archer's arrows and projectiles of the catapult mechanism of the enemy, which are usually aimed at their opponents from large baskets mounted on the backs of giant elephants, would rain down on their own people instead.

Come afternoon, the ruler sent his eldest son to the cape by the river's bend, to check up on the refugees to determine how they were behaving. He swiftly returned, and his eyes, already ordinarily bulging wide – this time, seemed barely contained by the confines of their sockets.

"Father, there are a hundred thousand of them already!" – he exclaimed impatiently, wholly forgetting the implied formalities that were expected of him, in addressing the Ruler. "And they just keep coming!"

"So, by nighttime, there will be more refugees than we have soldiers," – noted one of the Emirs in attendance.

Upon heard these words, the inner circle of the Ruler, consisting of Emirs and Generals, who were presently seated in two rows – one directly to his left, and the other - to his right, began to glance around at each other, not yet having had the opportunity to voice their opinions concerning the troublesome matter at hand. Almost immediately, the nature of the thoughts which were forming in the minds of his experienced military officials and closest court subjects, had become quite evident to the Ruler. To his surprise, it was not one of his military officials who had decided to break the silence, but, instead – the *Khazret,* who with a pallid, lifeless face, appearing almost entirely bloodless, sat in front of a silver stand, on which rested a weighty, leather-bound Koran. Gently thumbing his *chetki-tazbikh*, the holy Khazret forewarned:

"O, Mighty Lord, the result could be ill-fated for us all."

"The Khazret speaks the truth!"

"He is right! This could turn into an outright tragedy!"

So spoke the eldest son and the top vizier of the Lord, in response to the words of the Holy Khazret.

By late afternoon, the massive army, arranged in a dense formation, proceeded to march by foot into the valley. Unaware of what was to befall them, the swarming crowds of refugees cried out, welcoming them.

And in the blink of an eye, like a swift plague of winged locusts, the sky darkened, obstructed by a multitude of soaring arrows. The shrieks of joy and salutation soon transformed into a piercing shrill of horror and disbelief, followed by the moans of the wounded, the yelping and howling of women, and the curses muttered through the weakened, receding breath of the dying.

The blood-curdling wails and screams of the one hundred thousand massacred people filled the valley, reverberating through the steep chasms of the mountains, propelling themselves skyward, to the very heavens above. And in the distant watchtowers, it seemed to the nomads as though they were hearing the yelps of an enormous pack of rabid dogs, locked up and abandoned, caged up within the confines of the old camps. And the foaming, golden raging river, swiftly bending and twisting, snaking around the jagged, stony cliffs, roaring even more fiercely and wrathfully than before.

Subjected to the ruthless battery of the archers, the crowd, which flung itself in all possible directions within the valley, was noticeably reduced in size – those pierced by arrows fell one on top of the other, their bodies piling up – blanketing the ground. Those who had somehow managed to survive still, to avoid the fatal penetration of the arrows, began frantically stacking up the bloodied bodies of the deceased – to build walls, in an attempt to hide behind them.

However, it was inevitable that they would be met by the marching lance-bearing *naizagers*. Utterly helpless and entirely defenseless, the victims would abruptly jerk their heads back to the face the sky, when pierced by a sharp steel point, as though wishing for the last time to glance upon the beautiful, blue sky. Then, with head bent back, slumped over, prostrate, having finally and eternally rested their gaze upon the bloodied earth.

Now it was time for the spear-bearers to advance, who – without the slightest hesitancy, proceeded to topple the makeshift barricade walls fashioned from corpses and the dying captives, penetrating it effortlessly and – swinging their curved blades, began hacking at the unarmed people. Among the decapitators, was the raging holy Khazret himself, having not once in his life so much as slaughtered a sheep.

Subsequently, fated to the most agonizing of endings, the victims furiously charged into their last attempt at battle. No longer did they scream in terror, nor did they wail and beg for mercy – instead, they fought with the ferocity of lions. With nothing but their bare hands, they lunged at the murderers – grabbing and clawing at their throats. Cast down, they would latch onto the leg of an enemy running by, attempting to take them down to the ground, ruthlessly digging their teeth into their enemy's shins, while being struck down by their executioners. The fierce and feral screams, the hoarse wheezing of the fatally wounded, the gnashing and grinding of teeth, and the feverish cursing of the dying comingled with the cold, crisp whistle of sables slicing and slashing. Many, out of sheer despair, threw themselves from the steep cliff, down into the foamy, turbulent swift-moving swells of the waters below – only to become targets for the archers, who aligned themselves along the river's edge in a compact formation. And the foam, tossing its golden mane, lurched forth – newly stained by the deepest crimson of freshly spilled blood.

By the time twilight embraced the sky, everything had ceased – and the *askehrs* of the nomads were heaving the bodies of the lifeless war-prisoners into giant piles, that grew as tall as the soldiers themselves.

And the mighty army of the steppes felt elated and imbued with a newfound vigor and determination, due to the ease with which they had been able to exterminate such a vast number of these people, whose overall numbers, it seemed, were truly incalculable – much like a gigantic, swarming cloud of flies.

The valley once more was aglow, from the flames emanating from the fires, burning furiously through the night – fueled by the bodies of the inanimate captives of this capital city, continuously heaved atop the fires. The pitch-black sky seemed as though it had been smoked by the very pits of an infernal cauldron, in which sinners were slowly roasted. The thick suffocating smoke, and the unbearable stench of the smoldering flesh hovered over the ash-laden, blackened flames, which wildly, frantically licked at the confines of the cauldron.

The following day, having completed the morning's ritual *namaz*, the Ruler had called upon the holy Khazret, commanding him to read some passages from the Koran. So, the entirely dispassionate and detached Khazret, indifferent to the whole world, emphatically pried open the Koran, and began reading from the very place the Holy Book had opened.

"In truth, of what are we reminded by our earthly lives? She can be likened to the light that trickles down to us from the heavenly skies upon the land, which beget and breathe life into her into her flora and fauna, which by their design, are destined to nourish and nurture both mankind, and beasts as well. And so, when the vast expanse of the earth is draped with flowering vegetation – these worthless mortals suppose the world is so wondrously fashioned strictly for their sakes, and that it shall remain so – eternally. So, how is it that it takes merely one of our commands for all of this marvelous abundance and prosperity to disappear and melt away, like the faintest breath, leaving behind not even the slightest trace, or inkling of a memory of its existence to be found – anywhere."

Appearing ever so pale and emaciated, the Khazret suddenly slammed the Holy Book shut. He then took it upon himself to proceed to interpret that which was recited, in his own words – which were exceedingly, and unnecessarily ornate and at the same time – murky, much more so than that which was just read:

"My dear *Taksir*! The *surah* of the Holy Book – which was opened at random, forewarned of the fate of the multitudes of infidels, having found themselves face-to-face with our deadly blue blades!"

Seeing as the Lord was the highest-ranking Commanding officer, he ordered the entire army to wade across the River, and to line up in a proper formation across the wide plateau that faced the city. He traversed the camp on his battle-purposed *argamak*, inspecting his warriors. He determined the frontal strike forces, organized two side flanks – one on the left, the other one the right.

He appointed his eldest and youngest sons to take lead of the right flanking unit. Control of the left flanking unit – he handed over to his two middle sons. The main offensive strike troops were assigned to his main general and one of his sons. Each of his 'son-generals' was granted four Emirs, each of whom possessed his own private score of troops. The main body of warriors was to be headed by the Lord himself.

The enemy had established their own formation – consisting of twenty thousand cavalrymen, thirty thousand foots soldiers, and one hundred and twenty gargantuan elephants fiercely outfitted in various combat gear and rigging. Every elephant was snugly strapped in chains, each one connected to the next via their heads – arranged in a single row. On the backs of each mammoth beast was a mountable basket-like structure, which could hold as many as six standing archers at once. Between the elephants, were rows of mobile troops carrying heavy projectiles and slings; behind them were weighty catapult contraptions, with which they would launch bulky boulders and containers filled with some sort of flammable mixture.

In light of these towering – almost mountainous – elephants, the cavalrymen of the steppes, mounted on their wooly horses and armed foot soldiers, with their lances and spears, appeared somewhat pitiful, laughable even. It seemed as though, in an instant, they would be stomped and crushed out of existence by these gigantic beasts, mounted by fierce looking rider-warriors. And there was a certain, palpable puzzled bewilderment on the faces of the very same men who, just the other day, eager and bloodthirsty, disposed of the unarmed, helpless refugees. But it was the group that surrounded the Lord – the Viziers, Astrologers, and Treasurers – uninvolved in the actual combat, who appeared especially crushed by the sight that lay before them.

Just yesterday, he had asked them – "Where would you like to be at the moment of combat?" To which they all, in unison, responded, "We will be where the women and children are. They are afraid, so we must protect them!"

At which point, the Lord chuckled in amusement, and left them.

On the expansive plateau, two immense forces began to slowly advance towards each other. The ground began to rumble and quake underfoot, as the men, soldiers and elephants pushed onward. When the lead units finally faced each other side-by-side, the Lord climbed to the very top of the ancient *kurgan*, now elevated right alongside his main unit, the center of command, unfurled his prayer rug, and having turned his to align himself with the direction of the holy city of Mecca, began to pray.

Even in the midst of his prayers, he distinctly remembers noting that his lead offensive strike warriors began inching forward, slowly, reminding him of arched-back stance of a feline, beginning to curve and bend under the pressure of the one hundred war elephants, from which rained down dark, cloud-like showers of arrows, the bulky stones launched by the sling-bearing soldiers, and the decimating blows of the bulky boulders, propelled by the weighty catapult contraption.

The Lord rapidly rolled up his prayer rug, sent for his messengers, and released them with the following instructions – to substantially expand the right and left flanks with multiple additional units.

Once the enemy, which stormed into the opening with its main body of troops, had forced themselves forward quite a ways, the flanking tumen bore down on them from both sides, like jaws squeezing them together. Not having expected this at all, the invasive offenders quickly fell into disarray. The war elephants were cut off and isolated from the rest of the troops, which now found themselves surrounded on all sides by several thousand mounted warriors, deceived and ensnared. The archers that were mounted on the backs of the elephants were thrown into a chaotic state, and were quickly shot down by the archers of the steppes, mounted on rapidly moving horses, kept circling the helpless giants, who were all chained together. It did not take long for the most courageous warriors, having approached them closely, to begin stabbing at the creatures with spears, and slicing their stomachs with lances, ripping them open. The elephants, one by one, trumpeting and wildly swinging their trunks, crashed to the ground – simultaneously dragging down all the others, to whom they were attached. And in a short while, the battlefield was coated with the monstrous heaps of elephant carcasses strewn about – blood trickling down their massive bodies, producing thick scarlet pools upon the ground.

Seeing the ease with which these seemingly monstrous beasts could be taken care of, the nomadic warriors felt a new wave of uplifting energy, and began fearlessly attacking the remaining elephants. Having seized the catapult contraption, they began pelting the elephants with massive boulders the size of a horse's head. Soon, the enemy's troops were surrounded by two dense bands of warriors, and promptly destroyed. The vast battlefield was left in disarray, littered with the messy heaps of human and elephant corpses. The warrior's horses, with eyes askew, occasionally tripping on yet another victim's body, appeared confused and spooked by the sight of these immense mounds.

The fourteen year old grandson of the Lord, somehow able to capture one of the elephants, led the animal by the straps of its harness back to headquarters. Quite moved, and proud of his young grandson's bravery, the Khan beckoned to his grandson, and bending down to the youth's forehead, gave him a good sniff.

The same day, after half a day's worth of prayer, the army finally crossed the threshold of the city. All of the prominent officials that had not been killed, stood by the main gates of the city to greet them, their heads bowed to the ground. Appearing before the savage conqueror, they could but fall to the ground, faces pressed against the earth.

Intoxicated by their bloody victory, the warriors of the steppes, like an avalanche, burst through the wide open gates, which ceased to demonstrate any resistance. The fairytale-like riches found within this *giaour* capital city, were fully handed over to the victors for ransacking.

And while the mighty Ruler rested, having – along with his generals and close entourage, occupied the colossal, majestic castle – the thousands upon thousands of unbridled unruly warriors wreaked havoc upon the city. Having placed around the city, in all four corners, the Tyumen guards to create a barrier, the Lord allowed the remaining troops to pillage and maraud the city, having imposed no limitations, whatever their hearts desired. Let them pilfer in handfuls, filling their *korzhuns* to the very brim with stolen goods. May they grab as many slaves and beautiful females captives as they wish, and gratify themselves with whatever carnal pleasures they so desire.

The city was handed over for looting for an entire two weeks. In this time, the Lord, on more than one occasion, was able to confirm his suspicion that human greed truly knows no bounds. The other warriors had piled on their spare horses such great quantities of bags brimming with looted goods that you could barely make out the semblance of the horses underneath them. There were even those, amongst his heroic warriors and generals, that had claimed as many as several hundred slaves and slave-girls. Having bound them into long rows, they led them out of the city gates, driving them towards the main barracks in single-file row.

There was a time he bore witness to an incredible sight. Riding by the main square of the city, and surrounded by his nukers, accompanied by his usual entourage, as well as his new subjects – comprised of the local wise men, he witnessed two people fighting. One of the men was blind – a robust, elderly gentleman with a moustache, missing both of his eyes, and the second – who was fighting him – a sinewy, tan-faced, slant-eyed warrior of the steppes, who was unmistakably inebriated. With his long, crooked fingers, he mercilessly gripped the blind man's throat and in response, received a fruitless barrage of punches from his opponent, whose head simultaneously swung side to side, like a bell hanging from an ass's neck.

A little distance away from the two fighting men, who at this point – paid attention to no one and nothing within their surroundings, two horses were at a standstill, side by side. Attached to one of the animals, affixed to the uppermost pommel of the saddle, was a long, rawhide belt, the end of which was tied to dozens of captives, men and women – packed into a tight cluster, bound together by shackles on their wrists. Nobody had even bothered to observe what had taken place nearby, nor the kind of people that pulled up to them, stopping right beside them…

The Ruler could not bear the sight of this disgraceful embarrassment. He quickly leapt out of his regal wagon, without the help of his servants, as though he were some plebeian, and sprinted up to the rowdy fighters, unsheathing his lance, Damascus steel, and – generating power straight from the shoulder, struck down the slant-eyed warrior. The warrior instantly collapsed down to the ground, and having recognized the Lord, yelped, begging for his mercy and forgiveness and crawling over to him, began the groveling process that consisted of embracing and kissing his feet.

Realizing that some form of wholly unexpected assistance had come to his aid, the mustachioed blind man fell to his knees, stretched his arms out, grabbed at the ends of the Lord's clothing, and began expressing the most sincere gratitude:

"Who are you, my gracious savior? For it is but one thing that I possess as a memory of my dearly departed mother – this necklace made of stone, carnelian. It is worthless, but this greedy bloodsucker latched onto it and tried to steal it from me. Name yourself, stranger, so that I may know whom to thank in God's good name for the rest of my earthly days!"

"My unlucky friend! What good is my name to you?" – uttered the Lord, recognizing the language of the conquered peoples. "You fought well, blind man. If only all of your warriors had been capable of fighting as you did…and my name, you will later learn."

And soon after news spread, outran him even, in every city that they passed through on their return trek from their expedition: the Lord had stepped up for a unfortunate blind cripple, striking down his heartless, brutal mugger – essentially, the merciful conqueror of the world would under no circumstances permit evil or injustice to triumph in his presence.

Following this particular incident, the Lord had once and for all decided to adhere to this standard upon judging his trials. Having returned from this expedition, right in the midst of the celebratory feast, he took it upon himself to announce the upcoming executions of several slanderers, informants who had made it their business to disclose several secret occurrences that apparently taken place in the Lord's absence.

From that day forth, not a soul dared to approach him with some sort of "information" or tales of others. Evidence brought forth of information that was clearly a danger to the Lord, truly capable of carrying out damage either to him or his regime, he had passed down to him in the form of a series of clever hints and parables through his preferred sources – the trustworthy magi and fortunetellers of his court.

Based on the information the Lord would receive, he would accordingly begin crafting riddles for himself: does this story not seem unusual and somewhat redundant, taking into consideration the appearance of the spoiled apple twice presented on the golden tray? Is this a hint? And if so, what is its implication? Of what dangers are they attempting to forewarn me? And what could he possibly have to be wary of, within his own castle, in his homeland, sitting upon his own elevated and majestic throne? For he could not even begin to imagine a single kingdom or possible enemy in the territory surrounding his own, that would ever dare try to take a bite out of his…

The Lord tried to show the ambassador of the eastern country, exactly how much more extensive his arms and swords were, in comparison to others, and made it quite clear that it would not be long before he would actually direct his massive undefeated army to invade his kingdom. In order to convince the ambassador, and so he could verify this through his own eyes, the mighty Khan had decided to retain the ambassador for an entire two months, as long as the other was able to hold out on their return journey from the expedition. And only yesterday, he finally released the ambassador back home. As the other journeys home, the Lord will have already mounted his saddle.

Just yesterday, he had had a secret meeting with his personal spies and agents, who were sent to all of the far corners of the Khan's empire, under the guise of various Dervishes, possessed bahshi, and holy fools of the *Divan*. All reporting as one, they had informed the Lord that all was well in the Khan's kingdom, with peace and harmony reigning supreme – the Khan had no perceived threats, nor were any expected to crop up, anywhere.

In the furthest provincial territories of the Khan's empire, alongside the caravan routes and borders, he maintained a secret reserve of about one thousand riders – on camels, and yet another thousand cavalrymen, who rode around under the semblance of wandering merchants, roaming pilgrims, scouring far and wide for any sign of a rebellion, or inclination to revolt, brought on discontent with the Khan's rule. Yet, even from them, he received no information that conveyed the possibility of an impending threat.

And there was also no alarming evidence from his viziers or his treasurers, who were responsible for collecting the payments of taxes. No news came from his watchful agents either, who – in their service to the Khan – were implanted into the courts of the Emirs, as well as governors of the conquered cities and empires, all of whom were subjected to his rule.

So, could it be the nicked apple was not sign of some kind of underlying disorder, occurring in some land faraway from here, some distant province? Perhaps, while he was absent for four whole years, here – in the capital, in his very own palace – something had been stirred up, something corrupt – with the forewarning embedded within this crimson apple?

Each individual, from his inner circle that could have possibly arisen as a suspect in the Lord's mind, their loyalty falling under question – he made certain to keep by his side, so that the other could be seen at all times.

Upon having set out on his latest expedition, he had entrusted his top vizier with the responsibility of looking after his palace and treasury. It would not have been the worst of tragedies, if he had attempted to dig his nails into the boundless treasures of the Khan, though this was not particularly likely, for the vizier was a person of inestimable balance – in whom greed, wisdom, cunning and caution lived full-well, proving himself a valuable aid to the Lord in regards to maintaining his position of power. There was not much reason for him to pay particular mind to the rumors being whispered behind his back. The Lord was well aware, that within the walls of the royal court, those who are especially close to the main seat of power - the throne, always incite mudslinging and slander, which can most certainly be traced back to enemy lips.

And so, to what can this crimson apple – not only with the nick on its side, but also a worm at its core, possibly be alluding to? His native homestead appears to have held up, seemingly unharmed in the last four years he had been absent. At the last feast, every single one of his servants had been accounted for, except one. And, realistically, what could have taken place in his absence, in such a short time frame? And it was entirely possible that the dull servant-girl could have inadvertently done this, out of sheer distress at having to face the Lord.

And yet – any other person, the servant-girl aside, in having seen this apple, marked by decay, would have immediately thrown it out. So what must this signify – placing such an apple on the Khan's tray, a second time?! Without a doubt, there is something brewing in the background, here – and the apple was being served at someone's instruction, and not as a result of the absent-mindedness of the servant-girl.

Perhaps I should directly send for one of my Council? Upon his arrival from his latest expedition, the Lord had briefly met with his main spiritual advisor – and had been abrupt, instead of taking his time and engaging in lengthy, heart-to-heart conversations with him as he had done on all prior occasions.

The Lord was not in the habit of asking for advice straightaway when it came to the business of interpreting dreams or even the hazy fortunes doled out by his sages or prophets, until he had given himself ample opportunity to mull things over and arrive at certain conclusions himself. Back to the matter at hand – so what of this decomposing apple with the worm within its core…? Someone had undoubtedly chosen this particular apple. It must be a warning of some sort of turmoil, some deception within his own abode. But, what kind of betrayal is it signaling? And who might the perpetrator be?

Does such a brazen lunatic truly exist – who would dare to betray his Lord, in the midst of the era of his greatest sway, military might and power – while his immense stronghold towers upon the very peaks of magnificence, prosperity and abundance?

After having mentally assessed all of his most illustrious warrior-generals, he found himself unable to conceive of a single person, who had a single minute reason to deceive or betray him. Ordinarily, following a great victory, or prior to the commencement of a new military campaign, the Lord would liberally shower his most honorable generals with more than enough gold. Indeed, this was his "golden rule". And, in seizing the exorbitant riches of that southern empire, the abundant plundered treasures from the northern empires, the Lord did not behave in an ungenerous fashion - handsomely dividing all of the wealth amongst his generals and other lords. His rule had always been – reward them ten-fold for their loyalty and service. Then, they will eagerly follow him into any battle he so chooses.

Approximately ten years ago, when he was preparing himself for the expedition to the southern empire, he encountered discord amongst the men of the Divan. His eldest son, was determined, firmly supporting the campaign: "We will acquire all of the gold the empire has to offer – we will reign supreme, we will dominate the whole world!" The Emirs and Viziers countered this proposal in a cautious, calculated manner, skeptically crinkling and contorting their faces: "The people of those lands – they are more numerous than flies that circle manure. We may vanquish them, but will find ourselves amongst them in such pitiful numbers, that they will soon devour us, and we will dissolve in the midst of their vastness, and our children will be forced to forget their native tongue!"

Then, he commanded that they consult the Koran. The High Council hushed, and only the voice of the Khazret rang out: "Oh, my mighty prophet! You must go to war with the infidels – they who are ignorant of the true law, of the one and only Allah!"

The gold obtained from the southern empires, certainly helped to smooth out the contorted faces of several of the Emirs and councilmen – that expedition was very convincing, and with a newfound confidence, they finally seemed assured that they were capable of victory over a peoples – limitless in number, much like a massive swarm of flies, without losing themselves in the mix. And now, that the opponent was considering an expedition to the northern lands, where gold was no less plentiful, in fact – unquestionably more abundant, than in the southern lands – his fellow tribesmen, having over the years acquired a distinct taste for gold and treasure, would doubtfully oppose the goose, who never fails to produce their golden eggs...

So who is it this individual, who has cast a shadow of doubt upon their upcoming expedition to the northern lands? Or is it something altogether different – someone desirous of living out the dream, in the Lord's stead – to sit at the head this almighty Jihad? So then, who is this daring one?

Having lost himself in traversing the labyrinthine realm of his own thoughts, the Lord suddenly had a distinct feeling that he had approached this in all the wrong ways... No, the traitor is not here, not from this side...

The crystal-clear spring was mumbling something in a language all its own, something pure and childlike. And as they always had - the dense, soaring peaks of the trees – in this garden, which had been left up to its own devices, softly whispered amongst themselves, gently catching and cradling the delicate, fresh breeze that had smoothly sailed down into their gentle embrace – its means of arriving here, just as mysterious as its origins. It was as though every element of this atmosphere was created to cocoon and coddle - to lull the soul into the warm peaceful repose, so that it in its tranquil state, it would whisper: "Think...Think calmly."

But in this instance, clear reflection, in having collected himself with his thoughts, simply was not – realistically, taking place – either the soft rustling of leaves within this untamed garden, or the cheerful babbling of the brook nearby – all created a sense of distraction. And, as if maddened by his companions of solitude, the Lord leapt from the rock on which he sat, and started down the narrow path of the walkway. The intricate, serpentine path, much like the plots and schemes within the walls of his own palace, led him in the direction of the very same palace.

Immersed within the fragrant, velveteen balminess of the afternoon sun, the familiar garden had unexpectedly come to be unfamiliar, unrecognizable. It was as though it had been penetrated, pierced by this sudden, sharp pulse of pain – and it timidly squealed and squirmed, only to be flooded by a wave of gentle trills – the timid, resonating melodies of the birds therein. Their flock fluttered from within the darkened depths of the canopy, and having perched themselves up on the branches of a nearby tree, all but a stone's throw from where people strolled, they tweeted and chattered all at once, their feathered, puffed gullets bellowing vigorously – inflating, deflating.

As though she had been secretively peering out at him since early morning, from within the depths of the thick surrounding foliage, a golden doe gracefully glided by him, shielded only partially by a few sparse shrubs. Her delicately poised dexterity, and light, elegant prances revealed an undulation of the majestic musculature of her silken hips. The doe had, indeed, distinctly glided by, instead of dashing past, as occurs when stricken by fear, and her unusual expression seemed to betray a need to urgently convey a message of the utmost importance.

The meandering path had led him past an apricot tree, with her robust arms stretching out broadly in every which direction, and her ungathered overly-ripened fruits had fallen to the ground, rotting amidst the sea of grass that carpeted it, and huge, dark blue flies – as big as one's nail – swarmed over them in a dark and nauseating cloud.

There is no sight that is more disgusting than that of the decaying flesh of overly-ripened fruit. And somehow, not too long before this, the tree was covered in an exquisite, fragrant ivory cloud of fine, pale petals. Having shed itself of these, the tree was then filled in with the plump hints of what would eventually become a seed-bearing pod. The miniature, rounded little pods, like fragile newborns cradled in the plush green blankets of verdant vegetation, sucked on the nourishing milk of the earth, which had ascended from the deep, murky depths of the nurturing mother-tree, and with every fiber of their being – they absorbed every tiny little bit of life-bearing energy that the Heavenly Father had brought forth. Growing, swelling, ripening – the fruits of the apricot tree would slowly take shape, transform in color - a bountiful harvest, a self-born treasure – a genuine joy for the eyes to behold! And finally, it welcomes the long-awaited, wondrous fruits of its labor! And, what of it, then? Could it really be that all of this wondrous beauty was designed for the ruthless destruction of these despicable, useless creatures – with their filthy, bristly little legs? Truly, it must be so – one must recognize that the significance and dignity of this golden fruit of the apricot tree unravels exactly there, upon the highest of branches, where it demonstrates its splendor in full. And yet, if but once the fruit of the apricot chances to snap from its branch and tumble down to the ground, then its fate transforms with certain clarity: people will trample it underfoot, and what remains will be snatched up and devoured ravenously by the blue-black flies. And that which once seemed so wondrous, so pristine - will become but an abomination of decay ash, and as such will not only be utterly incapable of rousing the slightest bit of sympathy, but is sure to awaken a sense of revulsion and disgust... So what must one make of this, if at one point you find yourself positioned at the very top, much like the aromatic golden fruit, brimming with sweet life-giving juice?

The Almighty Creator did not choose to endow fruits with free will, nor consciousness so that they may firmly and stubbornly cling to remain eternally perched in their boughs up high, skillfully defending their God-given dignity. And as for man – well, for him to plummet from such a mountainous height – one that he was barely able to surmount to begin with, would mean only certain death. And yet, somehow this world of man is arranged in such a way as that anyone can keep scrambling higher upon the most uncertain terrain, and ignoring the unkind and envious glances piercing him from all sides – he continues to find reasons to hoist himself up even higher and higher...

The meandering path came to a halt at a small bridge, which rested above a circular moat filled with water, which surrounded the Khan's palace.

Here, the Lord transformed his appearance, once again slipping on the countenance of world ruler. His absent-minded, deeply lost in thought expression expertly and immediately altered, and took on their characteristic notes of severity, impenetrability and icyness.

And it was with this severe semblance slipped on that he strolled into his palace. Upon entering his chambers, he had already progressed into a state of veiled fury.

When the servant girl came in with the tray, the Lord, still absorbed by his silent rage, was seated in the center of the hall, alone, atop a wide elevated platform draped in tiger skins. A gentle, indoor fountain gurgled nearby.

The timid young servant girl, eyes downcast, anxiously biting her lip, like a virgin who finds herself in the bed of an experienced man, walked in, carrying the tray with food and paused before him. She placed the gilded tray on the round dastarkhan, which was spread out in front of the Lord. He gazed upon her with deaf aggravation: no matter how hard she may try to take on the guise of the bashful virgin, no matter how she mat bite her lip, he saw that her face gave up not a single shade of genuine embarrassment. No, this was the face of a cunning and experienced woman, marked by tasks of treachery and deception, a face on which not even a tinge of bashfulness could ever appear, for it was completely caked with a thick layer of powdery cosmetics – powder, blush, heavily coated lashes, and instead of a virginal reticence, her eyes revealed her well-versed familiarity with insincerity.

Hitherto, the Lord had not bothered to give any thought to honoring the servant girl with his attention, but this time around, he intently fixed his gaze upon her, probing her eyes for answers. Alas, his efforts to elicit any response from her proved fruitless.

So what does this mean, after all? Twice she served to me this rotten, worm-infested apple and did not even notice? And if, in fact, she did notice – how could she dare to serve it to me a second time?

The servant girl demonstrated all the usual care in her setting of the dastarkhan, and bending down low, she withdrew the room, slowly, moving backwards and bowing repeatedly, at which point she whirled around, and with a flippant and careless air, made her way towards the exit, the soles of her shoes stirring up the swaying hemline of her silken shawl. Her rounded hips were as alluring as they were ample, and she carried herself in a seductive and inviting manner, the kind of manner the people of her tribe were known for.

It was only when the door had closed behind her that the Lord began to survey what lay before him on the table. Almost immediately his eyes had zoomed in and isolated the crimson apple from the rest of the filler in front of him. And yet again it markedly displayed the same incision in its skin, except this time it had been widened, as if to make it seem all the more apparent. The incision had even affected the edges of the skin around it, which curled outward slightly and caused a yellowish crust to form on top. On top of everything, the crimson apple rested on a plate entirely by itself, as if desiring to call particular attention to itself.

And so it came to be, the servant girl knows everything.

Mechanically, and without as much as a thought, he pulled on the string attached to the bell, which hung from the headboard of his canopy.

The servant girl instantly appeared in the doorway, bowing.

End of the Legend • Abish Kekilbaev

The Lord had no choice but to put much effort into self-restraint, so as not to demonstrate his explosive rage. For this very reason, he initially found himself at a lack for words when the servant girl materialized in the doorway.

- This apple… You plucked from the garden?
- No, gracious Lord, it was sent over by the Great *Khansha*.
- You may go…

The servant girl gave a quick bow, turned around and vanished in the doorway. As she turned, the Khan had managed to catch a brief glimpse of a defiant smirk peeking through her bitten lip…

So, here he finds himself again in solitude by the spring. It was as though the unkind smirk of the foul servant girl fell upon the surface of brook bubbling forth from the fountain, and spread out in the shallow waters, appearing twisted and distorted. And the naïve little brook - innocent and welcoming, like a child, carried its crystal clear waters from the very heart of the earth. By his feet, flowing around the rocks, the brook tossed itself into cheerful smile – at times it seemed encouraging, sympathizing in his sorrows and dreams, and at times it would seem to tease him gently, kindly.

Hitherto, this quiet little section of the garden right next to the spring was his only island of blissful isolation, his only shelter from all of the unkind glances of the entire outside world, and now, it was as though some unnamed dark forces, some satanic shadows had mysteriously crept inside his blessed sanctum. And even the wide rock that was his usual sitting spot, seemed displeased, almost as though it was grumbling and shifting about underneath him, in an effort to fling him off his shoulders as swiftly as possible. And what if the dense foliage of the treetops is not simply swaying and rustling at the command of the wind, but fervently discussing the veiled mystery he himself is attempting to uncover?

In the past, the serenity and solitude the island provided had made it easy for him to work through any or concerns or doubts he secretly might have held onto, resolve any bitter thoughts or weighty apprehensions he might have had, which seemed almost instantly to melt of their accord, and scatter effortlessly in the breeze. Yet this time, one unpleasant suspicion seemed to pile on top of another, depriving him of his usual sense of relief.

"It was sent by the Great Khansha…"

On his last military expedition, his Baybishe and his eldest grandsons had come along with him. But due to the constant relocation of his army, the harsh conditions of the expedition had worn his children thin – they began to miss their home, so two years ago the Lord had bid the return, along with his eldest wife.

Last spring, having planned to return home from this expedition, he had sent a messenger back with the news, and he – having delivered said news, returned to the Khan's headquarters and relayed to Lord that all back home was indeed fine and well.

Upon his return from his expedition, which yielded nothing short of victory, during the uninterrupted festivities, he spent a month and a half living in the castle of the Great Khansha (where his eldest grandsons resided, as well). The castle was located about half a day's travel from the capitol. And yet, during that whole time living with the Baybishe, she had not so much as dropped a hint of any suspicious goings on, any possible treachery or deception within the Khan's home.

No, no shades of grief or concern had tainted his eldest wife's face during the festivities. So how is he to interpret this clear warning sign from her? And if whatever this treachery is occurred prior to the celebratory period, what does it mean – this greatly delayed forewarning of hers?

Even his sons had visited their mother's castle frequently, and did so not because their bond to their mother was stronger than their bond to their father, but simply because they desired to visit their young children, who lived their grandmother.

Or, perhaps, it was one of his sons who committed this unseemly deed? In that case, why would she approach their father with her concerns? For his children so greatly respected their mother, that she would never have to repeat any request or wish twice.

And what ills could her children possibly have acted out? Though, they do say that if one does not prepare himself for when the going gets rough, one should not expect any kindness... And as for the matter of the inheritance of the throne – this he had decided upon a long time ago, making arrangements in case something should happen to him; he had made sure to announce himself who would be heir to the throne. And he could not have possibly developed any insidious or underhanded thoughts against his father. Or, perhaps, his brothers had begun to come down on him? Even this the Lord could not seem to imagine. All of the brothers had come from the same place, they all shared the same mother. And his eldest son, who had joined the rest, born of his first wife who had passed on, had been sent far away to their southern lands, to fill the role of the active Vice Regent. The remaining three sons are far too young, and have not even developed a taste for such high-placed power.

Oh, Almighty, what on earth could have happened? Or was it that in the heat of preparation for this latest expedition to new faraway lands in the east that this cunning snake appeared, whispering subversive thoughts into the ears of his children? Is he one of those who opposed the expedition? For the truth of the matter is that, after having embraced their wives and children after many years of separation, his warriors have no burning desire whatsoever to shortly part them once more and, slipping their feet into stirrups, to gallop away on their battle horses to some unknown land far away. Knowing this full well, the Lord, in an act of truly regal benevolence, had graciously awarded those warriors, who had distinguished themselves in the last war. Though, might it be, that this particular decision was an excessively rash one? Maybe, the more prudent action would not have been to bestow limitless boons upon them all at once, but rather to withhold the rewards and honors for a select few, assuring them of their reception to the fullest extent in the near future?

At one point, he had advised one of his emirs – "Know full well how slim the eyes of Turks are, and know that their greedy souls are equally slim." There is but one way to ensure that they are to serve you honorably: you must appease their eyes with sight of gold and sooth their soul with words of praise. Praise them, and what you take from others, disperse as bribes amongst your own."

Does he himself not act in accordance with this rule, gathering up gold and jewels from the different corners of the earth, and using them to bribe his own vassals? Otherwise, what other possible means could he employ to tempt men into abandoning the warmth of their beds, where they lay in the comfort of broad's embraces, these lustful lads, who call themselves men?

Just yesterday, he had satiated a particularly gluttonous worm of his greed, having thrown into his gaping maw a generous heaping of gold, and jewels, and those who covet power and distinction, he made sure to supply with lucrative positions and titles of the highest ranks.

Let's see them try to wear a sullen expression or grumble in dissatisfaction now!

Who on earth is this stealthy disturbing intruder who has crept in and marked his presence in such a wholly insignificant amount of time?

As for the ambassador from the lands in the East, the Lord has made sure to keep him under very close observation, keeping a watchful eye out to ensure that all of their social interactions occurred one on one, and that not a soul was allowed to go anywhere near him – not his emirs, nor his Lord generals, not even his own sons.

Could it really be, that this sly, conniving swindler had effectively whipped up some scheme, that he had circumvented his uninterrupted surveillance and had somehow successfully slipped out, right under his very nose, via a secret trail or passageway of some sort?

Either way, this intrigue with the apple points to something dreadful and unusual, and the matter must be dealt with without further delay. And yet, the Baybishe had sent a messenger, and had sent a request for an immediate meeting. And he, thinking nothing of it, had postponed her reception indefinitely. And, it was at this point, it seems, that she grew impatient and began sending him messages through his servant girl by using crimson apples with rotten worm-holes. Now, to prevent potential deterioration of circumstances, it is imperative to assemble all of my sons for a proper interrogation. Though, if this matter does in all actuality have to do with some sort of sinister plot in an attempt to gain power and overthrow the throne, it may be, that this scoundrel, whoever he may be, would be on guard and would respond by attempting to bring his plan to fruition as soon as possible. No, he must not assemble his sons right now. And if one of them had truly allowed himself to have fallen so low as to plan a coup of the throne, it would be unlikely that the Baybishe, having uncovered this plan, would attempt to bring it to his attention. This would be the equivalent of pushing your offspring, born of your own womb, right under the blade of an executioner's ax, with your own bare hands.

In the case of the Great Khansha, the only person whom she feared and who she did not favor, was the eldest son of the Lord, born of his first marriage, to his late wife. It was the Khansha herself who was adamant that he be sent to the furthest ends of the earth as regent of those conquered lands.

Having enlisted in the help of the Supreme Council, and armed with a blessing from the holy dignitary – a hermit, who resided in a cave in the mountains, the Khansha had successfully steered her eldest son into the position of the successor of the throne.

The Lord, who was not keen on the idea of seizing his eldest son's lawful right, had sought to extend the announcement of who would be successor to the throne, but his son – whether from fear of a potential conspiracy against him by his fierce step-brothers, or perhaps out of pity for his father, who was pinned dangerously in between two fiery conflicts – had made the decision himself, opting out of his rightful inheritance of the throne and requesting the position of regent in a faraway land.

Remembering the decision his beloved firstborn had made weighed heavily on the Lord's soul; he chastised himself severely for his cowardice, and his heart squeezed itself into a tiny, pitiful little lump, reminiscent of a little fledgling chick fallen from its nest, still featherless. Though now, in having thought of his firstborn son, it was as though the weight of a thousand uncertainties, each question like a sharp claw digging and tearing at his mind, was suddenly lifted from his chest – and surrendered himself to the memories of long ago, memories of ordeals and persecutions.

All of his ancestors, going back seven generations, had been mighty warriors. His great-grandfather headed the tumen of the eldest son of the Great Khan of the Steppes. This path of generalship of their forefather was then inherited by every single generation to follow. Still in his youthful years, the Lord had served as an Emir, leader of the military forces of the renowned Khan of the steppes, who himself had given the future Lord his daughter's hand in marriage. The elderly Khan had loved him more than he loved his own children. So when father-in-law had perished at the hands of those insidious conspirators, his son-in-law had defended the throne by force, and established himself there.

In those times, the inhabitants of Mesopotamia had been divided into forty distinct tribes, torn apart by unending civil wars. And they were all subject to the descendants of the original Great Khan, whose militant multitudes where on the other end of the earth. Having ascended to power, he had at one point united all of these minor Khanates, bringing them all under the umbrella of his own nation. He accomplished this not so much through the brute force of his military, but rather through his political cunning. To each of these small-time Khans, predictably puffed up with hubris, the Great Khan had secretly sent a message containing nothing besides the following words – "We shall drive all of the others away. We shall rule together, just the two of us."

From each of these small fry the Khan received an answer, anxiously bubbling over with joy and gratitude, for the fact the He had picked precisely them. And in so doing, the Mighty Khan had accomplished exactly what he sought to do – each tribe had begun to wage war against the others, and soon after, the whole of Mesopotamia sunk in the midst of the war-fueled discord.

All the while that this was going on, the massive army of the Great Khan was marching closer and closer. Ahead of everyone else, the future Lord moved towards him, wishing to greet the Great Khan-Unifier. Certain that he would be able to win over the favor of the Great Khan, the young Khan-warrior hastened to outride the remaining petty princelings. But, the old ruler's offspring surrounded the Great Khan, showed much suspicion and distrust towards this new figure, and decided to strip him of his Khan's title, reducing his status to that of a war chief. Not long after, they had gone so far as to suspect him of a plot to overthrow the throne of the Great Khan, and took it upon themselves to secretly conspire to kill him off. But the Almighty pardoned him, it would seem, and the young warrior was able to intercept the letter which ordered his own death just in time. And then, he proceeded to run.

Just recently, while on his return trip from one of his expeditions, he and his army had crossed the very same Great desert, where he had desperately flailed about so many years ago, looking for a way to save himself, leading the miserable existence of fugitive. Leading his wife by the hand, the young warrior had struggled over a myriad of waterless, barren sand dunes in the un-ending desert. Their bare feet had left tracks winding up and down the sides of many dunes. And if these days the Lord finds himself walking upon special carpets stuffed with the softest bird plumage, then back then, all those years ago, there weren't any thorns or splinters in the tugai that wouldn't lodge themselves into the soles of their feet… Yet those tracks have been smoothed over long ago, erased by the ebb and flow of wind, forever shifting the sabulous swells. The painful abscesses caused by the poisonous thorns were healed by a more merciful time which was to follow. That agonizing exodus would only drift into his memory when

End of the Legend •Abish Kekilbaev

laying gaze upon his eldest son, and nowadays, when thinking of him. In fact, he cherished his eldest son more than all of his children combined, and felt closer to him than any of his prideful sons. And this is because, if not for his son, it remains uncertain whether he would have survived to this day, or even have attained the immense glory and might of present day.

...Roaming the desert, caught on the very brink between life and death, he somehow found himself in the hands of a particular gentleman, the chief of a tribe of nomads who lived in the Great sands. He, along with his wife, were captured and thrown into an underground *zindan*, plummeting over forty meters into the earth. Neither moonlight nor even a glimmer of the sun's warm rays penetrated down into the damp gloom of this prison pit. As if simultaneously teasing and torturing the prisoners, a faint spot of daytime sunshine flickered on the utterly unreachable top of the dungeon wall, far above their heads. Occasionally, one of the guards would poke through the opening, hanging his disheveled sheep's hat-topped head down, blocking the light altogether, thereby convincing two very weary and tormented prisoners that suddenly night had fallen upon them.

The deathly silence of the dungeon was disrupted every now and again, like the shrill neighing of a colt, by the rattling of the shackles binding his wife's wrists, when she shuddered from the piercing chill and dampness and tossed and turned on the cold, earthen floor.

The spouses had not spoken a single word to one another in countless days, not wishing to irritate or burden the other's spirit, already bleeding out in despair, exasperation and hopeless anguish. Every once in a while, someone would inadvertently breathe out a heavy sigh.

And so, in much the same fashion, forty-nine days and forty-nine nights crept by. On the fiftieth night, the milky rays of the moon splashed in, clearly outlining the bright, circular opening of the pit. It looked like a sparkling, silver platter.

All of a sudden, his young wife, hitherto imbued with a fierce persistence of silently demolishing all of the tortured anguish of being incarcerated in the dark and putrid pit of the dungeon, began to moan intensely from pain and began pacing quickly and rattling her shackles. The only thing her husband could do to support her, was to move closer to her and offer up his shoulder, so she would be able to lean up against him. The young woman continued to fling herself about in a feverish state of delirium, her skin beaded with droplets of hot sweat, as though the result of her blood boiling. And not understanding how she would to endure such an invisible and unbearable, excruciating pain, she began to knock her head against the clay wall of the dungeon. He shifted her attention to himself, offering up his own body instead of the wall, and then the solid, almost stone-like head of his wife began to bear down upon his chest blow after blow with a crushing force, along with the shackles, determined to pulverize all of his bones. Then, unexpectedly, his wife let loose an especially terrible scream – and immediately crumpled up and fell to the floor, completely limp. She had lost consciousness. In that very instant, he heard a new and unfamiliar voice drifting in through the darkness – soft at first, almost choked up, and then a progressively louder, piercing and demanding shrill scream, which deafened the ears.

The silver spot of light at the very top of the dungeon became obstructed for a certain period of time by a dark silhouette in a shaggy hat, and then once again, the light innocently began to pour through.

Unable to see in the murky shadows, he began feeling around with his fingers, and was able to perceive that some kind of small object, heavy and solid, had dropped down onto his chest. Probing the object at first with his chin, he managed to maneuver it clumsily upwards towards his shoulder, and proceeded to bite down on it. As it turns out, the weighty object was the key for the shackles.

Holding the key in his teeth, he twisted his whole body, and after several failed attempts was finally able to unlock the shackles binding her wrists. She remained motionless, evidently still unconscious.

Though almost immediately, as though woken by the distressing wails of a small child, she managed to come to, and began to stir in the darkness. Having regained her consciousness fully, she moaned again, and once more sensing the pain, she proceeded to cry out as before.

"Quickly! Take this key, and unbind the shackles on my wrists! Hurry!" he commanded.

For a long time, she fumbled about in the darkness, groping around for his wrists, searching for the lock on the shackles.

End of the Legend •Abish Kekilbaev

"Come on! Hurry up, faster!" he rushed her, impatient.

The hysterical screams of the newborn would not cease.

And so it came to be, they were now freed people. He immediately pinpointed the direction the newborn's cries emanated from, and carefully moved toward the sound until his hand had brushed by something warm, tender, slimy. The infant, newly arrived and still connected to his mother via the umbilical cord, was laying on the bare ground and was wailing desperately. His frantic vocalizations were interrupted by hoarseness, his sobs now sounding choked and even more pitiful.

His father bent over him, and proceeded to sink his teeth into the warm, trembling umbilical cord. He carefully tied it with a small lock of hair he had ripped from his wife's head.

It was only then that the tiny quivering bundle of human seemed to calm down, his screams finally replaced with silence. While holding the infant against his chest, the captive sensed an incredible influx of strength, serenity and certainty flow through him all at once, as though it was not he, who had experienced many months of troubles and hopelessness, running and captivity, it was not he, who had been cursed with an existence of perpetual fear for one's life, or the cruel punishment of unending physical exhaustion.

Someone then lowered down a rope tied in a noose-like fashion. The captive tied the rope around his wife's waist first. She was hoisted up. After she ascended safely, the rope was lowered once again, and pressing his small, naked child against his bare chest, he, too was lifted up to freedom. Their mysterious liberator, a black-bearded *djigit* donning a fluffy sheep's wool cap, loomed over the pit that led to the dungeon, watching them. The prisoner swiftly yanked the ruby necklace dangling from his wife's neck, and, placing it in the hand of their rescuer, he grabbed the sword from his scabbard and, unwavering, he clutched the wet infant tightly against his chest with the other arm, and proceeded towards the tent of the same tribal leader who had captured and imprisoned him.

Several armed djigits had already begun to approach the dungeon, but, upon seeing this determined bare-footed prisoner firmly gripping a sword in one hand and a helpless naked newborn in the other, they paused, unsure of how to proceed in the face of such a perplexing situation.

The prisoner located the entrance to the chieftain's pavilion, and upon endeavoring to enter, was promptly blocked by two guards, who crossed their blades in front of him. Yet, much like an angry dog restrained by the lashing of a whip, the young warrior's gleaming blade slashed through the air with two deft strokes, and the two guards crumpled on either side of the entrance – profusely bleeding, defeated.

His wife, who had been trailing behind, now ran up to him – and, grabbing her by the hand, the captive burst into the serene atmosphere of the pavilion. Once inside, numerous bodyguards instantly leapt upon him with their blades unsheathed, but before any blood was shed, the chief signaled with his hand raised high and his beard swaying side to side, and their attack came to a halt. The blades which hovered so closely to the prisoner's face, just as suddenly slid back into their sheaths, unused.

Many years later, when the favorable disposition of fate along with a blessing from the Almighty allowed him to crush his enemies – one after the other, and solidify his position as omnipotent ruler over every corner of these conquered lands, he had made the decision that he would gather his massive forces together one last time, and head out into endless desert which had once been the source of so many hardships and lack, and such bitter grief, whilst on the run. And here, at the foot of the river, whose murky waters were but a week's trek from the very lands where he had been held captive, he spied a densely peopled formation of warriors, all wearing similar caps – shaggy, and fashioned from sheep's wool. They were establishing themselves atop the tall sloping riverbank, stabbing their spears into the ground hurriedly, each one keeping a firm hand attached to their weapon.

When the two armies drew closer to one other, three men broke from the formation of the adversary, dismounted and approached them on foot. The elderly warrior, who was walking in the middle of the three, the Lord recognized straight away. The warrior in front of him was the same chief, who had many years ago had so cruelly held him captive, and then so mercifully released him. Stopping approximately five paces away from the Lord, the chief proclaimed:

"Here, we have the Koran, and right over here – a sword. If you were to take our word, we shall swear upon this Koran in my hand, a vow of allegiance to you. And if you do not believe us, you may slice our heads off with a sword. We shall not march on you with weapons."

End of the Legend •Abish Kekilbaev

The very same chief remained ever-faithful until his death, and was one of the first and most distinguished emirs of the Mighty Khan.

And that same first wife had abandoned this earth thirty nine years after she was born into it. And so, there was much she had not the chance to experience – so many wonders and pleasures, all the honors and boundless luxuries, which rightfully befall the Great Khansha. It was her duty, as his first, to serve the Lord by way of offering her trust and honesty, to be faithful and loyal through the harshest years, to endure the punishment and exile right by his side, and to bless him with the joy of fatherhood. Perhaps this gift, this joy, was the very gift she provided – warming his icy heart of the spiteful, bitter rage he possessed for his enemies; it was she who saved him from the fate of a savage. In her memory, as a sign of his deepest gratitude, he erected a mosque of unprecedented beauty, to honor his wife, never to be forgotten.

It was certainly no coincidence then, that his face grew brighter every time he chanced to encounter his eldest son, and in his eyes a flame would spark – of memories, which poured light and warmth upon his soul. His mind would then give rise to their youthful years, and the bright image of his beautiful, beloved wife. These days, he oftentimes finds himself thinking of his son, whom he had sent to those faraway lands not by the will of his own heart, but purely by submission to cold, hard reason. And if he happens to envision his son, in that conquered hostile territory – tormented, ceaselessly targeted by a thousand loathsome eyes, at any moment threatening to transform into a thousand fatal arrows, then the fear, like an icy chill, quickly creeps across his back. Even he pushes forth in the midst of a massive army, before whom the very ground itself does bow, or if he sits solemnly, the honorable one in the midst of a giant feast, surrounded by a magnificent royal retinue, consisting of four proud sons and countless grandchildren, without his beloved son beside him - the Lord feels hopelessly, incurably lonely. And this devastating feeling of loneliness under the vast, limitless sky, the universal river – henceforth, his irrevocable companion.

He remembers how his aging mother, from the disease ravaging her legs, which she was barely able to move about on her own, had told him in tone plagued with sorrow, in parting:

– My child… it seems you have finally attained your goals, towards which you have been reaching. And for me, it is time to depart – and all of my disappointment of dreams unrealized will go along with me. I leave you all alone, like a sacred solitary tree standing tall in an open steppe, left untouched for all to worship. And so, my son, allow me to offer you one last lesson. The throne, upon which you sit – do not consider more dependable than a pair of your shoes, permeated through and through by moisture, nonetheless.

She spoke cautiously, in a very low whisper, so as not to be heard by any foreign ears and yet neither her passionate ardor, nor the strength of her words was sacrificed as she firmly grasped her son's hand with her own small, withered fingers. Every additional word that came from her lips weighed on him heavily and only added to his growing consternation. Upon completion of her thoughts, her pallid feeble lips closed, her dark blazing eyes quietly dimmed, as though gradually detaching, disembodied, to dissipate in some distant, far-off expanse. And when her gaunt, sickly hand finally slipped out of his, and landed lifelessly on the edge of the bed the fierce Lord, the invincible leader, who – having conquered half of the world itself, found that he felt completely disoriented, much like a blind newborn pup, suddenly ostracized from his mother.

Ever since that day, when he returns from his campaigns in far-away lands, he remembers the counsel and forewarning of his dying mother.

And so, the current great Khansha was, in fact, his second wife, who had the taken place of his first, who had passed. She came from a wealthy, noble family. In those days, the Lord had already united the people, and had gathered what would be the empire of the Great Khan under his *shanrak*. His lucky star had shot straight up into the sky, far above the earth. Yet, he knew that the arrogant kind of his wife were compelled to perpetually spout toxic rumors, such as: well, the Great Khan does not come from "blue blood", yet he doesn't come from "red blood" either, so judging by his pedigree, we can assume that he can be only of "mixed blood". It seems that not a single person of such mixed pedigree has ever ascended the throne. And for this very reason, the Lord had chosen his wife from a noble lineage, to bind himself in marriage to her noble blood, and to terminate all of the attacks.

His new wife, seeing just how great and powerful her new husband is, watching the might of his blade topple the strongest kingdoms one after the other – this daughter of superior birth, understood once and for all the true power of the Khan, and was able to fairly assess and appreciate her husband, to whom she felt utterly bound, with her whole heart. Over time, she had begun to distance herself from all of the secretive rumors and inferences and whispers of her kin, who were in one way or another dissatisfied with the Lord, and soon enough she stopped listening altogether. And then her family gradually detached from her all the more so, after they realized that addressing the Lord directly was a much more lucrative application of their energy, and so they, ambitious and insistent, came to him for certain special privileges such as luxurious, high-grade linens – which the joyous, victorious Khan very liberally gave out to his imperious, entitled relatives – and did so gladly, without a heavy heart. And over time, even when the sun and moon, fearful of disturbing the glistening edge of the great Lord's sword with their rays, his new relatives had either given up entirely or forgotten their prior need to parade around their gentility, or remind others of who their ancestors were.

Further down the line, they ceased bringing up the topic of their ancestors altogether, and had decided to replace this with a new habit – praising their son-in-law, up and down. Yet, in the last few years, when the great Khan's sons had matured into adulthood and had begun to participate in his military campaigns, showing great valor and prowess in battle, the relatives of his wife, forgetting to praise and show gratitude to the Khan himself, have instead been praising and elevating his sons. Despite this, they did not forget to add: "And what of that little nephew of ours – as similar as two drops of water, he and our ancestor, the *batyr*! Mark my words, you will see – one day, the son will surpass even his mighty father!"

The Great Khansha had birthed only sons – gallant, dignified – the whole lot of them, and whom she raised all by herself. Over the years, the great Khansha had acquired a sort of regal assuredness, which in turn transformed her behavior. She no longer displayed the same timidity, nor the same attitude of servility and flattery. She created her own policy in the court – with the exception of the occasions marking the Khan's return from his successful military campaigns, where the entire main palace was filled with celebration and continuous feasting, the Khansha would live with all of her grandchildren in a separate palace on the outskirts of the city. And her husband concerned her least of all – if he wants to see her, then he can come to visit her at her personal residence.

Remembering his mother's admonition, he took for his younger wife a young woman from the tribe of his deceased mother. She was sixteen years old, and there was something about her mannerisms and her physical appearance that reminded him of his first wife of so many years ago. She had no foolish habits, nor was she capricious. She was gentle and mild. She was sweet-tempered and pure in her young age, like fresh, unspoiled milk. She had not yet been exposed to the toxicity that is power and the feeling of supremacy that all too often accompanies a position of authority.

On his latest expedition, as per their invariable custom, he took along his eldest wife – leaving his young wife behind at home. And as it turns out, in honor of her spouse, who had embarked upon this grand and daunting journey, his young wife had erected a majestic tower. Taller than all the other minarets and towers, she prevails, reigning over the city from the clouds above.

The isolated palace, where the Lord preferred to pass the time in peace and quiet, he bequeathed to his younger Khansha. What numbered days of rest he had left before his next expedition he planned on spending in that very palace. In his old age, when the years have taken what they can, he no longer preferred to ride around from palace to palace, instead choosing to settle down in one of his palaces until his final days. And it was the palace of the younger Khansha that he chose.

And suddenly, a realization loomed over his head: perhaps this was the reason behind all of this scheming business with the red apple and the Elder Khansha – born of the jealousy of the old Baybishe to the younger *Tokal*. Right in front of his nose, a bee busily flew by, buzzing, and he felt a pang of shame and blame, as though the bee had actually stung him: " Why on earth were you suffering so, how could such a simple realization and answer to this riddle not have dawned on you?" And then, as if to underline the authenticity of this crucial awareness, the leaves in the treetops above began to sway, and the leaves danced under the force of the wind.

Indeed, in his youth his thoughts did not circle around as they do now, in search of the truth – like a greyhound, overtaking with lightning speed and immediately taking it on the spot…

So, naturally, the proud Baybishe, very much aware of her own self-worth, would not take too kindly to her spouse, who for a time never stepping even a foot away from her, has suddenly taken it upon himself to retire in the presence of his young Tokal. The Khan remembered how the Khansha fell into a white-hot jealous rage not only over his current younger wife, but also at the memory of the Lord's first wife, who had passed on many years prior – when he had raised, in her blessed memory, a magnificent mosque. He remembered how long the Great Khansha continued to walk around frowning grimly, making certain her discontentedness and wounded pride were as visible as possible. And now, the newest installation – a majestic tower in sapphire-blue, once again painfully pricked the vision of his eldest wife.

How else can an elderly woman return the "favor" to her husband, if not through rumors about those closest to him circulating, appearing as a present and very real threat intending to do him harm? And the crimson apple – that was a sign that she had wanted to relay a message of an ominous nature. And yet, having figured out her true intentions, he had lost all his previous interest in the matter. The last role he wanted to play was that of victim in her staged female outrages. And what she wanted to relay to him was ever so clear, and was certainly not worth the headache of puzzling over. Having arrived at this conclusion, the Lord felt as though a massive weight had rolled off his shoulders. The worm that had been gnawing away day and night, seeding doubt in mind, had finally been satiated, no longer to prey upon his thoughts.

This night, unlike the previous night, he drifted off into a deep, and come morning felt well rested, invigorated even. Following breakfast, he sent for his personal carriage to be readied.

The grand gates of the Khan's palace were thrown wide open, and his luxurious, gilded carriage rolled through them, guarded on all sides by armed nukers, who escorted the Khan to the recently constructed tower.

Uniquely different, he was, in that having conquered half of the world, his eager thirst for the glory of other, yet unconquered crowns persisted. Indeed, so ambitious was he, that in order to have a capital city, its level of beauty and majesty would remain unrivalled across the globe. It is no coincidence that he enslaved hundreds of master-builders during his latest military campaign.

Every time, upon returning from various far-away lands, following an extensive absence, he would ride around the entire city, surveying the new structures that had been erected all through his absence. And the view of the capital, exceeding even the most wondrous cities of the world in its magnificence, elated his spirits.

And the sapphire-blue tower built recently by the Young Khansha especially brought him great joy. Having rightly felt in her heart his innermost aspirations, she had erected for him this minaret-tower. Its azure divinity even rivalled the sky itself.

The location chosen for the tower was chosen most successfully – no matter where you were positioned in the city, the minaret was always visible. The azure tower elicited the most rapturous enthusiasm, and seemed to smile to from afar to any who would approach it, their eyes glued to the site of her. Even the washed out sky, bleached by the sweltering heat of July seemed somehow rejuvenated by the bright indigo color, and the dome, situated atop the tower, radiated a certain profound exuberant azure.

The closer the tower is, the taller it looms in one's vision. The piercing smile of the façade of the tower seems to transform when approached more closely, appearing more grim and restrained. And when the Khan drove up to her in his gilded carriage, the tower stood before like some colossal giantess, whose head effortlessly jutted into the heavenly zenith.

The uneasy and conflicting feelings of the last few days, and the ensuing internal ferocious struggle and turmoil abandoned him once and for all. The magnificent view of this splendid tower quelled any remaining doubts that rested within his heart. He was overcome with joy from the knowledge that not a single capital on the entirety of the globe has such a striking, majestic tower soaring in the clouds. In other capital cities, if the Khan's numerous nukers happened to lay their eyes on any structure that would overwhelm their Lord's sense of pride or accomplishment, without a word of instruction, they would charge headfirst and with a loud cry, they would begin to break apart, crumble, demolish it with heavy tools. But here, in his own city, this awe-inspiring tower forced everyone to freeze in place for a while, mouths agape, and they would gaze upon her monumental spire in silent reverence.

From this point forth, this azure tower – like a Lord banner of the Mighty Khan – will be proudly displayed above the roofs of the entire inhabited world.

The minaret turned out to be a match for only one – the one in whose honor it was built: it was inviting, exquisite and perfect when viewed from nearby, in every imaginable way, and up close – the sheer power and unapproachable grandeur of it stunned and astonished.

The splendor of the palace fascinated the Lord. He stood in front of the tower with ecstatic expression, like some fervent youth who had, for the first time in his life, laid eyes upon an incredibly beautiful and unapproachable young woman.

Standing at the foot of the tower, he experienced an exceptionally powerful uplifting of his soul. And gratitude – for all that there was to behold upon this earth and subject to the brilliance of the human intellect. And gratitude for this majestic tower, sparkling like a sapphire. And for the beauty of the azure dome reaching into the sky. And for the inspired effort of the architect, who for the duration of many years filled with stressful labor, inch by inch, he built and heaved and raised up the tower to a height that makes one's head spin. Gratitude for his own unyielding heart, which though worn out, had survived all of the faraway campaigns and battles, and yet still wanted to keep hurling forward, like and eagle ripping through the clouds, soaring onward to the heavens with a keen, sharp-eyed, unyielding determination. And tremendous gratitude to his precious young wife, who had foreseen much – and had created such a celebration for him, that would surely not be ended in just one day. And, of course – boundless gratitude to this entire God-given earth, and the knowledge that, of all the mortals – he was the only one chosen for this greater glory and for the addition of the majesty and beauty of this azure tower to her lands.

Oh, you strange and mysterious sapphire tower! All it takes is a little bit of distance, and yet you still peer down for afar with the most inviting gaze! Your angular, geometric tiles glossed over with blue, seem to melt from a distance, emanating a languid softness. And the further the distance from her, the sharper and more distinct the outline of her silhouette appears to the eye. An unbelievable beauty, knowing her own worth, she dares not reward you with even a glance when you stand beside her – yet, from afar, she seems to beckon to you with such a promising tenderness, as though she is appealing to your attention and your embraces. And like a moth caught in a ring of the brightest light, you yearn to flutter no further than the illumined expanse of her charms.

And of all the numerous towers, castles and minarets he has seen over his countless journeys, along all the roads traveled upon this bright earth, to and from battle – truly, not once has such an alluring and magical beauty met his gaze. No logical explanations tried to work their way into his mind, such as why did contemplating upon this tower so charm his gaze, or why her intoxicating splendor had instantly bewitched this warrior's heart.

No acknowledgement or response would be given to those who were closest and coveted her. Her enchanting smile she would cast out into the wind, to her one and only – always so far, far away. She would greet him – he, who was marching closer and closer to her from afar, and the beauty would implore in gentle whispers: "Come…come to me!"

Oh, how subtly and impeccably did the architect convey the condition of the Younger Khansha's soul, pining so for her husband who was so very far away… Up close, the tower blinded with its beauty, but upon separation from her – suddenly, as if wrapping herself delicately in the folds of a mirage, the delicate beauty emitted only inexplicable sorrow.

As if dreading the impending separation, as if her objection was issued in the form of a plea: "Do not abandon me, darling… Do not leave. Come, stay with me a while longer…"

"Stop! Come back soon!"

As if actually hearing all of this in reality – he was confused, his train of thought abruptly interrupted, a knot rose up in his throat… Half-reclining and propping himself up, his elbows digging into the pillows, he suddenly bolted upright. Then he commanded they turn around, and head back.

It was not until the Khan had returned to his palace, that he dared to gaze back in the direction of the minaret. How the nukers of his guard would interpret his unusual behavior by the tower, he was not certain. He reclined again, easing back onto his pillows and closing his eyes, and so he remained for the rest of the trip back.

Unexpectedly, at the dining table, he felt a distinct burning sensation in his chest, and barely touched any of his food. He was only able to shove a tiny slice of honey-coated melon into his mouth. The taste of the melon relieved some of the onset nausea. This time, the crimson apple was not brought out. And the servant girl, wrapped in a sheer shawl, modestly kept her eyes low to the ground and her lips did not betray any shifty, secretive behavior. Today, the girl was nothing short of utterly obliging obedience, without the slightest hint of her defiant behavior from the day prior.

When she retreated from the room, he sat there for a while, silently staring at the crystalline waters of the brook spilling and gliding over the mosaic, paved with blue and pale rose colored tiles. Gazing upon the clear droplets of the fountain gleaming like bright, little tears that slid down and disappeared in the water, he felt that his outlook seemed brighter, softened, was becoming more sentimental. Much like packed snow in the winter that crumbles and then melts in the warm wind, so the accumulated weight of his severity and detachment seemed to dissipate from his soul; the rigid plates, like armor that encased it fell way – disintegrating like a broken curse, and his entire being was pervaded by a soothing tranquility, the serenity of solitude. And then in that very instant, he felt gripped by an unbelievable sense of self-pity, almost unbearable... For what? For whom? Perhaps for those clear little droplets sliding into the water, only to disappear in an instant in a pit of obscurity. Certainly not for the lonely azure tower remaining somewhere over there, behind him – in her transparent, vibrating vestments of smoky haze. The indistinguishable tender feeling, elusive, like the currents of water, led him to thoughts of the Younger Khansha. It was as though she had expressed all her feeling fully through the act of building the tower: her affection and yearning for him, her impatience and desire to be reunited yet again, the deep passion that remains hidden from the rest of the world, the unavoidable restlessness of solitude, the woe of injury and insult to her soul, brought about by the hostile environment of her surroundings in the court... As though her frantic moan was trapped within the tower: "Come to me! Hear me! Protect me!" And if dignity and tenderness, joy and sorrow, courage and mercy, longing and passion could all intermingle to form one word – ow can it not be love? For he certainly knew the meaning of love.

In his years of exile and roaming of the lifeless sands of the desert, his wife – wishing to prevent the disclosure of her extreme exhaustion was, at times, had no choice but to grab him by the elbow

and plead: "Hold me, hold me for a little while... I've no more energy."
In her fading eyes he could read her veiled feelings of despair,
frustration, and pain, but also her love and selfless devotion...

And when his eldest son approached him to bid his father
farewell before he left for his journey to distant foreign lands he, too,
tried ever so hard to push his overwhelming feelings deep down into
his heart, but in his eyes, the Lord could see the very same feelings as
his mother once had.

And today, after his engagement of visiting the tower, he sped away in
his carriage and looked back at her as one would look upon the person
closest to them in their moment of great soulful, passionate outpour. It
was only today that he able to grasp the mystery of miraculous beauty,
and the feeling of true, soulful passion – brought about by looking upon
the azure tower.

He immediately wanted to see his younger wife, so he may
once again look into her eyes and see that expression of suppressed,
despairing love.

A deep emotional tumultuousness filled his chest with an
spirited breath, and he braced himself in the sweet complexity of the
sensation, not yet fully grasping what worried him more: the long-
forgotten youthful feeling he was experiencing now, or the realization
that he had lived his entire life without any need for this heart-warming
sensation! And now his agitation and impatience fueled his desire to
see the Young Khansha right away. He hadn't the faintest idea of what
she looked like now. Their prior history did not include much one-on-
one time together, and when they were in public, he could not afford to
be seen admiring her beauty. Distraught by this, he tried to remember –
and suddenly, an image of her dark, sparkling eyes – somewhat faint,
floated up to the surface. Her demure, light face gave off a perpetual
appearance of humility and youthful kindness; her small, neat nose with
quivering nostrils; her sweet child-like mouth – neither thin-lipped, nor
thick; her chin – rounded, like and egg. They say that only the most
loyal women have such physical characteristics – they are bashful, yet
gentle and refined, and their eyes emit a certain sparkle, or ray of light
– not a blazing fire of passion, but one of elevated, pure, tender love.
These women charm not with bewitching, intoxicating smiles of
passion, but with their lovely sorrow, capable of capturing any real
man's heart, enough to drive them crazy.

The love of a woman such as this embodies itself in the form of this magnificent, man-made tower. The king and prophet Sulaiman, having penetrated the hearts of men, having grasped the hearts of women, having seen and studied thousands of the most beautiful women in the world – these particular women he likened to angels, who were capable of tying up any man without ropes of any sort, but with the power of their charming, earnest soul.

They also say, that the prophet Sulaiman, so as not to lose his taste for wine, drank it in in such minute quantities that he would place the tip of his finger into the goblet and then transfer it to his tongue. Afterwards, he could sit for hours, reveling in the complex bouquet caught in the persisting aftertaste. Well, if it were up to him, a warrior to the bone, such finesse truly sickened him. He has, after all, spent the majority of his life in never-ending wars. The Lord was never fully able to grasp the lessons of this legendary king of the olden days.

And as it turns out, it was not until this particular day, that he was able to taste the pleasures of that benevolent fate, which had set alight his blindingly bright star of fortune. His heart, hardened so very long ago, searched for but one pleasure – seeing the banners of his enemies fall to his feet, right next to the rolling heads of men topped with foreign crowns.

And always, if his heart desired a truly joyous celebration, then the body was bound up in the king's chains from head to toe, the crown pressed into the head, the throne was held, as if it were a trap. But then, what other fate could be expected from a person who had deprived forty different populations of their nation – living before him, waving around their forty swords amongst themselves, who took control of the of the reigns of all forty nations into his own, singular hands? And now he sits, disoriented and in isolation, driven there by the regulations of the palace, which he himself had created, and has no idea how to call his youngest wife to his side, though they reside in the same palace. Having witnessed much cruelty and treachery in his life time, having assigned himself the rule of severity when dealing with those who surrounded him – the Lord did not even allow the servants of the palace to approach him too closely, and to the peace and quiet of his numerous wives and concubines, he would retire only when under the protection of the veil of night. And unless large receptions with his ambassadors were involved, for it was custom for all of the wives and children of the Khan, from all the different nations, to sit together, he was not in the habit of spending time with any of them in the daytime hours. And now, the very same rules and order he created within his palace, were preventing any transgressions on his part, thwarting any possibility of realizing his sudden desire – visiting the Young Khansha. After all, the meaning of the red apple, with its obviously disfigured skin and rotting worm-hole, sent by the Elder Khansha is still uncertain. And the servants were likely to be working for her, as well. It is impossible to predict how a visit to the Younger Khansha would correspond with what the Elder Khansha had attempted to warn him of.

He anxiously proceeded to await the arrival of nighttime, when it would be possible for him to sneak into the women's quarters. Daytime – hitherto quickly flying by, like the easy whistle of a djigit, suddenly started to shift and waver in place, as though it were some hobbled horse. Even the sun, entering into the zenith, seemed to pause, motionless, in place.

The solitude of the vast, deserted hall depressed him, so he decided to go for a walk in his garden one more time. He arrived in his favorite quiet, isolated spot near the little spring, sat himself down on his usual rock, but was unable to harmonize his turbulence in his heart, and his thoughts started to wander about. And then he got up and made his way back, angrily glancing at the sun, which did not seem move in any particular hurry across the sky.

His heart, which not once had lots its nerve in the face of an enemy, grew timid at the prospect of approaching his marital bed, and – like some inexperienced groom, he was eagerly waiting for the sun to go down, for nighttime to creep in, so he would be able to sneak to the room of the Younger Khansha, and hide from all of his awkwardness and apprehension.

And finally, the shadows on the ground began to stretch out, longer and longer. The trees slowly lost their bright patches, sunlight spilling through the canopy, and their shadows spilled over, merging into one another. At the onset of twilight, the Lord returned to the palace. His whole day was spent in torment from anxious waiting, and by the end of the day, some form of doubt seemed yet again to creep into his heart. In his immense hall, illuminated by hundreds of lamps, he yet again found himself in a state of restlessness, dissatisfaction, boredom and was overcome with a feeling of ceaseless loneliness in this white world... Oh, for if he were standing in front of blue, bristling spears, aimed right at his chest, or in front of a horde of swiftly approaching enemy cavalry – he would feel no fear, he wouldn't even flinch. And if he was a young, ordinary djigit searching for his woman, he would bravely have stepped into the bedchamber of the Younger Khansha. But now, he is long past the age of unbridled, passionate love. It wasn't the old Baybishe he was intending to visit, just to sit and talk to her about this and that – no, he was attempting to see someone he barely knew – and though she was his wife, she was also a young girl. The Young Khansha had not once been bold enough to commence a single conversation for the entire duration of their royal marriage. And he, too, had not attempted to speak with her, either. What would he say when he would walk into her room? Though, of course, this young woman still belongs to him, as his lawful wife. But it is not as though she is the only on in the Khanate – the whole capital, every house in it, every person in those houses – they all belong to him. And not just the capital, but the entire nation stands still in a servile bow at the mere mention of his name. The inhabitants of half of the entire world slavishly stare him in the face. Despite this – there is not a single soul inhabiting this half of the world, with whom he can speak frankly and openly. Alas, his youngest wife is also one the other ordinary mortals, who lives under his authority and patronage. And over the last few days they have both been as prisoners – captives of this secluded, country palace.

She would not dare to overcome her timid and fearful nature in front of the Lord, and come to him herself – as a wife visiting her husband. Some living hell, this life is! It would seem that all living creatures, both body and soul, belong to him – squeezed tightly in the grip of his iron fist. And yet – here is the mysterious, ruthless truth: though everything appears to be his, it is simultaneously not available to him. Which means – it is other, foreign. He knew full well, that in the world dominated by his rule – every single person, with the exception of one, was living with an invisible noose wrapped around their necks, the noose being the power of his authority. And they all sit in their small cages, harboring the knowledge that there is nowhere to run, and that running is useless. He considered himself free from all bondage, and yet today he suddenly felt like a noose, flying in the opposite direction, had nabbed even him by the neck. People were frightened by his words, or his gaze and now – he himself is afraid of people's eyes and eyes, fearing he will undermine the rules he had set himself, in the eyes of the slaves.

And here he is, slinking around like a cat on the prowl, slipping out of his bedchamber. These insidious restraints, confining him until midnight, continued to drag behind him. It seemed that everything here – the marble-patterned vault and the matte-white blank walls and the stealthy shadows slanting along the floor and the stifled sounds of the footsteps pattering on silk carpets, and even the lamp he held in his hands seemed to be following him, noting each step; as if distinctly feeling the stares of many furtive spies, all communicating with each other through various signals: "He went there, and now – where?..." And thousands of nasty mouths, hidden in nooks and crannies and veiled in darkness – and all of these beasts readying themselves to gleefully roar and cry out the second he arrives at the threshold of the Younger Khansha's bedroom door.

Yes, thousands upon thousands of servile heads bow before him, yet he has no authority over the thoughts drifting inside of those heads, much like the feelings and desires of his slaves. He cannot reach thousands with his threatening gaze, yet – all of them put together, as one, can intently watch him... He could not possibly follow and watch every movement of a thousand hands, nor watch every step taken by thousands of feet, yet every action and movement of his own – is out in the open for all to see...

Even now, in this desolate palace cloaked in the darkness of night, they are closely watching him, their eyes wide open. Two gray-haired, red-eyed eunuchs encountered each other by the doors, and silently bowed before him, their right and left palms touching, then folded in front of their chest, their hands withered from years of slavery. Resembling corpses more so than living humans, they are ready to sweep to floor with the fearful quiver of their eyelashes, yet the second he passes by – they will raise their heads, and exchange meaningful glances with each other.

It felt as though the blade of a dagger had been lodged into his spine, and this sensation prompted him to turn around sharply. And right there in front him, he saw the two half-dead eunuchs turn to each other with animated expressions, yet the second they detected the icy gaze of the Lord, they immediately dropped their heads to their chest, lowering their gaze to the floor. The heavy oak door mumbled something as it opened before him and closed behind him, creaking on its hinges.

The Lord went into a large room, lit up by numerous lamps. In the corner of the room, someone's silhouette stirred in the shadows. It was an old woman – a servant who watched over the harem, and she slowly, unwillingly, lifted herself from her seat. This wrinkled thing, was the governess and nurse of the Young Khansha. All of the young wives of the Lord's harem had passed through her hands. So it had been since the beginning of his reign. Despite the fact that the governess not once came close to the Khan's quarters in the palace, every single wife the Khan has, has been educated in a secret science – how to conduct herself appropriately around the Khan, and what to be aware of as a fiancée to the Khan. The woman who watched over the harem was not like the other workers of the palace, her behavior was different – she was smug and pompous and minced her words when she spoke. Even now, looking at her, she seems almost unaffected by the presence of the Khan, unlike the other servants – and approached him in a dignified and even manner, overcoming the trembling of her leg. It would appear that even the Chief Treasurer himself, imbued with the power to keep his hand over the immensity of the entire Treasury of the State, could not afford to behave so arrogantly. She even frowned down upon the Lord and his many wives. As if it would be impossible for him to locate his wives' quarters in the palace without her as an intermediary. She had a tendency of being particularly difficult and unapproachable the first few days after his return from one of his long voyages. And now, in order to force the Lord to wait for her, she sauntered across the entire length of the hall with the most deliberate, leisurely steps she could muster – like some peahen, planning and counting its steps.

And so she approaches – the sickly, mottled skin of her face covered with deep wrinkles and cuts like the palms of her hands, and the wrinkles of her face in no way seem to align with her expensive violet satin frock. She was close enough for him to make out her thick, dark, bushy eyebrows, tinted a pale honey-yellow color throughout, except for certain splotchy patches of grey. Her hooked, owl-like nose, hung over her narrow, flabby lips. Her watery eyes were motionless, as though glued into her eye-sockets, and were firmly fixed upon the Lord, as though she did not recognize him. And only then, when he furrowed his eyebrows and scowled, did the old woman let her gaze drop to the side.

The old harem-overseer, feigning haste, proceeded to open the door for him, while awkwardly combatting her long, flowing sleeves with her arms, which had become entangled. Desiring to remove himself from oppressive, dim and deathly gaze of the old woman, the Lord quickly hurried into the bedchamber of the Young Khansha. The room was quite dim, and the air was infused with the aromas of pink oil and many subtle, mixed fragrances of flowers expelled through the swirling smoke of incense that blanketed the room. He did not notice the Khansha's chamber right away. It was to the right, and slightly elevated above a wide, flat ottoman. He made a step towards her bed. In the middle of the bed, among rumpled sheets, and flattened pillows, he saw two little lumps underneath a silk blanket. The Khan shuddered. It seems that the two little lumps suddenly came to life, expanded, only to deflate again, flattened and lifeless. And when the Khan finally surmised what movements must be causing such among the blankets, his body shuddered once again.

The area where her bed was located was dimmer than the remaining space of the bedroom. The smell of her young body, mixed with the aroma of pink oil and flower fragrances awoke in him a most powerful desire – one that he was certain had parted with many years ago, one that was deeply buried in the slopes of age. He felt now that his nerves, stretched to the point of pain not even a minute ago, were now relaxing, loosening, unwinding – like tanned skins treated with hot steam. His feet began to give way under him from the anxiety, and fearing that he might fall, the Khan came to a standstill, gluing himself to that spot.

The lumps underneath the blanket suddenly revived again. And here, the Khan saw a view, that all of his powerful desires suddenly subsided, shattering, as if their flight ended with a crash into the wall. His heart burst forth, then froze, motionless, and began to knock about inside his chest, causing it to quake.

Suddenly, from the center of this mountain-shaped bundle of pillows and silk blankets, two pale bare hands emerged – swept away the blankets, palms up, as if in prayer. Swiftly they fell, like birds shot down mid-air, and trembled atop of the blankets, then their fingers entwined, clasping each other gently, embracing in the shape of a ring... In this embrace, the woman's hands clutched the rumpled down blanket to her chest. It slid down, like a melting mound of snow, and her face appeared – flushed and dewy. The Khansha's neck, twisted under her head, which was resting on her pillow, was unnaturally long. Her black, disheveled hair was scattered all about her pillow, and what remained spilled over half of her face. Long eyelashes adorned her eyelids, which were firmly squeezed shut. Her mouth was slightly ajar, like a person who is ill and gasping for air from overheating. Her swollen lips, it seemed, would no longer be able to shut. Her clenched teeth were white as pearls. From some remarkable depth, a frail, barely audible voice leaked out – with a passionate and demanding moan. And the sound of this moan stung the Lord in the ear like a scorpion's tail. The Young Khansha moaned as if fighting something off, and losing her strength at the hands of some invisible force. The pillow, like a mangled white boulder, was lying to the side of her head.

Oh, such a strange, bleating, savage moan he had heard once, many years ago – as a fifteen year old youth. Since childhood, he was familiar with the sensation of playing alone, avoiding the company of other children. One day, he had jumped on his horse, deciding to ride into the valley, where he found a cliff, with its top shaved off, and decided to plant traps for the birds of prey. And then he noticed a woman, who had come from the direction of an isolated village road. She appeared to be draped in a long, black veil and was carrying a jug atop her right shoulder. She was walking in the direction of the spring. Once the woman had disappeared amongst the thick, tall reeds, which concealed the path to the spring – a rider appeared on the very same path. His beard was thick and black and shaped like a shovel, and he sat atop a shaggy horse, whose uncut mane hung almost all the way down to his pasterns. His hooves sprayed crumbled stones, which flew down the steep slope, tumbling into the ravine. Both the horse and the rider disappeared into the reeds after the woman.

The young hunter thought nothing of the appearance and subsequent disappearance of both the woman and the man in the reeds. Completely absorbed by his passion for hunting, from his perch, he was observing a hawk gliding overhead, tracing circles in the sky right above the exact place where he had erected his trap and rope noose. And then, an unexpected cry pierced the air, emanating from the direction of the ravine. The screams were likely coming from the woman, the one with the jug. He instantly jumped out from his hiding spot. The screams and wails intensified. The boy grabbed his bow and arrows, and set off in the direction of the shrieks. Two times he fell, cutting both his knees against jagged rocks, and both of his palms were shredded and bleeding. He did all he could to ignore the pain, pushing on, rushing to her aid, but as he moved further up the ravine, he heard the cries grow quieter and now they sounded entirely different somehow – unlike the cries inflicted by pain and suffering.

And all of a sudden, he was hit with the realization that these screams were not due to any type of painful, unbearable torture, but that they were the choked moans of some sort of incredible enjoyment. The sounds were akin to the bleating moan of ewes in the sheep pens in spring time when they would lead the lambs up to them, and make the drink the colostrum… Confused and disappointed by his mistake, the boy kicked over a large, loose rock which was balanced on the edge of the cliff face, and stone tumbled downward, noisily carrying other fragments of rock and soil along with it. Angered by this trickery – a deception that had triggered his purest intentions – to come to the aid of someone in trouble – the boy returned to his snares.

After some time had gone by, he saw the shaggy horse with its long mane being mounted by the lone traveler – the djigit with the shovel-like beard – and saw him cross the stream at the bottom of the ravine, and scramble up the steep slope on the opposite side.

And soon after, the woman in the *parandja* appeared, with the jug on her arm, as before, and with a light-hearted step began to walk along the road, her hips playfully swinging side to side, her strong legs stepping handsomely.

And knowing nothing of any misfortune, the hazy smoke emerged from the chimney of a small hut, twisting and turning, only to fly up into the capricious, clouded sky.

His torn, bloodied palms searing in pain – which he had undergone, as it would seem, for no good reason. Considerably more painful than his burning palms, was the boy's disappointment that he had been an involuntary witness to that beastly behavior of which people partook, in these isolated, mountain areas by the spring. His heart was overwhelmed resentment and disgust.

And now, here, standing over the bed of his young wife, the old Lord had finally grasped the full essence of what was taking occurring before his very eyes. And in his heart, the distant disgusting memory boiled up again. And that same child-like disappointment, when he so strongly feared for one's well-being – for their life, proved to be a preposterous anxiety – instead turning into the unbearable pain brought on by the shame of his error.

Before him, was the same disgusting, bestial act, as then, and boiling over with contempt, he immediately removed himself from this sweet-smelling, luxurious bed, the sight of which had instantly transformed into something so loathsome. He did not leave – instead, he ran – as quickly as he could, to escape all that he had witnessed in the Young Khansha's chamber.

End of the Legend • Abish Kekilbaev

He could not even recall bolting through her doors. He raced down the long corridors and halls of the palace, attempting to rather reach his own quarters as quickly as possible. And as he drew closer to his quarters, it suddenly struck him, that for some odd reason, during his humiliating flight from her room, he saw neither the old harem-keeper, nor the two eunuchs who resembled reanimated corpses. Yet, he was also certain that these harem servants would gladly spread news of this incident the very next day – seeding gossip of the Khan, who, for no fathomable reason, had quickly and unexpectedly bolted from the bedroom of his youngest wife. His heart wailed and bled out, as if it had been shredded to bits by a pack of wild dogs. And it seemed to him that his bedroom, his current destination and safe-haven, was located on opposite end of the earth, and would take several years to reach.

He finally reached his private quarters, but was his energy was near-spent. After shutting the door, he had the distinct sensation that he was not alone: as if thousands of prying eyes motionlessly gazed at him, blaming him in some fateful slip-up. In the large hall was completely silent, except for the bubbling and trickling of water in the indoor pond. All the nooks and crannies of this enormous palace seemed to simultaneously churn out these dark, murky masses of silence – thick, oozing, suffocating. He tugged at his clothing, baring his chest and approaching the pool of water, and then slid into it until he was knee-deep. He desperately desiring to be quelled and calmed, grounded through contemplation of the peaceful, gentle current of crystalline water. But his urge for rest was ultimately rejected, as if his steel body-armor had been torn from his chest, which was now exposed, and once again made vulnerable at the mercy of hands of boundless fury. He rose to his feet and slowly approached the window, its view unfolding before him, stretching out into the nighttime garden, enshrouded in darkness, only faintly illuminated by the horned moon. In the round courtyard in front of the palace was a fountain, much like in the Lord's quarters, and the second he stepped into view, his silhouette visible in the well-lit window, he noticed the flickering of numerous shadows on the lawn, scurrying and scattering in front of the fountain. The myriad soldiers of the Khan's personal guard, as a result of boredom, probably arranged some kind of innocent socialization in the grass in front of the fountain pool, and seeing the figure of the Khan himself in the window frightened them, scattering in different directions, like cockroaches, rushing to once again occupy their various posts along their numerous patrols – in their hideouts, lying in wait in the gardens and forests surrounding the palace.

The moon had long ago pressed its horns to rest upon the very edge of the earth. In its faint light, the vague outlines of the front walls and entrance of the Khansha's palace appeared, surrounded by the pitch black shapes of the wild, overgrown garden and forest. The sliver of moon sank into the trembling, rippling surface of the water in the pool outside, and it reflected back the illuminated windows of the house. The strange, wavering lunar night, replete with cloaked cunning, ascended her throne above the Khan's enormous palace and garden. But the Lord's quarters are impenetrable – not even a single beam of light can be creep in from the world outside, and when all of his lamps are extinguished – his enormous room resembles a large, overturned kettle, with smoky, blackened walls.

Oh, night! That sly night, which binds the eyes of every man, which deafens the ears of every man. As though all of mankind, with his fussing, agitation and anger of the day, has been dosed with a poison which lulls him them sleep – and they would fall, without consciousness, seemingly lifeless. And the realm of total authority of the power of the thick shadows and silence descended down upon them. And so came the time to commence and complete all of the deceptive, devious, wily matters. The entire world was, it seemed, smothered with the suffocating mantle of illicit undertakings. It was the time to open oneself to all of one's monstrous carnal longings – the kind of thoughts that, without great shame, cannot see the light of day. And so, the timeless witches' Sabbath has begun, when the world and all its people are in the devil's hands. His creations, innumerable assemblies of the sin-drenched night, which remain deeply buried in the daytime, away from God's light and the eyes of righteous men, under the veil of night - the vermin creep out by the hordes, and the swarms of filthy bats come pouring and fluttering out of all of the dark and narrow crevices and burrows of stinking squalor. It is only in the daytime that people appear before each other as decent, worthy human beings – for when night descends, that man transforms into nothing more than an animal: one that snores in his sleep, sweats in his stuffy bed, and if a woman perchance is laying nearby, he will become enraged, like a bull, and will proceed to mount her as nature has permitted. But the next day, when the sun rises up into the sky, his human eyes will be pried open, greeting the day, and the animal in him will instantly melt away – metamorphosing into their two-legged bodies, nothing more than ordinary people. They will all be filled with feelings of shame, and will hide their shame with the daylight, embarrassed by troubling and judgmental words and opinions thrown

End of the Legend •Abish Kekilbaev

their way by people who are not at all different from themselves. However, night again approaches, and each one of them will once more be able to slip off the burdens of this human condition, like a robe, to be freed from their feelings of shame, and to once again become nothing more than what they truly are, themselves – to be alone and free from the necessity of being dependent upon the will and desires of the remaining people. Night of bestial liberty! For, it is there in all people, but for him – the ruler of half of the world, no such liberty can exist, or be afforded. All around is the endless night, and it is as though he alone is sitting beside the bright bonfire, and feeling thousands of attentive and unfriendly gazes like spears, crossing each other, their eyes fixed on him, trailing him in the dark. And the Lord himself cannot even begin to wonder what is out there, in the pitch black stone wall of this night… The concerns and tribulations of daytime he drags behind him, no better or worse than anyone else, yet in regards to his nightly pleasures – this matter certainly has nothing to do with his honor.

There is no torment more terrible, than to be sleepless in the warm, dense night in the solitude and confinement of one's luxurious bedchamber – surrounded on all sides by the two-legged creatures of the night, as they shift about in their beds – those heaving, vile movements, expelling in all directions the smell of dripping females and the smell of sweat-drenched males burning hot with lust. Compared to this – they were a real paradise, those short nightly respites during their campaigns, the night before the battle, impregnated with the stink of the foot-cloths, hung up to drying above the dying embers of their bonfires. They were like genuine angels, the serenely snoring soldiers, who had fallen asleep clutching their spears, their saddles tucked under the heads. Not a single one of them knows whether their judgement tomorrow leads them to fall in battle and meet their death, or if they shall survive to remain in this existence, along with the rest of the living. And is not greeting the new dawn, time and again immersing oneself in the endless slumber and then immediately awaking, in order to think over the cavalry's attack in the morning – not the most extraordinary bliss one could experience in their lifetime? And so, for what reason did these fierce and courageous soldiers, comrades of his for many expeditions, push so zealously to return home sooner? What paradise did they expect to find at home, sitting around the fireplace?

The Lord's thoughts suddenly lost their streamlined order and all seemed to blend together, and then the current of thoughts stopped altogether, as if the water in a ditch was overflowing, and spilled out to the side, to flow into the earth, never to return. He recalled his wife's chamber, from whence he had just returned, where he heard her lustful feline moans and yelps, worthy of the devil himself. He shuddered in disgust and this revulsion enveloped him, as if some vile, creeping creatures were sliding further and further up his body, all the way to his throat.

He turned abruptly away from the window, and again approached his chamber. Longing to be reassured that all of this was not just some horrid nightmare, the Khan began carefully, slowly looking around, inspecting all the familiar objects that were in his chamber. On a raised platform, he saw his bed – empty. Suddenly, he felt a cool, crisp breeze on his sweltering face, emanating from the water in his indoor pool. He reached his hot hand out to touch the slender, gold tube – the source of the bubbling, sparkling transparent water, and its icy caress, which had forced its way up from the innermost depths of the earth, stung him.

He sharply jerked his hand back. His whole body was strained, as if anticipating some kind of mortal danger.

— O, Allah... As it turns out, this is indeed a crimson apple...

The second he proclaimed these words, he collected himself, fell silent, fearing that someone might be listening. No matter how intensely he tried to control himself, restrain and drive the entire devilish dance of doubts, suspicions, and revolting assumptions back into the deepest hiding places of his soul, it seemed that they had surrounded him from all sides, carrying their whips with them, ready to lash out at him mercilessly. And his common sense, like a poor horse, lost all of its composure, the cobblestones of unanswered questions tearing into its broken hooves, ripping them to shreds. And yet it carries on ahead, blindly pressing forward through the thick fog of doubt.

Yet, without a doubt, the old Baybishe, having twice sent that red apple with the worm hole, was hinting as something – and that something was the Younger Khansha. Oh, these two women, like rams butting heads... Climbing out onto a familiar pathway, his horse – thought, wanted to trot along it, and yet another question floated up into his mind, and then, another... and his hand pulled at the reins, the old horse came to a stop, and bowed its head down low. "Yes, rival-wives, this is so... Yet, did I not see with my own two eyes how she was laying there, baring all for love, exposing her bare chest to someone? Why else would she be swooning in her sleep, moving around in all manners of obscene ways – a young woman, who has not even known motherhood? What else could it be, if not out of desire for a man's caresses and kisses on her chest?"

And who was this man, who has roused in her such a frenzied passion? Could it be that he was this man? This seemed unlikely. They have not been married for long enough. They have not yet had the opportunity to have gotten used to each other enough, either, for her to have developed such a passion for him. During those two-three nights spent together those few years ago, his young wife had not shown anything he could have likened to insatiable or tireless love and passion.

The girl was nearly a child then, and was terribly confused and oppressed by her feelings and silent obedience... Whoever that person was, to whom she was giving herself away entirely in her sleep – was certainly another man, and not the Lord himself.

His heart began to ache strongly. Its seems that he is fated to go on, a stranger to all, until the very end of his life – with no one to love him, and no heart to call his own... And his own heart, hardened by the ice-cold winds of fate, suddenly began to sink, like a jagged, crumbling lump of melting ice. The wound, so bitter-cold and penetrating, like a freezing draft, chilled his very soul... Yet, who is it that he's resenting, in front of whom did he nearly shed a tear? And at that very moment, a red hot rage erupted within his chest.

What insolent audacious person, what sacrilegious thief who knows no bounds dared offend the Khan's honor, and with their sinful body defile their blessed, conjugal bed? And how is it that he alone took it upon himself to lay the shameful blow upon his whole kind? Who would have thought, that in all of the great Khanate, there would be a person who would want so terribly to offend his own soil in his name? Indeed, all of the most valiant men of all of the different peoples under his authority, marched by his side in their campaigns to lands so far away – could it really be that one of them had done such a thing? Oh, Allah... Could there really be someone that has captured the eye of the Young Khansha? So, who can it be? He must be lured out and captured...

He grasped onto this thought, and his whole body tensed, as if he was a golden eagle – readying himself for an attack, and seeing clearly his prized outcome. He must not do this hurriedly, he must strike accurately and with certainty.

But, who could that Young Khansha have been seeing – having bid farewell to her husband who had gone off to war, surrounded only by the environment of her palace? The courtiers that were left behind were either older than he was, or were nearing his age. With all of the strictness and order of the harem, it was entirely unlikely that some handsome, young djigit could have made himself known to her, let alone captivated the attention of the Young Khansha. He mentally sorted through all of the names of the employees of the palace, yet none of them cast even a shadow of a doubt. There was not a single man among them who could have seemed exceptional in any charming way, nor was there a single man who could have caused the Young Khansha to swoon.

But then, who could it be? Who? Who is this mysterious tempter, that could have evoked all of these feelings within the Young Khansha, who could have enslaved her heart and her ability to reason, giving her peace neither in day, nor night – persisting in pursuing her not just in reality, but also in her dreams?

After many fruitless attempts to pinpoint the suspect within the entire circle of possibilities, the disheartened Lord had to reevaluate the situation again from the very beginning. Who could it be, who? The terrible tension and the useless mental gymnastics yielded a sharp, throbbing pain in his temples. His heavy eyelids were inflamed, he felt a stabbing pain piercing both of his eyes, as if hundreds of thorns had suddenly punctured them. These inflamed eyelids glued themselves together from the sheer gravity of their weight, and when – in an attempt to fight off sleep, he wants to open his eyes even wider, he had to employ much of his strength to accomplish it. Half-delirious, his head and body seemed to grow heavier and heavier, and his failed pursuit of the invisible specter exhausted him entirely.

But, was it worth it for him to fall into such nightmarish worries, to have his soul thus consumed, over the simple accidental sight of some restless, perhaps somewhat unhealthy dream of his young little wife? You never know what could creep up in the unknown depths of one's imagination, in a person's darker dreams? And why is it so difficult to assume that the lover that was within her sensual sleep was not the Khan himself? Indeed, the answer is simple and apparent: the several years of separation have led her to greatly miss his kindness, his presence, and in anticipation of their next meeting – day after day, her sleep-tainted mind could no longer remain chaste or restrained. And in her restless, covetous dreams she sought the idea of him!

And if she did not long for him, then why would she have ordered the construction of such an awe-inspiring, marvelous minaret which he had just inspected earlier that day? What could possibly inspire raising such an enchanting, azure tower – if not the longing and pure love of a woman? Indeed – this is the minaret of her love.

Hanging above a bottomless pit, and ready to collapse into, the Lord's last hope was to cling to the small, blooming bush called "love".

It is indeed so – the living image of this azure tower expresses a frantic, boundless, all-consuming love. But, towards whom is this love directed? And whose is it, this otherworldly azure femininity, foolishly ready to give all of itself away? Is it possible that his wife, so badly longing for her husband to return, passionately outstretches her arms to him – across the barren wastelands and great sands, and the lifeless time of their separation? Or… is this the guilty enchantress calling out to her secret beloved? And so, the architect who personified the amorous desires of the young Khansha, who planned and constructed this miraculous sight – who did he have in mind, with these hidden intentions? The husband…or the lover? And is it purely by chance – that when the husband of the longing wife approaches the tower, her wonderful head is built unreachably sky-high, as if proclaiming her lack of desire to see him? And look at how she opens up, in all of her strange, melancholy beauty – only when he departs further and further from her, to gaze upon her from an unattainable distance. What is hidden amidst the folds of this mystery, this riddle, built into the walls of this incredible tower by the architect? And why does this tower call out to you with such passion, the further you move away from her?

Hey, architect! I have figured out your secret! You have not built the minaret to express the love of the Young Khansha for her husband, but in your own unrelenting, burning, passionate desire for her! Your secret has been revealed – you have been caught, architect!

Finally, it has been solved – the bewitching enchantment of this azure tower – this tempting force of the devil.

The Lord became infinitely more gloomy, since he was not certain if he should be pleased or feel devastated, now that he has finally solved the puzzle of the ceaseless disturbance gnawing away at him since his visit to see the azure tower of the Young Khansha. It had come crashing down, and disappeared, the prison of doubt in which he had been tightly locked away, in his cramped and suffocating cell. And then, in an instant, he was once again swept into this tortured, feverish state, that threw his body into fits of burning heat and freezing cold.

This entire furious fever of thought shrank, and condensed down into only that conclusion, which was known by heart (thoroughly known): an answer to the mysterious hints of the Baybishe and her worm-bearing red apple, had finally been discovered.

And now, it is necessary to collect irrefutable proof and evidence, something equivalent to catching a thief by their grubby hand at the scene of the crime. Finding witnesses should not prove difficult. It merely requires a sit-down with his elder wife, a few questions, and she will gladly sort everything out for him. And the old-woman who oversees the harem will stick to her like glue. And the eunuchs will undoubtedly have information to report. But most importantly, the elder master-builder is the one who can truly deliver the most significant and reliable information. And for the time being, it is necessary to determine with whom to begin the questioning.

The Lord placed his palms against his forehead and stilled his body in thought. His thoughts were no longer swirling about aimlessly, they had finally settled in place. Soon after, he had figured out the proper first move – the fastest, safest, most accurate one, as well as the one that was least damaging to his honor and merit. There is no need for questioning everyone in a row, no need to make this inquiry known to the public. And at the first sign of certainty, it is necessary the criminal be swiftly dealt with. And those who are aware of the crime, knowing the Khan's severity towards informants or those who speak idly, they will be certain to hold back their tongues. They will stay silent, as if their throats were packed tightly with sand. He will do the following: he will summon just the architect, and he will interrogate him one-on-one. And before the wrathful gaze of the Khan, the whole truth will come tumbling from his lips. He will wait until dawn, and then dispatch a messenger for him…Or, perhaps, it would be better to call upon the elder master-builder, and have him bring in the architect? Yes, this will be the proper action to take. And no man who knows of this will be able to conceal the whole truth of the circumstances surrounding this matter. And the elder master-builder will certainly not miss out on a chance to perform such a large favor for the Khan.

The Lord got up and approached the window. He only now noticed that the dawn of the new day was approaching. The sky was bathed in a washed out, bluish-pink light that streamed into the

End of the Legend • *Abish Kekilbaev*

window, making visible all of the small specks of dust carelessly floating through the air. The water in the Lord's indoor pool reflected the colors of the dawn sky, and appeared to be covered in a fine, bronze patina, with the occasional splotches of the most minute specks of ash, like some vestige of a fire that had burned out many years ago. He had but to touch all of this, for it to all crumble and scatter, disappearing before his eyes.

In the final hour of the hazy dawn, the Lord stood in solitude, pensive.

MINARET

1

If only this sudden, treacherous cough would not attack! If only he could control it and suppress it – the Khan's entourage, following him at a respectful distance, solemnly studying a sword, would surely have just passed by. But suddenly, as if by the devil's work, he developed an unbearable tickle in his throat.

But, what devil is there, really… His knees began to quake when he heard the news: "The Khan himself thought that it would seem fitting to conduct the namaz in the mosque." And like a small boy, who did not know how to hide his poorly concealed terror, he looked pleadingly at his surrounding masters. And he noticed on their surly, severe faces not happiness, nor fear, but some sort of inexplicable, agitated expression.

And only a few of the elderly masters were able to preserve their peaceful composure and dignity. These men, with an air of self-importance, were twisting the tips of their whiskers, as if to say: "Well, so it shall be… If he sees fit to visit – then let it be so, let him visit!" And merry little flames flickered in their confident eyes. But the young ones were a different story – their minds were disturbed, their souls in upheaval – they did not know from experience, what to expect from this honorable visit – whether to fearful or be filled with joy. And so the young builders walked around with expressions befitting their internal upheaval – heads hanging low, their perplexed and disturbed faces frozen as such. And whenever the young architect happened to see the yellow striped carriage of the Khan in the courtyard of the mosque appear, he secretly felt an ominous chill, a dark premonition run through the very depths of his soul… Each one of the several hundreds of workers who swarmed the construction site from the ground all the way up to the roof of the cupola, unwillingly emitted alarmed sighs and exclamations: "Would you look at that… He actually came!"

End of the Legend •Abish Kekilbaev

And then it was seemed to young architect that these exclamations, which were simultaneously pulled from so many chests, rolled down into the resonant air of the silent morning right down to the Khan, who emerged from his gilded carriage. And the entire day the young architect involuntarily continued to glance at the unraveling construction site of the enormous *madrasah*. The architect himself stood on the cupola of temple minaret, and directly under him swirled the sloping sides of the enormous cupola of the mosque, and the tiny dots of the builders flickered all along the scaffolding. It was as if the young architect heard the exclamatory whispers of each and every one of them, the exact same words: "Look, he has actually arrived!" – and the indistinguishable, latent fear caused him to shudder, as if a sharp arrow had been jammed into his neck from behind, right under his skull. In the wide courtyard of the madrasah stood a large circle of the Khan's guardsmen, each decorated with the feathers of an eagle, and holding a spear in one of their lowered hands. Not one of them moved from their place, each standing confidently and quietly at his post, and looking at them – the young architect's soul seemed somehow to be put to ease. Nevertheless, when the striped, gleaming yellow carriage of the Khan, led by terrifying horses, black as night, was surrounded by the guardsmen of the cavalry, did not disappear as before from the courtyard of the madrasah, the soul of young architect was in such upheaval, he was utterly beside himself.

In the springtime, on the fourth day of Ramadan, the Lord was present at the laying of the first stone, for the construction of the mosque. The young architect had not even dared to raise his eyes to gaze upon the Lord, who stood, densely surrounded by his nukers. The two masons on hand, alternating, handed fired bricks to the architect, and he nervously, hesitantly lined them up in a row, unable even to uphold the strict line of their placement due to his shivering nerves.

Then, four months had passed. That whole time, five hundred people worked up in the mountains, splitting and cutting large masses of rock. Two hundred people were cutting the marble down to tiles, grinding and sanding them to a brilliant luster. Ninety-five elephants carried the loads from the mountains, delivering them to the construction site. And each day the striped yellow carriage rolled into the spacious courtyard of the construction site of the madrasah, and in the evening hours, accompanied by an armed escort, it majestically rolled back in the direction of the palace. Every single day for four months he heard the same words: "See, he wants to watch the progress himself…"

End of the Legend •*Abish Kekilbaev*   83

And now, it has been three days since the completion of the mosque. Four hundred and eighty columns, each one taller than seven fathoms and altogether they supported the imposing stone framework. In the mosque, which was constructed from marble and gilded to finish, the faithful will raise their hands up and pray for the health of the Khan and for his victories in his various military endeavors. The gentle azure-color of the main temple cupola and the smaller surrounding cupolas of the minarets made the sapphire shade of the sky appear an even more vivid blue.

Today, on the third day, after a long and impatient wait, the voice of the *muezzin* reverberated through the air, flying above the great city, and vibrated within the heart of every single faithful person. This was the call to Friday's prayer. The Lord exited the temple, but did not ride back immediately following the service. He walked around the mosque, admiring the beauty of its clean lines and its elegant finish. The minarets were placed above the four corners of the temple structure. And standing with his back against the base of one of the minarets was the young architect himself.

As the Lord approached closer and closer, the young architect became utterly paralyzed with fear and confusion. He dared not raise his head, and it seemed that the large, sleek azure minaret behind his back, its enormous sharp peak piercing the sky, would suddenly crumble to pieces, collapsing and burying him underneath the ruin. His throat felt dry and stiff, breathing seemed difficult, and his heart felt like it was being squeezed. He decided to humbly and obediently surrender to whatever may follow, so he closed his eyes and bowed his head down low, in reverence. And at that very moment, as if by God's punishment, his throat began to tickle again, as if something was stirring inside it, pushing against his Adam's apple, and he frantically tried to move it round, to suppress the inevitable – and so he choked, a hoarse cough emerging from his throat. And he kept coughing, helpless to stop it, his face turning deeper and deeper shades of red from the strenuousness of it all…

And at that very moment, the Khan and his entire entourage, closed in on him right then, abruptly stopping right in front of the miserable architect. All of a sudden, his coughing ceased. Teary-eyed and pink, he daringly raised his head to look up at all of the noblemen – and saw, in the center of this mass of people, a man – not particularly tall, who stood with his head thrown all the way back, gazing up at the blue dome of the tower. Not through reason, but pure intuition the architect had determined that this undersized man was in fact the Great Khan in the flesh. Not for a moment daring to look at him, the young architect quickly lowered his head and stared down at his feet.

"Which artisan is responsible for building this?" a quiet, yet clear and audible voice asked, as if strained through his teeth.

"A master of the Ortyube clan" the familiar deep voice of the senior Master-Mason resounded.

When the thundering hooves, ringing of the harness bells and rattling of the sabers signaled the entourage of the Khan had taken off, the young architect boldly raised his eyes and noticed that the nukers of the Khan's cavalry passing by were gazing intently – and paying particularly close attention to him. They were no longer admiring the minaret, in imitation of the Khan's behavior, but with a certain curiosity, they were eyeing the young architect himself.

The following morning, a crowd of sixty people stood in front of the bulky gates of the palace, which were adorned in beautiful, swirling patterns of precious and semi-precious stones. Among them, was the Master-Architect from the distant Ortyube, who called himself Zhappar.

The tempting aromas of food drifted in from behind the palace gates. Then, seemingly out of nowhere – from some sort of hidden doors, guardsmen emerged, running with poleaxes atilt in their hands.

The gates were opened, the guardsmen funneled the crowd inside. And immediately, the humid, hot air transformed into a pleasant, cooling breeze. The countless fountains, bubbling away all around the garden, pulverized the invisible humidity of the air. The various paths winding around the garden were moist and clean, and lined with blocks of red limestone, as if some unseen drizzling rain had just finished passing through.

On both sides of the main pathway, and on each skillfully pruned tree sat an exotic peacock from overseas, and on their bright feathers, painted vividly with every thinkable color known to man, hung large droplets of water, resembling diamonds of unprecedented sizes.

Six splendid Indian elephants, tall as mountains, their backs draped with large satin cloths were mounted with intricately decorated wood palanquins. Not particularly willing to carry out the loud commands of their drivers, they clumsily descended first to one elbow, then another, and without much coordination they rose to their feet again, their heavy bodies swinging from side to side.

Six very dark-skinned trainers with long, tufted mustaches and enormous turbans, the ends of which hung all the way down to their elbows, sat in the *palanquins*, cross-legged, and desperately shouted to their gigantic pupils as they swung and struck them on their ears with long, slender canes. And these huge creatures, strangely enough, obeyed these ridiculous, self-confident little fellows in their oversized turbans, their eyes popping out of their head. Some of the elephants, upon losing their equilibrium due to these unnatural movements, would fall sideways, then for a long while, and with great difficulty they would rise back up on their feet.

The auburn roe-deer curiously observed these exotic, unfamiliar wonders, but upon noticing the large crowd of people approaching them, quickly scattered in all directions, relocating to the overgrown depths of the garden.

Sixty renowned masters, from all around the world, first approached the three boys who were sitting on a magnificent Persian carpet in the cool shade created by an old enormous mulberry tree. Getting down on one knee, with their hand on their chest, each one of them descended in the traditional formal pose of a greeting. The young descendants of the Khan then rose from their places and continued to guide the masters further into the garden, where on an elevated platform, covered with thick carpet bedding, upon two folded pillows reclined the great Khan himself. With a dull, detached expression, his gaze was suspended in front of the marble pond, its blue color offset by the bright crimson color of the deserted apples gently bobbing up and down in the water. In the middle of the pond was a large, white foaming fountain, which sprinkled tiny iridescent beads of water all around itself. Even from a distance of approximately twenty steps to the Khan's raised platform, the masters started lowering themselves to their knees and began casting themselves face down to the ground in prostration.

The Lord stretched out the tip of his hand, which emerged from the spacious sleeve of his simple, unembroidered *chapan* and made an unknown sign to his seven viziers, the champions of his entourage, who were sitting by his side.

The chief vizier, who was seated in the middle, turned to the prostrate masters and uttered something in a low voice. The young, black-eyed architect Zhappar, who was sitting in the very last row, could neither hear, nor make out a thing.

Then a group of djigits approached them, each holding a chalice in their elongated hand. Holding these chalices over the heads of the masters, the djigits proceeded to spill out their contents – gold and silver coins – right over their heads. Then another group of djigits bearing trays replaced them, and with a quick bow, they produced a tray for each master, upon which were laid fist-sized tightly packed satchels, tied with a silk cord and finished with tassels.

The prostrate masters began pounding their foreheads against the earth as a sign of their utmost appreciation for the Khan's kindness and generosity.

As a sign of his acceptance of their gratitude, the Lord gave a slight, nearly imperceptible nod. And at that very moment, the oblong blood-red ruby, as thick as one of his fingers, mounted on the very front of the snow-white Khan's cap, in the shape of a rounded peak, seemed to explode with gleaming light, splashing glistening icy red rays in all directions.

The chief vizier waved his hand, and Masters-*Ustad*, certainly deserving of the Khan's favor in having done wonderful work for the glory of the Lord, all rose up from their knees. Shuffling backwards slowly in reverence, they removed themselves several feet further from the platform to make room for the Khan's festive arrangements on the elevated platform, and they gathered to rest in the shade of the mulberry trees.

Then the Lord consented to the commencement of the reception of foreign ambassadors. Like the masters they, too, held the same or orderly arrangement: first, they bowed to the three boys, the dear grandsons of the Great Khan. But, with the envoys, the young boys took documents from them – credentials rolled up into small tubes – and took off with them, running in the direction of the Khan's platform. When they were about three steps away from the Khan, they fell to the ground, and – crawling up to him on their knees, they bowed and stretched out hands to pass the scrolls to the Lord. Afterwards, they bowed down to the ground another three times, and once again returned to their original seats.

Each of the ambassadors, having respectfully placed both hands at their sides, the high-ranking court officials were brought before the Khan's dais. Behind the ambassadors were palace servants, all in a row, bearing the gifts brought by the foreign envoys.

The ambassadors waited at a distance of ten steps, after lowering themselves onto their right knee, their palms pressed to their chest, their heads bowed low. The noblemen of the court who accompanied them, in an obsequious manner, took several steps back. Now rising from their places, the viziers were directed towards the ambassadors and, holding onto them by their elbow, in an alternating fashion, they were led up to the Khan's platform. Stopping after roughly five or six steps, the ambassadors arranged themselves in even lines, and again, all at once, they bowed down low. To this, the Lord responded with a quick wave of the hand, signaling for them to approach more closely.

The ambassadors timidly advanced – their palms still folded as before, without raising their lowered heads, and proceeded to sink down to their heels.

Then the Lord began to ask questions. The ambassadors responded. The masters were huddled together closely under the sprawling branches of the mulberry tree, outside the hearing range of the diplomatic conversations. Many of them were allowed into the palace garden for the very first time, and out of admiration for their surroundings, struck by the magnificent splendor of the Khan's reception, the masters sat with open mouths, greedily consuming everything with their eyes, fearing they might miss even the slightest detail.

The ambassadors were seated on a low platform, on the other side of the garden path, next to the Khan, and opposite the viziers.

And at this point, the djigits that formed the domestic crew of servants, proceeded to bring out vessels requiring four handles to be carried out. The metallic vessels were enormous as boats, and shallow, and were dusted with gold, heaped with mountains of steaming meat that had just finished cooking. Each group of four servants placed a vessel at a respectful distance from the Lord, then, sinking into a low bow, they exited, going beyond the limits of the banquet space. And immediately, they were replaced with butchers wearing leather aprons, who unsheathed their sparkling kitchen knives, and with uncanny dexterity and swiftness, started slicing up the meat into small pieces.

Even more dishes of meat were brought out on large leather trays, and with the aromas of strange flowers, the cool breeze wafting from the fountains created an intermingling of scents with the entire bouquet of rich, hearty meat aromas of tender lamb, sausage-kaz'i, made from raw-smoked horse meat, the tender, juicy dried rump, the amber-yellow meat of a foal's nape. A solid ten trays of meat were trimmed and cut within a matter of minutes. The prepared portions were quickly doled out by the nimble hands of the meat-cutters, who placed them in various deep chalices made of silver and gold, which stood in rows. One the djigits finished, they took a bow and left.

A new band of servants arrived carrying wooden, painted basins. They were filled with hot, splashing *surpa*, and were carefully placed down onto the ground. Into the bouillon spices and salts were poured, and – having thoroughly mixed the ingredients together - a spicy-salt brine had been prepared. The hot bouillon flooded the sliced meat that was in the cups from painted wooden ladles, and on top of that, every bowl was topped with quadruple-folded pieces of *shelpek*, the finest flatbread made from thinly rolled dough, which was then fried in oil.

Upon finishing all of the necessary food preparations, the servants took their leave, and the managing-elders of the palace's ceremonies picked up two dishes, and began handing out refreshments to the Lord, the ambassadors and the viziers. The regular palace servants waited upon the less important guests.

Fruits were distributed after the various meat dishes. The meal was completed with a sweet *koumiss*, with honey mixed in.

Once the dinner party had concluded, a group of palace servants appeared in the middle of the courtyard, in front of the Khan, bearing the gifts of the foreign envoys. This entire time, they had modestly stood off to the side. Desiring a thorough examination of all of the expensive gifts by all, the gift-bearers intentionally moved very slowly and solemnly, holding in front of them all of the gifts that the ambassadors had brought with them: swords with patterns embossed in the steel and mother-of-pearl handles; Sable and beaver fur-coats, covered with exquisite stitching. Large Iranian carpets were unfurled, large gold ingots laying on tray, and further were displayed pearls and corals, emeralds and sapphires, as well as the skins of rare, exotic beasts from across the sea. Upon approaching the foot of the Great Khan's dais, the gift-bearers bowed down to one knee, and became still. Right next to them, was the ambassador of the giving country, who also bent down in a servile bow. And so, the Lord, with a regal flick of his hand, indicating that the gifts were satisfactory and thus, accepted.

The rows of gift-bearers continued to approach, while those who were already seen were sent in the direction of the palace.

The Lord rose from his seat, indicating to everyone present that the reception was finished. All who were present also rose up, and were directed towards the gates.

Six enormous elephants dropped to their knees, unraveling their long trunks, to properly bid farewell to everyone who had attended the Khan's reception. The guards at the gates lowered their spears, and acknowledged the guests with a friendly nod.

The same day, the Lord made an announcement to the Great City – in honor of the completion of the new mosque, a massive celebration would be held in the capital.

On the spacious meadow behind the palace garden, almost always empty during the summer and winter seasons – today, come nightfall, transformed into a lively area where many bonfires began to blaze, and tents suddenly began cropping up alongside them. Some time ago, many a crowded celebration had once been held there, and all the well-off inhabitants of this city had special sections allotted to them, where they were allowed to place their tents along the temporary streets and alleyways. Two ditches, filled with noisy, flowing water, ran alongside them.

On the morning following the Khan's announcement, the vacant meadow seemed to come alive with colorful tents and pavilions. On the outskirts of the meadow, the small tents of shoemakers, tailors and various other artisans and craftsmen were clumped together. The closer one was to the middle, the more magnificent the tents became, which belonged to certain wealthy noblemen. The previously vacant meadow was suddenly, in the matter of a day, completely obscured by tents, which gradually escalated, like steps, rising up towards the center of the town – like some kind of enchanted headquarters of a diverse mass of people, directing their apex towards the sky. This apex was the dome of the Khan's tent, which had four corners and four sides, each spanning about the height of one and a half men. The tallest dome, supported by twelve incredibly long poles, spanned a height of twenty men from the ground up. Stretching from the ground to the top of each pole, were long, colorful silk ribbons, which swirled and rippled in the wind. The powerful poles, grounded in the four corners of the tent and crisscrossed as they moved upwards, culminating in middle of the dome. In the center of the tent, there was constructed a small turret, which was crowned with a spire, and topped with a crescent moon.

Inside, the tent was lined with purple cloth with gold stitching. In each of the four corners, at the base of the dome, hung symbolic images of eagles, their wings spread out, as if in flight. In the Khan's enormous tent were located the eleven *yurts* of his wives, each yurt was hidden behind a stretched silk curtain of a particular color. Furthermore, the Khan's personal tent was connected to each wife's yurt by a separate, whimsical and labyrinthine, pathway that did not intersect with any of the others.

The eleven yurts and the giant tent of the Khan, were hidden behind a large fence, and the fence itself was fully encircled by a row of oak-wood kegs filled with wine.

Six stations of armed escorts guarded them day and night, without any shut-eye. Without the personal permission of a chief vizier, not a single person was allowed to approach his tent. And the guards would only lower their sharpened, gleaming steel spears in front of those exceptional few who were personally invited inside.

And so, in just such a manner, the person who passed between the tilted spears was the young architect from Ortyube. He was shown one of the greatest honors – receiving an invitation to wine and dine with the Ruler of the World at his personal dastarkhan, on the first day of the holiday celebration in the capital city.

The majestic throne of the Lord was set in the very middle of the large tent, and directly behind him, some steps and a platform were arranged to facilitate the elevated placement of the Khan's extensive family.

The guests had just finished settling down in their seats, when suddenly – cries were heard, accompanied by the tinkling of bells and pendants, signifying the arrival of the court jesters. In the main space of the tent, in front of the throne, they performed an amusing scene: one in which they ridiculed the despicable Shah-rulers, who had been conquered by Amir in his latest military campaign.

The guests, however, did not dare laugh in the presence of the King and host, especially given his solemnity – his regal dignity would not be tainted by even the faintest of smiles. And so, it seemed as though the jesters were simply entertaining each other.

And when the performance came to an end, the treasurer of the palace threw an embroidered sack with coins onto a tray which had been presented by the main jester.

The jesters bowed low to the ground, and maintaining that position, taking tiny, quick steps backwards, they scurried out of the tent, disappearing behind the curtains.

At that moment, the adjacent curtain shifted and spread, and out stepped the Great Khansha. She donned a magnificent, lavish crimson ensemble, decorated with jewels and precious embroidery. A luxurious necklace hung down to her chest, which attracted everyone's attention, and consisted of alternating rubies and pearls. The long hem of the Khansha's dress was carried in on outstretched hands by fifteen very young women. The Baybishe's face was densely covered with makeup and her eyebrows were blackened, as well. Her transparent, cambric veil skillfully concealed the faded beauty and youth of the Khansha. A small, exquisite turban in the shape of a minaret rested atop her head, entirely adorned in jewels. The ends of the turban tumbled down in small waves, and came to rest above her shoulders. A small gold crown with three large rubies that blazed in the light, was the finishing touch to her minaret-turban. The large feathers of an eagle-owl, framing her face, hung all the way down to her long ears. The complex (intricate?) attire on her head required the constant attention of her female servants, who – when it began to strongly sway, proceeded to hold up her hair-do from both sides. A massive entourage of a hundred, dolled up ladies of the court accompanied the Elder Wife of the Asian emperor.

The procession of the Khansha and her entourage was led by a group of frail eunuchs, who emerged, surprisingly, with the most impressive gait, and were nearly bursting from their own self-righteous smugness and pride. To all of the invited guests, who were greeting the Great Khansha with a low bow – the eunuchs gazed at them with condescension, making no attempt to hide their disdain.

The Khansha sat directly behind the Lord, and a bit lower.

In the next moment, another colored curtain shimmered and moved to reveal the entourage of the Young Khansha – no less magnificent or well-dressed. The Young Khansha then took her seat behind and a bit lower than the Elder Khansha. And even lower and further behind Young Khansha, were seated the seven daughters-in-law of the Khan.

With the arrival of all of these young, beautifully adorned women, the Khan's tent began to resemble some sort terrestrial paradise, occupied only be eternal beauties and *houri* virgins.

In the midst of the multitude of Masters, was the young architect, who has the distinct sensation of being in a dream. With bated breath, he watched the unbelievably beautiful women, in their marvelous outfits of silk and satin, bedecked with gold, silver, and diamond jewelry. The young man was dazzled beyond words, his head spinning from the visual onslaught of colors around him.

When both the Young and Elder Khanshas and their entourages - their dresses rustling, their jewelry tinkling, finally occupied their proper places, the servants began to bring out the wine and koumiss. Here, in front of the feasting party, appeared the princes-Khanzada – with snow white cloths resting atop their hands. The stately, skillful djigits followed behind them, carrying gold trays, on which stood small, gold cups with various beverages. The princes-Khanzada clasped the small cups with their white, silk cloths and carefully carried them over to the mothers, both young and old. When they were about halfway there, the princes lowered themselves onto their right knee, in a long, ceremonial bow. After approaching the mothers and giving them their beverages, they again dropped down on one knee, and with a long, respectful bow, they proceeded to give out the cups. Then, the princes modestly stepped back, and having yet again descended to one knee, with downcast eyes, waited for the mothers to finish drinking and return the cups. After all of that, taking just as much care in grasping the empty cups with their white cloths, they handed them over to the servants. Having completed the ritual, the Khanzada bowed once more, and left the tent.

Among those who were invited were the sixty masters-ustad, who were seated on another wooden platform, separate from the Khan's. To drink to the very bottom of the Khan's generous cup was an immutable law. And by sunset, upon leaving the Khan's tent and dispersing to find their own tents in the midst of the celebratory town, the guests were noticeably swaying and stumbling, unable to process a thing.

Summer nights had arrived, setting the stars alight – winking in the black expanse of the southern sky. The sweltering heat of the daytime had subsided, as though it had been dissolved in the shadows. Countless bonfires were crackling and blazing in between the tents. The people – cheerful and excited, came in to crowd around them. The holiday continued into the night. The velvety, peaceful silence of night had suddenly ripped clean through by the powerful bellow of the trumpets, long as poles. The sound was complemented by the incessant discord of the rattling tambourines and drums. The melodic call of the *dutari,* reverberating from all sides, best expressed the intoxicating joy and enthusiasm of the partying crowd, greedy for the feasts and spectacles. The murky gloom was pierced either by the shrill sounds of the *kylkokbyz* fiddle, or husky vocalizations of the *Sirnaya* pipe, or the delicate trilling of the *Sybygzi* reedpipe. The large circle of light, illuminated by the bonfires was suddenly disrupted by the arrival of many tall youths in skullcaps, wearing an assortment of light robes tied across the waist with colorful sashes – moved by their own boldness, they instantly launched themselves into an irrepressible fiery dance; or they would effortlessly swim in, aflutter in their silk outfits, their long, fine, jet-black braids, languidly turning ivory-skinned beauties in agile dancing.

Certain seasoned men, engulfed by a lethargic daze resulting from a intake of copious amounts of food and wine, separated themselves and, in small groups, huddled around the large copper *samovars*, drinking tea to their heart's content, partaking in djigit merriment, like telling each other small jokes.

The lively fires vigorously crackled and popped under the giant cauldrons, and when the *aspazshy* cooks shifted their wooden lids to the side, the aroma of the mingling spices and steaming foods filled the air, beckoning to all in close proximity. Portly men with thick, black mustaches, spotted with dewy droplets of sweat, having rolled up their sleeves – began to tend to, in a manner bordering the sacred, the skewered meat frying on spits. Others were dexterously turning the metal rods with skewered kebob-meat above a saxaul fire, and the sausages – just started to form a rosy crust as they oozed out fat, hissing as it fell on the burning coals, creating a blue flaming splash in the midst of the orange glow… Wine flowed in great abundance, soaking the whiskers of both the young and the old.

Ears were seized by sweet captivating melodies, nostrils quivered from mouthwatering aromas.

The crimson tongues of thousands of bonfire flames danced and licked the air under the

The crimson flaming tongues that rose up over thousands of bonfires quivered under the mammoth expanse of the jet-black sky.

On this favorable summer night, the merriment only continued to increase, and the laughter only got louder.

The Khan's holiday was a great success – all were merry and feasting. During such holidays, it was strictly forbidden to fight, harm one another or quarrel or bicker in any way whatsoever. In the hour designated for the most merriment, there should be not one petty squabble. Nor should anyone overstep the specified boundaries of decent behavior. Those individuals who do not take the written law seriously – those men who are rude and eager to fight, well... for those the authorities have made special arrangements, some distance off atop a small hill – a group of gallows, should anyone need them.

Once the festivities had come to an end, the Lord set off towards the new mosque, to fall on his knees in front of the Almighty, and pray for his blessing of the highest *hazrats* for his new campaign in western lands.

2

...That year, the Warrior-Khan had already marched off to a distant land, when the nobleman *bey*-Akhmet, who owned the house in which the young architect, Zhappar, was staying, had given his daughter's hand in marriage.

For than two weeks here, in the quiet alley, where Akhmet-bey's house stood, dozing in the quiet heat and gentle babbling of running water – something stirred, a great fuss erupted – there was much noise, an inconceivable confusion arose. Though most of all, before the honest people, the pre-wedding feverish displays were the result of bey-Akhmet himself.

The arrogant merchant, long before the wedding was due to occur, had commanded everyone to search the trunks for their expensive outfits for the festivities, to grab them and hang them up. Unable to resist trying his outfits on himself, he put them on and twirled about in front of the mirror from morning to dusk. Bey-Akhmet was arrogant, conceited and ambitious, especially regarding matters of a social nature. In his eyes, the conundrum of which turban to don when appearing in front of the guests, was no small or irrelevant matter. Therefore, he wound the turban around his head not one time, nor two. No, having built himself yet another glorious splendor, he looked in the mirror, perpetually dissatisfied. So, he would unwind his masterful creation and reconstructed his turban in a different fashion. Yet again, a deep sense of disappointment and sorrow clung to his soul. Then he shouted:

— Hey, wife! Come here!

But his wife, who was either watering something in the garden or kneading and pounding out dough to make flatbread for *tandyr*, could not immediately hear the voice of her husband, calling out. Then, he proceeded to really cry out:

— Hey! Woman, are you deaf or something?

And then, from some distant corner of the compound, as if emerging from the depths of some cave, sounded the weak voice of his wife:

— Hey! What happened, bey-eke?

Bey-Akhmet, spitefully, was practically hissing the like a red-hot frying pan:

— Come here faster! Where are you sitting over there? Come here!

Wiping her hands, soiled in one thing or another, on the way - she appeared at the threshold of his room.

— Hey! Look to me, wife!

— Well... I'm looking.

— And what you do see?

— Well, it is you I see, bey-eke.

End of the Legend •Abish Kekilbaev

— What are you going on about? Well, well, well…

Bey-Akhmet's already minimal patience shattered – he ripped off his turban, which was as plump and heavy as a head of cabbage, swung it, and hit his wife on the side of her head. Frightened, she quickly gave flight, and bey-Akhmet, livid, tore after her, and had begun to chase her around the garden.

Proving to be an involuntary witness to this family spectacle, the young architect Zhappar, who had been resting in the gazebo in front of the house, turned away quickly, in an effort to conceal his smile.

Soon, the cries ceased, and short while later bey-Akhmet emerged from the house. He was magnificently dressed and looked absolutely stunning. On his head, looking like something akin to a round, densely stuffed bag – sat his enormous turban. Atop his thick, fleshy shoulders rested a bright, coral-red chapan, and his feet boasted azure-blue Moroccan *kebisi*-slippers, which had long, tapering points which bent in an upward curl. Large, tight and somewhat askew – the bey's belly was pulled in and fastened with a gigantic leather belt, about a fifth of a meter wide, and studded with silver rivets. Under the patterned collar of the chapan, which was thrown open, was a blindingly white silk shirt.

Smiling smugly while he stepped up into the gazebo, he asked his tenant:

— So, how do I look, oh, venerable one?

— Magnificent, honorable bey-eke!

In anticipation of this grand, imminent social success, bey-Akhmet waddled down the steps and left the gazebo, briskly wobbling through the garden towards the gates. He stopped about half-way there, looked side-to-side, in attempt to locate his wife, and shouted:

— Hey, wife! Tell everyone: as of today, my trading is finished! Yes, the store is closed!

He then continued walking, widely swinging his hands around his belly. Suddenly, he collected himself again, and assuming a dignified stance, proceeded to trot further in short, little steps like a hobbled horse until he disappeared past the gates.

He returned in the evening-time, around twilight, and before he had even made his way inside, he was already yelling:

— Hey, wife!

— Well? — an answer emerged from some uncertain location.

— Wife! Have you got any water in your *kumgan*?

After lowering his feet into the copper tub filled with warm water, he began to speak with a lively, clear voice about all that had happened to him on this day. He was in such good spirits, in fact, that Akhmet-bey wanted all of this to be heard by his wife, who was pouring water onto his feet from the *kumgan*, and the young tenant, who was politely retiring to his room, and his daughter, who was preparing tandyr, and the donkey in the shed in the corner of the garden, that was continuously chewing on straw, and the abandoned ox-cart that was a tad closer and long since in need of fixing, and the pitted, decrepit clay wall of the courtyard, and the first few stars in the darkened night sky, and the quiet street with its monotonous, gurgling little stream, and all of the neighbors from near and far, and all of the Emperor's palaces and their enchanting gardens, and the entire city – the capital city of the Emperor, and, why go on listing them, why waste time on such trifles – the whole inhabited God-given world...

He spoke with such liveliness, as though he wasn't telling stories of himself, but of some other, clever, different Akhmet-bey, who – upon returning from the ends of the earth and time, had accomplished numerous glorious deeds, such as: showing off his new outfit, getting into a bit of a tiff with someone, fighting with someone else, and really getting into it with a third; he'd had more than one kettle's worth of tea, he had turned someone down, and rightly so, they'd clearly deserved it; he had placed successful bets on an acquaintance's quail... Concluding his narrated tale of the mighty deeds of the forever departed day, Akhmet-bey yanked off his turban off his head, placing it in the outstretched hand of his wife – on top of which he also piled his kaftan, his pants, and above all else, like a Tsar's crown, he delicately removed and handed over his azure-blue shoes with curled points and gold stitching. His wife, loaded up to her very head with his clothes, using her chin to help keep them from falling, was about to leave, when bey, recalling something important, stopped her with a question:

— By the way, how many quilted blankets have you sewn?

His wife reported — this many blankets were prepared..

— Look here, you'd better not be mistaken, the wedding is nigh at hand! – he warned her, as a formality. They were referring to their daughter's dowry.

Finally, having expressed everything that had been on his mind, he reached for his snuff-box and loaded up his nostrils with generous portions of tobacco. The subsequent sneezing and bellowing, the roaring that shook the silence of courtyard, and with this dramatic outburst, as though they were frightened little birds, all of his anxieties and concerns seemed to fly off, depart, like all hitherto known words. And from this point on, until the very end of the day, he did not utter a single word.

After his generous supper, all that remained was for him to reach the man's half of the house and crawl into his bed, which was right next to the bed of Zhappar, and collapse his head on his pillow and snore continuously until morning.

This snoring – at times increasing in volume and terrible, at other times would sound almost like sorrowful music – these "night sagas", sung by the nose of Akhmet-bey, would every now and then, keep the young architect from falling asleep until morning.

It was quiet in the great capital of the Emperor. Dying down to flickering ash, and smoke rising up into the air, the bonfires finally were finally extinguished, even in the noisiest areas.

All the normal, peaceful men of the city are sleeping, only one Zhappar is wide awake. For a long time, he twisted and turned from side to side, and in some instant – finally broken by the fatigue of the day, he slipped into a deep, deep slumber.

Suddenly, the room was filled with some sort of devastating, ringing silence, from which Zhappar immediately awakened, in a state of panic. Initially, at a loss and confused, he then realized that it was the lack of Akhmet's snoring that disturbed him, and the bed next to him – was empty. Then, he heard a distant creaking of a door, somewhere in the other half of the house – the women's quarters. Smiling through his sluggish state, Zhappar calmly reclined on his bed.

At last, it was the day of the wedding, who no one waited for longer, or with more enthusiasm, than Akhmet-bey himself. In the courtyard, they installed four massive cauldrons, for the cooking of pilaf. At some distance from those, on saxaul coals, they were frying kebab. Over the entire duration of the celebration, lasting several days and nights, the tandyrs had not cooled even once.

All of the pleasant odors drifting out of the house reminded one that this celebration was nothing short of a wedding. In the courtyard, it smelled like meats; the male side of the house smelled like rawhide leather, wine, and sweat, and the female side smelled like fresh fruits, sweets, and incense.

Day after day – was the continuous, uninterrupted consumption of food, switching from one type of food to another. The swigging of certain wines and drinks, only to be replaced by others… During the breaks, in between the food and drinks – the merry sounds of the dutar and tambourine could be heard. If one were to take a peek at the men's half, one would see how in a circle large men, there would be a young boy of about twelve, who would be skillfully twirling and dancing, not a care in the world, snapping his fingers, while the large, dark-haired men, swaying to the beat of the drums, beat their fists against their hairy, sweaty chests. If you were to take a peek at the women's half – they, too, were dancing: winding and shaking her fleshy hips was the unmatched dancing of a girl, who was surrounded by a circle of women, who, too, were swaying to the music, and clapping their hands with great force, completely unaware of the pain it was causing.

When the smoldering sphere of the sun toppled over the edge of the earth, during the appointed hour, a man who had been called to the wedding feast, arrived. He was a priest-*kazi*. Into a painted cup filled with clean spring water, he threw a silver ring – preparing the marriage chalice. At which point, he called over the groom and the witnesses of the bride's side of the family. After instructing the future groom to drink from the chalice, the kazi handed the chalice to the bride's witnesses, who, one-by-one, passed the blessed water down to the soon-to-be bride, and when she took a sip, the chalice returned once again to the kazi, who in a booming voice, read a prayer, and then – in the presence of the witnesses and parents of the future bride and groom, he gave his blessing to this, now sanctified, marriage.

Once again, the dastarkhans were spread out, and the wedding banquet and merriment continued. And time had rolled on past midnight. The groom had passed on a message to the female side – a request, to be allowed to pass to the female section, and to be allowed to see his bride. The women erupted in a state of confusion and panic. They lit several oil lamps, and carrying them in their hands, began to walk towards the fiancé. In the bride's room only the bride remained, hidden behind a curtain.

The groom, surrounded by a noisy band of his djigit friends, began to confidently move towards the female quarters. But, the second they threw open the door – everything turned into an unbelievably frenzied, topsy-turvy mess. The women schemed to fight with the djigits, in no joking matter, in an attempt to try to capture and seduce the groom. And so, began the rite of the "pulling of the groom". The rabid, howling women did everything, not holding back in any way. They burned the men's beards with the oil lamps they had been carrying. The air smelled of burnt fur. Certain especially hirsute gentlemen were still preoccupied with the fires raging on their faces, and in sheer horror, they seized the hems of their kaftans and started whacking their faces, trying to put out the flames. The ladies were able to abduct the fiancé, after all. One woman stretched her arms under his shoulders, and reached around to pull his neck backwards, and in this fashion, she began to pull him behind her towards the bride's room. The entire horde of women whooped and howled, excitedly giving chase behind them.

Having lost the groom, the djigits glumly returned to the male half of the house, and sat down at the dastarkhan.

At the same time, the groom was seated at another dastarkhan, in the female half of the house, and generously gifted all of the friends and witnesses of the bride, in order to bribe them into allowing him past the curtain. In an attempt to cheer up the groom, and propel him towards a generous demeanor, the young women and girls sang plenty of songs, danced and gaily joked.

Meanwhile, among all of the widespread cheer and merriment, the bride, still alone, was in complete wearisome solitude behind her curtains, sitting on her throne, in the most absurd form – surrounded by the forty quilted blankets of her dowry, which would be taken the following day to the house of her new husband. The groom was only permitted to pass to the bride's curtained quarters once he had satisfied all of the sordid desires of all of his bride's friends and kin. A large bowl of pilaf and fruits was brought to the young couple.

The dastarkhan in this half of the house remained lively, noisy and in good spirits, as were all the women who occupied it.

Then came the dead of night. The young bride and groom were left alone in their room, surrounded by the massive heaps of the wealth of the bride's dowry. Because of the piles of clothing that were scattered on various racks and hung on ropes, the numerous boots, shoes, leather stockings and slippers, which lined the walls, the marital room looked, more than anything, like a dreary clothing shop. In the end, it was for the better, that her mischievous friends, having tucked the bride snugly into the bed, did not leave any light in the room with her.

Despite having left the two newlyweds alone, the experienced aunts did not wander very far: leaning their ears against the door and sneaking outside to the windows with the loosely drawn curtains, they stood absolutely still, dying of curiosity. At first, they could not be heard, and then, in accordance with what was occurring in the room between the newlyweds, excited whispers and giggling were heard. "Hey, don't laugh! Be quiet, you!" – One aunt said to the other, as she grabbed her by her fleshy side, pulling her away. "Otherwise, people will figure out that we're laughing about what the young couple is doing in there!" However, when the all of the sounds in the room befitting the situation seemed to cease, the *zhenge*-aunts lost all interest and stopped giggling right away. Huddled in a small circle, they all began to quietly deliberate: had it transpired, had it not transpired? And if something had indeed transpired, then precisely to what extent? Finally, they had decided to send one of their own in to the newlywed's chambers, so off she went. She approached the door and knocked.

Hearing the knock, the groom rose from bed and opened the door just slightly, and the messenger slipped in. She appeared soon after, carrying in her hands a gift that was customarily given by the newlyweds. But, this was not all. Resuming their huddled positions again, the council of aunts had figured it all out: it was time to go pay the parents of the newlyweds a visit, to demand gifts in exchange for the wonderful news – everything had turned out in a most satisfactory manner.

The next morning, the young husband returned to the room full of djigits, in order to celebrate like a bachelor alongside them for one final time. From this point on, he was to be the head of a family, and associating with other bachelors was no longer in the cards for him.

When the young djigits surrounded the new husband, and began congratulating him, one-by-one articulating their congratulations and greetings, the young Zhappar emerged from his room.

He was experiencing a splitting headache from the unceasing two-day long commotion. He slinked by, head lowered, to the courtyard, until he reached the lonely mulberry tree, which grew by the gates. Zhappar felt broken, weak, as though he had just come to from a fainting spell. He distanced himself from the surrounding people.

The wedding celebration finally dispersed around noon, and the young husband returned to his home, while the young bride remained here, with her parents, for the time being. Unwilling to part with his festive finery, bey-Akhmet scurried about the house and the courtyard in his embroidered kaftan. The bride had not yet emerged from the room with the curtain. About half a dozen good, neighborly women were outside, helping with the washing of dishes and the drying of expensive utensils, all the while gossiping – either loudly and boisterously, or whispering carefully.

All day some sort of agonizing, nauseating heat hung in the air of his room, which come nighttime, had turned into an insufferable, sweltering humidity, and Zhappar, unable to relax or find any comfort, did not even lie down once in his bed all day. He thrust his feet into his leather kebisi, and went outside into the garden. Above the house, the full moon brimmed with a silver, milky radiance. And the old, decrepit duval looked as though someone had forcefully blanched it, without sparing any of the lime. The silence of the nighttime was so all-encompassing, that he clearly heard how, on the other side of the courtyard, the old ass was munching away, breaking apart the straw with his teeth.

Making his way out onto the porch, Zhappar leaned his back on the post of the shed, opened up the top of his shirt and turned to feel the cool caress of the evening breeze against his chest. Suddenly, he heard a dull sound, like the sound of something falling – *thud*! He glanced to the side, over by the gates, and then to the other side – yet he saw nothing. The very same heavy "thud" which came from above and landed on the earth, now repeated itself, except this time, it was as if it had landed in sand – no repercussion, as if nothing had even happened. Astonished, Zhappar froze in place, and strained his ears. Yet he hear nothing – no sounds aside from the crackling of straw in the teeth of the ass, all the way in the distant shed. Would it be possible to figure out

now, just which side the sound of the drop was occurred? No longer
desiring to guess blindly, Zhappar decided to investigate on his own, so
he descended from the porch, trying to walk as silently as possible. Yet
the wide kebisi shoes he was wearing, made a treacherous squelching
noise, and the soles of the shoes made an audible slapping sound as he
walked. And then, he thought that he saw a dark figure race over to the
parts of the courtyard that were submerged in shadows. Zhappar stood
still, deliberating how he should act. Should he take a step towards
some unknown danger – or should he take a step back, avoiding the
battle… He decided to wait a bit longer, to observe – see what comes of
it, perhaps make out where it's headed. He distinctly made out the
sound of his own heart beating furiously in his chest. This was certainly
fear. Shamed by his own cowardice, he gathered up his willpower and
decided, be what it may, and threw himself headlong into the shadows.
Instantly, something sprang up before him, knocked its dark body into
something, and started running very quickly towards the clay fence.
Desperately slapping the kebisi against his heels, Zhappar broke into a
run himself. The pursued figure, having reached the fence in just a few,
quick leaps, threw his hands up, and grabbed the top edge of the clay
fence, readying himself to jump over it… Then, suddenly, the escaping
figure froze in place, let his hands fall from the fence, and then turned
around to silently wait for the approaching Zhappar, completely still,
until he closed in. When he was only an arm's length away, the pursued
figure suddenly said:

— Oh, so it's you? And it thought you were bey-eke…

Judging by his voice, Zhappar recognized the mystery figure –
it was the groom from yesterday's wedding. Pointing his thick, heavy
eyebrows, beneath which sparkled his inexplicably smiling eyes –
which expressed neither sorrow, nor regret – the groom calmly looked
at him, and saying nothing more, slipped into the shadows that ran
alongside the house. Emerging in an illuminated section of the yard, he
began to walk towards the entrance to the property with a wavering
gait, and his slanting shadow dragged behind along the earth. This
man's gait – so unhurried, so confident, displaying nothing of that
primal panic and confusion which had shown itself during that
shameful flight just a few moments ago. He disappeared round the
corner of the house, but his shadow continued to drag along the ground
for a while, until it suddenly straightened out, growing erect, like the
tail of a thieving dog, and – passing along the clay fence, instantly
disappeared from sight.

As if he had just seen an apparition, Zhappar could not come to, shifting his detached gaze along the courtyard, from one spot illuminated by moonlight, to another.

But, beginning with that night, for precisely one week, he continued to hear the same dull sound of something dropping, followed by the noise of the squeaking door coming from the women's half of the house.

According to an ancient custom, the bride was to remain at her parent's house for an entire year after the wedding, and so the impatient husband was forced to sneak around at night, to secretly visit his intended. Not to mention, his visits would have to be carried out noiselessly, he had to sneak in to his wife's chambers, like some invisible night-demon, so as not to inadvertently catch the eye of his mother-in-law or father-in-law. But soon, the groom ran out of patience trying to observe this inconvenient custom, so in all of one week, he arrived and very decisively took his young wife away back to his house with him.

And now, each evening when he returned home from work, Zhappar approached the house with an entirely different feeling in his heart, than before. The hose and the courtyard seemed unrecognizable, almost foreign to him, although he was surrounded by the same jagged crust of the uneven clay fence, standing as tall as a man. The same old ox-cart was frozen in the corner of the yard, its bulky handles pointing up towards the sky and behind them, its large, dark wheels. And the gray ass twitching its ears, and as before, was munching loudly on straw in the distant shed. And yet, something had left, something had abandoned this familiar yard, and left it feeling dreary and barren. Bey-Akhmet, seemingly purposeful, still walked all around the courtyard, scratching his plump belly while darting about, and yet – even he seemed unlike himself, somehow. It was as if he had finally reached this point of self-restraint and earnestness – what was intended for him by fate, and what had not been given to him by nature during his birth. His wife, already a women of few words, now seemed to utter barely a sound. That it was no specter that was ambling about the house, but in fact a living, breathing person was made evident by the shuffling of her feet across the ground, and the way her clothing would flutter as she moved – the black parandja - which covers women all the way down their ankles, and above the head, yet another, brown, chapan.

And the room of the bride, where she had lazily waited behind the curtain, now belonged to Zhappar himself. The wedding chamber, where new bride had spent her first few nights of love with her husband, had not yet aired out the aromas of incense, powders, pomade and kohl. And every time he would lay down upon her bed, which was placed in the middle of the room, he would recover all of these delicate aromas – sensing them as something familiar, kindred even. And in the listless excitement of his soul, he could not remain lying in one spot. All he had to do was shut his eyes, and a vision appeared to him: somewhere, from the far corner of the room, a virgin, draped in sheer cloth swam through the air, the waterfall of her luxurious hair not hidden from the world. Yet, when he opened his eyes, there was nothing in front of him, except for the dim radiance of the moon in his window.

He would lay there for a long time – first, with his eyes closed, then, with his eyes open – until he experienced the sensation of his eyelids being filled with lead. Weighed down by this invisible force, eyelids seemed to be shutting on their own, immersing his soul in a deep, deep sleep. But in his dreams, the spectral virgin would not abandon him: she was right there, a mere arm's length away, making her bed. She reclined on her snow-white down-feather bed, sinking into it entirely, and then was still, unmoving. Unbearably flustered and burning up, he fought with himself – wanting at first to leave, and then nothing more than to firmly remain rooted to that very spot. Yet he still made the decision to get up. Suddenly, he was experiencing the strangest sensation – inexplicably, his whole body felt like it had been pumped full of plaster. Not a single part of his body would budge, his head felt as though it was buried in wet sand: he wanted to turn and face the young beauty, but no did not have an ounce of strength that would allow him to turn his head – the weight of the universe had heaved itself onto Zhappar. He made an incredible effort and concentrated intensely, yet the result was pitiful – he was only able to wiggle his hand. He yearned to lengthen it, and stretch it out to the adjacent bed, where the virginal beauty was resting – he stretched out almost far enough to run his finger along the edge of the down-feather bed, when all of a sudden, his hand landed on something solid, and cold... This startled and frightened Zhappar, and he came to.

After numerous disturbing and dreadful nights, riddled with nightmares, he began to feel drained, despondent and hag-ridden. Something inside him snapped after the daughter of Akhmet-bey had married and abandoned her parent's home. The young architect became noticeably antisocial, closed off, and for seemingly no reason, would fall into a panicked, anxious state, or get drift off into a haze of uncertainty.

Before leaving for his campaign to the distant western lands, the Lord declared a new edict, forbidding any type of trade or commerce from occurring in the parks or gardens, in the open courtyards or streets – in order to rid the city, the largest capital city in the whole world, of its noise and bustle, the screaming, the soot and the dirt, the dust kicked up horses hooves, the piercing braying of the donkeys, the bellowing of camels. To facilitate a market, the Khan ordered for a large, covered street to be built, which would span the length of the entire city, and booths and shops could be erected on either side of the street. And among the rows of covered market plazas, they were to construct deep pools with fountains and devices for watering.

From that moment on, construction of the area designated for the market plaza was in full swing and the racket it created was unavoidable, every twenty-four hours a day. Slaves were driven out of their dungeons, and they proceeded to clear the area where the future commercial plaza was to be built; they demolished houses and carried the clay duval fences. And on the following day, on the exact spot where the ruins stood, a clean, flat area materialized, like the palm of a hand, cleared for the building process to commence. And the efficient crews of masons – along with the architects, the carpenters and the remaining workers – all gathered in the primed courtyards, and began to erect a string of sheds, benches, storage areas and warehouses and special pathways for the immense, covered marketplace.

Soon, the commercial area took a step within the boundaries of the Khan's capital. During the winter, the earth froze deeply, and so all of the ground operations were held up, that is, putting off the deadlines for completing the project.

Zhappar would tire easily in such construction sites – from the fussing and quarreling of hundreds of masons, laying down walls, and the view dazzled his eyes, and the young architect – either exhausted, or perhaps just having lost his zeal for living, finally stopped experiencing restless nights and strange dreams. Even his recollections of sweet Zukhra, which had ceaselessly tortured his soul – now, over time, had faded, growing dim in the fog of oblivion. In that year, which had given him the opportunity to live under the same roof with this dear girl, to see her every day – had eventually led to a sense of kinship of their souls. And now, she was forgotten, lost amid the confusing streets and alleys of these majestic cities. She was hidden behind some clay wall, in a house in an unknown location, in this teeming human anthill — and there is no hope whatsoever, of seeing her dear face again, smiling. And nevertheless — during each sudden, unexpected and mad recollection of her, his heart would grow cold and drop into his stomach, because one thing was absolutely clear: no, there was and could not be any hope of perhaps seeing her sometime, accidentally bumping into her in a crowd of people passing by, among these teeming streets and crowded alleyways. His painful, springtime dream – and the bitter, icy hopelessness of December: these two emotions soon ceased to fight one another and agreed, or so it seemed, apparently, to surrender… or, rather, to arrive at some resolution, whatever it may be.

And so, Zhappar arrived at the realization that he was no longer the same man he had been before. The young architect collected himself, rolling up every bit of his will into a ball, as if he was preparing himself for something decisive. In his movements, his actions, his behavior and the attitude of his soul, there was a certain level of restraint present, a certain severity and self-restriction. It was as though he had taken a pledge, vowing not to be distracted in this life, by anything, to be occupied with nothing but the laying of bricks, which would rise to greater heights daily – and in the most rigid and perfect order.

When he is the one taking care of laying down the brickwork, the bricks lay down perfectly in a row, rapidly, one after another – a beautiful system, they are firmly et in place, forever – how his new thoughts and feelings, purified of the dense fog of hope, vague griefs and withering passions. The covered street of the marketplace grew longer each day. And already, almost two full years have gone by, since the Lord marched westward, taking his entire army with him. The Chief master-ustad is in a hurry, whipping and commanding everyone to build more quickly, so the Lord's orders could be fulfilled in time, just in time for his return from his campaign. Each morning, the Chief-ustad arrives long before the work for the day commences, in order to look around and approximate the amount of work that has been accomplished by the shop masters.

Also, today, after leaving his cart at the entrance to the construction zone, he immediately set off for the sites that were located

End of the Legend •Abish Kekilbaev

under the main awning, where the masons were raising the walls of certain commercial structures. But, in doing the antithesis of what he usually would in starting off the day, the chief ustad did not approach the masons, who had gathered together to begin their work, nor did he even address them. He immediately entered the brick box that was being constructed, without paying even the slightest attention to all the bustle going on around him, or the extra workers who were transporting wheelbarrows full of bricks or filling stretchers with a certain solution, he approached Zhappar, who was speaking with other masters, most decisively. The young architect thought that the chief-ustad would walk by, but no – he was headed right towards him. He stopped and placed his foot on top of a pile of bricks. First he caught his breath, and then said:

— Oh, Zhappar, just quit it all and let's go…

The young architect looked at him, bewildered. What could this mean? Where are we going?

— We need to go to the palace. The main vizier demands your presence.

The shaky carriage of the chief ustad stopped in front of the white stone mansion of the chief vizier. Zhappar obediently followed the chief master, walking past numerous guards. After clearing several spacious, breezy halls, they finally appeared before the chief vizier, who sat on a tall, carpeted ottoman, in the center of a beautiful blue hall, beside a large, round pool. He graciously accepted the bows of the master-builders, and then he fixed his eyes upon the young architect, and gazed at him for a long while, examining him from head to toe. After the prolonged silence, he opened his mouth slightly, in what appeared to be an attempt to express something of great importance to the architect, but then he suddenly shifted his gaze to the Elder-master and ask him:

— Have you told him why I demanded to see him?

— No, my lord, I have not. — responded the Elder-master as he lowered himself, bowing.

— Then hear me out, ustad Zhappar. Our honorable, majestic, radiant Young Khansha would like to please the Great Lord upon his return from his travels by erecting a minaret in his honor. We have decided to bestow the great distinction of its construction to you, ustad.

Once he finished speaking, the vizier immediately turned his gaze away from Zhappar and lowered his deep eyes, which, like bottomless cups, spilled over. But when he raised his eyes again, slowly, he locked his eyes on Zhappar, with the glare of a python, and the young man felt the entire magical force of the piercing eyes of the Great Khan's first-in-command. And not daring to look into those unblinking eyes, the young architect bent down, bowing low.

The chief vizier's all-seeing eyes trailed along the bent backs of both masters, and in an apathetic, icy and negligent tone, he proclaimed:

— I do hope that all is quite clear?

Zhappar inquisitively glanced at the chief-ustad, as if requesting an elucidation of what is to be expected in such a case: joy or woe or terror – and what answer should be given in return. But the chief just stood there, without expressing any feelings regarding what the vizier had said.

Fearing unpleasant consequences for his tense and inquisitive glance, it suddenly dawned on Zhappar, that the answer the vizier was waiting for was expected from Zhappar himself, at which point he hastily and nervously blurted out:

— Yes… everything is understood.

The entire month after this unexpected incident, Zhappar travelled around the entire city in a ox-cart, searching everywhere for a place where he could drive his first peg into the ground, and begin measurements for future construction. In the entire capital city, there was not a single neighborhood that Zhappar did not visit in his month of exploration. The architect searched not only suitable areas for the minaret, but also the terrain, slowly, carefully inspecting the farmsteads, properties and houses in the vicinity, spending hours standing somewhere in a secluded corner, scratching his head with a concerned expression…

One day, the ox-cart which Zhappar had been using to drive around stopped for a long time in a meadow on the south side of the Khan's garden, the area surrounding the palace of the Youngest Wife of the Khan.

That particular place was reminiscent of some kind of ancient burial mound, but nevertheless significantly, and in this case –

favorably elevated above the line of the city's urban landscape. And the soil here was dense and stony – and suitable. Over time, the sinking foundation will be quite insignificant, and will not harm the future of construction, and will also not lose its current height. And so – the location of the tower was a success – it was far from the throng of urban buildings, yet it was still yet in the suburban area outside of the city. The famous capital's mosques with their minarets and cupolas, the intricate madrasah and palaces of the Khan did not surround this place, so it was wide open and had great visibility. Nothing could detract attention away from it, and the palace of the Young Khansha, which was nearby, could only complement the impression made by the tower, which was erected per her wishes. Then again, the palace was almost entirely hidden from view, engulfed almost to the rooftops by the thick verdure of the forest-park.

Well, now that the decision had been made, he picked up a peg and drove it into the ground.

Stretching all the way towards the ruins of the ancient sepulchral mound, which was completely riddled with gopher tunnels and burrows, row upon row of two-wheeled ox-carts loaded with supplies were being hauled, raising dust up to the skies. Red, fractured ridges had grown into mountains of transported bricks. The slaves, stripped nude above the belt, their dark, sweat-drenched backs glistening, started to dig up the soil, laboring intensely under the supervision of a multitude of guards, as well as one overseer – a vigilant and incredibly cruel man – and continued toiling under the merciless sun of the southern sky. To the same extent that the slaves were digging up the soil beneath them with shovels, they were increasingly sinking down into the ground below them, and soon enough, they disappeared entirely out of sight, immersed in the ancient, yawning bosom of the earth. The taller the edge of the construction pit grew with every day, the fewer the indicators that those slaves with their nude, dark, glistening backs were not buried forever in the very graves they themselves had digging down into the ground. Zhappar was ceaselessly rushing around the foundation area, refining the measurements for the future minaret, crawling from one end to the other, from one corner to the other, meticulously bringing out the stone substructure that would be the nest for the future greatest minaret of all-time.

And then, finally came the day, when the forty remaining slaves were raised up to the surface from the foundation area, and

Zhappar himself went down into it. And although it was considerably cooler in the deep earthen pit, than in the scorching summer heat above, after a certain amount of time had gone by, he started to feel oppressed by the subterranean gloom and deathly silence of the crypt. Some kind of invisible, but palpable otherworldly force was siphoning the very strength from his soul, attempting to drag him away to the realm of shadows once and for all. And barely coping with this strange and otherworldly terror, Zhappar laid out the first rows of bricks, which had been lowered down to him in large leather satchels.

But finally, he had singlehandedly laid out the most critical part of the foundation, and he scrambled back up to the surface. Beyond that point, he only oversaw the construction, observing how from the depths of the tomblike earth, a monstrously thick man-made stone tree began to grow vigorously toward the sky. In the near future, all of the passers-by, or travelers whose path led them near the site, would always pass by closely, compulsively stopping to marvel at the miracle unfolding before their eyes. And seeing this, the young architect was silently filled with a sense of pride for their accomplishments. And when hundreds of workers and masters from different guilds approached him, pointing at him from a distance, when they searched him out and rushed to him with questions, and he, too, rushed around the entire site – the young architect would not grow flustered, nor did he tire of this throng, this human anthill. On the contrary – the intense fatigue, the aching of his tense muscles and creaking joints, the agonizing lethargy from lack of sleep – all of this melted from him, washed away by the warmth of human eyes directed towards him.

He, too, would line up with everyone else for the laying of stones, and together with his tower – growing a little bit every day, and slowly moving further up and away from the sinful earth, from the faceless mob of slaves, endlessly lugging stones and mixing the solution in leather tubs. The slaves were drag the stones and carry the mixture upwards, via the internal spiral staircase of the tower. And soon enough, he was already rushing around the thin, tapered neck of the tower, where only two workers could fit upon the scaffolding, and even then – with great difficulty. The crowd of onlookers surrounding the site had thinned out over time. They observed the new tower rising up, how it stretches taller and further skyward, in front of your very eyes, growing brick by brick – and scrambling bravely to the highest point – its very own fearless architect. But the vocalization of their amazement and captivated looks no longer mattered to him: the tower had ascended to such great heights, that it was no longer possible to distinguish a single human face, or hear any voices. From the top of the tower, people appeared as nothing more than a tiny, stout midget with miniscule, plump legs, spread apart. Without the attention of the onlookers, the bricks seemed much heavier than usual. Much like the unnatural gait of a hobbled horse – everything that was caught up in the strict, long since imposed rules of building – bound his creative flight with its routine, and this weighed heavily on Zhappar.

And now he impatiently had to wait for the slaves to climb up and unload yet another heap of bricks in the small working area. Attuning himself only to that, which was audible, he listened to the initial sounds, which he connected to people arriving at the entrance, at the very bottom of the tower: then, he heard the loud crash of doors, the knocking of the stretchers; then steps ascending the spiral staircase, coming closer and closer; some words were spoken. The majority of the slaves were prisoners from distant countries. They do not know his language, and the architect did not understand a single word they spoke. Yet, from the beginning of the created world, it has probably gone something like this: the blood of kin, native blood – draws people to each other with incredible force. Let's say a hobbled horse is standing in a ravine, munching on grass; then, it senses the sharp smell of other horses, passing by, over the hill, and it will not be able to control itself – it will, without a doubt, give the rallying tribal sign, and neigh in a vibrating, high-pitched voice… When the slaves appear next to Zhappar, carrying the piles of bricks in leather stretchers, and the stench of the sweaty, unwashed bodies stings his nostrils – he does not turn away from them, choosing instead to greet them with a few friendly, encouraging words. Barely alive enough to carry their back-breaking loads, the slaves – not comprehending a single word, bared their teeth in a joyous smile.

Meanwhile, the tower continued to grow in height, and presently matched all of the tallest buildings in the city. Much like resting in the palm of some hand, it was possible for him to observe the fuss of the narrow side-streets, and the teeny, tiny courtyards of the urban *Mahallah*. Resembling black dots and lines which stitched up the areas between the toy-box houses, the crowds of urban dwellers scurried about in all directions, either walking on foot or riding on horses or asses. And all of this appeared so disorderly, yet quite meaningful to oneself, and the commotion of the urban crowd seemed to resemble an ant hill. It was amusing to watch this chaotic flurry of people, this stampede, rushing about. And even the most beautiful, most expensive luxury goods which easily draw one's eye when walking by the stands in the marketplace – now, from here, appear as nothing more than cheap trinkets, pitiful baubles. One does not want to believe that this entire senseless, petty, joyless, pitiful running around in circles of humanity was designed with a hidden agenda: our own self-destruction. It is almost as if they aren't able to live in the out there, in the boundless space, each his own king, god and divine hero! No, we have doomed ourselves to this miserable existence – driving ourselves into cities, laying out narrow, confusing streets so we cannot walk anywhere without butting heads with one another. They fear open expanses as if they were bloodthirsty tigers, ready to ambush them at any moment, so they ineptly bury themselves, surrounding themselves with the four walls of these stuffy, stone boxes – one no different the another, a result of the wretched intent of their builders. So shameful they've proven to be, in their creation of this nightmarish anthill nation, clambering ahead by stepping on each other's heads, in a desperate attempt to, via all that is true and untrue, to get out on top. From here it is easy to see, how all of these attempts are in vain, and how the inhabitants of this human anthill are gradually turning into madmen – frantically risking to reap some sort of benefits, butting heads with each other, fighting, mercilessly taking each other down, to secure their place and come out on top. And so – if not for this order, then what? Is it not a possibility that another way should be discovered – where one would be able to take care of and represent himself, in these great wide open spaces? And would some enemy suddenly materialize, that would be able to locate and destroy each one, scattered throughout the world, one-by-one? And what of this infested human anthill? Certainly, there will be numerous powerful villains, who will conceive of a way to crush them all with one blow, leaving nothing but an ugly, bloody pulp behind? The mighty conqueror, who mercilessly captures other, foreign anthills to increase the size of his own, making it even more densely populated, allots even more grandeur for his taking. And for what purpose is this new minaret being built? Is it not for the ever-growing grandeur? In the eyes of the foreigners, it will rise up in glory – yet another majestic anthill. Or, perhaps – this massive tower was erected for another purpose: to serve as a warning from afar, for his brothers living in freedom, in the spirit of the wide, open steppes – so they would not hurry to replace the freedom in their life, with the stale existence and suicidal swarms of the city life? So, what is all of this for? These cities, these minarets… He – the architect-builder, has no answer for this, himself…A year ago, he obtained an order from a snake-eyed vizier, and now, he is fulfilling it… As they told me, per the

Young Khansha's request. And she is probably sitting in some garden gazebo, monitoring his progress; and then – monitoring the tower's growth. And, this minaret, what in the world does she need it for? What on earth prompted her to dream up this tall termite-nest? When such crazy thoughts penetrated Zhappar's mind, it was in those very moments that he yearned to climb out of the labyrinthine clay walls of the city, and into the fresh air and vastness of the open plains – to take off to the endless steppe, dozing in the midday haze. But, no matter which way you look, if you are anywhere within the confines of this immense city – everywhere your gaze is confined by clay walls and fences, bleached white by the scorching summer heat, and in autumn – splashed with the thick, dirty mud of roadside puddles, propelled by wheels and hooves, from below. And as if attempting to escape from this mud, fearing he might sink in these puddles of silt, he swiftly clambered further and further upward, by tower, to touch the shining blue skies.

It was only at this moment that he realized why towers and minarets were necessary to people. They express the aspiration of the proud spirit and vigilant mind of man – toward flight, above the bustle of the frail world, to ascend to the greatest heights on the wings of a bright, bright dream. And there, on a mountain peak, looking down at the world with utter clarity – one begins to understand and appreciate the truest values life has to offer When it isn't crammed into a box of walls made of stone, the soul is able to unearth genuine insight, and understand the value of true freedom; and the mind will recognize and distinguish those lofty human thoughts, carrying them to mountainous heights, from the lower passions and desires, which go no higher than the tail of an ass. Also, the mind comprehends what distinguishes the fussing anthill of terrestrial existence from the lofty, exalted life of the soul; and knows how to, in human matters, distinguish the insignificant from the great; to learn to confuse the genuine measure of things from the proportionality in comparison with other things; to learn how not to trust all things imaginary and random, disguising themselves as the truth and law; how not to not confuse the manifested appearance of a thing with its genuine, internal essence. Indeed, even the negligibly small mouse sometimes leaves its damp burrow to warm its back under the rays of the universal sun, to look around with its inquisitive, roaming little beady eyes, and to admire that life which occurs on a larger scale, and to determine once and for all, that the whole wide world is actually not as confining and gloomy as its underground burrow, but wonderful and boundless instead. And then, realizing that life on this earth does not consist merely of a mouse's concerns, grievances and sorrows, but also of the wonderful majesty of the universe, the wee mouse is overwhelmed with joy and raises his squeaky voice to the sky and sings his praises.

Perhaps, this minaret, which was pulled out from the Earth's soil to form this wonderful pillar, is not only a powerful obelisk honoring exceptional human courage, but is also a gentle, trusting hand stretching out from the submissive, dark earth to the bright sky, which hangs above it. It seems, even yesterday, these common bricks were nothing but worthless clay which right there, at the foot of tower, was kneaded into existence by the hooves of a depressed, gray little donkey... But now, as if inspired by a certain magical force passing through his hands, palms and fingers, the bricks fall into place and are transformed into something that is visible to all – a marvelous structure, bewitching everyone. Normal clay dust, the delicate dust of the earth is transmuted into the proud, graceful, slender minaret, its peak the center of every man's gaze...

Last year, after driving the first peg into the ground, he began to tensely look to the distant horizon, hoping to see there, in the blue skies, an image of his future minaret. For a long time he would gaze into the pale, azure sky, but saw nothing. And once, for no more than a second, an elusive spectral image of an ordered tower finally flickered before his eyes, disappearing as quickly as it had come. He rubbed his eyes in order to see the enchanting tower once more – with its foundation driven into the earth, and its peak butting against the sky, but the tower did not appear once more. It vanished, without leaving a trace behind, as if in an instant the earth had swallowed it up whole. But even then, as he was standing on the large ancient mound punctured by gopher holes, he knew for certain, that he would grasp this spectral vision and give it a physical form – raising it from the earth into a majestic blue stone minaret.

...Eight years have passed since that day, and time has flown by – unnoticed.

Scrambling up a sand dune with great difficulty, while dragging two striped korzhun bags tied to its back, a small grey donkey led the way, and two followed – a father and son. Their long, monotonous journey has continued for several weeks. Traveling through the dry, unyielding desert, they encountered wells with potable water only once every two to three days. The wells were tucked away

End of the Legend •Abish Kekilbaev

from the scorching sun underneath the branches of saxaul trees, and were covered on top with bundles of weeds. And so whenever the travelers would encounter one, they would briefly rest and wash their feet in the cool, refreshing water.

Pacing himself behind the small donkey, the father walked on in front of the son. Walking without stopping, the father did not attempt to converse with his son and only from time to time, having conquered yet another steep incline of a dune, he would bend over, arching himself, pausing for a moment on the crest of the dune. Digging his fists into his hips for support, he would slowly bend his body, stretching out his back.

And only the small grey donkey did not show any outward signs of fatigue. Pricking his long ears up and back, his skinny legs trotted along the surface of the sand, almost like he was sliding from dune to dune, without raising his lowered head. Long since obedient to the cruel will of the two-legged beasts, the animal no longer struggled to oppose it, for he had a firm grasp on his fate – he knew that he would never again know the meaning of rest. The little donkey only clung onto one thing, hidden somewhere in some corner of his consciousness – that at some point, beyond the ashen stillness of these sands, awaits the prospect of slurping up some crisp, cool water and munching on some tufts of grass. The two-legged ones do not arrange this leisurely pleasure out of pity for him, but do it strictly for themselves. But this made no difference to the donkey, for he knew the sequence of their actions by heart, so his little legs vigorously trotted away, patiently undertaking the task set before him.

The demeanor of the seventeen year old youth, on the other hand, was quite the different from that of the donkey. He displayed an obstinate and gloomy disposition. The young Zhappar was growing weary of this endless journey.

For the duration of the entire winter, his father was bound to his bed by illness, but had finally started to recover by the month of March. Where his energy suddenly came from was a mystery. But still – he ploughed his paltry plot of land, raked across, and finished by sowing some seeds. In the courtyard, in front of the small adobe house, which had sunk into the earth, tiny, stunted saplings poked out of the ground, and his father set about trimming them and loosening the soil in a circle around the each stem.

All of this was done without any excess words, and after he finished his work, he gathered the children around him, and assigned to each their personal domestic responsibilities in detail. That is, to each child, except for Zhappar.

Not long after, he left for his journey, taking only Zhappar with him.

The inhabitants of the small cabins, forgotten in the vastness of the steppes, ran out of their houses, and, stopping by their gates, stood and watched them for a while, until finally they vanished from sight.

When they were departed with their donkey in tow, who was hung from all sides with old korzhun bags – the neighboring women, the curious creatures that they are, inquired of Zhappar's mother:

— And what market is the honorable potter-ustad headed to?

Puzzled herself, his speechless mother could do little more than shrug her shoulders.

And where they were off to now, even Zhappar did not know. Many tall tales were told about their father, yet not even his children knew which ones, if any, held any truth.

Even the potter's appearance in these parts was an incident filled with mystery – where did he come from? How did he end up here? One day, sometime in late autumn, he wandered into the village with a passing caravan, then stayed behind, and from that moment on, here he remained.

Not particularly inclined to spilling matters of the soul before others, the tall, dark, strong djigit turned out to be an artisan, whose hands molded life into raw clay. Very soon he was able to live on his own, independently, earning a living through his potter's craft. He took in a wife – a poor, orphan girl. By God's favor, the man acquired a house, a farm, a family. He had children.

Of them all, he prized his first-born son, Zhappar, the most. He constantly kept the boy with him. The ustad was severe, had a strict disposition. His eyes were always gloomy, his gaze fixed, tenacious, prickly. Due to his strictness and particularly close attention to the behavior of the children, he was the one truly raised them. Not once did he ever leave a single misdeed unpunished, not even the smallest, and only at the sight of Zhappar, his severe demeanor would soften, his expression even exuding a certain tenderness. Yet, in never manifested itself in any words or actions – he never stroked his head, or patted him on his back – not once did he press his face into the forehead of his favorite boy, to take in the scent of his own favorite child, his own flesh and blood. And nevertheless, the cold and sharp harpoon of his gaze, which mercilessly penetrated the remaining children, who had in some way misbehaved or wronged him, seemed deliberately to fly past the target, and splinter into pieces, whenever the matter concerned Zhappar. The boy himself did not understand how he could have possibly gained the relentless, unwavering love of so severe a father. But, no matter what happened the last year or two, whenever he would fulfill any task doled out by his father, Zhappar did not experience the same fear of his parent as he had before, had he done something wrong, nor did he shiver and shrink from the latent anxiety, as if someone was taking aim from a bow, intending to pierce him right between the shoulder blades...

From time to time, his father would travel in the region in search of necessary clay. Early in the morning, leading the donkey by a leash, he would leave his small road, which was on the outskirts by a small river, which neither streamed into the larger river by inflow, nor did it emanate from it, instead forming a lengthy channel. All day, passing through places along the steppe familiar only to him, he would return home in the evening, bringing home two large korzhun bags packed to the top with clay. One day, in the springtime, his father took Zhappar with him on one of these journeys. The boy, who had never ventured beyond the perimeter of his own road, was placed on top of the donkey, and was instructed to diligently push him forward, to ensure that he didn't lag behind his father, who strolled ahead in a leisurely manner, but whose wide, sweeping gait soon put him far ahead of the boy and little donkey. First, they made their way through a narrow hollow, which was usually filled with lambs and kids grazing under the watchful eye of the local shepherds, and then they emerged on spacious, grassy hill.

From that elevation, they could see the entire oblong, open valley, surrounded by multi-colored, striped dry valley taluses, a spacious valley, on which, like a handful of *dzhugary* grains spilled out on the dastarkhan of a pauper, were sheltered the small village's cabins. From a distance, the tiny allotments near each cabin, whimsically arranged into small gardens and tracts of land for plowing, each delineated by sun-bleached yellow, pock-marked duval fences, resembled the curves of a drawing or some kind of naïve mosaic. Chimneys poked out of the tops of every house, and hazy curls of smoke poured out of each of them, expanding, like orderly, elegant clumps of shaken wool. The local region, which, before, seemed as infinite as the universe – and beyond its limits, the end of the world, and there, none of the fabric of order or structure that existed in the world remains – appeared to him now as an unremarkable backyard on a small plot of land in a riverside valley. But the sensitive, gentle heart of the child, ready to tremble out of pity and sympathy at the sight of anything small or defenseless, or to be penetrated by conflicting sensation imposed by the manifestation of anything spiteful or unjust in this world – Zhappar's heart ached from the feeling of helplessness and barren pity for the wretched cabins of his native land, which were squeezed into this obscure valley, the poor dwelling places of the those who endlessly toil in the steppes.

Striking the heels along the sides of the small, grey donkey, the boy hurried after his father, who had walked sufficiently far ahead by this point. Gradually, the grass turf ended and beyond that, the ground became flat and even, like a stone plateau. The horizon – the line where the sky meets the sun, back in the village, seemed to be entirely close, and now, since their ascent of the hill, with each additional step, it seems to move further and further away into some previously unfathomable distance. The world, which previously seemed like a narrow bluish strip, now – unexpectedly, expanded exponentially, and the sky, pouring in from above, previously dragging its blue canopy along the earth, in that instant, seemed to suddenly leap up to dizzying, incomprehensible heights.

His father marched onward impatiently, his form consistently rigid, as if he'd sworn never to give himself peace until he'd reached the edge of the horizon. However, that way Zhappar had had time to understand that this apparent edge of the earth – not the neighboring world, which would tremble and quake in his vision as he rode the donkey all day, but the insidious plateau, eluding any attempts at calculating the number of steps to reach this elusive edge, which only seems to slip further out of reach. You will move towards it, along the road, and it will obediently unfurl itself before your feet, and yet you never will be able to defeat the devious, pesky visible horizon.

The tension had turned father's dark, ruddy face a painful red, but he marched on without stopping, just as quickly and decisively as before, not paying any attention to the scalding desert sun, which had already surmounted the zenith. And the smooth, rounded alabaster mountain, which had seemed very large from distance, by midday, rose up before them. Yet, as they drew closer, the white mountain had receded and appeared much smaller, as if some chthonic monstrosity had begun to swallow it up from below, and when they approached it even more closely, the mountain seemed to disappear altogether and evened out with the other neighboring hills.

His father climbed the wide summit of the white hill and, stopping, stood motionless for a while, staring off somewhere into the distance. He had left the house today with the intention of seeking out some clay, and yet, on the way, he had never honored the white mountain with his attention – never noticed its form, nor the color of its clay outcrops on the slopes of mounds and ravines. And even upon reaching the intended target – the white mountain, he did not immediately proceed to inspect the soil under his feet, instead he looked out at the unattainably remote horizon, which seemed to sink in the quivering haze. As if attempting to lock away its secrets from the fixedly prying eyes of man, the horizon hatched a plan, creating a game of light – first pouring out a blinding iridescent ripple at the base of the sky, then shutting itself away behind a diverse multitude of clouds with shimmering, luminous edges, and finally igniting the evening horizon with a fire-breathing haze. From his very first meeting with the stunning expanses of the terrestrial and celestial worlds, with its commanding silence and pronounced, mysterious pacification, the boy stood, motionless – neither living nor dead, as if bewitched, recognizing within his soul some special, indescribable state. He felt the prickly chill of horror slide slowly across his back — as if some monsters had appeared before him, of gigantic proportions, and he stood before them – nightmarishly small and frail. And even the donkey somehow seemed to tune into this unusual state that the humans, the father and boy, found themselves in — the slanted eyes of the donkey started watering out of grief, his eyelashes began to quiver quickly and often, as if the donkey himself was on the verge of tears...

But, nothing intelligible, distinct or weighty was perceived by the boy, nor was he able to grasp any lessons in all of this to carry with him – from the washed-out light on the horizon flooding his eyes, to the focused and perpetually sullen expression of his parent, who – the more he turned his gaze towards the spectral limits of the celestial game, the sadder he would grow, and more gloomy...

After that journey with his father, it seemed to him that the confined valley, in which, as if in the narrow space of his cupped hands, their cabins were arranged, was often oppressing him, suffocating his breathing, taking away his ability to fully stretch and straighten out his chest. And over time, he developed a habit – using any situation as an excuse to run off to the steppe. And now, working in the small vegetable gardens near the house was such a burden to him, yet tending to the *aul's* herd of lambs and kids was pleasurable, it was a task he accomplished with great zeal. Distancing himself as much as possible from the narrow, confining valley, he would release the herd of little ones to roam around freely, and recline in the grass, looking up at the sky for a while, and would drift away in his daydreams. Suddenly, as if waiting for his arrival, the ringing silence of the steppe was filled with a full-fledged spectrum of the sounds of wildlife. At first, from the top, it seemed, from the foamy clouds of white, which floated along the blue celestial river, the frequent trilling sounds of larks came spilling down; and the other delicate singers of the air and the earth caught on to its canto, sending forth cheerful, eager chirps and peeps, tweets and cheeps, having climbed out of numerous hiding spots and stuffy burrows, warming their backs and chubby sides in the rays of the generous sun. Then the gophers joined in, whistling gaily, not at all hiding their satisfaction in hearing themselves sing. The sounds of the herd of lambs and kids which reached him, the pleasure with which they munched and chomped the juicy spring grass – this, too sweetened the mixture of sounds flowing into his ears – as if this was, in fact, the bewitching melody of life. He was filled to the brim with the sweet music of the life of the steppe. His gaze was bursting with the sea of blue of the affectionate sky.

Having left the everyday bustle for a time, after remaining, in solitude, with the perfumes of the natural elements, the boy lies on the warmth of the sunbaked earth, floating away in a fancy of fantasy. It was as if he had for the very first time been introduced to the realm of poetic images, to the depths of the mystifying secrets of creation, of the universe, which he could not even express in his own human language. He is awed and enraptured by the imperturbable serenity of the structure of the world, which cracked itself open to him, a child, if only for a moment — by tranquility, uninterrupted by the bustling and fussing and scurrying about man. His eyes absorb the sky gliding over the earth and entire peaceful celestial expanse. Here, the rounded cirrus cloud, with it smooth, grey underbelly effortlessly glides to the side, pushing itself off from the horizon, as if leaning against the earth and

End of the Legend •Abish Kekilbaev

searching for something there, and his whimsical shadow, with its ever-transforming silhouettes. It was almost as if the shadow itself was watching him, sent from the sky by the Arbiter of Peace with the following task: "Go forth, study and learn everything there is to know in the whole wide world." And this soft, full, downy, fluffy cloud soars above the very head of the boy – the cool shadow she produces blankets him, like a gentle, affectionate hand.

He shuddered, as if tossed up by some mysterious higher power. But the sudden fright of it passed rapidly, for the sun peeked out from behind the edge of a cloud, and eagerly splashed its rays downward, and his body languished again. His young, clean chest – not once yet having felt the stinging ills of life, freely and deeply inhaled into itself the radiant life of spring – and was blissfully washed over by the sweetness of light, clean dreams.

Then, his back went numb, followed by a pricking sensation in the small of his back. He lifted himself up and off the ground. The sounds of life died down all around. The sun was tumbling down and westward. It was almost as if she were worried, making sure that the shepherd did not remain behind, in solitude, and in a friendly, but concerned manner watched over him, suspending herself above the horizon. And the second she ascertained that the young boy had risen to his feet, located the whip laying at his side, and began to walk towards the herd of little lambkins and kidlets, she immediately plummeted over the edge of the earth.

And when twilight arrived, the shepherd chased his small herd of young animals, with several milk-bearing female camels, frantically bellowing and bleating excitedly, as they ran towards the side of the valley with its familiar roads, leaving behind the thickening expanse of haze of the day past.

Father seemed to approve, that, steering clear of the band of other local children, the humdrum of those playing games on the littered backyards between the aul roads, the son preferred solitude. As it turns out, not without reason did the father once lead only Zhappar by the hand into the pottery workshop, where the master, with the secrecy of a thief, never allowed a single outsider.

The workshop, where he molded clay and straw with a fast hand, at the angle of an adobe duval fence, bore a mixture of smells – of dampness and heated ceramics.

The second his father's feet touched the potter's wheel, the silence of workshop was disrupted by a gnashing, scratching sound, as if the air in the half-lit workshop was being sliced into strips, like belts. The black top disc of the machine tool began rotating so swiftly, which dazzled the eyes. The clay, procured by father almost at other end of the earth, hauled back on the donkey's rump, mixed in water to a viscous state, cast onto the black rotating disc in a sticky lump — in the hands of potter, the wet clay truly sprung to life. First, in the middle of the swiftly revolved black disc, in the palms of the master, the clay started to swell into a bright dark, bluish, glossy bright sphere, which gradually, directed by the skillful fingers of the potter, was transformed into either a deep cup or a beautiful jug.

Zhappar's entranced eyes followed every movement of his father's work – as though he was watching the magic of some out-of-town fakir – how the resiliently flexed the bare calves of his legs, which rotated the squeaking bottom disc, how the emotionless, concentrated stern face of the master suddenly filled with a warm, vibrant light, which did not tear away from this future ware of his, not even for a second.

For the first time ever, the boy discovered the degree of magical perfection the actions of the human hands can attain. He was amazed by how, even from the simplest of materials, obtained from nature and of seemingly no value – from plain, old clay, raising dust underfoot somewhere in the brush of feather-grass and wormwood, kochia and buyurgan, ordinary water, ungraspable, slipping through our fingers, and also from fire, which crackles to life above the branches of a saxaul tree, and then disappears somewhere, after releasing a stream of smoke – all of this, without being able to see that which exists, that which leaks and flows away, and that which burns – can still give birth to things of such immense beauty, that we cannot tear our eyes from them.

And so the time came, and his father placed him at the potter's wheel. And only having touched the holy of holies, the work inventory of his father-ustad, he understood, that for the preparation of such an elegant, lovely jug it is necessary to possess – aside from the sifted clay and clean water, smoldering saxaul coals and exerted, wheezing bellows and with a good furnace – an exceptional bodily strength, which, being utilized to the maximum, nothing held back, you will leap about in a dance. One must also have excellent, tireless sight, equally sharp from beginning until the final completion of the ware. To possess the skill of uncompromising concentration, to remain focused on that which is important, when all ninety of your veins and nerves, like yarns stretched taut, tremble and scream impatiently – altogether as one, and then individually. To know how to manage the intricacies of hopes and doubts, unifying the forces of inspiration and demanding work. To uncover the ability of not allowing yourself to become a slave of success and happiness, but to be the king of your own passions; and to finally give birth to that small thing within oneself, that we call patience.

On the old, torn, tattered camel saddle, in the corner along with all of the other rubbish, on which Zhappar usually sat while watching his father work, now sat his father. His father sat silently, paying close attention to his son's every move. His face did not manifest any signs of tender affection or enthusiasm whatsoever. The sharp, piercing gleam of his father's eyes disturbed Zhappar.

This was the appearance, as his son would understand much later on, the desire of his father to harden the character of his son with his severity, to prepare him for heavy trials and tribulations in the future. His father was not prepared to pass on his legacy to a lazy, indolent or weak-willed lump.

Under the close, watchful eye of his father, who, from morning to evening accompanied Zhappar to his job, he came to understand one additional truth: a true master sculpts and sharpens his eyes and strict concentration. And finally, Zhappar also grew to understand why his father-ustad did not allow any outsiders or random people into his pottery workshop. A true master would not risk revealing any secrets of his craft to unknown, wandering eyes. In this instance, he can be compared to a beautiful woman, who skillfully hides all of her charms and her virtues under her silks, but lest you look upon her as she tilts her head just so, or if you happen to catch a glimpse of her fleeting lunar gaze, until the end of their days, those djigit's hearts will belong to her. The drops of perspiration, rolling off the brow of the creator, mustn't fall into a person's eyes — and they should not see his faces, contorted by stress, nor his furrowed brows of dissatisfaction with himself. Let people see only the joyful creation of his hands — and may they twist and turn their heads before it, awe-struck. For the master-ustad, the artist, there is no higher expectation than this. A true master cannot be made of someone who is not irked by the fixed, testing gazes of his rivals, just as those who are not proud of their unique, creative successes also cannot be called masters, nor can those, who are not intoxicated with joy to the depths of their soul, when they see the enchanted looks upon the faces of people examining their wares. Zhappar's father was not so much pleased with the elegant, high-quality products his son was producing, but more so the ambitious attention his son paid to the positive sentiments regarding his work. And so, he was convinced of the fact that he was not mistaken in his observations, the master thanked fate for the fact, that he was not one of the other, ordinary children – that his son was gifted and moreover, possessed a healthy, artistic ambition. With this newfound faith in him, his father started to seriously and thoroughly train son in this craft, desiring nothing more than to pass on to him all the knowledge, skill and practices, which he possessed himself.

In the morning, Zhappar would enter the cramped, damp hovel of the potter's workshop, and would leave it no earlier than evening time. At first, the parching smell of fired clay irritated his throat, but, over time, he grew accustomed to it, and eventually stopped noticing it altogether, much like his ears grew accustomed to the gnashing, scratching sound of the potter's wheel.

Even though, as an adolescent, he grew tired of the monotonous nature of this, essentially, routine labor, he did not feed his aversion to it. Each and every day, some small, new secret was revealed to him, adding to his wealth of knowledge, and this guaranteed his captivation with mastering the art of the potter's craft.

In order to not over-work his son, potentially causing a state of disenchantment with his studies, his father would sometimes leave the workshop closed for as long as several days, or even a week, so that his son could go and distract himself by doing the things that children do, to take a good break from the burdens of the difficult craft. But such interruptions and idleness quickly bored the boy, and with great impatience he waited for the day when he would once again be allowed to enter the workshop infused with the smell of hot, fired clay, and sit down at the potter's wheel.

Soon, the jugs Zhappar had made began to appear, and were dispersed throughout the village. When he first saw the girl, who was walking with a jug resting on her shoulder – one of the jugs that he had prepared with his own hands – he proceeded to follow her, at a distance, all the way down to the river. The slender, lithe, petite girl bent down, filling up her jug with water, and then, so as not to dirty her wet boots with dry dust, with the jug firmly resting on her shoulder, she walked along a strip of densely packed, wet clay soil and started walking straight for him, at which point Zhappar quickly ducked behind a duval and hid there, bent down, for fear of being seen, or that they'd figure out why he was sneaking around and following the girl.

Soon, there came a time when not a single house in the village was without a jug crafted by Zhappar's own hands.

But then came the day, when for some mysterious reason, his father set out on a distant journey to an unknown place, making sure to take his son with him.

In this scorching desert expanse replete with burning sand, it seemed as though they were the only living things – the two of them, wandering to who knows where. At times, overwhelmed by the ceaseless sands free of people, they would see the fuzzy, black speck of a person appear somewhere in the distance, approaching them either by foot or on horse – but as they approached more closely, it would become apparent that this was nothing more than a small bush or branch of saxaul poking out of the sand.

And this wandering in the sands of this arid, waterless desert, following a snowless winter, with not even the foggiest idea of where you're headed – makes the already practically intolerable journey that much more difficult, because it seem so utterly pointless.

Deprived of all his strength, Zhappar collapsed on his back into the sand, and his eyes, squinting from the blinding sun, trailed after the energetic little donkey, which trotted alongside his father, scrambling up the steep incline of a dune. Above Zhappar's face, the faded, blank azure sky melted into swirls. Not one cloud interrupted the blank, blue expanse of the sky. Only above the uneven, wavy horizon, he saw a stripe of gossamer, grey-blue haze stretching across it. The further upward one's eyes would roam, the more frightening and dark the sky appeared. Desperately looking around at the terrible, foreboding, barren sky Zhappar forced his body to comply and rise up, to catch up with his father. Caught in quicksand rising above his knees, he forcefully loosened himself and hurried after them, observing the little donkey's trail, who – of the three of them – seemed to be the only one with a true sense of where to go.

The deep creases that had been etched into the sides of the dunes suddenly smoothed out before the setting of the sun, the journeyers finally reached the end of the desert, and walked out onto a sandy plain. Here, finally, the father stopped for a while, and began to look around, inspecting their surroundings. Tensing his deep, dark sunken eyes, he intently inspected the uneven circles and long stretched out shapes molded from the wind-blown sand – as if he were reading some mysterious hieroglyphs inscribed into the earth, by all of nature's genius loci. He attentively observed the distant surroundings, his expression pensive, his eyes – downcast. Then, he turned to the donkey and urged him onward, slightly east of the sun.

And soon, where the sands became enmeshed with the brown earth, an enormous, oblong-oval depression in the earth opened up in front of them. Due to the particular way in which the sun was descending, the gigantic tilted shadows of the dunes slowly extended outward along the earth, playfully intermingling with the long clouds stretching above the horizon – like terrestrial and celestial counterparts.

It appeared as though the little grey donkey was slowly being dipped into a dark pool – the road was steeply plunging into the shadow of the valley. Avoiding the possibility of pushing further into the gloomy depths of the natural basin, the father picked out a spot, from where the edge could still be seen and tied the ass down to a sinewy saxaul stem. He led Zhappar about twenty steps to the side, found a concealed place, from where the outermost edge of the basin could still be seen, and positioned his son there.

— Sit quietly, do not make yourself visible until I return.

Parting the tightly spaced branches of a saxaul tree, his father began to carefully wade through the brush somewhere off to the side. Soon the sound of branches snapping under his feet died down. Evidently, his father had also found himself a shelter.

In the tugai brushwood, it was damp and cool. The efflorescent saxaul and the grassy smell of the zhuzgen pleasantly animated Zhappar. The blood-red rays of the crimson sun seemed to have become entangled in the thick, prickly crowns of the saxaul, and hung there, like fiery cobwebs. The thickening twilight seemed suspended, like a pitch-black web hanging amid the trees. Through some fiery, illuminated gap, the narrow, sandy strip of the edge of the basin could be seen. Zhappar timidly shivered, fearing the solitude, and he peered all round him, tensely listening. But nothing in particular peaked his attention.

Soon he was overcome with fatigue, his eyes started to close by themselves, and he instantly plummeted into a sticky slumber. Only with the utmost effort, was he able to pry open his leaden eyes again.

And in the fiery chasm between the dark-blue webs of the forest haze, Zhappar suddenly saw movement. He rubbed his eyes and focused more intently. He immediately distinguished the moving shape as a man sitting atop a camel. After winding around the tightly spaced, prickly thicket where Zhappar was hiding, a man in an enormous turban was spurring a long-necked brown dromedary and then disappeared in the direction of the red sands. On the front pommel of saddle, something rounded, flexible yet firm, was swaying. This must be a winebag, the boy surmised. Only now, Zhappar started to feel as though the entre interior of his mouth was dried up. Maybe he can call out him, ask him to partake of his wine? Yet, father did tell him to sit quietly, to not call attention to himself... His head started spinning and he desperately watched his hopes ride off into the distance on a camel. And he had just enough time to notice that in his right hand, which hung at his side, tightly gripping a white staff, was covered in numerous small, sparkling, jingling and rattling objects... This means that this man must be one of those strange holy fools, a wandering magician and conjurer. The boy remembered that these types – unlike other people, dressed in rags, didn't cut their hair, were generally disheveled, and would occasionally drop by their barren village.

For some reason, Zhappar now entertained the idea that this magician, at this very moment, must be headed in the direction of his beloved village. And an inexplicable gut-wrenching anguish gripped the boy's very soul. The lonely rider on his dromedary soon disappeared in the thick evening haze.

His head continued spinning. He felt pressure and sharp pain, so he picked at some moist clay by the roots of the saxaul tree, lumped the pieces together and placed the cool, damp clump of clay against his forehead.

The setting sun disappeared behind the dunes. The small aperture, through which the boy looked out at the area surrounding the edge of the basin, was enveloped in a dark, grey shroud. Very soon, the entire basin, all the way to its outermost limits, was swallowed up by the thick twilight haze.

As if deciding whether or not to jump into the thicket of the of the forest haze, the flickering reflection of the sunset was hooked on the very edge of the gigantic natural basin. The northern part of the sky turned a pale grey. Under its canopy, even the white sand on the rocky slope turned an ashen-grey. The trees, which surrounded and covered Zhappar, head and all, enveloped him in an impenetrable, uniform darkness.

Narrow, like the blade of a knife, the whitish strip along the edge of the cliff gradually grew thinner and finally came to nothing. And already, in all the different corners of the sprawling sky, one could see the twinkling of stars – at first winking at us timidly, reluctantly, as if troubled, that they dared to immediately climb up to and occupy the most honorable places in the sky. But little by little, as more stars came out to take their places, the light they radiated began to shine even brighter still. And so, it seemed as though the little fireflies up in the sky seemed to notice that down there, in the forest, like in night's tall grass, amid the desolate desert – hiding from someone, were two beings – a man and his son. Suspended above their heads –the whole myriad army of fireflies in the sky began to observe them with great curiosity, cheerfully winking to each other, as if discussing the matter.

The pitch-black cover of night draped the edge of the hot desert with an infinite assembly of silently flickering stars. The twilight's half-sleep state, in which Zhappar recently found himself, had dissipated, as though he had been splashed in the face with a handful of spring water. His eyelids, still swollen from sleep and weighed down by gravity, now fluttered wide open, and the gaze of the boy, directed at the night sky, became lucid and meaningful.

All around, the opaque, jet-black night was unpredictable, dangerous, like an agitated male camel in heat. The dull, dead silence penetrated the air – there were no sounds, no rustling. Such uncertainty gives birth to fear, and he felt like some terrible, unknown danger could be lurking, creeping slowly like an agile feline, silently circling him. His heart was beating so loudly, he thought it might just jump out of his chest. The boy, frozen, stunned with fear, waited for the threat to, once and for all, come crashing down, and sink its sharp razor-sharp claws into him. However, the night lingered, as if changing its habitual behavior and now, like a wolfhound of the steppe, standing motionless for a while, it cautiously observed your every movement from a distance, waiting for the perfect moment to pounce, and finish off its prey. The boy understood this of the night, locking it away in his memory for the rest of his life – in order to survive the treacherous, concealed dangers lurking in the silence is much tougher than facing an enemy head-on, walking toward you out in the open, sword in hand.

The night completed its customary cyclical rotation, steadily moving in its allotted time. Out of nowhere, a loud noise broke through the silence, emitted from the edge of the saxaul brush. It almost sounded like someone was breaking clean through the brush, snapping and crushing the branches effortlessly as they went. Soon these sounds were joined by others. Then, a violent, ear-splitting crack pierced the air, the kind of sound usually heard during immense, roaring forest fires. But, there was no visible fire, despite the growing intensity of the cracking noise. Zhappar huddled there, tightly clutching a saxaul stump, which he had clasped onto at some unknown point, and the stump itself, also gripped with fear, began to tremble from the monstrous, annihilating noise in the night, in the warm embrace of Zhappar. From a very young age, Zhappar had heard of many different kinds of hideous monstrous creatures, which populated the wild thickets of the tugai. Attempting to, in the very least, catch the scent of the creature wreaking havoc nearby, the boy began furiously pulling air into his nostrils, though this method ultimately proved unsuccessful.

The loud cracking noise in the forest did not cease, as if a herd of wild animals was pummeling through a narrow gorge, trampling across fallen trees, all the while playing around with each other.

Zhappar's throat completely dried up. He wanted to unclench his hands, which embraced the stump, but was unable to do so right away – his fingers tense, interlocking stiffly.

The advancing cracking noise reached its loudest peak – and then, out of nowhere, started to recede. His numbed fingers finally loosened and released their grip, when suddenly, a springy branch, which he had been grasping along with the saxaul stump, escaped his grip, swung to the side, and noisily snapped several adjacent branches. The noise was loud enough, and Zhappar thought he could make out a rattling sound that resembled an avalanche of rocks! And those creatures that had searched for him, and then receded back into the tugai, heard the unexpected racket, and stopped, motionless, waiting to pick up on the slightest noise amid the stillness that could give him away. In tense anticipation, the boy squatted and, not knowing what do with his awkward, interfering arms, wrapped them around his knees and clasped his trembling fingers together. He was doomed. And to his great relief, more accurately, to his amazement, the unimaginably loud noise in the forest had subsided completely. It was replaced with a deathly silence. Not believing his ears, the boy cautiously waited for a long time, but no noises returned.

And then, to his complete surprise, he saw the tongue of a flame shoot up into the sky. Believing he may have imagined this, he firmly scrunched his eyes together, and then opened them again – but the fire did not disappear. The bonfire, which was just a stone's throw away from Zhappar, licked the black night air with its long, winding tongues, like snakes. Having rapidly grown in size, the fire extinguished the distant stars in the sky, which, through the thick smoke and heat of the flames, began to stretch and coil, like fiery glowworms. Sending small crimson sparks shooting out if its sides, the bonfire seemed to leap about, throwing its head high into the sky, and then slyly glanced around, side-to-side, like a bandit. Next to the bonfire he could see people that looked like shadows, swaying and dancing around. Some of them stepped out of the darkness, and into the circle of light, bringing with them handfuls of something, then throwing them into the fire. This caused the fire, which had died down for the time being, to leap back up high into the sky, belching out dense, velvety scarlet-black clouds. Zhappar could not figure out what the people, moving in and out of the firelight, were doing. The large flashes of the flames created long, slanted shadows on the sandy edge of the bottom of the cliff. They resembled a lengthy row of abandoned, ghostly black poles. Once Zhappar's eyes had grown accustomed to the darkness, he saw a row of horse's heads, and he realized that on the border of the firelight was a hitching post, to which all of their horses were tied. The horses that stood closer to the light of the bonfire, were easier to examine, and he made out the gleam of swords, as well as quivers filled with arrows hanging from their saddles.

However, something still puzzled the boy. Who are these people, the likes of whom he has never seen before, and what are they doing here? If we were to discuss this realistically – then who, aside from thieves and terrible villains, ends up in a tugai forest, on the edge of the desert, in the dead of night, with weapons in their hands? So, were these the people that his father feared, when he sought out safe shelters, when he hid himself and his son in the evenings? There was one time, when he told him a story about gangs of robbers that attack traveling caravans and rob them. So, in all likelihood, these people are robbers as well. But what wealth can a simple potter lose – is it not silly for him to be afraid of being robbed?

Nevertheless, the boy continued to cautiously observe the slanted sandy cliffside, where the bonfire was burning, and these people continued to swarm. But it seemed to him, that these people were hardly interested in that which they didn't know, nor were they interested in what was happening in the surrounding thicket. They crowded around the bonfire and chatted about this and that, their heads nodding and their hands waving about.

Zhappar, astonished beyond words, observed them for a long while – examining their slanted shifting shadows moving along the cliffside, their wooly hats and their curved blades dangling from their belts. He did not expect anything good to come of these people, but his fear of them was nothing compared to the terror of before – the terror of the silent, desolate night, the wilderness in the forest thicket that had scared him out of his wits not long before their arrival. The boy even experienced a sense of relief that the horde of bloodthirsty monsters, with sharpened claws and teeth, which had been trampling through the forest, had now disappeared into the night forever. And in a short while, he almost peacefully looked out at the distant bonfire, which had begun, little by little, to grow dim, disappearing out of sight altogether... Finally relaxing both his body and mind, the sweet languor of sleep crept up and embraced the boy, and he slipped into a deep, peaceful sleep.

When he finally came to, his father was standing over him and shaking his arm. He opened his eyes, and his father silently motioned with his hand – "come here". The two of them made their way through the thicket, emerging in the spot where the little donkey was tied to a saxaul stump, patiently waiting for them. His father grabbed the donkey by the leash, and they set off towards the sandy slope, the same area where, on the previous day, they had descended into the basin.

And the instant they waded out of the thicket, the powerful morning sun fell upon their face. And now, in the bright light of day, they saw a large, black burnt spot on the ground. So, it was here that the strange people lit their bonfire on the previous night. And now, they had all disappeared.

Not yet fully awake, and yawning as he walked, Zhappar hadn't even noticed that the desert was completely behind them. Now, they found themselves walking along the large caravan road, and his father marched ahead of him, his feet pounding the deep, swirling dust – ground down to the consistency of fine flour by the feet of thousands of travelers and countless heavy wagon wheels. Upon raising his head, the boy saw before him the enormous, striking, angular silhouette of the mountain embankment, its sharp peaks jutting into the lofty firmament. And considerably lower, somewhere at the very foot of the mountain range, Zhappar saw the outlines of a large city, sinking into a bluish haze. Along the very top of the angled slope, a magnificent, richly adorned caravan, unlike anything Zhappar had ever seen before, came into view, and was heading in the same general direction. In front of the caravan, and densely surrounded by nukers, was a huge elephant. It was equipped with a large, decorated harness, draped with long beautiful fabric, and carried a bright, golden palanquin on its back. The caravan was accompanied by a protection detail of nukers on horseback, one on each side. When the tail-end of the procession slowly slipped from the plateau into the valley, the convoy of guards closed in tightly around the end of it, and the cavalry unit of lance-bearers was slowly drawn into the basin, as they marched behind the caravan. The father and son, sufficiently impressed with this menacing display of soldiers with lances and swords, trailed behind them at a respectful distance, yet making sure not to fall too far behind. As it turns out, it was precisely this unit of guards that was safeguarding the caravan that arranged a brief stop in the saxaul forest. They were sent out ahead to ensure safe passage through the thick brushwood. And now, Zhappar came to understand why his father went to such great precautionary lengths to hide them in the forest. Had they ended up in the idle hands of the very same guards that were on the road, who knows how this would have ended for these travelers? For these places they had passed were, unfortunately, well known for harboring gangs of robbers, and the process of checking the roads continued day and night – and the guards were strict, severe and had a predilection for questioning every person who happened to pass by – in the wrong place, at the wrong time... And in the forest, leaving his son alone in his shelter, the father purposely hid separately, but not too far away, so that, if need be, he would be able to distract the guards away from his son.

Zhappar was not yet aware, that a night watch of guards had been sent ahead to provide safe passage for the caravan with the elephant, for the palanquin that it carried contained none other than the younger wife of the Lord, the dignified Young Khansha.

He learned of all this later, after wandering along the meandering side-streets, weaving between the endless, nearly identical clay huts and uneven duval fences of the Khan's Great City, where, with great difficulty, his father finally located a particular solid, squat house with a flat roof. Going no further than the gate, he called out to the owner – a plump, verbose individual – a merchant by the name of Akhmet-bey.

And Zhappar has lived in that house ever since that day.

When he and his father appeared before him, Akhmet-bey, froze in place, and was disoriented for a moment, as he attempted to recall where he had previously encountered this vaguely familiar man. The dark skin of his face twisted up in folds around his beady, little raisin-eyes, which expressed a certain suspicion and distrust.

His father, in a humble, yet dignified manner, began to explain:

— Honorable bey-Akhmet, you probably don't remember me... I am your old acquaintance, the potter from Ortyuba. Whenever you visited our village, you always stopped by my house as my guest. And under the roof of my very house, you told me, on numerous occasions: "If you ever find yourself in the capital city, do me favor, and make sure you stop by." Well, I made it to the capital city, so here I am, bey-Akhmet.

As if recognizing the guest only now, bey-Akhmet politely placed his hand on his chest and bowed his head. He opened the gate, letting in the little grey donkey.

Hurrying ahead, he bustled about, leading his guests into the house. In the men's quarters, they sat down for tea. Here, sitting at the dastarkhan, the merchant laid out all of the most recent news of the city to Zhappar's father.

After listening to him, his father addressed the matter of his appearance in the city, and the reason behind it.

— I brought my son here. While I am still alive, I have decided to place him in your care. A dervish had popped into our village recently, and from him I learned that the Khan has ordered the construction of a new mosque, and for this purpose, they are gathering masters from all around... Please, help me to get my son in there...

As it turned out, bey-Akhmet had a good relationship with practically every single powerful figure in the city, aside from those who serve the Khan directly in his palace. A few chats with various city merchants in the market over a pot of tea was all it took – the merchants, who deal day in and day out with the screaming and arguing of their workers and the loud luring of customers into their dark, cramped shops, and in only a week's time, the question of employment of both of the guests was ultimately settled. Both masters from Ortyuba, father and son, were officially enrolled in the enormous collective – as builders of the mosque.

But the building process had only barely begun, when Zhappar's father once again fell ill, bedridden with the same ailment that had tortured him the entire prior winter.

Zhappar had only worked with his father for two months, and the poor young man was completely lost and nervous, when he had to climb platforms of the eastern minaret on his own, without his father-ustad. With every day that went by, the minaret tower grew taller and taller, and, finding himself on the planks on the top platform, the boy-master felt very nervous and uncertain, constantly turning and looking around, like an orphaned little sparrow. It only took one, curious look from any other person to create such a sheer state of confusion, prompting him to thrust his chin against his chest and lower his eyes. And in this manner, it continued – his desperate eyes darting about, then looking down, embarrassed, trying to avoid the squinting, prodding, oftentimes openly scornful stares all day at work. The young master followed the path of the sun with his melancholy gaze, urging it along towards sunset. He watched the adjacent masters as they worked on the scaffolding nearby, cautiously examined the large building of the madrasah, which, as rumors and whispers claimed, was the precise location the Great Lord used to oversee the construction of the mosque.

Giving all of himself to his work, it was as if Zhappar lived on burning coals – he could not be sufficiently close to his sick father, and one evening, when he returned from work, he found his father, dying. The second his son walked through the doors, with a weak gesture of his frail hand, his father called him over to his deathbed. Tears instantly filled Zhappar's eyes, and he could not even distinguish the familiar features of his dying father. It was as though the room suddenly sank to the very bottom of lake or swamp – the outlines of very object in the room seemed to be washed away, then they swayed, then floated, as if enveloped by a murky haze. His misty eyes, gushing tears, and only when he leaned in closely, was he able to distinguish the unnaturally bright white body of his father in his undergarments, as if it was sprawled out at the bottom of the swampy waters... The screeching, frail wheeze, which had just begun to transform into coherent speech, abruptly stopped. His father fell silent forever, and his large, leathery, rigid hand, which firmly grasped his son's in a rock-hard grip suddenly softened, unclenched and fell to the bed.

And so now, remembering all of it, sad and inconsolable, he was once again laying bricks in circular rows of the growing tower, looking above the brickwork to the infinite distances opening up before his eyes. In the surrounding area of the city, packed with identical houses made of clay, imagining itself as something akin to a faded old blanket, and from there, out of its dilapidated folds – to see the clean, bright gleaming horizon, would be like some unattainable dream. And yet, the minaret being built here rises above all of the other minarets and towers in the city, and they wretchedly look upon their rival from below, as it continues to press up and into the sky, as they remain on the same old level of the city, monotonous and formless, like the sad, tattered sole of a shoe. Far from the urban structures, one could see bright-green strips and dark-green patches of wool – the fields, vegetable-gardens and orchards on the outskirts of the city.

And a strange and uncommon job has been entrusted to Zhappar – to clamber upwards into the realm of the skies – a realm without structure, support, weight, or measure. There is nothing to cling to there… And the strange, charming, wondrous peculiarity of laying bricks in the circular tower: the higher you raise her up, the more you feel yourself, upon entering in the morning, sinking into some great depth. And gripped with fear, like the terror that is felt when drowning, submerged to the very dark bottom of a pool, you desperately struggle up, up, to the small blue round window, to the rescuing light.

With each day, the objects and specks of the earth's surface decrease and move away from him on their own, looking pitifully reduced, as though crushed and flattened by some colossal invisible giant, until he converts the entire nondescript view from up top into an unattractive picture, something akin to the bottom of a puddle when dry. But instead of this unattractive reality, the tower proposed the flight of a view from heights overlooking new horizons, which expanded with the new elevations of the constructed minaret attained each day. And it was left far below, the smoke and the dust that eternally hangs above the city, like a looming hazy shroud – the foul breath of the city revealing the tall wall of blue.

It was afternoon, and the sun was free of clouds, and shone in the sky, vibrant and inspired. A transparent azure flooded the entire firmament from top to bottom. And suddenly, far away, at the very edge of the horizon line, light began to pour forth, spilling down in a long, golden-yellow stripe. Not believing his eyes, Zhappar discarded the trowel onto a stack of bricks, wiped the sweat from his brow with his hand, and with greedy eyes fixed his gaze intently upon the depths of space. Yes, it is undoubtedly so: much like one can see the bottom of a deep lake through the transparent thickness of water, so too, through the thickness of celestial azure did the golden yellow color of his native steppe burst through!

Hanging over the edge of the wall, and extending his neck outward, Zhappar leaned as far forward as was possible. He had secretly yearned to see this for so long! And, as if in response to this clean, youthful impulse, the golden expanse rose up from its place and flew up towards him – to this deep natural basin, where this great city stood, differing in appearance from all of the surrounding natural landscape, like a bald spot on a camel differs from the rest of its hide.

Picking up one brick after another and adding them to the row, Zhappar impatiently peered into the blurred horizon, half-expecting that from the far-flung distant reaches, a powerful wave would roll forth and envelop every tugai and bushy forest, every garden and palace, every minaret in this city and all of the pitiful little houses slapped together from clay and straw, and finally all of the horrible, balding crooked duval fences. The golden shimmering light, the fierce expanse of the steppe will fly here and liberate him, this new-comer, this orphan, ripped from his beloved steppe and entombed alive in this tower of bricks.

Today Zhappar did not climb down from his tower platform until the sun completed it travels through the sky and the twilight thickened around him, letting in the blindness of night into his eyes. And the next day, having left the house before the sun's rays had dawned in the sky, he was already rushing through the dense darkness towards the tower, and with a kind of joyful relief in his soul, he scaled the tower to its crowning, luminous circular aperture. This entire week flew by for him, in a sort of inspired feverish state. Just having reached the work site, he threw his first impatient glance over the brickwork in the direction of his distant, beloved steppe, which he missed to death. Zhappar felt the calming sensation of his beating heart. Despite his comforted state, his heart, nevertheless, did not find relief – for the steppe did not rush to reply to his passionate call, nor did it fly towards his growing impatience. Instead, it lazily stretched its golden-ochre smoky body, lacking any desire to fully awaken. But, by midday, her mirages had decomposed and dissipated, clearing away any remnant haze, leaving only the crisp, cleanly delineated horizon, and Zhappar's gaze rested not upon his beloved fluid, spectral steppe, but the bare, sensuously smooth desert nearby. And the tender soul of the young man experienced such great pain at this unsightly substitute. The desert – the same muddy-grey shade as the city, had been insolent and merciless with him, like an unceremonious, vulgar market wench, who – after robbing him would hide in her sweaty, sticky clothes, in all of her smothering hiding spots, all that he would have liked to behold and take in – having stolen everything that he held dear to his heart. And having expertly swindled him, picking him clean, this bazaar-bandit looks at him – brazen and wide-eyed – and pretends that she neither knows nor wants to know a thing.

Oh, how changeable are feelings, feelings born of such great heights! Just a week ago, he was soaring on the wings of joy, above cities, and everything, that he had experienced, standing on that platform of the tower – and today, he felt like he had been cast down into the gloom of despondency, total disbelief in the flight of his dreams and reality. The previously secluded height of the minaret seemed like the most reliable place for solitude, a place where his confused spirit could accomplish its flights from these musty and cramped labyrinths, where he was subjected to the cruel will of fate. And there was no salvation in that. Yes – the tower grabbed him by the collar and raised him above the suffocating plane of the average city-dweller's existence, — yes, he was raised above all others by this tower, for he had built it, and yet – this, in essence, changed nothing. Just as the gray desert had unraveled itself before him, eternally existing in some somnolent stupor, both then and now. Just as the golden steppe had forgotten about all of its might and limitlessness, so it remains to this day – laying beyond the horizon in its numb, lethargic indifference. Yet, only a little while ago, he – having raised the tower but a mere inch from the ground – rejoiced and was proud, as if he had conquered a whole mountain. But as it turns out, all of his efforts and joyous labors, were useless — the tower grew, but nothing around it had changed.

And now he saw in himself that same rash failure, which had thoughtlessly decided to cross a river by stepping stones, pouring them all out into the river himself — and, after paving the river to the center, the self-assured fool finally understood, that even this is no task he is capable of completing. And so there he remained, standing in the midst of these rapids – unable to step forward, and not daring to step back. Now, leaving for work in the morning, Zhappar almost hostilely squinted at the tower jutting out of the earth – like a living reproach to any imperfection, ineptly penetrating the ground of a feeble person.

He scaled the spiral staircase to reach his work site up on the scaffolding, but even this proved to be difficult, and choked him. Each new step ached and painfully constricted his joints.

Work was no longer a prosperous affair – everything fell from the hands, he gripped the trowel without any of the customary pleasure, as it had always been before, and he put much effort into overcoming this condition. It seemed as though the sun was frozen in the sky, as though it were tethered, and the day seemed to stretch out infinitely. But beyond the outskirts of the city, just as frozen as it is sluggish, lay the faded, discolored desert. In the very city itself, all the houses stood, motionless, as if hammered into the earth. The streets, perpetually infested with people were suddenly desolate, barren. It seemed like even the air was thick with a kind of all-encompassing drowsy stupor, and became dense and viscous, like spoiled milk. And even here, on the highest scaffolding of the tower, the last few hours, not a single gust of wind could be felt.

The mercilessly sunny days scorched the whole region with their intense heat, and now the fiery sands and the green stripes of the gardens around the city where almost the same unified yellow-gray color looked like the ashes of the *adyraspan*-grass, which was used to make alkali during the dying months of autumn. Like some kind of massive giant witch, having rolled up her sleeves, turning the entire round earth into some sort of great cauldron, in which she began to boil the scathing alkali. And the merciless sun was helping the witch – and setting her eyes, boiling with blood, upon the cauldron, the heavenly body proceeded to stir the fire beneath it.

Among the entirety of this sucking, pulling, bog-like, killer heat and land, Zhappar became sluggish, indifferent towards everything, No matter how hard he tried to push away the laziness of his soul, to concentrate on his work – his attention was scattered, at best, unable to retain a thing. When suddenly, a strong, intrusive memory appeared – a picture from childhood: the deep, oblong basin, compressed on either side by the layered, steep slopes of cliffs, and at the very bottom of this basin – were the small, wretched houses of his native village. He could distinctly make out each little lambkin and

End of the Legend •Abish Kekilbaev

baby goat, from that distant herd of youngsters, excitedly clambering up the hill…Swaying her back side to side, he saw the young girl walking with a jug on her shoulder. And the jug – is his, Zhappar's, his first independent work…

At that moment he felt a sharp pain in his side, as though someone had forcefully struck him. He sat up, trying to grab a hold of himself with great difficulty. It occurred to him, that he had fallen asleep on the job, in the midst of clear daylight, drained by the sweltering heat and the hazy melancholy of solitude. Returning to reality was unpleasant, alarming even, as if he had stolen a small piece from her, for his unforeseen sleep. Zhappar looked around on either side of him. Yes, everything looked just as it did in his sleep. It was a heartless, blistering midday. He was in a stone tower. It keeps growing up, up – and below – the city lays there, like a corpse fried by heat. Above him, is the ashy-grey sky, looking downward, lying prone.

And as if restoring his dissipated dream – one picture after another, with great care, Zhappar gathered the memories of his native village. So, why did he not remain there forever – to mold, fire and sell his jugs and pots until the end of his days? What difference is there, between those who mold pots, bargain in the market, herd sheep, or walk beneath God, building minarets? All of these things are to subsist – in that is their destination and justification. Which of them brings man greater satisfaction? There is no answer – but, perhaps, the most righteous one of them – is he who stands the most firmly upon the earth, he who considers the pressing, terrestrial matters, especially without thinking– the middleman between man and Allah, dooming himself to experience eternal doubt, sincere self-torture, and sentencing himself to the lifelong imprisonment of solitude. Why did they not continue to live on in those tiny cabins, forgotten by God, knowing nothing of the torments of solitude of the desperation in the midst of a throng of people in the streets of a large, bustling city? Why has his deceased father, on the steep slope of time, suddenly reached out, pulling this human anthill and his son along with him? What happiness did he yearn for, what was his hope with all of this? Not even half a year had gone by, before he was taken ill and plummeted to his grave. His ashes are buried in foreign land, not mourned by his relatives or close ones, without so much as a clump of his native soil to be cast into his poor grave. Yet, even on the very precipice of death, he'd pronounced with his last, dying, wheezing breath – "Do not leave…" Why, father? Why was this necessary – what is the point?

The kindness, it remained, but where does the reward lie? What good did he see here, in remaining in this city? Here, a truly pitiful existence dragged on, to be perpetually lacking confidence in one's strength, and he nurtured himself more with hope for a better future, than with earthly food.

Poor father, why did he so passionately want to see his son grow into a great master? And why not bless the calm, peaceful work of being a village potter, which provides one with deserved sustenance and the confidence one requires, until our very last days? So that it would be possible to live by the simple wisdom of the working people: if we work, we work 'til we drop, and if we eat, we eat 'til we're full... Once, when they had journeyed to gather clay from the white mountain – father stood on its peak, gazing off into the distance for a while, his eyes watery and foggy. Was it really then that he'd dreamed up this future for us – to live in this ghastly, deathly city, that is now laying under his son's feet, like some dirty, dusty rag?

Well, it seems that his father's dream has come true – his son carried out his will, and now risking falling to his death on a daily basis, he scrambles up a spiral staircase to the very top platform of the tower, which he himself is building. And here, finding unsteady support for his feet, each day, brick by brick, he raises this future minaret skyward, with the perseverance of a condemned man, sentenced to raise the tower to the very foot of the celestial throne of the Almighty himself. Oh, the madness of this thought – to lay their foundation upon the abyss, to lay one's hopes on impermanence!

No, this is not the result of some heat stroke, nor is this any emerging dissatisfaction of the soul with itself – his eyes darkened and everything around him seemed to float, like in some pre-fainting state. Fearing that at any moment he might keel over, he descended two steps, down to the platform area. From here, his eyes gazed down upon the rows of porous bricks that had been placed today. Not yet covered with plaster they, too, had begun to swim before his eyes, the fired-clay color fading, blurring together into one grey mass. It seemed to him, that the brick wall was dripping, melting downward, and he, himself, is soaring somewhere between the heavens and the earth. And only the round hatch beneath him, which people use for walking up and down all day – was distinctly blackening before his eyes, in the light of day.

All of a sudden, a bright light gushed from trapdoor, and scattered into blinding white and yellow sparks, which seemed blow about the entire platform, as if propelled by a whirlwind. Suddenly, they compressed into one big ball of light – and, taking the form of some kind of living being, accomplishing fully intelligent movements and fluidly swaying, it began to approach the spot where Zhappar stood, rooted to the floor. Then, this animated cloud of light advanced and became suspended exactly like Zhappar – between the sky and the back abyss of the towel well. For some reason, it seemed like they would collide, and both fall down into the yawning gap of the tower shaft. But, the apparition of light stood up and firmly planted its feet down onto the platform, face to face with him. And then Zhappar's entire essence was gripped by what seemed like a strong spasm. The animated apparition dissipated before him. Then, the walls of porous, red brick distinctly and solidly rose up before his eyes. The trowel, smeared with solution, lay on the very edge of the brickwork, possibly falling down at any moment. This nightmarish world, unpleasant, like sensation of touching a sticky cobweb, instantly disappeared, as if caught in the midst of a silent, invisible vortex, and then, spirited away. But Zhappar's soul, which lost its grip on reality, and was transported to some realm that borders on sleep and waking, did not know what to believe. If this hazy specter really had appeared before him, where did it vanish to, all of a sudden?

But, to what world, spectral or material, could she belong to – this woman with the radiant face, enshrouded by a veil embroidered with the finest golden brocade? What could she be doing here, on this construction site, covered in dust and spattered with silt? Or is this just the poor mind of the young master, tormented by heat, suddenly gripped again by some fit of madness, creating visions of one more ghost?

Through the transparent veil with gold embroidery, he could see two dark eyes, like black currant berries, gazing calmly back at him. The face was so white, that if not for these black eyes and shining black eyebrows, it would have merged with the veil and then then it would have seemed to the youth that the wind had taken some a beautiful silk veil hostage, tossing it up to the minaret. Yet, before him stood a living mysterious beauty, wrapped from head to toe in a cloud of white silk.

In that moment, he decided to figure out if that which appeared before him was, in fact, a vision or a genuine person. Zhappar worked up the courage and, throwing his eyes wide open to glance at what was before him.

And the passionate, young, sincere eyes of the master-architect found themselves immersed in the smiling, gorgeous eyes of a true beauty. It seemed, that at any moment, his gaze would cause the beautiful gold veil to spark and catch fire.

And, seeing his confusion, she turned and moved to the side, her movements confirming that she was in fact, a real, living woman. With two slender fingers she picked up the long hem of her dress, and taking a step towards the edge of the tower, she bent over it and looked down. But in silent exclamation, as though worried that her high *saukele* might topple from her head, she quickly straightened her body and turned away. And at that moment, a beautiful red ruby sparkled on her forehead, and it was massive – about the thickness of a finger, and half its length.

She even wanted to start with some friendly words, but didn't know, apparently, where to begin, so she only smiled nervously with downcast eyes.

From this smile, from the blush of pink that suddenly flared up in her cheeks, her entire face appeared to be smiling. And the young architect was struck by her dazzling beauty, and in a secret moment of madness he thought to himself – he recognized this bewitching voice and he was certain that somewhere he'd heard this beautiful laugh. In his secret madness, he began to wonder in what life he could have possibly been lucky enough to have succumbed to her feminine charms, or felt some kind of wonderful, deep feelings towards her…

It was then that she turned and headed toward the stairs spiraling down – yet another confirmation that she was not from a spectral world at all – she picked up the hem of her dress, for a moment showing her white, satin *salwar* pants, which tightly covered her lean, rounded calves.

In the dark aperture of the platform, where the stairs spiraled downward, the white silk veil swiftly shot up and then went into the darkness, as if absorbed by the gloom of the cave.

Zhappar remained standing there – numb, shaken. The divine image shone brightly before his eyes, though the white wonder was absorbed by the darkness. The smile on her cherry red lips and her gleaming, black eyes – seemed to have stayed forever here, on the top platform of the of the minaret mid-construction. Fearing that he might frighten his visions, he stood there for a long while, immersed in it all.

And yet – where could he have seen these cherry-red lips, these radiant black eyes, the color of ripe currants? He had the distinct, strange feeling that not only is she familiar to him, but close, like a relative…Even the motions of the body – the way she stands in place, or perhaps her gait remind him of some incredibly close person, almost like someone he would encountered every day… Though on a daily basis, he could have encountered only – the owners of the house in which he lived, the chief ustad-builder and the half-bare, blackened slaves, who would transport bricks and mix the solution. And so, as it turns out, there is no one familiar, whose gait and movements he could have grown accustomed to? Is this Zukhra, the daughter of the owner of the house, where he resides? If this was Zukhra, then realistically he could have seen her on a daily basis, until her father gave her hand in marriage. Always with her head wrapped in a bright white shawl, she'd briskly and gaily walk through the courtyard, her lithe, curvy figure easily distinguishable under her long silk garments. However, even in seeing her in the courtyard each day, he never fully saw her face or encountered her in the house, since women, from the olden days, have remained only in the female half of the house.

One day, he had returned home from work, but the merchant and his wife were gone, though someone was in the courtyard, gently singing. Who could this be? Walking out to the gazebo, the young architect saw Zukhra in the garden, who, like a goat, had clambered up the apricot tree, and shaking the branches, densely crowded with ripened fruit, and fully absorbed in her activity, she did not notice how her shawl had slipped from her face, which always remained hidden. And, feeling the sudden sting of foreign eyes gazing upon her, she turned around sharply and, seeing the youth, she fixed her shawl, again hiding her face. But he had already had time to see her wide forehead, short straight nose, and her lips, like plump, juicy cherries, the corners of her mouth harboring a seductive smile. As if frightened by the prospect of being observed by a strange, unfamiliar man – she quickly leapt from the tree and ran into the house. And he looked after her, not strong enough to overpower the urge to watch the swaying folds of her dress, which did not conceal, but rather revealed the sight of the woman that she was to become.

From that day forward, after coming home from work, he always searched for Zukhra. If he did not see her, then he transferred all of his energy into listening, trying to catch the distant sounds of her voice. Whenever she would suddenly pass by – how filled with joy he was at the sight of her rustling dress… He often stayed close to the mother, helping out in various chores around the house. And from that day, where she had accidentally shown her face to the strange young man boarding in her house, she too, made herself more visible, especially on days when her father was not home. She began helping her mother in the yard, where her mother bustled about every day. Zukhra became considerably more productive and helpful than she had ever been before. And the young Zhappar's heart, at the sight of her swaying, rustling dresses, was ready to bloom, as if springtime had arrived in his soul – radiant, overpowering – his first true feelings.

Just how devastating of a fire was swept over his modest, unseen feelings, Zhappar learned the day that Zukhra was taken to the house of her new husband. Her beloved, resonant, bewitching voice made silent forever, and the rustling sound of her swaying silk dresses dead to him now… In his chest, to this day, the burning fire of repentance for that indecisiveness and helplessness that he portrayed eats away at him, unable to protect his most tender, most genuine feelings. But what could he do? For some time, the youth had reconciled himself with the thought that nothing would have come of it, and the potential loss he would have suffered was foretold by fate, and was not something he could ever return from. But why was Zukhra, the very same Zukhra that he had lost forever, appearing at the very top of his exorbitant stone tower? And how could her husband, the one with the shaggy black eyebrows, have let her come alone, to this unbecoming place? And what will come of her now? But the strangest, most absurd element of all of this, was something different altogether – how could this have come about? After that loss, he, after by some miraculous twist of fate having encountered her again, still had not dared to utter a single word, just like the first time around! As if he had swallowed his tongue, turned numb and weakened – and lost her yet again, not having expressed to her the one thing that still burned deeply within his chest. Oh, she probably despises me for the frailty of my soul! Today, Zukhra has left forever, and he is dead to her now! So this explains why she coldly and disgustedly shook him off with her leg, draped in those white, silk salwar pants…

And now, recalling all of this, he threw a glance over the edge of the tower, peering down at the world below.

At the foot of the tower, he saw four carriages parked in place, and people crowding all around them. One of them resembled a small white puff floating through the air – this was the woman in the white silk veil. She was followed by several people from the crowd. One

End of the Legend •Abish Kekilbaev

pushed ahead to the very front and, opened the carriage door, decorated with dark blue curtains. Two women in yellow shawls helped the woman in white into the carriage, each one supporting her by the arm. At one point, the white cover on her head swayed to the side, slightly opening up a view of her face, but then swayed back, ensuring it remain protected from strange, prying eyes. The impatient horses quickly jerked forward, and the blue curtains fluttered in the open carriage windows as they took off.

The young ustad, with a fixed, uninterrupted gaze watched the caravan of carriages and spear-bearing guards, until they rapidly receded into the distance, leaving behind them only a thick cloud of dust. The carriages proceeded to the garden, where the palace of the young Khansha was located, and then it disappeared behind the gates of fence. Finally, the young architect realized who his mysterious visitor was, after all.

It seemed as though the entire world around them crumbled the structure of life that has already been established for many centuries, and now – the realm of spectral visions and mirages reigned. Casting down everything in its way, the dark gloom of night swept over the city. From the peak of the raised minaret, Zhappar descended down the spiral staircase of the tower, using the last little bits of his strength. At the bottom, he washed up, in no particular hurry. The slaves had long since been driven into the dungeons and locked away in the casemates. He was the only person still at the construction site of the tower, and only one carriage remained, which the architect climbed into and took home.

The following morning, climbing out of the same horse-drawn carriage as the night before, he gazed upon the bare bricks of the circular tower, and saw that the entire surface seemed to be pitted, as if covered in pockmarks, by the unevenness of the bricklaying. It looked almost deformed. The reddish-brown tower itself, its body ascending somewhere upward towards the skies, appeared rough and unattractive on the dark blue of morning sky, especially transparent and fresh into these early hours.

Today he was struck by the fact that he had succeeded in raising this huge thing all by himself, and sometimes it seemed that it could break even the great earth-mother's ribs, on which it sat – that glorious, monstrous idol. Also, for the first time, he perceived the heartless, merciless haughtiness of the tower. Its essence was that of the tyrant-conqueror. Perhaps this automatically crept in from that hatred, which he felt for the empire of the curved clay slums of the city, that unceasing melancholy, and the freedom and pure air of steppe, with which, in the feverish superhuman stress and labor, it was raised, one after the other – all of the reddish brown bricks. He must raise it to that level, where he can examine the far-flung distance of his native steppe… The entire night prior, his sleep was filled with but one vision: a white silk veil that sailed above the unsteady haze of an autumnal mirage, and flying downwind was the blue curtain, which swayed in the windows of the covered vehicle.

Into these parts the obvious signs of a commencing autumn had arrived. A resilient wind, multilayered, was blowing its chilly music of a cool morning and carried with it the dense aroma of overripe fruit and the smells of satiety, succulence and zest for life of the coming harvest. An unprecedented blue and boundless clear sky commanded humanity, reliably protecting it from the as-yet distant signs of tear-inducing wintertime… And in this most generous, tranquil and pensive period, when one wishes to forget all the suffering and at each moment of existence to take pleasure in one's occurring joys of life—the maladroit, huge tower seems ready to collapse with all its heartless mass upon this peaceful, divine gift of autumn. Zhappar felt as if he is the unintentional perpetrator of this threat, and it seemed as if the entire weight of the twenty ton tower had been placed upon his shoulders, had crushed him and deprived him of his breathing.

And now, as if he had acquired a new habit, after placing each brick in the wall he gazes above the brickwork in the direction of the park of the Khan's Young Khansha. He imagines that she also is looking at him from one of the windows of the solitary palace, which lies comfortably amidst the curly greenery of the park. Surely it must be that the appearance of the untidy brick giant has an oppressive effect upon her, and it is quite likely that she prophetically foresees that it is precisely this future minaret which shall bring dishonor and doom to all her reveries, delicate and transparent like her parandja, the veil worn by Muslim women…

Picking up an arbitrary subsequent brick, a particularly bright and unusually red one, Zhappar instantly put it back into the heap of bricks. Some grave premonitions overwhelmed him.

Like a lake during a calm after a storm, the sky was clear, lucid and peaceful.

Zhappar knew not what to do with his life... His ceaseless, heavy labor of many months, his agonizing doubts of the architect mastermind, the rise and fall—for him all these had lost their meaning. Of course, he knew already what to do in a similar situation. Without giving it a second thought, one would need to grab a brick and throw it on the mortar levelled by the master craftsman...grab the brick and stack it unto the wall. But does one do this when one's hands do not obey one's commands? They do not trust him, that one must do precisely this. To lay out the wall obtusely and mindlessly with brick... His long-standing initial goal—to get away from the oppressive, peeling clay duvals, walls made of clay and straw, to rise as high as possible above the diminutive adobe huts—Zhappar had already accomplished. For some time now he has been admiring the bluish, as if it were a strip of sea, distant horizon of the steppes. But this horizon, rather than flying towards Zhappar's ardent call, on the contrary, is running away from him; the higher he raises the tower, the farther away it moves. It seems as though it is an offended friend from a neighboring village, who had received a black eye in a trivial friendly fight. Earlier, the minaret he had been erecting seemed to be a kind and appreciative giant, who is happy that he has been pulled out of the earth, where he had been pressed by a heavy force of burden from all sides and had been breathing his last... But now, having been freed, the giant had begun to oppress others, having gradually changed—from a tall tower lifting up those who would gaze at the bluish horizon of the steppes—unto a zindan, the subterranean cell carved deep in the rock, which did not go underground but rose to the sky. And unto this zindan the viewer of these far horizons had been thrown. And he can be found now in an unusual, suspended situation—neither able to descend to earth nor to fly unto heaven.

Indeed, all the known earthly zindans are better than this heavenly one. In the deep dungeon you may be shackled hands and feet, but on the other hand you are hidden from the evil looks of hostility. But here not a single passerby will walk by without staring from below at the architect and not blurting out some insipid statement. Is there anything more horrible than evil tongues and unkind eyes of strangers? These eyes are like fateful weapons of enemies: one becomes frightened and turns around in order to run away, while the arrow will just then pierce your back; or should you rush towards them, straight ahead—your chest will be penetrated by a spear, with a crunching sound splintering your bones, and, thrusting through your ribs, it will exit as a red-hot spear out of your back. Is there any worse and acute agony for your soul than the one where from afar, looking at you directly, the people are talking in low voices about something, and there is no way for you to find out what it is they are saying. It is not unlike standing before a cave's entrance where a lion is located, and to guess what would provoke and irritate him most to jump out of the cave and to attack you. But a vain person is not even afraid of a lion; at the risk of being torn to pieces, he will continue to hang around the cave just to remain in plain view of the people.

Although real hell is precisely that public place where they exhibit you in order to please the despicable rabble. This is the true dungeon from which you can't escape. In this dungeon your pillow is a rock, your bed the damp floor, and in this absolute darkness you're not able to see what vile creatures you have to fight off, what predators are circling around you, and you have no idea how to find your way out of there, if that is at all possible. And later you meekly accept this fate of yours, and you will begin to treasure it above all in the world and to guard your prisoner's robe. In an actual dungeon you are at least aware that you live a predictable life, a difficult one, but one commensurate to your sentence. But in this prison, in plain sight of the crowd, exhausted by rules of propriety, you are unable to explain it to yourself why you should be walking nude in front of everyone, forced to smile sweetly and bow to each and every passerby, and thereafter, stepping aside, in an agonizing way attempting to speculate why some in seeing you are grinning while others are threateningly rolling their eyes. And yet, considering all this, people still dream to achieve fame and glory. He, too, has been infected by this human frailty, and he is forced, as if he were a sheep's turd pierced by a straw, to be ever present in plain view of everyone on the top of the tower—the tallest tower ever!—and to put up with all chatter and cavil by every rogue and cheat. It had now become clear to him that his father had also been infected by this pernicious thirst for fame and had driven him to the city. After all, down with consumption, he would have been well advised to remain in his tiny and obscure settlement, in his small winter hut, lie down in his own bed and be the master of his house, to produce earthenware pots and jugs, and in such a manner to earn a living and the respect of people, to cough a bit here and there and live out his life at his own hearth. Poor father...

Here he is, Zhappar, self-assured, sitting on his winged racer called *dream*. But how many injudicious, haughty men there had been prior to him who were able to jump on such a horse and even to take off, but then tumble down from it, unable to hang on. And, rubbing one's injured side, would be muttering: "This horse is nothing but a wooden rocking horse; one can't get very far on it."

And on this clear morning today, when the sun had not yet become scorching and in the hot air the translucent blue expanse had not dissolved as yet, he was standing at the brickwork site, holding a pile of bricks in his hands, and in deep concentration he was seeking new ways to overcome his own convictions and to commence his accustomed work.

Below was still the same city. As if they were bits and pieces of sheep cheese nibbled on and sullied by children at a poor man's dastarkhan, a festive meal, the humble small houses were scattered about and protruding. A clear sky, but entirely empty, without the slightest hint of any mountainous news. Now the trained eye of Zhappar, the architect, did not leave out the slightest detail of human existence, turned this time towards the park of the Young Khansha of the Khan.

Today he noticed that the area in front of her palace, usually hidden from the people's eyes by a dense greenery of the surrounding garden, suddenly revealed itself to him from his new height as if it were from a bird's eye view. The tower had grown to such an extent that from its upper level the palace, watched over by armed guards and surrounded along its park's edges by an impregnable wall across which only flying birds could reach, now turned out to be right under the architect's feet and became accessible to outsiders' eyes. All of the park's lanes became visible, the flower beds were like brightly woven rugs, and the variously sized ponds were like glittering mirrors.

Suddenly, within him a powerful and voracious desire to work had awakened, and his hand reached for the trowel. During his time of despondency and profound doubts heaps of bricks stacked by the slaves had surrounded him from all sides as if they were mountain ridges. Now it had become utterly clear to him that the minaret should be built even higher, considerably higher than it had been planned earlier. Then this mysterious palace and all the space around it shall be entirely visible from above. Not a single obscure corner shall remain inaccessible to his gaze. And he will become the only human being in the entire world who will be able to see from a bird's eye view life in the palace of the Khan's beautiful wife, in its entirety or in parts, which the almighty *Lord,* the great Amir, the terrible and blood-thirsty Lord, who had conquered half of the world, managed to hide from the view of all the people at a quiet suburb of the city. Even the Khan himself does not have the fortune to observe the wondrous pictures of life of his young wife in such detail and so reliably as can the architect, the creator of the minaret.

The mountains of brick at his feet vanished rapidly. That day Zhappar, the architect, did not even notice when evening came. Next morning, while cleaning his trowel, he directed his renewed attention in examining the park of the Khan's wife. It is quite likely that sitting at some window she also looked at him, following his every movement. Now he decided to build the minaret of such height so that from the top of the tower one could look over the entire park and the courtyard in front of the palace. And the one who would be below, no matter from what vantage point he would be looking up, he would perceive that the minaret is suspended directly over his head.

He quickly rid himself of that lack of confidence, the spiritual torpor, and these profound doubts, upon laying of the brick, he would have for many hours of pondering. Now his work proceeded briskly, nay, at a gallop, and much was achieved, at times, during the day's work. If one would be continuing at the same rate of success, the minaret would achieve the planned height already in a week's time. And then, what would remain was to face the entire structure. This had to be done in such a manner that those who were to look at the minaret would have their hearts standing still from sheer delight, and they would be unable to tear their eyes away from it. One must arrange it so that the color combination and the pattern of the facing are such as the azure skies with their delicate clouds in their natural essence. And the greyish-brown earth, on which the tower is standing, could be a delightful view from down below and upwards upon the wondrous light-blue regalia of the minaret. And its tip cannot be built flat and obtuse like the top of a stick cut off. The minaret should not look like a segment of a pipe. It must terminate with a dome, graceful and ethereal for the sky, which will embrace it for its flight. Nor can one make the tip excessively pointed, lest the tower should resemble the sharp point of a spear, threateningly pointing towards the sky. Nay, the apex of the minaret must become a light blue cupola, marvelously harmonizing with the huge dome of the sky itself. And the orifice of the tower's tube must be hidden from spectators' eyes, for it must be artfully culminated by a slight elongation of the rounded cupola. Everything must be sculptured in such a way that the viewer of the tower would not be able to comprehend whether it is soaring into the sky or descending from heavens down to earth. This is precisely the type of ravishing miracle of equilibrium the architect sought to achieve.

He wanted to avoid certain extremes: on the one hand, the minaret's tower should not be oppressive by its domination and dimensions of everything smaller around it, and to arouse fear among people; on the other hand, it should not create the impression of an easy toy, which anyone who had admired it might wish to take under his arm and walk off with it. Moreover, the tower should be dressed in such a facing, adorned in such wondrous masonry regalia, that the minaret would instill in people the idea of an infinite perfection of the Creator revealing on this occasion another one of His miracles of His infinite wonders of His Providence. Should the people walk off without being imbued with it here and now, they will still retain in their memories the image of a miracle, they will always remember him, and deep in their hearts they will retain the desire someday to come back and once again become absorbed in their contemplation... And the architect recalled how softly the window curtain in his carriage had fluttered.

Here it was, the major decision for the tower to be built: the minaret should be azure, graceful and ethereal, just like that curtain! Zhappar was indescribably happy for the hint from heaven itself. Indeed: 'He found on earth that which he sought in heaven.' Be it so! The tower will become precisely such an ethereal one, floating in the air, beckoning... Let anyone who sees the minaret for the first time imagine this to be the arm of some beauty yearning for love, reaching out for heaven in her supplication towards the beyond-the-clouds habitat of angels. And let the Lord, returning soon from his strenuous and distant campaign, also see this arm, joyously welcoming his arrival.

'One would need to get hold of some prussic paint, prepare as much as possible *dermene*' the master made a mental note. 'Also I'll have to tell them to burn plenty of tumbleweed to get its ashes. All this for the prussic paint...'

A sense of impatience gripped him to come to a close with the bricklaying of the tube structure and to commence with the artistic completion of the minaret. The decision for the latter came from above, and one need not procrastinate in its implementation. On this wondrous morning with its translucent blue skies, the minaret stood out clearly before him as if it had been a painting drawn in space... And suddenly he had this vision that emerging from nowhere some sort of energetic demon began attacking this painting, shredding it to pieces with his crooked claws… The vision of a lovely blue tower disappeared, and no matter how much Zhappar tried to call it back, the painting did not reappear and only the copiously blue sky flowed in front of him in the waves of the sweltering air.

But then below, under the tower, that very same Khan's park remained. Right in the middle of the green lawn in front of the palace, like staid white geese, several women were pacing back and forth. Zhappar did not even notice when and from where they had emerged. The small group of womenfolk headed for the spacious pond, which was sparkling with its patches of light at the southern end of the lawn. On the pond's shore were two towers, similar to minarets, between them a brocade white curtain was stretched on a rope. At the very edge of the water small piles of something red could be seen. Coming up to the pond, the women lined up in a queue and began to undress. On the green grass small white islands of shed clothing appeared. The nude young women who were emerging from these headed straight for the emerald pond.

A resounding shriek could be heard and the pond's water foamed with a massive spray as if under a hail of falling pearls.

White bare female arms flashed in the water; the women were shrieking and splashing each other with water.

Three bathing beauties with lovely hips jumped out of the water and ran to the red piles which were right by the water. They began to grab and throw lush red apples into the water. The shouting and shrieks once again resounded with renewed strength; the womenfolk in the pond were jumping high out of the water, seeking to catch with both hands the flying fruit. Apples were falling all around them, disappearing for a moment in the water, but instantly resurfacing, they were sprightly wavering amidst the nude bathers. The latter began to attack each other with joyous shouts and taking the apples away from their competitors. As if infected by the merriment coming from the lovely bathing beauties of sumptuous bodies, the water in the pond began to rise with frequent ripples and the frolicsome, white-crested winged wave would suddenly fall upon the young pointed breasts of a jumping playful beauty and kiss them with gusto. The long, black hair of the women, being wet, would fall in strands upon their breasts and back, seeking in vain to protect their mistresses from the covetous and shameless hands of the playful waves. In an instant, the tranquil and sleepy pond had suddenly erupted in an unprecedented merriment, broiling, splashing unto its banks, broiling with white foam as if a large school of carp had entered it. When the well-endowed, healthy young women were colliding with each other in the water, and someone among them would commence in tickling her girlfriend, a tempestuous jumping about in the water would start, accompanied by deafening shrieking and the water spray became a huge fountain. Before Zhappar's very eyes an incomparable merrymaking unfolded on the water.

But, at long last, the playful womenfolk in the pond settled down. Forty nude beauties sat around it, and, placing their feet into the water, began to get warm in the sun and to dry. Thereafter they commenced combing their hair, followed by helping each other in braiding and assisting in arranging their hairdos.

Suddenly, as if by command, they all got up and hurried to the lawn where in the green grass their clothes were spread in small white piles. Forty nude women, pink from bathing and the sun, disappeared behind the white curtain... Reappearing one by one, they gathered in small, white geese flocks and once again peacefully walked across the meadow, this time towards the palace.

As soon as the last of the white flocks had disappeared in the tree-lined walk leading toward the palace entrance, from all sides and various corners of the park men were darting out, be they servants or guards, and they began to fish with hand nets on long poles the wet red apples out of the pond.

While the young architect by this time had a new concern: with the total intuition of an artist he felt that the tower should not rise any higher. If one should raise the brickwork of the tower circle even by one additional brick, then that would not adhere to the necessary proportions and would not achieve the desired image of the minaret. But, according to the former calculations, the tower had to be raised higher, but it did not wish to be raised even one iota. It seemed as if it had been grabbed by its feet and was being dragged down. In this contradiction between the calculations and the architect's perception he had to find a way out and to come to some sort of a decision. Thus, work was ceased temporarily.

Now each time when the Khan's wife and her court ladies along with their female servants came to bathe in the pond, he observed them continuously, even though he cautiously expected that someone among them would look in his direction. But not a single one of the forty beauties, frolicking in the pond and sitting around on its shore, resting, had ever raised her head to gaze at the tower looming over them. And he had been able to observe them to the point where they got dressed and would leave their place of bathing. And all of the forty women, as if by a secret conspiracy, would return to the palace but not even once looking in his direction.

After their serene and tranquil departure from the paradise park nothing therein had an attraction for him, did not beckon him and did not enchant him. The silvery mirror of the pond would instantly become motionless and lose its luster as if its surface had received a dusting layer of grey ash. The flower gardens and flower beds would also lose their bright colors, while prior to this they would strike the eye as they do on Persian carpets.

Along with the park and its loss of luster, a mood of despondency would befall the young architect. With a nebulous gaze he would look from above at the park's paths, where just recently the young Wife of the Khan would have been walking, accompanied by her retinue. And appearing to taunt him, the pathway at its curve, having long lost the warmth of the lovely feet of the Young Khansha, would suddenly twist in a contorted smile, and it seemed to him that these were someone's maliciously pursed narrow lips. Attempting in his thoughts to walk along the very same path following the court ladies, he invariably reached the overhanging and trimmed branches of trees along the path—and thereafter he remained alone, for the ladies disappeared from his sight. And as if marking time in his indecision, remaining in place, not daring to step across an invisible line, he then turned back, downcast.

When on occasion the Khan's Wife does not appear in the park, he begs of the sun not to hurry in its sunset. At other times, after having had her walk in the park in the late morning, the Khan's Wife no longer would come out of the palace. And the young architect, as someone hopelessly in love, would be all but dried up and would become all drawn in the face and losing his natural color. And the terribly brave, hot-blooded argamak of thought in an instant changed into a pitiful mare of despondency which dejectedly roams along the trodden path of gray banality. And, ultimately, Zhappar began to realize that for him, a dirty commoner, a potter unto whose palms so much clay had adhered that it cannot be washed away by all the world's soap, for him even to think about a forthcoming love from the Khan's Wife, even to assume of any of his desires towards her would be most base, a sin and a sacrilege. Fearing his own thoughts, he would look around guardedly: is it possible that someone had been able to figure out his temptations which are worthy of the very devil himself? However, who cares about this lonely madman who brings himself to frenzy from the joys of paradise, which he shall never experience? But then, what the hell, why and by what valor does he differ from that little disheveled sparrow, which had strayed from its flock and is sitting all alone and chirping on a treetop? Is this perhaps the reason why the young Wife of the Khan and her retinue, knowing perhaps what sort of man is sitting at the top of the tower, did not favor him with even a single glance. This is such a worthless person that one may have no qualms about undressing completely, bathe in the pond, and thereafter, without so much as looking at him once, return to the palace.

Well, all right! So this means that in order for the proud Wife of the Khan to look in his direction, digressing from a constant contemplation of her greatest Husband-Residing-in-Heaven, this master architect must create a minaret of such unprecedented beauty and such magnificence that has not been seen by any of the residents of Mesopotamia from the beginning of time! Then we shall see whether the Khan's wife would snub her little nose at the minaret, which he will built in such a way as he had planned initially, when he had seen its clear image in the blue celestial space! Let then those forty of her female servants and confidants loudly cluck their tongues, praising his great structure, while this haughty Wife of the Khan, of course, shall not fail to cast her keen, foxlike glance of an evaluating female upon him...

His heart, which formerly had been languishing with sadness, once again dared to rage in his chest. Thus Zhappar vowed to himself that he would face the minaret's tower in such an unusual manner, so marvelously that the Khan's wife and her forty ladies will have nothing else left but to go mad with delight.

Under his personal supervision in the proximity of the tower, they constructed and fired up ten huge tandyr ovens, each one the size of a six-panel yurt. They brought and piled up next to the ovens heaps of bundles of dermene and juniper, all of this was burned in the ovens and the ashes collected to make the paint base. Thereafter they commenced with the baking of the facing tiles, which were polished and glaze of an azure-sky color poured over such tiles. For an entire month, ten master craftsmen, suspended on cables, were facing the tower with the glazed tiles. The architect found himself to be on the rack, constantly circling around the tower, silently watching how it was gradually being dressed in its azure sparkling regalia of an unusual superlative blue hue. At times the architect would leave town on his light cart in order to check from afar the evenness and correctness of the tilework for the glazed surface of the minaret.

As if it were a thin pole against the background of a blue sky—pale blue on blue—the minaret was contrasting well with the other tall structures in the area, and it provided a new concept of the interacting heavenly and earthly ratios.

The minaret became the first major brainchild of the young architect, and therefore, still not comprehending what the newborn child was blabbering about, the creator would take a long and hard look, and examine his creation. He stood on his cart looking at it. He would look at it getting down from his cart to the ground. Some other time he would place the palm of his hand at his forehead in a visor way, and would look how the sun slowly circumvents the tower, and he would smile a kind smile. At times he would amaze people quite a bit, examining the tower, slanting his neck as if he were listening to some voice from heaven to which he would point his protruding ear. It seemed as if he is listening rapturously to some instructions, which were imparting some significant and prophetic knowledge to him.

Then suddenly and abruptly breaking loose from that mystical place, jumping on his cart, he would rush headlong to some other place. Having arrived there, without getting off the cart, he would stare with unblinking insane eyes of a dervish somewhere out into space, and he would sit there without changing his body's position as if conducting a stressful spiritual encounter with some unseen adversary. There were occasions, while walking somewhere, he would stop all of a sudden and as if he had spotted something extraordinarily grotesque, he would shake his head, clasp his hands in dismay and squeamishly spit in all four directions. Or suddenly, for some reason falling into utter despair, he would squat down, cover his head with his hands and would thus sit a long time, squint as if the entire world now was unkind to him. Or yet, as if he had banished from his soul all youthful and bright that life has to offer, he would moan and mumble, clenching his teeth in such a manner that his cheekbones would swell and his jaws would lock. His consciousness would drop off into a gloomy state, with widened eyes, thereafter he would witness, one after the other, violent scenes of frightening and absurd visions. Time would cease its movement and his milieu would be immersed deep into darkness. But hark! It seems that a rescuing lucid moment is imminent—suddenly, equally as spontaneous and unexpected, all these oppressive, awful and ridiculous events have dissolved into thin air, all troubles have vanished, and he once again has his eyes wide open. They are watering from the excessively bright light of day and the architect subconsciously wipes them with the sleeve of his robe and becomes deeply absorbed in a new thought which had just flashed through his mind: how to refine and bring to an utmost perfection the facing of the newly built minaret. At that point he jumps up and dashes headlong to the construction site in order to implement as soon as possible that which had inspired him. His real and human appearance comes back to him, and his face regains the color of life and his youthful, kind and joyous smile reappears.

Here he goes, jumping on his cart and rushing to the construction site. Swift as a whirlwind he bolts into the tower, like a madman he runs up the spiral staircase. Having reached the master craftsmen builders, who are scampering about, up and down and across the tower shaft on wooden scaffolding, he begins to explain something to them. The young architect is getting all worked up, moving his arms. Having convinced the master craftsmen, he instantly calms down and once again rushes down the staircase in order to look at the just now arrived mosaic tiles. Grabbing several as samples, he is instantly dashing off to the *tandoor* ovens, where these tiles are going through the kiln and glazing process.

During this past month, Zhappar had exhausted himself beyond recognition. His face had acquired a sallow earthy color, he had gotten so thin that his clothes simply hung on him like on a stick. Of the former handsome youth only his eyes remained, burning in a feverish flame of inspiration, lively, perceptive, not omitting the smallest detail at work.

Quite recently still, an unsightly, intimidatingly huge, an unwieldy brick tower, hovering as a large, cumbersome and lifeless object above the city, now it had transformed in plain view of everyone, wondrously becoming more attractive each and every day as a maiden before her wedding. Growing crowds of town folk come to look at the final phases of the minaret's construction, and talk among the people had it that there had never been—be it in the capital or the entire country—such a marvelous, enigmatic and captivating structure, which was hiding within itself something magical.

Depending on the sun's position in the sky and time of day, the tower's color also changed into the most extraordinary hues of blue.

Everyone who came to view this phenomenon was astonished by this. And everyone remained mystified by the secret of this magic.

Thus the day came when the master, as a bird flying high, in person put the finishing touches on the dome with his own hands.

In these warm parts, where winter only bears the name, yet another winter period had passed, the new spring had arrived, with its sun and warmth, when even at night oil does not solidify. The trees in the Khan's park were covered with clouds of new blossoms. The wealth of flowers was such that it seemed a myriad of white butterflies congregating in the garden, and uniting its wings into one huge cover, they had now enveloped with it the entire palace courtyard of the Young Khansha of the Khan.

The time of late morning was approaching when the young Wife of the Khan, as usual, would be going out for a walk in the park, accompanied by her retinue of ladies. Zhappar had been waiting for this moment with particular impatience. And, ultimately his wait paid off, glory be to the Almighty One! So here from the whitish-pink clouds of the blooming trees along the path the ladies of her retinue appeared, dressed in their magnificent attire. But coming out into the middle of the lawn, they suddenly congregated and froze in their tracks. Then, forgetting their prescribed affectation, they began to run and jump in the direction of the pond. But not for the purpose of shedding their dresses and going into the water. Everyone without exception, the ladies raised their heads and, mouths open wide, were looking at the huge light blue minaret, which seemed had jumped out of the ground at their very proximity. Now at last they showed desire to notice it! Rejoicing and triumphant, Zhappar grinned in satisfaction. But suddenly his breathing stifled and his eyes became wet with tears. These were tears—be they from the bitterness of a late retribution or from a jubilant joy of victory.

The blue minaret had constant additions of new, minute and detailed decorations, but it was nearly finished. Only from the side of the Khan's palace, right under the very dome a rectangular dark gap was visible. This was an opening where bricks have not been placed and through which the architect was secretly keeping watch over the park of the Khan's Young Khansha.

Now he was able, remaining unseen, to observe how the forty beauties after their morning meal were stately walking about on the lawn in front of the palace. In the very midst of the crowd of ladies was the Young Khansha, whose with her sparkling jeweled turban, marked with the red ruby, was distinctly different from the headdresses of the other ladies of the court. Zhappar was in no hurry to close the opening, his observation window through which he could admire the heavenly *houris*, who were frolicking without a care in the park.

When standing in a half-circle along the pond's shore, the women began looking at the minaret and shouting with excitement, Zhappar felt almost like being the Creator, who is looking down from the mountainous heights upon the praise and glory offered by the people below. The masonry minaret, for which he died a thousand deaths and came back to life again, had become for him as much as a winged *Tulpar* of happiness. Its mythical wings shall carry Zhappar to the heights and the threshold of a perfect world.

However, something deep inside his soul caused suffering and anguish. Something horrible, incomprehensible and gloomy would surface as if from the depths of hell. And, having a premonition of something malicious, he thought that the bird of success, which he had grabbed by its wings, would one day for certain slip away from his grasp. His soul moaned and wept as if seized by diabolical dogs.

At that point, he made a desperate and insane decision. He would not seal the opening under the dome and would not descend but will remain here in order to die. Let the guards with their poleaxes come and get him in order to chop off his head or forcefully to bring him to the executioner. For down there, below, he will perish anyway—he had a premonition about this with his entire despairing and tormented soul.

Sensing that something is wrong in Zhappar's behavior, the chief builder climbed the stairs to the upper level of the tower's throat. He came, by the way, with an important bit of news: the Lord is returning from his great campaign. Prior to his arrival in the capital, one must completely finish work on the minaret, and the entire area around it should be levelled off and cleaned to a spic-and-span condition. According to the observation of those comprising the caravan, the minaret can be seen already quite well when leaving the Great Sands. During the festivities staged on the occasion of his victorious return, the Lord will generously reward the outstanding batyrs, and, it is possible that the Lord will also reward the architect, who had erected into the skies such an outstanding tower. And after this, the master's fame, who had created such an unusual minaret, shall spread throughout all the corners of the civilized world.

While the chief builder spoke, Zhappar looked all this time through the opening, without turning around, as if he didn't hear the former's words. After noticing this behavior, the old master stopped abruptly, and examining Zhappar with a lasting and probing look, he immediately realized that the young architect is a captive of some disconsolate, all-consuming passion. And tracing Zhappar's look and gazing out of the opening, the chief builder saw far below in the distance, on the green lawn, the Young Khansha with her entourage of court ladies, who had raised their heads and were looking at the minaret with curiosity.

Without saying another word, the chief master builder left Zhappar and descended down the staircase.

News about an imminent return of the army from its campaign had been circulating, and it was the major event of this week. The residents of the city's mahallah area, where Zhappar resided, were talking about nothing else all day long. It was only Zhappar who could care less.

Now the city residents, after getting out of bed, the first thing they would do is to look at the new minaret, which could be seen from all points of the huge capital city. Only after admiring the light blue tower, the city dweller would sit down to have breakfast. Anyone who would approach it closer would notice the unsealed opening, which loomed darkly right under the cupola and was facing the Khan's park.

But none of them, those not wishing to see the shiny poleaxe in the hands of the executioner—neither in their dreams nor in reality!—had given it even a thought to voice their observation. Recalling the harsh law of the Lord, who would have the informer executed first, thereafter the criminal, each and every one held their tongue about these events.

As it would seem, only Zhappar did not know what horrible rumors concerning him were spreading in the huge city. But also the young Wife of the Khan, not aware of these rumors, had become alarmed by the audacity shown by the young architect. She also noticed the dark gap under the minaret's cupola.

On that day when a messenger had been dispatched to the Lord with the report from the capital, two carriages left the palace of the Khan's Young Khansha and were headed towards the minaret.

Zhappar, who did not leave the opening in the tower, had noticed the departure of the carriages and knowing that they did not have far to travel to the minaret, began awaiting them impatiently. A short time thereafter, he heard a door slamming loudly at the bottom of the tower's tube, thereafter footsteps could be heard on the staircase. Someone was stubbornly clambering on the narrow spiral staircase, which was so narrow that only one person could either ascend or descend at one time. Suddenly, out of context and place he noted that the sound made by someone's feet in the staircase and his heartbeat initially coincided, but thereafter his heartbeat began to sound more accelerated, much ahead of the sound of the footsteps. In his agitation and in some form of irresistible yearning he cast a glance towards the palace of the Khan's wife, and he saw that the green lawn was empty. The trees, without stirring, stood under the sun at its zenith and had their leaves tucked in. The entire world, along with Zhappar, was listening to the ascending sound of feet in the tower, and it understood, just as did Zhappar, that bringing him his doom were these demons of death, which had filled the black zindan of the minaret

An icy chill of a dreadful premonition ran down his spine, but Zhappar was not terrified. The tower... Zukhra... the Khan's Wife... a light blue fluttering kerchief... weapons of torture, a sword and poleaxe...Angels of Death Munkar and Nakir. No, he was not frightened of death—it was simply an unpleasant feeling, as if one's body and one's eyes are pierced by thousands of sharp icy needles. Not at all! During these horrible minutes of Providence he behaved in a balanced and fitting manner. Thus, without confusion one awaits death, if one has done everything in life already and it had disappointed one long time ago and completely.

He continued staring at the opening in the floor of the platform, wherein darkness of the inner tower loomed. The sound of footsteps from below got louder. Zhappar became rigid as a pole. His leg muscles got tight as if in a spasm. His entire body became taut like a bowstring.

Now, now... something should be menacingly flashing in the opening... perhaps a sword or an executioner's poleaxe... He would not be able to avoid a death penalty, when the merciless Lord is greeted with the tallest minaret tower ever, and with a gap under the cupola at that, and facing the park of his young wife. Who could even dare to have such thoughts… But hark! Here, right on the spot, they will chop his head off, and the chief master builder will have the task assigned to him to close the gap.

Zhappar was unable to divert his eyes from the dark pharynx of the staircase opening. But the distinct sounds of footsteps are no longer originating from the tube of the tower, but rather from somewhere from above, falling on his head with abrupt jolts. 'Bear with it!' Zhappar urged himself on. 'Bear with it to the very last!'

To bear with it to the end and to stand before the world's evil to one's death—this is the sole consolation that his fate had prepared for him. His throat felt as if it had totally dried up, everything callous, can't swallow, can't inhale or exhale. 'It's better that way,' Zhappar thought. 'Now the executioner will swing his poleax above my head, and I won't be able even to cry out. I'll suffocate and will die even before he kills me. And at that time no one will hear my mournful wail.'

The sound of footsteps is right next to him. At the last moment he was drawn to turn around and look down at the Khan's park. 'To see her one more time before the executioner gets me…' But the green lawn was empty. The sun had already set behind the zenith, and on the ground short shadows appeared. There was also no one at the mirror pond. 'That means she didn't go bathing…'

The footsteps could no longer be heard.

Some sort of chilly gleam flashed in the darkness of the staircase opening. No, this was not a flash of an executioner's axe. Something white and graceful floated above the dark chasm of the tower. His face perceived a fresh and aromatic breath of air. Then he saw a delicate feminine hand adorned with a large pearl shining in the darkness of the tower tube…

'Here she is… She came alone… Yes, yes, that's her.'

So this is how it can happen… She is standing right across from him, just as she had during their first meeting. The Khan's Wife. That very same snow-white long dress and the same transparent white chador on her head, not hiding her black, as a succulent currant, eyes and her plump-cherry-lips.

The Khan's Wife did not ascend the top step, remained standing indecisively on the staircase, as if she had concerns that a powerful blast of wind coming from the tower would sweep her away. Then she resolved to ascend to the platform... At this time, the burdensome shackles of fear and doubt, which had agonizingly oppressed him all day, had concurrently dropped off, he perceived that he is alive and free, and thrusting his arms forward, he stepped towards her.

The Khan's Wife recoiled, for she had not expected anything of this sort.

Coming to his senses and becoming ashamed of his actions, he froze in place in confusion. But soon he gained confidence and raised his eyes and began looking her over attentively. O, my, she is a just a young girl...

He recalled what her eyes looked like when she had come here the first time. At that time she appeared embarrassed, almost frightened and apprehensive. But she did not perturb him with her childish fear, she did not recoil from him in panic. That young girl, almost a child, looked at him with some sort of concealed hope... And this one, exactly the same way, looked at him with the very same eyes, where soon fear had disappeared. This one also had a ruby sparkling on her forehead, but this ruby was different and smaller, and the covering on her was different, shorter. But she looked at him with some concealed appeal, as if calling for help... O, so much like Zukhra, leaving the garden. And if right here and now he will not resolve and tell her everything but everything! After which one would not even be afraid to die, if he should once again be oppressed by fear and would not admit to her, then he once again is missing his fateful opportunity, which had occurred between him and Zukhra! Just as she, this girl-woman shall disappear from his life, leaving forever in his heart a wound of bitter remorse...

Finally, Zhappar brought himself to say something, he summoned up his courage, nervously cleared his throat once, then again...but words just didn't come to him. While the young Wife of the Khan, actually just a young girl, continued to look at him intently and expectantly, as if she was pleading with him. And when Zhappar once again reached out his arms to her, she did not back off. At this point he perceived that he was losing control over himself and that his entire existence was crumbling, flowing and immersing into some tender and flaming, effulgent vision. And he learned that such a vision is indeed

End of the Legend •*Abish Kekilbaev*   165

the brief moment of human happiness. He learned that it presents itself only once in a lifetime. And one should not let it out of one's hands! Knowing all this full well, he pressed to his chest the tender, like down, virtually melting body of the Khan's girl-wife. At the same time he also felt that he is helplessly, uncontrollably melting from the touch of her lips upon his.

The minaret was completed on schedule. After long years on his campaign, the Lord was greeted by the light-blue, newly-erected tower with a beckoning and mysterious smile. Brightly illuminated by sunlight, it sparkled in a gamut of colors and hues of light blue on a blue celestial expanse.

Zhappar had been already sufficiently informed of the Lord's will as a Khan to personally visit and look over the new minaret, and that he had been standing before it at length in admiration and then had departed back to his palace with a look of satisfaction on his face. However, time passed and there had been no news for the architect forthcoming from the palace.

And when one late afternoon, in a routine and quiet manner, without so much as noise and shouting, a special messenger came and ordered Zhappar to follow him to the palace, the latter instantly realized that he should not expect to receive rewards and honors. So the young man decided not to withhold a thing and not to refuse to admit his guilt, when he was confronted by an old man with a morose and hoary face, who was sitting under the central arches of the palace, sulking like a vulture, raising his severe, penetrating and horrific eyes at the visitor.

LOVE

For the past three months the Young Khansha had become extremely emaciated. From her constant sojourn in a room with windows of a colorful stained glass, her face acquired the lifeless hue of bone by alkaline bleaching. Her long and rounded throat and neck, just recently captivating the gaze of those marveling how with such grace and pride the mistress of these properties carried her charming head and how lively she responded to the call of others, had dried up to such an extent that the veins on it became drastically pronounced, while in the back one could count her vertebra protruding through her skin.

Her dark eyes no longer exhibited their former brilliance, and there were shadows under her eyes, which were gloomy and sad like the semi-darkness of her bedroom.

By accident, espying her image in the large, circular mirror, the Khan's Wife quickly turned away as if she did not wish to encounter some of her unwanted rivals.

No movement, no sound all around, except the whispering fountain of the khauz, the water basin, to which the huge and empty palace is listening apprehensively. The Khan's Wife, too, is listening as if suspecting everything to be a conspiracy. But day and night, the fountain's whispering is the same, and the khauz is listening to it and the palace is sullenly listening, but nothing happens. Tired and angry by their chatter, the Khan's Wife jumps up and runs to the basin with its dimly gleaming water, and she is at the point where she is ready to tear it apart. But at the sight of the innocuous tiny spurts from the fountain, barely soaring, instantly falling with a babbling sound back into the water, fated to spread along the smooth water surface, so that the furious mood of the Khan's Wife suddenly changes to one of a silent sadness, and disheartened she drops to the silk rug, which had been placed on a low platform next to the khauz... After sitting at this spot for a very brief time, she gets up and leaves.

But all she would have to do is move away a few steps, and the fountain and the khauz, which pretended to be angelic and humble, once again commence their truly diabolic and derisive whispering and conspiratorially odious mumbling. Wishing to terminate this nest of intrigues and gossip, the poor Wife of the Khan decides to wear down the resistance of the conspirators and remains sitting near the water, for in her presence they do not dare conduct their conspiratorial conversations. Thus she had been able to sit at length until she would begin to get sleepy. But all she had to do is to get up and make a mere step aside—the empty, semi-dark hall once again would be filled with sinister whispers.

And with each step away from the fountain, she hears the sounds of its dense spurts, initially erupting through the bubbles from the depths of the khauz, thereafter falling back as if strengthened and mixed with the sounds which were wafting through the huge, lacquered and gilt-covered oaken door: the muffled voices of the eunuch-slaves, the peremptory shouts of the old harem keeper, and the affected chirping of the court ladies.

End of the Legend • *Abish Kekilbaev*   167

Outside the stained-glass windows the park had a multitude of trees of a varied species; their branches were covered with a variety of leaves, and each one of them, if it had acquired a mind and speech of its own, it would rustle and susurrate many a gossip about her. Her walks in the park, which had become rare now, the Khan's Wife sought to conduct at a distance from all people, along the most remote paths, passing through the dense undergrowth. And in these secluded hideaways of a park grown wild, she would only encounter keen red deer and roe deer, who would secretly observe her from the bushes, monitor her every step, or would overtly gaze at her with their glistering, curious eyes, peeking from the forest clearing: 'So this is how she looks, this very same Khan's Wife, of whom so many are titling and tattling everywhere!'

Lately she has become a total recluse; should there be no weighty reasons, she would not leave her chambers at all. From her husband and master there had been no news, no greetings at all. Every morning she would be darting secret glances at the faces of her servant girls, who came to dress her, but their eyes were noncommittal, and their mouths shut tight. It appeared as if they were guessing that the other day she sought to eavesdrop on them in the vestibule to find out what they were gossiping about, so now they behaved in a strained manner, overly polite, coming and going in a humble manner, trying not to linger about and avoiding conversations with their mistress.

After all, not so long ago, particularly during her initial years of marriage, the rooms of the Khan's Wife were perpetually resounding with the joyous flurry of activity and happy laughter. Everyone in the palace was delighted with the appearance of this young and beautiful new mistress, and even the harem supervisor, a stooped old woman with a plump nape of her neck, without raising her eyes off the ground, with the arrival of the young Wife of the Khan to the palace seemed to perk up and as if cheered up, slightly straightened her hunched—like that of an ox—back. On the threshold of some festivities, the old woman tried her utmost best, sending out her servant girl-spies to the residence of the Senior Wife of the Khan in order to ferret out what sumptuous attire the Senior Wife would be wearing, and what pomp and ceremony she would employ during her entrance with her court. All this would be done in order for the Young Khansha by any means—even if not surpass the Senior Wife—but at least not cede to her in splendor of attire and pomp of ceremony. It was a sight to behold how the two old harem keepers of two rival harems of the Lord, meeting in his large tent, are shooting supercilious and scathing gazes at each other! The young Wife of the Khan could not stop laughing from such a sight.

It would seem that the old woman indeed cared for her lovingly and protected her like her own child.

Well, the rest of the court ladies and female servants of the Khan's chambers were treating the young Wife of the Khan, it would seem, with sincere adoration, because almost all of them were much older than she and they wanted not only to show their respect to her as a spouse of the ruler, but also to watch over her, care for her lovingly and to pamper her like a little sister. And just as she was considered to be their little sister, who was fortunate to become the Chosen One of no other than the Lord, the ladies and the servant girls were proud of her. It seemed as though for them there was no greater pleasure in this big, wide world than to dress their young mistress, comb and dress her hair, bring out the beauty in her face and to take care of her tender body. Getting up in the wee hours of the morning, they would come tip-toeing to the bedchamber of the Khan's Young Wife and in a crowd would gather at her door, waiting impatiently when she would wake.

As soon as she would open her eyes, an entire swarm of servant girls from the harem of the Khan's Young Khansha would descend into her room, and a furiously joyous commotion of servant girls reminiscent of a cheerful dance of white butterflies on a sunny meadow commenced. Frightened by such a multitudinous onslaught, the not yet fully awakened girl-Young Khansha of the Khan sought to crawl back under the blanket, but she had no chance to escape the dozen or so inexorable loving hands. And when these soft and dexterous hands touched her pampered, fragile and as-yet-disobedient, just awakening young body, and began to gently stroke and slap it, she would close her eyes and obediently submit in her lassitude.

This was at the very beginning. And one evening after her meal, the harem's mother-mentor, with one command ousted all the female servants outside and remained with her alone. Not knowing the reasons for such mysterious actions of the old woman, the young Wife of the Khan looked at her curiously and awaited subsequent events. The mother-mentor's eyes were incomprehensibly and even frightfully gleaming. At this point, the old woman with her crooked as a sickle nose leaned over her ear and began to inform her of something in a whisper, rapidly moving her narrow like strings purple lips.

She mumbled at length as if reciting some sort of incantations. The young wife of the Lord, unable to turn her eyes away from those glued on her like leeches, the insane eyes of the harem mentor, sat before her transfixed. The entire room, as it appeared to her, began to spin around her from this witchcraft of the old woman.

She was able to move only when the harem mentor had stepped away from her and backed out towards the door, continuously bowing to her. But even after her departure, it seemed the rooms retained some invisible evil whirlwind. The lights of the numerous suspended lamps did not shine down but rather were all directed at the ceiling, and the huge room remained in a dim semi-darkness, vaguely indistinct just as the instructions of the old woman. Perceiving a somewhat labored breathing in her chest, she walked over to the cool basin with the fountain, and here is where at the door she espied the great Lord, who came to visit her. The inexplicable strange semi-darkness, which just moments prior to this had heavily shrouded her bedroom, suddenly vanished completely, with an even bright light taking its place. The floor under one's feet, which had been swaying as if a vessel on waves, once again acquired its solid state and equilibrium—and all this had occurred as if her life's expanse around the Khan's Wife had instantly ceased its arbitrariness under the intransigent gait of the Lord.

She froze in place, not daring to move her gaze from the approaching fearsome man. When he had reached her, she recalled who he was and how all mortals are required to greet him. But she had barely bowed low when someone, approaching her from the back, seized her under her elbows, and then easily lifted her with his hands. Embarrassed, the young Wife of the Khan, dared to lift her head and she saw the bright and gentle smiling eyes of her Husband and Lord.

When she awakened in the morning, she was alone and endlessly happy, and she waited impatiently when her servant girls would appear. She felt how her face was glowing, and she did not know how to conduct herself in front of them. Ashamed, she hid under her bedcovers and listened…

Subsequently the heavy oak door opened. The first to step across the threshold was the old woman harem keeper, bending her neck with the plump nape, and following her now and pushing each other aside, rushed the servant girls and court ladies into her bedchamber.

Hiding behind her locks of voluptuous black hair, which had fallen on her face, breasts, and had spilled all over the pillows, the Khan's Wife did not raise her eyes.

The joys of the court ladies and the girl servants were boundless. One after the other, they would come up to her bedside and kissed her on her forehead, and they were chirping something very joyous and happy, not seeking to hide their playful emotions.

When, however, after this first night the Great Khan spent with his young wife another two or three nights in a row, the rejoicing of the servant girls and court ladies of the Khan's bedchamber had no limit.

But very soon the Young Khansha experienced the first piercing taste of jealousy from the Baybishe, the Senior Wife. At one of the festive receptions for foreign ambassadors, passing her keen gaze over her huge entourage, the Baybishe stared at the Young Khansha with a penetrating, scrutinizing and tenacious glare. In response to this the young Wife of the Khan dared to lift her gaze at the yet beautiful, well-groomed and haughty Senior Wife of the Khan, and she observed signs of concealed anger on her face. But this did not frighten the Young Khansha, on the contrary, it somewhat instantly calmed her and imbued her with a feeling of infinite confidence and profound satisfaction...

She shall learn of this awakening in her of the eternal feminine spirit of rivalry, bitter as a poison and sweet as honey—she will learn of it later. However, from that day on the Young Wife of the Khan had freed herself from her tormenting feeling of inferiority, which was akin to her youth and inexperience, because of which she felt ill at ease even in front of the most ordinary servant girl in the palace. Her feminine mind had suddenly and fully awakened in her, and she immediately realized the truth that to wear the Lord wife's tall turban-saukele, heavily studded with precious stones and gold ornaments, is quite an easy task, when hundreds upon hundreds of ecstatic loyal citizens' eyes are gazing at you with rapture.

Whilst earlier she paid no attention to the passionate gossip of her old woman, the harem mentor, concerning the type of luxurious and costly pleasures which are tolerated in the palace of the Senior Wife of the Khan, she now began to listen to such with a great deal of interest, seeking not to miss any detail worthy of her interest.

Preparing to commence his new campaign, the Lord had moved his residence to his military headquarters in the center of the capital at the palace inaccessible to visitors, where even members of his family were not permitted. The young Wife of the Khan heard only rumors of the way he lived there and what he did; these rumors were at times conflicting or even distorted. They dealt, for example, with the time frame for the new campaign or with the palatial gossip concerning which of the close and trusted *Beks* had a successful speech at the meeting of the Great Divan and what he had said. But all the news reaching her had been word-of-mouth, not obligatory and ambiguous lay rumors. Much of it, upon checking, turned out to be total nonsense and idle figment of the imagination. The sole truth turned out to be the one that on this particular campaign the Lord had decided to take along with him his grandsons, and along with them his Senior Wife. Judging by such planning, one could easily guess that the campaign would take not a mere year nor two, but a considerably longer time. After learning about this, the Young Khansha lost her peace of mind and on several occasions wanted to visit the Lord at his main residence without his prior invitation. However, she never did make a decisive move on that count. But it became particularly unbearable when the Lord's decision concerning his Senior Wife's accompanying him on this campaign had been announced publicly. Now the Young Khansha was unable to look into the eyes of the ladies of her retinue due to her feelings of shame, and they in turn were unable to look in her face from their feeling of awkwardness for her. It seemed as if a time of mourning had been established at the Young Khansha's court. The former merry and carefree frolicking walks and games in the park ceased by themselves, as if they had never heretofore existed.

During the next several months, the Lord did not show himself, but then suddenly one evening he showed up at her palace. When her servants reported to her that he had left his golden carriage and was walking in the direction of the building, she did not run out to meet him, but decided to stay in place and wait. But the Lord did not go directly to her chambers, but went to his and did not reappear for a long time. He made her await him in languish until midnight. The Khan's Young Khansha suffered greatly and like a lost soul drifted from room to room in the women's part of the palace. Having lost all hope, she was standing near some window and, leaning with her forehead against the cold window, looked out unto the nocturnal park. At this point she heard the distant noise of the opening of the oak door. And the Khan's Young Khansha, losing all patience and forgetting about the proper sense of reserve, ran with all her might to meet her husband and master.

Alas! not a single one of the convincing, necessary and nurtured in her heart words, which she had prepared were uttered during this, her cherished and long awaited night, when both were alone.

The only thing for which she had courage enough to express in words:

-   My Lord Master, will your campaign last long?"

With due care, gently peering into her eyes, the Lord replied:

-   This only Allah knows.

Having said this, he took her trembling fingers in his hand and slowly stroked them with his palm.

Next morning the entire city was shaken by the thunderous thousands of battle drums. The Lord mounted his horse and the great campaign commenced. The armies left the city in a festive formation.

The Young Khansha felt lonely, unhappy, and deserted by everyone in her huge palace. Only now did she realize that as helpless as she was, she was tied to the entire wide world only by this seemingly stern, many years her senior, this man with piercing, all-consuming eyes. But when he gazed at her, with his cold eagle's eyes, in their very depth, suddenly lively sparks of gentleness and kindness would appear. And she realized one more thing that when he would be nearby, even if not quite next to her, her life would seem for her not as empty and lonely as heretofore.

Seeing how depressed and saddened their mistress was, all her servant girls and ladies of the court would instantly take on a similar appearance as if each and every one of them had suffered an irreparable loss.

During these days the Khan's Young Khansha, who had barely reached seventeen years of age, had fully tasted the cup of agonizing loneliness.

During her solitary walks in the park her yearning for him did not leave her for a moment. No matter where she turned her gaze, at any tree branch, at any tree bearing ripe fruit and covered with mature leafage—each one of these rejoiced participating in the universal holiday of life and in adorning the world. A multitude of tiny birds, fluttering from branch to branch and twittering in their overall chorus, and the keen buzz of bees, flying from one honey-source flower to another—all living beings were extolling their happiness of worldly existence. From time to time a mischievous whirlwind would suddenly attack the trees in the park, swaying their crowns, and blowing about in their leaves which would begin to dance along with the merry wind.

Instead of coming back after her walks vigorous and refreshed, the Young Khansha would be worn out, tired and unhappy. This frightened her, because in her as yet short life she had never experienced anything like it. Gloomy loneliness after the departure of her husband, unappeased passion in an awakened soul and a corporeal ardor consuming her, an inescapable sadness, a total helplessness, and a hopeless despair were excruciatingly torturing her. Not knowing where to hide, how to find peace of mind, she would be sitting at length, hiding in some obscure corner of the palace now unloved and hated by her.

Trying to divert her from this oppressive mood, the girls had decided to entertain her with their artistic talents, to sing and dance for her, but contrary to their expectations their good intentions led them to an opposite result. Rather than cheering her up, the songs of the girls and the languorous music had such an effect on her as would salt placed on a wound, and the wriggling arms and necks of the dancers, their provocative, cultivated licentious gaze and their porcelain shine of snow-white teeth in sensual smiles seemed as insipid attempts of nannies, bustling about in front of a bawling little master in order to make him laugh. The Khan's Young Khansha sat with a blank look, observing indifferently the great efforts made by the girls in their quest of their useless art.

At times she would get to feel so uneasy in front of the ladies of her retinue and the well-meaning servant girls, who had their best and noble intentions in this useless entertainment for her—to the point where she had thought of an entire range of refusal tactics, starting with "don't feel like it" and culminating with "I have a headache"—only in order to spare herself to be present at just another one of these entertainment events.

The old harem keeper had racked her brain and got her headaches, trying to think of, attempting and not being at all successful in steering the Khan's Wife away from her abnormal seclusion. One time she would lead the Khan's Wife into the park, showing her exotic foreign flowers and plants. Another time she would spread small boxes, some made of birch bark, or would untie small bags containing jewelry such as gold rings with diamonds and other gems, ear rings and pendants, necklaces and brooches studded with diamonds. All these treasures were from the trousseau of the Khan's Wife or comprised the gifts by the Khan, his high officials and military leaders, provincial governors and foreign ambassadors. Or the old woman would unroll before her bales and bolts of cloth brought from all parts of the world with their fairytale-like names: *ualat, mahfis, rauiya, shamsiya, shadda, mashad, tafsila, gyulistan, misriya, abiariya, luluiya, saburiya, miskaliya, safibar, kidn, atlas, kamka...* offering the young Wife of the Khan to choose any of these she would like for a dress. She also offered her to select anything from the unused furs stored in their treasury: expensive fur coats, hats of sable, beaver, marten, ermine, snow leopard, and the fire fox. But—alas!—to all of this the melancholic soul of the Khan's Wife remained impassive.

After becoming convinced that she cannot be lured by luxurious items and valuables, the old harem keeper decided to steer her towards more lofty conversations and in this fashion to distract her from her sorrowful thoughts, and not to leave her in her pernicious loneliness. Thus she acquired the habit to drop in at the Khan's Wife at any given moment, without any permission granted on behalf of the latter, and to relate to her endless stories of events at the palace. But the rumors circulating on the lofty court level were of no interest to the unhappy Wife of the Khan; she did not listen to them, but sat silently with a blank look in front of the old woman.

But the worldly and wise old woman did ultimately find the right key for a conversation topic, which would be able to stir the half-dead soul of the young Wife of the Khan. One day, the harem keeper began to relate what honors are bestowed upon the Senior Wife, the Lord's Baybishe, when she visits the conquered countries. And this is when the somber, frowning eyebrows of the Khan's Young Wife began to move excitedly, and her eyes, previously staring at some point in space, turned to gaze at the old woman. Not yet believing that she had at long last located the sensitive spot of her charge, the harem keeper began to relate in detail about all that she had seen and experienced at the court of the Senior Wife, where she had worked earlier. Understandably, fearing the all-powerful Baybishe, the old woman was reticent in her assessments of the Senior Wife of the Lord, however she was not hesitant in denouncing her court personnel and servant girls.

Based on the words of the know-it-all old woman it turns out that since the day that the Lord had settled for a lengthy period at the palace of his Young Khansha, she had acquired some fierce enemies in the camp of the Baybishe, and they were ready to get rid of her from this world of ours. *For* it had now occurred that all the honors, gifts and awards, which heretofore were flowing to that court from all corners of the world, now are bestowed not only to the Baybishe alone. For that reason the innards of the Baybishe are on fire as if poisoned, while all the secretive talk that the best and the most expensive gifts are sent by the Lord to his Young Khansha, originate from the mouths of the very same Senior Wife and her daughters-in-law.

The harem's old woman glanced askance at her lofty ward, seeking to ascertain whether she is exhibiting any signs of displeasure or rage, and when she became convinced of it, she continued to embellish her story even more. At that, her face with her hooked, sickle-like nose, with a dense network of tiny wrinkles, with her flaccid lips resembling strings, the corners of which were sharply drooping downwards—this face of the harem keeper reminded one of an autumn spider net, while the convulsive mouth resembled a spider itself. This spider operated non-stop in order to capture the fly—the Young Khansha .

As if stringing beads, the old woman related in succession everything being said about the Young Khansha at the court of the Baybishe. All that could diminish the dignity of the young wife. They say that her main merit is her tender age and her fascination of youth, whilst with the rest she has nothing to sustain her imperial pride: her origin is not of a direct lineage of heirs of some eminent dynasty; and her forefathers are famous not so much by their ancestry but rather more by their fertility; and on her maternal side her ancestors are not at all conspicuous. To be sure, by taking her for his Young Khansha, the Lord only acted obediently in accordance with the death wish of his late mother. Malicious gossip had it unofficially at the Baybishe court that even though the Lord is holding on to his throne on this earth, time is relentlessly marching on and the time is coming when he will have to relinquish his imperial seat to go to heaven. When this occurs, Allah forbid, then who will support her, the unfortunate one, who had been married off to an old man, from whom it is doubtful that happiness of motherhood will come to her and the lap of her skirt will not be stained with the holy blood of motherhood? And she will remain her entire life alone, sitting somewhere in a corner, hugging her own knees...

The spider swaddled its victim with its spider's web and trapped it; thereafter it crawled up to her and, grabbing her with its front paws, pierced her with its poisonous mandibles.

Its deadly embrace the spider loosened only after becoming convinced that the poison had spread throughout the body of the victim, and her eyes lit up in a pre-death crimson flame as glimmering coals would fanned by a gust of wind.

Not yet aware to what extent of mental frenzy she had gotten her victim, the old sorceress started to lick with her own filthy tongue the bloody wounds, which she had inflicted with her poisonous mandibles. Pursuant to the nature of primeval feminine treachery and hypocrisy, she began to refute, one after another, her own calumnious statements, as if seeking to cleanse the lucid world of her own filth and to lick off her very own dreadfully odorous slander.

The language of jealousy is much like ice and fire; words of jealousy freeze one's soul and burn one's cheeks with fire. Knowing this full well, the old woman was competently holding her own by relating how these dimwitted skunks who were serving the Baybishe were considering the young Khan's Wife to be a silly child, who has just been weaned from her mother, and they want to order her around. After all, she is the meritorious daughter of an ancient service class dynasty, and at present it is not only the amassed wealth of the great state which is flowing into her young hands, but also the most profound consideration of the Lord himself is passed on to her. Thus all the vain attempts by these toadstools will turn out to be groundless, and they will only vociferously foul the air and nothing else. The Lord, so far, has been standing behind her completely, and all this malicious gossip, ravings, and idle chatter of the bootlickers of the court of the Senior Wife are meaningless for the young Wife of the Khan—as is the howling of a transitory wind or the buzzing of dung flies near the cattle yard. But still one should seek ways how to conduct oneself with the Baybishe in such a manner that the Senior Wife would cease thinking how to get the best of the Young Khansha—and only for the reason that she is the senior one. Let her imagine whatever she wants, but she should know when enough is enough, and should not transgress the boundaries beyond which her rules and regulations of her territory are no longer valid. Allah be praised that her Lord of the golden mind, while he is of sound mind and clear memory, shall not permit anyone, even himself, to destroy their family hearth and their genuine marital happiness.

The old harem keeper got worked up in all seriousness. The narrow nostrils of her hook nose were fluttering; her head on her hunched neck stretched upwards like that of a turtle, and her voice began to sound like the long trumpet karnay. Her sparse, bristling rat-like mustache moved awkwardly, moving above the upper lip of the old woman, right under her hook nose.

Noticing that the harem mentor is about ready to fly even higher, the Khan' Wife stopped her with a look of amazement, and the old servant, realizing that in her candor she went, perhaps, a bit overboard, she instantly went silent and, presumably remembering some urgent matters, she jumped up from her seat and fidgeting and grimacing galloped off.

Nonetheless, this not very pleasant conversation of the harem servant with the Khan's Wife did bring some useful information for the latter. Her soul's stagnation which lasted days and nights and did not allow her to see herself in a true light was instantly removed by a thrust of alarm and sense of danger which invaded her heart. A heavy weight of doubt dropped off her and she suddenly felt at ease these times. She understood that she needed to have a more decisive attitude. The hairy lassoes of despair and hopelessness she had on her hands she instantly tore apart and discarded them into the weed-overgrown ravine of despondency, while along these a wide and even pillar-studded road opened up for her thoughts.

And thus the possibility had come to calmly and meticulously sift through everything that the old woman had tattled to her. In the heart of the young Wife of the Khan a desire for a fight had awakened, an outright immediate battle with the dark shadow of the Baybishe, which had spread over the inexperienced head its crooked copper claws of a merciless sorceress.

Even though the young Wife of the Khan reigned and ruled in her magnificent palace, she well understood that the Senior Wife of the Khan, with the experience of many years of rule, this Baybishe would not allow any form of rivalry, would not acknowledge the Young Khansha as her equal, and considers her a weak and childlike dimwit.

Despite her youthful years, the intuition of millennia prompted her for the sole and appropriate response to the threat of the copper claws would be only a threat by equally as dangerous copper claws as well. With this thought, her face exhibited a malicious trace of the future revenge, and her formerly kind, dreamy, black like current, beautiful eyes sparked frigid flashes resembling the blade of a sharply honed sword. She jumped up from her seat and began to walk about the palace, and her gait and all her mannerisms became quite decisive, nay, even militant.

This change occurring in the behavior of their mistress was at once observed by all her servant girls and court ladies. This made them happy, even though they did not dare, as previously, to rush to her with shouts of ecstasy and to surround her joyously from all sides. And their faces reflected the light of her newly found cheerful and merry state of mind.

The first thing the Khan's Wife did was to order all the valuable unused furs to be brought from the treasury, those which she had recently rejected with indifference, all the fabrics, clothing and jewelry—nothing of which she had chosen earlier.

Now she was instructing the old woman what fabrics to select and what to sew. In areas where the reigning mistress had doubts, had difficulties in choice, the harem keeper, with an appearance of a connoisseur would intervene and offer her advice. But at any rate, before her now no longer stood the former timid girl, who would agree to everything, mouth open in ecstasy. Now she would calmly hear out the advice, and unhurriedly think everything over before announcing her decision.

The old harem shrew could not help noticing that her charge at long last is getting the taste of power. She now gleefully rubbed her hands in anticipation of a furious internecine war of the two Wives of the Khan. Expecting much to be gained, the old woman had changed in appearance as well. Not thinking badly about her rather complex past, the illustrious harem keeper sought now to recoup her losses, forgetting all about her aches and pain, about her creaking joints and her stooped, like a cow's, old body, and she exhibited an amazing vim in settling matters of her mistress.

Going on an inspection round of all the storerooms and treasuries, she listed everything therein and made a report of it to the young Wife of the Khan: what is on hand and what has not been acquired yet, although it is due by virtue of the position of the beloved Wife of the Khan; if such item is not there, then where it could be obtained and from what countries, areas and cities it could be delivered.

After compiling the list of everything which ought to be in her possession, the Khan's Wife dispatched her demands to the Chief Vizier with the old woman harem keeper.

But the chief vizier, it would seem, did not take kindly to this sudden appearance of the old woman with her mission and sent her back where she came from without further ado. When she came back emptyhanded, the humiliated Khan's Wife this time sent off an official messenger from her court and ordered the vizier to come in person before her. Realizing that the beloved Wife of the Great Khan is insulted and angered, the old vizier came immediately and already at the threshold fell on his knees. He reported that her royal mission shall be implemented completely and without fail, and that he had already compiled and dispatched documents to the state repositories from whence special couriers will deliver all the listed furs, animal skins, costly cloth, jewelry, exotic ointments and fragrances.

In seeing the Lord's very own respected and valued Chief Vizier, obediently bowing at the feet of the Young Khansha of the Khan, the harem keeper experienced an immense sense of satisfaction, as if it were not in front of the Khan's Wife, but rather in front of her that the Superior Vizier had been genuflecting.

Now when in all the palaces the news had spread that the Young Khansha had gathered for herself the most famous tailors in the capital in order to have them fashion her wardrobe, the court staff of the absent Senior Wife of the Khan had their hair stand on end, for they were intimidated by her anger.

The Young Khansha of the Khan, however, had commenced with all her fervor to implement her new endeavor. Meanwhile, the Senior Wife of the Khan, being with her husband during his military campaign, heard the news of the sewing of incredibly expensive clothes and the delivery of unheard-of valuables and luxury items for the Young Khansha of the Khan, which was the main event within the great empire of the Lord.

Soon the Young Khansha got to hear, and thereafter regular updates from the Senior Wife were coming in, wherein the latter did not spare caustic remarks and virulent statements towards her young rival.

The Young Khansha was not at all perturbed about the news how the Senior Wife of the Khan was ranting and raving; on the contrary, it amused her and became the curative balsam upon those wounds of her soul, which were initially inflicted upon her by her rival. With an exquisite subtlety, her calculated blows of retribution and their most precise reaching of target were bringing the young Wife of the Khan an incredible delight, an intoxicating joy of a well-earned victory. And she was ready to develop more and more innovative and refined methods in her war with the residents of the Baybishe palace.

As though in defiance of her recent depression and despondency, she now experienced an incredible love of life. She conducted her walks in the park along with her entourage more than she had formerly. The Khan's Wife liked particularly the apple game during their bathing in the pond she had invented. To this end, early each day her servant girls would pick the fruit from the trees, would stack them in heaps under light awnings along the pond. Closer toward the heat of midday, when a strong wafting in the park around the pond of a sweet aroma of ripe apples could be perceived, the Khan's Wife with her court ladies would appear for their bathing.

This was a refined and exquisite, beautiful and sensuous entertainment—young, bare bodies of voluptuous women, frolicking in the blue waters amidst a multitude of apples: crimson, golden, and rosy, very much as the glistering, rounded and firm dancing fruit alongside in the aroused waves. Altogether—apples, women and waves, all equally starved for caresses and contentment, were unrestrained and enjoying each other in the embrace of sensuous love. The waves kissed the nude female bodies, penetrating with their kisses all their delightful recesses. The women were rapaciously, ardently sinking their snow-white teeth into the flesh of the sweet fruit, and these were kisses of death for the apples.

These sensuous water games were distracting the Khan's Wife at least for some period of time from the deadening routine of regulations and duties at the palace. Throwing off the mask of a haughty sway and throwing off her exquisite royal garments, as though returning to an innocent childhood, to feel oneself free and happy! But this thirst for freedom did not quench it fully, even though they did find here, at this small pond, moments of total permissiveness... Thinking of this, the Khan's Wife walked at length alone around the quiet pond.

One day after bathing, after drying, she lay down on a mat in the shade of a light awning, and her servant girls commenced to massage her. Along with the appealing scents of the park there were additional aromas of exotic ointments and refined fragrances, and from all of this the air around the bathing beauties on the lawn became truly heavenly.

During the massage of the Khan's Wife the touch of the slim and flexible little fingers of the young servant girls only caused a tickling sensation for her; her tender body was not sufficiently kneaded, therefore she requested older women, whose fingers were rougher, stronger and harder to massage her. The experienced servants understood well what the body of the young woman needed, and they didn't spare their strength on a prolonged and thorough pressing, rubbing and kneading of the languishing relaxed body of the Khan's Wife. Relinquishing herself to the mercy of their dexterous hands, she became entirely relaxed and obediently quiescent, covering her eyes with her eyelashes, and immersing herself into a blissful semi-slumber from which she did not wish to emerge. But she knew that this blissful rest would not last long, and so she left, floated into a kingdom of fantasy, and the Khan's park all around changed into a heavenly garden, and she, her servant girls, and the ladies of her retinue became immortal houris.

Her real days of life were thusly marked with all these heavenly blessings.

But why then is it that the full-fledged Lord of this heaven on earth, where the birds of happiness, so greatly desired by people, are nesting, this very same Lord does not remain here for long, but is recklessly tearing along with his army somewhere where the world ends, staying away for months on, and even years? What is the reason, why does one have to go on to wars to find happiness? What a strange desire, is it not an insane cause? But remembering suddenly that she had permitted herself a sinful deed indeed—to cast doubt concerning the sacred acts of her crowned husband, to defame the lofty ideals of the Great Lord, the Khan's Wife swiftly removed such seditious thoughts from her head. And as it happens in hunting with a dog—the borzoi is out in the field and is almost reaching its prey, when of a sudden it is detracted by something else and at full speed jumps to the side—thus the thoughts of the young Wife of the Khan leaving her Lord without paying him any mind are at full speed following the tracks of the Baybishe... The question arises, why did she get attached to him, why did she have to drag along on this military campaign?

Now here is where her awakened demon of contention acquires a splendid feast, and the Khan's Wife gets no less pleasure out of this

End of the Legend •Abish Kekilbaev

than from the dance of little fingers kneading her back. Turning on her back, she notices the hot sun shining in her face, and it seems to the young Wife of the Khan that this is her hated rival, the Baybishe, who is spying on her with one bloodshot eye. With a smile, she therefore stretches out and with pleasure offers the massage girl her young and vivacious breasts as if reiterating: since you're spying on me, look, you poor soul, on the wealth you're lacking; eat your heart out, you old bitch, lick salt when you're tormented by thirst. You will no longer have such a beautiful body and such youthful vivaciousness.

The Senior Wife of the Khan is cursing the Young Khansha's youth and charm which have torn her from the Lord's embraces. She also hates her rival for moving her, the Senior Wife, into the ranks of brood hens destined to cluck over their brood, to keep them company and to feed them. And wishing to avenge herself for this common defeat in life, the Baybishe endeavors to regain her husband's good graces by dragging herself along with him on his military campaign, wishing to personally take care of him and to please him in everything. But how can she please him? How can she be dear to the Lord's heart? Of what use can she be during his campaign? Perhaps only for washing his foot wrappings? No, this is not the way to conquer the heart of the World's Lord.

He shows up at the Senior Wife's residence only out of respect for the mother of his children, and also in order to visit his progeny, his sons and grandsons. But to visit her, his young wife, the champion Khan, would come after a long military campaign and bloody battles, and her residence for him is a garden of repose for his soul and a monastery for his soul cleansing of his sorrows, and a source for renewed strength. This is the essence of it all, there is no other... And certainly, it would not become a great warrior and monarch wearing a diamond crown to spend day and night with his Tokal—Young Khansha—and to cling to her like a soft and sensual young man. But, should he, by whose will and name all four sides of the world are supported, should he leave in peace and quiet his subjects even for a mere two-three years, the entire despicable rabble of the conquered provinces and of the entire nation will secretly hold him up to ridicule: saying that the Khan is no longer the same as afore, and instead of feats on the battleground he now prefers feats in the warm bed of a woman. No, this shall not be! She will not—if she can help it—proffer her husband for the humiliation of the despicable rabble. Only now did she realize what delusion and frivolous blasphemy her thoughts had been in regards to all campaigns and conquests of foreign lands being such a senseless and cruel cause.

This is indeed the apex of selfishness on her behalf—to seek keeping him tied to her apron strings—prior to his campaign or after, only by the mere fact that she had become a late love for this great warrior, his last song of tenderness. It is around the crowned Lord like around the axis of the world that life of his entire infinite empire is revolving. Each step he makes, any movement—all are in plain view of the entire nation. Therefore, in the nature of things the Lord duly visits the residence of his Senior Wife, who had presented him the happiness of fatherhood. In the large and comprehensive family of the Khan, there are numerous sons and grandsons who are hoping to inherit the throne, but order and harmony must always prevail, and just for this alone he must visit his Baybishe more often. For this very same reason he has taken her for the entire duration of his military campaign. Even from time to time in the presence of his military leaders during the war council meetings, he might ask for her opinion. All this, of course, is mere show in order to adhere to their ancient customs exalting motherhood. But in essence, what sort of military advice could this ruffled hen provide, whose paucity of brains did not even suffice in order to refrain from rivalry with the Tokal, who on the basis of her age could be her daughter? It could never happen that in a narrow hen's chest there could be concurrently a selfless concern for one's consanguine children and a jealous battle for a man and husband. All said, she must be saying something to him when they are together and alone in a family conversation?

Suddenly, her train of thought interrupted, the Khan's Wife tried to open her eyes and raise her head from the pillow, but she decided not to show her servant girls that she had awakened, and she squinted even harder seeking to capture and continue her evasive thoughts.

No matter how she tried, but she could not imagine what it could be that the Lord would be discussing when alone with his Baybishe. All of her attempts brought her to the same degree of perplexity: what is it that two aged persons would do except have a conversation? In this respect the Baybishe has total freedom: in contrast to her, the sensitive young girl, who would forget all the words she would say when she is alone with her great, one-and-only man.

On this occasion, on the eve of the commencement of the military campaign, she wanted to cry her heart out at his chest, to tenderly reproach him for leaving her all alone, to weep and long for him during their lengthy period of separation. But she simply could not bring herself to do it; she was too diffident. Next morning, when saying their farewells, she sought to remind herself that she is not simply a young girl in love, but a genuine Khan's Wife, and with poignant and fitting words appropriate for such an occasion, to express her conjugal love for him, and without inhibition tightly embrace his neck. This she couldn't bring herself to do either. Thus she stood at the threshold, looking at his back moving away. Sensing her gaze upon him, he stopped and turned around. He wanted to go back to her or say something; he raised his arm reaching out for her. But then he looked aside, into a side corridor, once again turning away from her and walking off without looking back.

Desirous in learning what it had been in the adjoining corridor prompting him to look, the Khan's Wife rushed out of her bedchamber and came to the corridor intersection. She looked into the adjoining hallway, and she saw standing side by side kowtowing eunuchs, the harem's guards. Obese, fattened up, the eunuchs were squirming like mealy worms in flour. Realizing how she had made a fool of herself in front of the despicable slaves, she ran back to her bedchamber, and in a fit of anger she slammed the door behind her. But recalling how the Lord had stopped and in a kind manner, with a smile had looked at her, she instantly forgot her resentment and calmed down.

She was the only person in the entire world who had seen how the eyes of the Great Khan, the Warrior, were shining with love! Yes, his eyes rather than his words were telling her that he loves her with all his heart.

The Khan's Wife suddenly began to feel that her flushed cheeks were aflame as if caught on fire... But she did not want to let her servant girls know that she is aflame with happiness... She tried to contain the flow of her emotions and thoughts of reminiscences, proffering herself almost with a sensual pleasure...

But what happens thereafter, when the torch of love for the two lovers burns out completely?

What will take up the void in one's soul after the former garden of love loses its bloom and its fruits, when it withers and its dry leaves fall off?

Perhaps, like that spot, where once a yurt stood in the steppe, the garden will also be overgrown by wild weeds and will be covered by the sands of oblivion?

Even though the cool voice from the depths of reason had declared: 'Indeed, without fail this is how it is going to be'— somewhere from a greater depth yet, from the subconscious, a discordant, gay feeling of protest was rising. This feeling, not unlike a friendly hand, took her hand and drew her to new heights of a tumultuous imagination.

But if love passes and does not even leave seeds for its continuation, then why is it that spouses who have gone cool towards each other cannot part with each other and are leading a sorrowful existence to the very end? Is it not perhaps for fear of the inevitable old age and a predetermined inglorious departure?

And this is understandable why mere mortals live with such fear, because their power does not extend beyond the threshold of their home. But will the Lord fear this, He, who rules over half of the world, cared for lovingly by his boundlessly devoted wives, kept by the State, extolled by his dynasty's reputation, surrounded by countless troops and law-abiding, industrious people? Nay, something is amiss here, and the meetings with the Baybishe are sought by the Khan not for the sake of hiding together from life and death. There is another emotion lurking here. But which?

Perhaps in the soul of old people on the bonfire of a long burned out love there remain some hot ashes, which are called mutual respect. And, until it cools, one of the partners manages to depart to the Other World.

The Khan's Wife experienced some degree of happiness after solving this complex riddle. But then suddenly she remembered all this meant that the Lord and the Senior Wife of the Khan are tied precisely by this unceasing to the very end, mutual respect which has not cooled... She suddenly perceived a piercing pain in her chest. It seemed to the Young Khansha of the Khan that her entire body, kneaded and stimulated by unceasing, pressing fingers, began, in convulsions, to tighten and become numb. Just a bit more and her body would be ground into a bloody mess. She got up quickly and pushed the masseuses aside. They began to dress her, and here is where even the finest silk cloth began to singe her skin as if it had been pierced by thousands of tiny needles. She started getting the chills. She was hardly able to withstand the procedure of braiding and setting her hair by her servant girls. And she hastened to leave that place, which she had but recently considered her paradise in the park, and she hurried as quickly as she could, as if she had seen an angel of death lurking amidst the trees.

Once again a gloom of despondency overwhelmed her consciousness. She realized her meaningless rivalry vis-à-vis the power of the home-loving, fertile, and for this the much respected Baybishe. And the pain from the injustice of fate burned her soul. In despair, she wished for the fire of love within her to burn out as soon as possible, the ashes to be cooled down and be blown away by the winds of oblivion. Just a short time yet to endure—and this horrific wish shall come true...

Nay, better not to think of anything of this nature. But these thoughts had metamorphosed into persistent flies which had covered her in dark swarms, flying in pursuit of her everywhere. She felt a loathing from the touch of their furry little paws, she shuddered with her entire body, and she would tightly close her eyes in order not to see the dark clouds of fly swarms. But it was of no use—behind her closed eyelids there began to hover even more detestable swarms of minute gnats, whose annoying whine was more unbearable than the buzz of flies... Terrified from how she felt, the Khan's Wife, with great difficulty opened her clinging eyelids. 'Did I get sick?' she wondered.

In her fear, jumping up from her seat, she hastened to a corner of her bedchamber where a large mirror was located. But her own image calmed her at once, as if putting her to shame for such reckless fears. An unrivalled beauty gazed at her from the mirror. Neck, breasts, face and rosy cheekbones—just treated with ointments and fragrances— were shining victoriously. Only one aspect of her looked untidy, which was her hastily and not tightly braided tresses were somewhat fluffy. But then, on the other hand, she knew rather well that this suited her, providing her an alluring lively look of languor.

Her straight nose with its white, round end would palpitate capriciously with the slim wings of her nostrils, as if the sweetish aroma of exotic rouge on her cheeks had irritated it. As if they sought to come to the defense of this capricious little nose, as if they were justifying the sacred righteousness of their indignation—from under the frowning brows, her large, clear and somewhat somber eyes were looking on with sincerity and incorruptibility.

Not quite trusting that this was indeed her image—the lonely girl who is looking at her from the mirror with an offended look—the Khan's Wife moved closer to the dark glass of the mirror. Indeed, such a naïve girl must resort to great cunning in order to stay afloat in this world and to remain unharmed! Any adult person, who would see her for the first time, would feel neither so much love for her, nor admiration or even amazement, but rather a paternal pity: 'oh, child, oh poor girl...' So that the twinkling little sparks she had observed in the eyes of her husband, the Khan, were nothing more than a manifestation of a brotherly compassion, but not the small flames of a fierce love...

It's not for you, immature puppy, to enflame the passion of the Great Khan, the fearless Khan, plunging half of the world into a state of trepidation. His heart will not tremble even if confronted by a blazing sword, so that your passionate gaze poses no danger to him. You are a mere morsel of sweet pink flesh for him, the means for warming the Khan's bed, now that the Khan's Senior Wife is no longer of interest to him as a woman. For, after all, he is also a male, as all the other men warriors. And you, foolish one, had considered his instant caresses as a manifestation of lofty love... So bite your tongue and be thankful to fate for showing you the honor, selecting you as the young female pup in her first heat, providing you the right to be close to the Lord himself and to have placed you to reside in a palace of your own! Are you truly worthy of being a rival of the Baybishe, who has by right and in practice all the love, all respect and loyalty which are inherent only to the earth shaker, the Great Lord? And do not attempt to stand in her way, and do not make her angry for no reason.

You, with your pitiful views, how can you compete with the very experienced, heedless-fearless wisdom of the Baybishe, against her genuine common sense, by which she wins over everyone, induces the despotic Lord to listen to her, although he can't stand those who seek to come to him with their advice and admonitions? Where, o where, into which secret pocket, can Allah, the Gracious, place even the tiniest piece of the substance of Baybishe's wisdom, on which, much like a baby nursing her mother's breast, clings her crowned warrior and husband, seeking her support, counsel, and consolation during the difficult times of his campaign of many years?

Joyless, the Young Khansha of the Khan, seized by distressing thoughts and sinister forebodings, not knowing where to hide, led a miserable daily existence, submitting herself to the nagging and destructive throes within her.

She heard someone's breathing behind her; frightened she turned, as if some stranger had encountered her nude. Before her stood the harem keeper, hugging a heavy lacquered jewel case. At the sight of the frightened, wide-open eyes of the Khan's Wife, the old woman managed something of a smile on her face by drawing apart her wrinkled mouth and moving her rat-like whiskers.

"This has been brought for you by the Supreme Vizier himself. He stated that it came by special mission from the Great Lord, who is on his sacred campaign," the old woman declared with great solemnity.

Still at the mercy of her oppressive emotional experiences, the Khan's Wife listened to her absentmindedly, not fully comprehending what she should do and how to respond to the harem keeper's report.

The old woman went inside and placed the case on the Khan Wife's bed. Then she came up to her and taking her by her hand pulled her to her bedside. Not daring to open the case herself, the harem keeper retrieved from somewhere in her deep sleeve a shiny small key, she held it with two fingers placing it quickly on the palm of her mistress.

The latter did not realize at first where the lock for the case was located, she just stood there holding the key in her hand. Seeing that she would not be able to do this on her own, the old woman took the key and opened the case. When the lid had been opened, she looked on in fright with bulging eyes: looking now at the Khan's Wife now at the contents of the case.

The Khan's Wife was blinded by something whitish, shining from the bottom of the case with a radiant brilliance. She squinted her eyes, and then again opened them, and her gaze encountered fairytale like brilliant jewels. There were white pearls in necklaces and separately, they were sparkling in a mother-of-pearl iridescent luster; coral jewelry in refined configurations; ethereal carnelian with a deep glow; and multicolored—as if embossed spots—jasper. White and yellow diamonds, sparkling with a spectral of light; unusually clear sapphires, blue like the September sky; smiling, eternally youthful green-eyed emeralds; scarlet-red rubies and crimson-red corundum—and many other precious stones, never heretofore seen by her. And on top of these truly priceless treasures, brightly glittering like a magic lake in moonlight, there was something entirely unrelated to these jewels, as if floating in water, a verdant live stalk with a large white flower.

The Khan's Wife took this white flower, which had miraculously not-yet wilted nor lost its luxurious aroma, and gently pressed it to her breast. The tormenting iron hoops, which were constricting her soul, at once were torn one by one and broke off from her. Hot tears streamed from her eyes, coming down like spring rain across wintery deserts— contrary to all laws of nature. Her heart, which had almost come to a standstill after such a multitude of grievous doubts, concerns, and fears, at once started beating easily and happily.

Her tears flowed in streams, the Khan's Wife was weeping like a small child, and she didn't care about the presence of the old harem matron. With each tear shed, with each renewed sob, the Khan's Wife freed herself from these fierce demons who had surrounded her, were tormenting her, and were drinking her blood like leeches—the blood of her spiritual faith in goodness—and they were devouring piece by piece her human dignity. Glory be to Allah that He gave the Lord a wise feeling of pity towards his little wife, who would have perished without him in great sorrow and doleful loneliness. And so from another part of the world he had sent a messenger, who galloped across half of the universe in order to deliver the Lord's gift.

The Khan's Wife carefully and lovingly showered the lovely white flower with her kisses.

The understanding old woman left for the young empress to be alone with herself. The Khan's Wife reclined on her bed and, taking out the marvelous valuables from the case, began to examine the jewelry, then to spread these on her breast. And soon the white, yellow, green, and light blue little stars with their radiance and glow, like with the power of magic, carried her off to the world of a fairytale dreamland, under a multicolored stellar rain.

Her gloom dissipated, her sorrow left her soul, and she brightened like the spring sky. Her happiness overflowed like a wide river during a flood. Oh, if only now, casting aside inhibition and shame, she could cuddle up to him with her entire body burning with love, bare her breasts welcoming his kisses, to give in to him unrestrained, completely—and to accept him in such a way as earth desiccated by intense heat accepts a long-awaited downpour.

But in this huge palace there is nothing for her to hug except the empty gloom of her bedchamber.

To admit her boundless love by writing her Lord a letter? No, this is not acceptable... Send her words of love by messenger? Can't do this either. What then should she do, poor soul, if she is dying from the impossibility to state her love immediately, right now? After all, her beloved Amir will not return so soon; it will be neither tomorrow nor even the day after that he will cross the threshold of her bedroom. But what shall she do with herself and the powerful emotions stirring within her in a whirlwind of love's desire? And how can she prove to her Lord that she is ready to be his victim, to prostrate herself on his road to victory? And how can she announce the words of her great and sacrificial love in order for her beloved, her husband, the Great Lord to hear them? And for all these trivial, evil and hostile people, with the Baybishe leading, and this entire huge city, and the entire big wide world? It appeared to the Khan's Wife that if she does not immediately tell the entire world about her love, her heart, filled with an irrepressible joy, will break up in pieces.

She could even now follow her Lord, but wouldn't this high-handedness hurt Amir's feelings and bring forth his dissatisfaction? What more, thousands of evil tongues will not fail to defile her virtuous deed.

In no hurry to remove the valuables strewn about on her bed, the Khan's Wife stretched out on its edge and gave rein to her high hopes. How could she repay her Lord for his great and regal regard for her? How could she make him happy on that day upon his return from his distant campaign? The best present, the most welcome news for him would have been the news of her forthcoming motherhood. And if the campaign would be prolonged, and she would give birth to their child much before his return—what could be more marvelous and wonderful than to meet him at the little cradle in which would be the newborn radiant prince? O, then Baybishe and her henchmen always flaunting with the fact that she had borne children for the Khan would for a long time hold their mouths.

But, alas! All of this remained merely in her dreams. At this point, for his lofty affection, she could only respond to her Lord with her selfless love. She has nothing else to offer...

Well, then there is nothing else left but to find a means to declare her love, so that it would be a message not only to the Lord, but also to all peoples on Earth. On behalf of her one would need to erect such a grandiose monument, so expressive and beautiful that by this gesture the Lord, having returned from his campaign, before everyone else will guess without fail, will see and hear the exultant song of love: her love for him. The song of tenderness, purity, devotion, and of a prudent, patient waiting. She has the means to create such a song, such a monument. She shall not, like the avaricious Baybishe, sweep under her belly all the valuables and treasures given as presents, and to hold them solely for her own use. She shall spend on the erection of an unprecedented monument—the tower of love—all the jewels and treasures she had received from her beloved Lord. And let the great *Lord* be the first one to be amazed by its beauty, and thereafter any passing person in this world. This shall be a tower surpassing by its height all existing minarets of the great city. And the people shall be captivated by the power of pure love and shall give all due to the outstanding young Wife of the Khan, who had planned and implemented such a marvel.

That night the Khan's Wife fell asleep in a happy state of mind.

Next morning, scarcely awake, she dispatched a messenger to summon the Superior Vizier. When the Young Khan made her royal wish, the Vizier initially only stared wide-eyed with his already by nature bulging eyes. He seemed as though he froze in a stupor. By his appearance one could not determine whether he is astonished by this noble impulse of his young empress, or whether he is enraged, regarding it all as her wild whim. On his elongated bony horse-like face not one vein trembled. The Vizier just stood there, pale, distracted and impassive. But when the Khan's Wife finally stopped talking, the Vizier bent with a most profound bow and then, placing his knotty and strong hand on his chest, declared:

-    All shall be done as Her Highness commands!

Not even a fortnight had passed when a master, designated by the chief builder, came and reported to the Khan's Wife that the minaret will be erected by one of the architects who had participated in the construction of the mosque honoring the late first wife of the Lord.

A swarthy architect like an ant is on top of the structure and is particularly busy, running about along the entire wall and constantly leaning over its edge and is looking downward. But what good is his busybody activity if the construction is proceeding so slowly? Have mercy Allah! What if she would suddenly not have the opportunity to see how her pet project would rival in beauty and magnificence actually with the ageless sky? She feared the thought that the minaret may remain unfinished—as a reminder of the futility of human passions, as an appalling stump of an untenable vanity, insulting human gaze with its unsightly appearance.

So that the Khan's Wife wanted to ascend the topmost platform of the tower being built herself, in order to look in the face of the shameless architect, the ant, call upon his conscience for him not to prolong this work for such a long time. And, if necessary, to ask him about this, wringing her hands in supplication. Not knowing how to handle this matter, she decided to consult with the harem keeper, and the latter, usually ready to run at breakneck speed in order to carry out any request of the Khan's Wife, on this occasion became simply speechless, froze from shock and could only blink her eyes in bewilderment. She thought at length, and then she proposed timidly: "But perhaps, at first, it would be best to send people so that they could gradually find out everything, how work was progressing, and then would report to you?" That is how they did it, and the agents of the Khan's Wife soon made their ascent of the tower, returned and reported: "The construction is proceeding at full speed. Every day one thousand bricks are placed. The tower to date already surpasses in height the highest structures in the city. To such a height it is rather difficult to lift the building materials. This is why it takes such a long time. The construction of such an unheard of huge tower structure is proceeding at its utmost limit of possibilities, and to accelerate the construction in a shorter time frame is not at all possible."

But for the Khan's Wife these work tales were mere empty excuses, which were fabricated by them in order to distract and to calm her—only so that she would not bother them. No, she will not remain calm until she sees everything herself. No longer heeding the admonitions of the cautious old woman, one day she announced her wish to the Supreme Vizier himself that she had all intentions personally to visit the construction site, for which purpose she demanded an appropriate retinue to be arranged for her.

On the scheduled day, accompanied by the Supreme Vizier, the chief master builder, and a flock of servants and supreme guards, the Khan's Wife went to inspect how the building of the minaret planned by her is proceeding. A pompous imperial cavalcade departed through the gates of the palace—and instantly along its road hung a huge giant of a structure made of reddish brown brick over them, and it became taller and taller the closer they moved to it. It seemed to be moving up a steep staircase towards the sky. And when the imperial cavalcade stopped at the base of the tower, as if at the bottom of an out-of-this-world gigantic tree, and the Khan's Wife got off the carriage, it appeared to her that this reddish brown brick tree had filled half of the universe. The Khan's Wife seized by a mad ecstasy, did not perceive the ground under her feet, and had it not been for the ladies of her retinue, who were holding her arms, she would have swirled up lighter than a tiny flake and flown to the top of the tower. Turning away from everyone, the Khan's Wife began to walk decisively to the entrance of the minaret.

The area in front of the tower had been cleared of construction debris and smoothed out; all along its edge a crowd had gathered: construction workers, slaves and just gawkers. Not paying them any mind, far removed from her suite and guards, the Khan's Wife entered the tower, accompanied only by the stooped harem keeper, three servant girls and the chief master builder. Impatiently, she hastily walked up the staircase. In the back, one could hear how, breathing heavily at the steep ascent, one of the servant girls could barely keep up with her. As one ascended higher, the darkness within the tower shaft had become denser, and soon it would have been pitch dark, if not for the servant girl walking in the back illuminating the spiral staircase with a lantern. The inner walls along this staircase had been blackened by the torch fires of the construction workers. The young Wife of the Khan, picking up the lap of her skirt, was climbing quickly and skillfully. After some time the darkness in the shaft of the tower began gradually to dissipate. At the very end of the vertical tower tunnel the midday sun shone brightly, blinding one's eyes. Finally, the Khan's Wife reached the upper construction platform in the tower. Because the hazardous close quarters of the upper part of the shaft had narrowed, where even two persons could not pass each other, the servant girl with the lantern had fallen behind for some time now.

Either this was due to the drastic change from coming out of the darkness to bright sunlight or from the unaccustomed height, but the head of the Khan's Wife started to spin. Catching her breath somewhat, she looked around. Under her feet was the wooden scaffolding, the brickwork had been raised up to waist level, and over and below it she saw the city from a bird's eye view. The capital lay there below, at her feet in a disorderly and huge spread. The slender and proud minarets next to the stern mosques, the lofty palaces, from below appearing almost like the roof of the world, from here seemed minor, amusing, toy-like little houses, thrown about by a child's hand.

End of the Legend • Abish Kekilbaev

An unparalleled joy seized the Khan's Wife. To no purpose had she been so upset and distressed earlier; the tower's construction has been already finished, and it was marvelous! It was now absolutely towering over the entire ancient city. The Khan's Wife was avidly, with an insatiable gaze, looking at the huge spacious city, and suddenly, turning aside, she noticed not far from her a man standing motionless, leaning at the edge of the brickwork. She surmised that this was the master, but being all covered from head to toe in mortar, probably embarrassed for his unsightly appearance, he had the appearance of a frightened boy. He did not utter a sound, and did not make a single movement. It was amazing and amusing for her to see that this most unique skilled craftsman, able to raise to the heavens such a colossal and immense structure, can act like a wild, small hare hiding under a bush. Whether it was from compassion towards this pathetic man or due to his wild and amusing appearance, the Khan's Wife smiled unwittingly—her cherry-shaped lips widened with a sparkle of the whitest teeth. Although at this unbelievable height, on this snug construction platform they were entirely alone, and no witness could have seen her smile directed at this unworthy stranger, in her mind she censured herself and once again puckered up her lips in their customary cherry-shaped form. She also realized that it would not become her to tarry here any longer, and she picked up the lap of her skirt and headed for the staircase opening, where her servant girl awaited her with the lantern. At the turn, getting ready to step down into the opening, she looked back at the master and noticed only now that he was very young, still but a youth. His face had pronounced cheekbones of a native of the steppes, his nose was straight and his huge eyes, taking up half of his face, were mysteriously sad.

While boarding the royal golden carriage, she raised her head and once again looked at the top of the minaret. She managed to see the master looking down, but it was impossible to discern from this distance his facial expression. She only smiled, lowering her head and remembering how confused and amusing he had appeared to her.

After this visit, the Khan's Wife no longer was concerned, as previously, about the fate of the minaret being built. Upon her return to the palace, she once again resumed her former pastime and amusement, went on her daily walks in the park, and held at the pond lively and merry bathing sessions. But now, to her heart's delight savoring the hands of her masseuse-girls, she no longer would clutter her head with various somber thoughts. Day in day out she would calmly observe how the object of her dreams—the tower—was growing. But one day, she became alarmed in all seriousness when she did not see at the edge of the upper platform the architect, who usually, all alone, would be laying the brickwork for the round wall, which noticeably became narrower at the very top, at the orifice of the tower. In other words, the master, who would usually be moving on top of the minaret like an ant at the tip of a straw, had vanished somewhere. Concerned about this, the Khan's Wife sent out people to ascertain whereto the builder had disappeared. The messengers returned with a reassuring report: nothing has happened to the master, he has merely moved down to the ground for a few days to prepare for the finishing work.

Summer had passed and autumn had begun. Then, unnoticed and quickly, as is usual in these lands, winter had passed. Prior to this the brick minaret, which without its facing, had the appearance of a dilapidated, bare giant savage, had now begun to be dressed from the bottom up in a checkered armor of construction scaffolding. Then, through the frequent wooden cubicles, would filter a remarkably blue, bright glaze. The blue expanse spilled from the bottom upwards.

Now for her long walks in the park, the Khan's Wife with her retinue had acquired a new goal: they followed the progress of the blue glaze rising on the wall of the tower. It was virtually before one's eyes that the minaret was acquiring this blueness, as if it was some gigantic, magic, plenteous ripening of fruit.

Donning the color of the azure sky, the tower, at times, would blend completely with it, and the people puttering about on the construction scaffolding like dark squiggles, were seemingly crawling along the veritable blue sky.

Ah, if only one knew how overjoyed and exulted the Khan's Wife had become to observe such a wondrous event! She even prided herself, as if she had designed this herself and built it with her own hands.

Every time now, when she, having had a good night's sleep, would in the morning run to the window, the obscure little people scampering about the body of the light blue tower had prepared a new surprise for her.

Now the tower would change its image every day. If earlier the crimson-reddish log would gradually become a gangly ungainly pole stretching onto the sky, having dressed in blue garb, the tower now became filled with such a gentle and poignant beauty, which now would be difficult to describe by mere words. Moreover, within the minaret's scope, now that it had donned its azure glaze, something quite understandable and even familiar to the Khan's Wife had appeared. And suddenly the thought struck her that the tower reminded one of someone's hand raised upwards in a gesture of welcome! She was astonished how precise the master had expressed the most significant and timid secret of her desire! Why, that is precisely what she had intended to instill in this future great tower forced so painfully out of her heart: the anxious longing for her beloved, to whom she conveys in distant lands her welcoming wave of her hand!

Another time it would seem to her that the tower is some remarkable herbaceous stalk, tender and juicy, of a milky ripeness, grown in the world's most fertile area of the lap of nature. And it can be barely seen swaying in the breeze, warmed by the tepid vapors of the fertile soil.

But having compared the tower with a slim stalk, the Khan's Wife is now concerned about her own created image that the powerful autumn and spring storms would not break the stalk, while the fiery heat of summer would not desiccate it.

She had ample imagination with each new day to picture the minaret either as a trusting tender small child with naïve camel-like eyes, or a warrior on horseback in shining armor, with a long spear in hand. Or another time, as a ridiculous tramp on the road, begging for alms, stopping at a house and looking into its window. At times she imagined that it is the Emperor occupying the tallest throne in the world, flouting the sky with his crowned head...

She wanted to understand the reasons for such a multifarious nature of the minaret. Another incomprehensible matter was, why despite the obvious fact that the work had been completed, the master architect still continues to putter about in the cupola and simply won't announce the completion of construction? Moreover, right under the cupola, from the side facing the park and the palace, the master, for some reason, had left a gaping opening and is in no hurry to close it. And she, the carefree one, has been bathing there in her birthday suit, not attaching much thought neither to the gap in the tower nor to the master puttering about on the cupola.

But now she became careful, because a suspicion had arisen in her that this man-ant on the tower had already managed without pangs of conscience to study her nude body to its innermost and little secret recesses...

Now, going out on her walk just as previously, she would come up to the pond and from there look closely at the minaret. And a daunting feeling would seize her that the tower seeks to commence with some sinister and risky negotiations... The tower would send some coded language signals known only to the two. No one in her entourage should find out about these negotiations. The tower always waited for her and became very lonesome if it couldn't see the Khan's Wife even one day. When she went into the palace, the tower looked down in sorrow into her bedchamber windows, and when she went out for her walk, the tower would instantly sparkle with joyful patches of light.

It seemed as if each day the minaret came increasingly closer to the palace. Days and nights it stood right at the fence to the park, not daring to jump over it, and it looked in her direction with melancholy and hope.

It appeared to the Khan's Wife that there was a love message encrypted to her in a mysterious language in the minaret, and she would sit at the window for hours on, as if a scholar in front of ancient and decrepit scrolls unable to uncover the secret of bygone letters.

She found that this masonry structure reminded her of her own person. After all, inside of her under the cover of a magnificent appearance without sorrow, a profoundly hidden melancholy was lurking for an unexplored meeting with someone who would remove from her soul all the sadness and would appease this soul. Incidentally, not only did the tower irritate her soul concerning unexplored matters, but it also hinted with a secretive compassion: 'Don't tell me that you still have not comprehended a thing?' And following this reproach the vision came to the Khan's Wife of the architect's youthful face with his hopelessly sad and huge dark eyes... It seemed to her that her heart is overwhelmed with emotions of gratitude towards him for the fact that he was able to guess so precisely her yearning and had depicted her so aptly in the configurations and hue of the masonry minaret.

But perhaps he had depicted his own yearning for his vain hopes by this azure tower? And these are his magic eyes continuously looking through her windows at her with reproach?

What reasons would he have for reproaching her? Is it possible that it is for the fact that she had provided him the opportunity to exhibit his talent and his art—in all of their exalted perfection—to the entire world?

And why is it that he is delaying with the final completion of his creation, and he doesn't lay the bricks there and does not seal up this unsightly gaping space under the cupola of the minaret?

The Khan's Wife ordered the royal coach to be ready and once again she went off to inspect the minaret. The timid and humble appearance of the tower, which presented itself when viewed from the park by approaching it by road, began suddenly to change drastically. Rather than exhibiting timidity, she saw in it the arrogance of an unapproachable beauty! This time the Khan's Wife did not ascend the tower. She only deigned to enquire from the chief master builder when the construction will finally be completed, to which he answered in a rather vague way: "Once the master finds that one tower line that he had planned and will stretch it outside, on that day everything will be completed!"

On her return trip, the Khan's Wife constantly looked out of the coach window, and her eyes did not deceive her: the more they were moving away from the minaret, the more it would lose its menacing and arrogant appearance, and changed to an ingenuous-marvelous giant.

As she entered her chambers and looked out the window: it was still this same desultory head of a roadside beggar protruding above the wall of the park border, suspended on an elongated haggard body and a thin neck.

The Khan's Wife realized that all these changes in the minaret's image were not accidental.

Despite his youth, the master architect is eminent and talented. He had profoundly mastered the conception of his royal patroness—to express in this minaret all the pure love and yearning of the Khan's Wife separated from her Lord, who had left on a distant campaign. And he has brilliantly created it in such a manner that at a distance, from the most remote approaches, the minaret appears as if it is calling forth with a raised hand: "Hurry, my love, hurry up and come!" But then why is the tower so arrogantly turning up its nose when one comes closer to it? By doing this, will the master not infuriate the Lord? Will the great Amir like this strange disposition of the tower, which at first, from afar lovingly beckons, and thereafter, nearby, disdainfully turns away from one? And yet another delusion: looking at the minaret from the palace—it appears mournful and as a gravely offended person. But this is not the case—on the contrary, it should be that the minaret must express the boundless happiness of the young Wife of the Khan after so many years of loneliness waiting for her master to come back from the wars, and then holding her in his strong yet tender embrace…

This master is gifted and powerful like a magician, except perhaps unable to compel stones to shed human tears. It shouldn't be just a chance occurrence that such strange attributes are granted to a tower. This is not a chance occurrence, but has rather been done deliberately. How shall she react now, if this secret intention by the architect would become public knowledge, not only to her? And in the markets evil rumors, prone to the point of vilification, will spread… And here is also that gap at the very top, and that has been noticed by the people…

The Khan's Wife summoned the old woman of the harem and ordered her to send out throughout the city spies and informers, in order for them to sniff out and listen to what people are discussing concerning the near-complete minaret. But these spies—who were called the "Soulless Ones"—were not able to report anything of a specific nature: saying that the people are captivated by the great wisdom and noble act of the Khan's Wife for preparing for the *Lord* such a wondrous present, and they are equally praising the talented young architect, who had been able to implement her idea into this awesome creation.

The Khan's Wife was not quite at ease concerning the validity of these reports, compiled by the venal spies, the Soulless Ones, but nonetheless she felt certain pangs of conscience, calmly telling her that she is getting worked up and rushing about to no purpose because of some nonexistent triviality.

There should be no reason to fear malicious rumors. Virtuous city folk see in this marvelous minaret the embodiment of her sincere conjugal emotions towards the valiant Amir. Thus, coming back victoriously, the *Lord*-warrior will still from afar perceive in the tower all of her boundless yearning for him, and coming closer, he will be convinced that the tower does not notice anyone next to it, but remembering the only one, the desired and long-awaited one.

The young architect had splendidly and exactly rendered all of her emotional secret desires, not having met and talked to her previously, and now the great Amir, having seen the tower, will only find perfection in its rendition, and a flawless purity of its design. May that day come soon! And when it comes, she shall transform into a white-winged bird of paradise, flap her wings, and hearing the mighty and ardent breath of her Lord, she will soar over the clouds to the heights of happiness. While her rival, the Baybishe, will have nothing left but to burn up from envy and impotent malice. This old hen now surely imagines how she will upon her return from the campaign boastfully list her achievements—how many roads she had travelled, how many conquered lands she had seen, on how many elephants and camels they had transported their war trophies, given to her personally… Well, let her, her small wings, though, will drop off and like a shot bird she will tumble down, when before her, in all its splendor, the gigantic azure minaret will appear, the new miracle of this world! She would not see this even in her dreams! And the Lord, at long last, shall be convinced that such a majestic victory reception his Senior Wife would not have been able to arrange, no matter how long she would have lived with him and whatever trials and tribulations she would have gone through with him. The Khan would have been convinced completely that no matter of what noble birth her origin, Baybishe, whom he had raised to the throne with great solemnity and in every way sought to ennoble her in the eyes of the people, she is only but a tightwad trembling over her treasures and a primitive female, capable of getting pregnant from even a careless touch of her husband's hand.

The great Amir can see right through people, he reads their thoughts without guessing, and it would not be difficult for him to learn how pure his young wife is in her love for him, and in all her emotional intentions, and how wise and with a foresight beyond her years. But she will not seek to build herself up in vain, stressing these words: just look, what a wondrous present I have prepared for you! No, she will conduct herself as afore, humbly and pleasantly in a natural sort of way. Her passion, as if it were a sea filling up her soul, she will restrain, she will not spill even one drop in vain, but in a chaste manner, diffidently and passionately, as on a first, nuptial night, will return this passion to the one who had been able to summon it in her. But let this timid restraint not impede his understanding that as a woman who knows the value of her happiness and is able to value her man, she is able to respond to his royal love with like royal dignity.

If only that day would come sooner when she will flood the entire palace in the waves of her unrestrained jubilation!

The azure minaret is fated to become the staircase on which she will ascend to the heights of her dream. And she is ready to kiss the golden hands of the master who had erected it, step by step to the stellar sky. If only he would not hold back the construction, and would, as soon as possible, seal up this awful gap right under the dome. However, how will the Lord feel, when he notices, naturally, the tower's mask of dejection and offense, when one looks at it from the side of the Khan's palace? Or will the Khan calmly, simply solve the riddle which torments it? Certainly, he will solve it, for there is nothing in this world of secrets and puzzles inaccessible to the intellect of the Lord, who has forced four sides of the world to their knees. Meanwhile, before his return, she has to resolve the problem of the strange distinctive features of the new minaret all by herself.

But what if…this melancholy mask on the minaret ready to come alive, what if this is a horrible sign of a secret feeling, for which, even by mentioning it, a fierce punishment is due by severing the tongue of the sinful speaker? The Khan's Wife recalled—at which point she looked back cautiously—that yonder, on the top of the tower, she had seen the expression on the face of that young master… He had raised his eyes, and their eyes met. And she had read everything in his desperate, frightened and insane eyes. No mistake about it, he was in love…dying, with a love without hope. And he had expressed it all in the form, lines and hues of the gigantic and wondrous minaret. What will happen now when the all-perceptive mind of Amir will learn of this at the very first encounter with the tower? He cannot pass over this matter which had become obvious even to his inexperienced young wife.

Moreover, the Khan's Wife had been frightened by her own unexpected conclusion, audaciously intruding her lovely head like an assailant at night. The azure minaret, ever present in her window, appeared now much closer and seemed, without compunction, defiant. As though it confirmed: 'No, there is no mistake about it, it is precisely so. Glory be to Allah, at long last you have fathomed it all. And be it so, what will you say, what answer will you give?' It appeared to her that the minaret had detached itself from its burial mound elevation, made a huge step forward, jumping right up to the building. It is about to jump into her bedchamber… In a burst of an absolute terror she recoiled from the window, ran out of her bedchamber and towards the part of the palace where one could not see the frightful minaret through any of the windows.

How then could one rid oneself of such persistent attention by the azure tower? And how should one reprimand the creator of all this, the madly insistent architect?

Her first thought had been to issue an order to forcefully bring in the obstinate one, who had lost his mind, and to subject him to punishment for his deliberate delay in completing the construction of the minaret. One should, by the scruff of his neck, grab this youth possessed by demons and shake him to his senses, so that he would forget even thinking about his insane love and would be praying to God for his head to remain intact. Such unheard of insolence by this youth without kith or kin was driving the Khan's Wife out of her mind. Her soul raged like a thunderstorm, ranting and raving. Just look at him, what puny creature to turn up, a frail famished one, who did not even dare to lift his eyelashes, but look at him! No wonder, after all, this despicable snoop, this loathsome skirt-chaser, crawled around for hours on his watch tower! One needs to remove him from sight by all means! Otherwise, from thousands of vile-smelling mouths of marketplace habitués will crawl out and flow the most dreadful and filthy gossip. And this wicked screwball, reaching out his hand towards the moon in order to nab it, but in a timely fashion one has to bring him to his senses. It's not very good if someone without kith or kin, a vagabond, a dirty builder dares—be it even in his thoughts!—to encroach upon the chaste purity of the Khan's marital bed! Even if one living soul in this world would learn about this—grief will come to the young Wife of the Khan, and her dreams to glorify throughout the ages the name of the Lord of the world and to extol her pure, passionate, and boundless love for him—grief and shame! But while she is the great empress, the wife of the Amir himself, she has the power with one motion of her hand to remove from earth this savage commoner and his blasphemous solicitations. She will now call for the harem keeper for the latter to report to the Vizier, and the Great Vizier shall no later than the following dawn put away the scoundrel in the deepest bottom of a stone zindan. The matter shall be resolved by a diligent executioner with his axe, who shall chop off his head along with its criminal thoughts, and then no one shall get wind of the heinous tricks of the mad architect. Thus, instantly and at its full gallop the life of the unsurpassed master, who was able to create the greatest work of architecture, but could not master his carnal appetite, and had been unable to subdue his built up passions, shall be cut short. And he should blame himself for this! She is pure and not guilty—before Allah, before the people, and before her Lord.

In any case, one needs to make haste. The news that the Lord had turned around his army to return home she had received just recently. No rumors could have reached him as yet. The state of affairs stands at this moment thusly: one has to end it with this pervert, and to assign the finishing work and completion of the minaret to the chief builder.

But it is unlikely that one can cover up the traces of the committed crime entirely. Is the great Amir really blind as not to notice the degree of diabolic treachery and shamelessness with which the azure tower is virtually invading the bedchamber of the Khan's Wife? Can one have an omniscient mind and not notice that behind all of this, an unbridled desire and a most candid and violent amorous lust is lurking?

The Khan's Wife did not notice that in the burst of her somber thoughts she had bit through her lip. What can one do? How can one act here most judiciously? Or, perhaps, one should round up all the slaves, convicts, prisoners and criminals from their prison cells, and order them to destroy this disgraceful minaret down to its foundation? But…but what will the peoples' rumors consider this to be? How will people, who live on the other side of the fenced palace grounds, construe this? They have known this for some time now, while she had only begun to discover this lately. Perhaps amidst everyone she is the least informed… After all, the saying goes that there is no smoke without fire, so that for the people it shall become even more so suspicious should she order to destroy the minaret, which is her very own brainchild. And would she be able to explain the reason for her inconsistency to her Lord?

The Khan's Wife returned to her chambers and came up to a window. The tower was still in its unfinished state—in the gap, the eye under the cupola's drum, as previously, something is constantly dashing to and fro. And it is only this unsealed dark gap in the minaret's forehead which destroys all the vibrant and wondrous elements in this otherwise grandiose structure. With such appearance the minaret does not hide it in the least, but rather cries out without words about its disgrace. It is beyond anyone to remove it except by the master himself. Like a mighty sorcerer who is able to bring to life the miracle of the azure tower, he does not wish to do this until he obtains his object of lust. She realistically pictured the image of the swarthy dark-haired youth with huge eyes, who, yonder in the tower had cast a timid and pitiful glance in her direction, but at the same time a glance of doomed intransigence. O, unhappy lad, you are indeed madly in love, and you're not afraid of dying, if you have so overtly coveted this…

The entire secret of sorcery for this tower lies in that the master had no other input into his work but his recklessly blind love. It would appear that long ago he had already forgotten what had been required of him as a true builder, a skilled architect, and he had been completing his work not to the strict rules of his craft, but in a total intoxication of his amorous feelings. And he, unhappy poor devil that he is, had embodied in the azure tower all his unrequited and doomed love. Looking from afar at it, it may seem that one cannot notice a thing, aside the welcoming sweep and the sad blueness of distant and expectant eyes. Coming closer one perceives the pain of despair and an uncontrollable yearning for love for the sake of which one is not afraid even of death. By this it is not difficult to surmise that this madman had decided to remain there under the minaret's cupola, staring through the gap, and to die without leaving the place, and he will not for anything come down by his own free will. Therefore, one needs to go up and explain to him the total futility of his insane claims, and should this not be effective, then one should tearfully plead with him: 'Be so kind, do finish your work quickly. Do not incur to your detriment your own death, and to mine—an everlasting shame of dishonor!' If he truly loves her, he will not be able to refuse her request. However, if his youthful soul, by now profoundly perverted by the *shaytan,* the devil, would have to be brought back to the true road, making adjustments with the executioner's axe, then, all the same, the news about the pernicious desire which had arisen will come down with an appalling voice from the top of the minaret, through the dark hole of the remaining gap, and will dissipate all over the world. But then, o woman, only one thing shall remain: to artfully circumvent the circumstances, to outwit the shaytan who had tempted the young man. In order to save the life of a traveler dying of thirst in the desert, there is only one method: to give him water to drink to his heart's content.

Then he, leaning back from the vessel, closing his eyes, shall hear the song of angels. For a lofty master, who had built such a wondrous vessel of beauty, who had imbued in it all his anguish of love and sealing it with a magical seal, it is not difficult to unseal such a vessel, if one provides him with a painkiller to alleviate his pain, rewarding him—may it be only for a brief instant—with what people call happiness. It would seem that one needs to artificially create such an instant of happiness, and to reward the master with it, in order to motivate him to finally release from the sealed vessel his own created beauty, now already inspired by his experienced instant highest pleasure in life. But as far as the guile, that 'kitchen of miracles' and that farce of conversions, reincarnations, visions and apparitions in broad daylight—all these mysteries she, the Khan's Wife, shall invent by herself, and of it neither all the honest people nor the great Lord himself shall ever find out, for all eternity! No one will ever learn about the strange and monstrous solicitations of the young architect. Everyone will only observe one thing: the image of the universal joy of the Khan's Wife, who finally, after her long wait, has welcomed her valiant Amir the Warrior. After many years he had come back safely from his campaign and had embraced her in his warm conjugal embrace.

Let it be thus. Inshallah! And may the master of the rebellious hope and the architect of the fleeting thought find an end to his suffering.

Finally, the Khan's Wife had been able to bring into one stream the forty small running rivulets of her thought and she felt reassured. Coming to a concrete conclusion, it seemed as if she had tightened her belt, standing up straight and confident.

Early in the morning she summoned the harem keeper. All the other servant girls and the court handmaidens she had chased off from the entrance, and ordered them not even to approach the threshold. All these maids, masseuses of fragrant ointments, lady's maids, everyone who had been instrumental in bathing, rubbing, dressing, and sprucing up the Khan's Wife, were all crowded together in confusion in the vestibule. The old woman came out of the bedchamber and entered the vestibule only towards noon. Such had been her lengthy conversation with her mistress. The harem keeper cast her predatory look at all the servant girls, who at once became quiet, then she chose one, ordered her to remain, and the rest she told to immediately go to their tiny cell-like rooms, The court ladies and servant girls, who did not learn the reasons for such an unusual manner of starting their morning, went to their rooms shrugging their shoulders, bewildered. In the afternoon, the carriage of the Khan's Wife with her suite left through the gates of the palace park in the direction of the minaret.

End of the Legend • Abish Kekilbaev

As if it had been tied down to the poles outside an indoor market, the horse and carriage royal column remained a long time under the tower. Then, raising clouds of dust, the decorous carriages dashed back in the direction of the palace.

The following day, going for her walk in the park, the Khan's Wife noticed that something is stirring in the dark gap under the tower's cupola—and almost right before her very eyes, the ominous opening began to fill up, and then it closed up completely.

Three days later, the minaret's facing had been completed. Coming up to the window, the Khan's Wife saw that a pleasant new acquaintanceship awaits her: the azure minaret, unrecognizably joyous, tall and graceful, presented itself to her.

...When the great Lord had returned victoriously he held a grandiose feast, at that time, despite his young years, the architect of the azure minaret was honored and rewarded with a full chalice of gold dinars.

Accepting the *Lord's* gift, the architect cautiously glanced in the direction of the royal enclosure where the Khan's Young Khansha was solemnly sitting, not responding to his thievish look, she did not even so much as move her eyebrows, but hastily scanned Baybishe's retinue. But the Senior Wife and her attendants had no expressions of suspicion on their faces. And the heart of Khan's Young Khansha, many a day beating irregularly from various doubts, suspicions and fears, finally became calm and re-entered the everyday stream of life.

At the end of the feast, when her crowned husband deigned to stay at her palace, the jubilation of the young Khan's Wife became boundless. Impatiently she followed the course of the sun. The summer sun, which had become lazy, just wouldn't leave the sky. But as soon as it had descended into its nest and disappeared beyond the horizon, the Khan's Wife along with all of the living and nonliving world breathed a sigh of relief, bidding farewell to the intense heat of the day, which had earlier appeared from the desert. Now one could settle in the cool semidarkness, ridding oneself from all the oppressive worries of the day, near the tranquilly babbling fountain. O, how many years has the cauldron of her love's suffering been heating up, but now just a bit longer and it will seethe and throb like a mountain spring!

Her interest was centered on the door through which her beloved would appear. Yet no matter how she awaited this moment, when the door, ornamented with gold, would swing open—this moment, however, was in no hurry to arrive.

This night passed for her in an unbearably agonizing watch of the door. The chambermaids in the morning, entered with lowered heads, although she was able to read their words of consolation in their eyes: 'Nothing to worry about. It's merely that the master is rather tired after all these lengthy ceremonies at the great *toy* feast. It's not proper for a Taksyr, a gentleman, to run immediately like a young and impatient groom to the bedside of his filly.'

All day long she drifted about the courtyard, not knowing what to do. She thought first perhaps a walk in the park, now grown wild, but she refrained from doing this, fearing that by chance she might disturb the Lord, who loved to spend time in solitude near the quiet spring.

The first few days she reined in her impatience, showing the Lord her consideration: 'After all, war is not a child's game, and he must be dead-tired, let him now sleep to his heart's content, rest and recuperate.'

But days passed and he did not come. She listened attentively at every sound beyond the door. But the Lord did not walk his half of the way to her place. Now, throughout the nights she would toss and turn without sleep in her bed, which seemed to her as if it had been studded with thorns.

She began to look closely and with distrust at the faces of her handmaidens, and kept an eye on her old harem keeper. But they, rather than bringing her all the latest gossip of the court, they themselves were ogling her in expectation. And then the Khan's Wife sought to stand firm, trying not to show them how utterly gloomy and depressed she had become. But is it possible to hide this from the attentive and watchful eyes of servants, who had been trained in such a fashion as to understand without words and to anticipate every wish of their mistress? And thus they are tiptoeing around, not making a racket and not rollicking in laughter, as usual when they had frolicked in the past together with the Khan's Wife.

She had now become almost a recluse, would not leave her chambers even for her favorite lawn. In her bedchamber she indulged in solitary dreary thoughts. Her head would begin to ache and she would come to the window. The azure minaret, as if detecting her in a

End of the Legend • Abish Kekilbaev

crowd, sent her a friendly smile. Then she just stood at the window a long time, as if complaining to the tower that the great Amir is offending her with his inattentiveness and incomprehensible change of attitude towards her.

But the ecstatically self-complacent minaret, sparkling in its blue attire, wanted nothing of the suffering of the young Wife of the Khan: it was gaily winking at the celestial luminary reigning over the universe. Ah, but it no longer peeked into her chamber looking like a dervish beggar of a despondent appearance standing at the fence. Now its appearance was much like a self-satisfied city dweller, who had achieved considerable success in life. And for the young Wife of the Khan it was somewhat distressing to feel this disdain expressed towards her by this dandy all dressed up in blue. After all, it had been her idea; she had initially created it in her imagination, then she let each brick go through her heart and each step in the staircase. While this self-complacent minaret began yet to remind her with malicious pleasure: 'Do you remember, my dear, how you had ignored me, looked in my direction in an arrogant manner, as if seeing no one? I asked just for a droplet of attention, just a sip of mercy, but you did not quench my thirst, you did not feed a starving one. Now what? Is it good to be hungry? Is it good to die of thirst?' At this point the Khan's Wife suddenly remembered the architect. On the last occasion, at the feast, she had been able to get a better look at the young master craftsman. A wide, receding forehead, sharp cheekbones and a straight nose... And those huge dark eyes, wherein the radiance of a lofty mind filters through some sort of alarming sadness. Should be interesting to know what does this youth with a talent given him by Allah, what does he do now? It didn't seem at all that he had been greatly enthusiastic about the present of the gold dinars in the large chalice. He doesn't resemble a money-grubber or moneymaker. It's obvious that he is heart and soul dedicated to his brainchild. Indeed, he shall not forget his azure tower so soon, particularly the last days of its completion... When he had been so cruelly, rudely and shamelessly deceived.

At first, the Khan's Wife was incapable of recalling that incident without breaking out in happy laughter. And from this good-natured, somewhat frivolous laughter her heart would become light and pure. As if her soul had been cleansed by a vernal high water. Each time she would laugh, imagining the ingenuous, inexperienced youth. Yet at the same time she would feel a tiny bit ashamed that she had played a trick on him—and in some incredible way her compassion would be on his side. During such times she experienced compassion and even a liking for him. How had it been that the unbearable slave servant girl had recalled jokingly: 'I will never let you go, stay here with me, and stay here forever!' Isn't he great, this djigit? See what he desires? Seems he's willing to hug the Lord's wife in his embrace all his life!'

Relating in detail this entire sordid story, the young servant girl kept on giggling, and along with her, her most august mistress would break out in laughter. But later, and rather soon, she had virtually found control over herself, and ceased laughing. And this was not due to her considerations that she felt it improper to laugh along with her slave girl. Listening to a by no means chaste detailed narrative of her servant, who had performed the mission as assigned by her mistress, the Khan's Wife suddenly perceived a dagger piercing her deep in her heart. Her blood started flowing from this wound after the Khan's Wife realized that the words, which the youth had been babbling in his ravings of passion before that girl, were not intended at all for her... And then the Khan's Wife, with a frozen fish smile on her lips, began to pose questions herself, and came up with an entire pile full of them. But the more details she learned, the greater the pain increased in her chest. And each movement of the passionate youth, each of his words, and any distinctive feature of his male mannerisms, of which she now learned, were wounding her heart more and more.

She didn't take her squinting eyes off the slave girl sitting across from her, and with some grimly concealed jealousy listened to her, examining attentively her now glowing cheeks, her eyes sparkling with joy, lips swollen with passion, examining the movement of her svelte and lithe body, which bore within it some sort of secret unattainable for the Khan's Wife... That precious, rare feminine secret, which bypasses many people in this world. And if it so happens that it should suddenly open up before a woman—the happy chosen one shall hasten irreversibly into the flow of emotional caress of the one who worships her with his great love.

Some of us are fated to experience such happiness, while others, on the other hand, are denied this completely. Should be interesting to know to which category does she belong? And if she has experienced such happiness, can it be repeated? Or all one can only do is reminisce about it with a tranquil smile—for many years thereafter or one's entire life? Is it possible that happiness could find its way of returning from the past? But at present, however, it happened that the

End of the Legend •Abish Kekilbaev

love for her, which had erupted in the heart of the young architect, she had by her own will personally passed on to another woman.

In those days, when she had consulted the old woman harem keeper on how to save the life of the genius young fellow, the architect, as well as to save the great creation of his, carefully selecting from among the numerous methods of action that one-and-only perfect one which should bring about a successful result and the fellow back to the living—they had chosen the option of dressing up the slave girl in the clothes of the Khan's Wife as her substitute. A slave girl closely resembling the Khan's Wife was to be sent to the top of the minaret. Her bedchamber servant was chosen. Now she was ecstatically relating what she had to go through in the embraces of the cheated architect, and judging by her story, one got the impression that she had not been at all distressed by this role which had befallen her.

During her as yet none-too-long life, the Khan's Young Khansha heard it often said that the pain of a belated regret about a lost opportunity for happiness, nagging at one's heart, is known to each and every woman. Therefore, recognizing this event and considering that it does not pertain to her directly, the Khan's Young Khansha sought to forget about it at the earliest possible time. As to her own unintentional sadness and heartaches, she regarded them as a passing whim. She tried not to give it much thought any longer, while the perilous secret which only three of them knew—herself, the harem's overseer and the slave-servant girl—she tried to totally erase from her memory. Next morning, when she saw that instead of the gaping aperture under the minaret's dome there was a blank wall already covered by an azure glaze, the Khan's Young Khansha gave a sigh of relief, feeling that in her heart also some sinister and fatal breach had been closed. Yesterday's tempest of alarm had calmed and had changed to a light breeze of hope rendering salvation. And when she learned that the Lord had personally inspected the minaret and had been satisfied by this creation of the architect, she calmed down completely. But now panic and alarm once again overwhelmed her, and the reason for this was no doubt the fact that it appeared as if the Lord had forgotten the way to the female part of the palace and had not even once deigned it fit to visit his Young Khansha. Her entire being was depressed from her unfulfilled hopes—not unlike an abandoned puppy running from one dump to another in search of any morsel to eat in order to survive. But she, the Khan's Young Khansha, of a true blue-blooded and white bone heritage, could she possibly seek pleasures on the side, as if she were some sort of a tart-concubine, who, having left the bed of her Lord spouse, is headed to the first available stud?

That last thought was most intrusive: "..left the bed of her Lord spouse…" But did she really have such frequent bed-visits? Perhaps only on sleepless lonely nights… squirming as if on a table of torture… seeking thereafter to lull herself to sleep. Why should one be so sacrificial and faithful and patient—all for the sake of such a bed? Did she ever dream of this earlier? Was it for this that she sought to please her Lord, giving all her treasures, which were presented to her by him, in return for the building of the azure minaret? But then what is a case of valuables for him, who had swept into his domain all of the world's treasures, and for whom it is nothing to throw these valuables to beggars, for it will not deplete his treasury. And what of it now, having shown such generosity he can allow himself, being under one roof with her, not even once to drop by her bedchamber?

Remembering what images of the most lofty of homages in meeting Amir, the Conqueror, she had fancied, the Khan's Young Khansha would blush in shame. And isn't her love for Amir an even greater delusion? Be it so, but how painful is it to part with one's sweet dream world? Even though it may have been merely illusory, but it was a hope nonetheless! The sweet throes of madness harbor expectations of a celebration! And such madness fills the world to be relived from generation to generation.

And is it possible that in any one's heart a genuine, indefatigable love can awaken if another such heart cannot be found? Without a responding mad love, could one possibly experience love of distraction? Yet, on behalf of the Lord, her spouse, who is wearing his crown of diamonds, did she ever sense even the slightest sign of such love? In that case, what constitutes love as drawn by her fancy but is the making of her own imagination? Would it not have been precisely such a delirious whim which had imbedded itself in the head of that ridiculous madman in the azure minaret?

Terror gripped the Khan's Young Khansha caused by her own confession to herself that she had allowed for a certain doubt to arise concerning the sacrosanct marital union with Amir. And this is equivalent to casting doubt on the sanctity of the very Creator of the World. Completely terrified, the Khan's wife whispered a prayer from the Koran three times. But the prayer could not purge the burden of doubt from her heart.

On that day she felt entirely worn out, she even moved about with difficulty. Her flesh seemed as if it were separating itself from her bones. Evening came to her as a desired salvation. She fell right unto her bed, when her servant girls had departed she instantly dropped off into a deep and hollow sleep like in a tomb, a sleep like a semi-fainting spell. Pleasant warmth filled her body. An invisible, mighty ray of bliss thrust itself from its mountainous heights and descended upon her, penetrating her skin and flesh, and penetrating into the depths of the skeletal structure of her entire being. A solar downpour gushed with its iridescent rain, cleansing her soul of her alarm, sadness, sorrowful thoughts, anger and vexation—everything concomitant with misfortune. The invisible mountain ray restored all her nerves which were tattered like bowstrings after a fiery shooting. "Rest to your heart's content, have no worries at all, and do not regret a thing"—as if they were seeking to instill confidence in her, the miraculous finger rays were stroking her hair, and upon their touch her immense headache, which was pounding with a sharp beak at her temples, was instantly eliminated. Swaying gracefully, some pliant shroud enveloped her from all sides. Now she saw nothing but this mysterious shroud before her eyes. The Khan's wife could not fathom whether she was asleep or awake. But no matter where this was taking place, in her sleep or in reality, before her eyes there suddenly appeared and froze in place, as if it were a pillar of light, someone's luminescent silhouette.

It was this last remnant of her slumbering consciousness—the most steadfast nocturnal watchdog—which made her concentrate on this silhouette. And the last remnant of her common sense called upon to guard her being, suddenly had become alert and began to waver anxiously at the very edge of her consciousness, irrepressibly dropping off into sleep. But now her watchdog sense perceived someone's approach.

The heavy gilt ornamented door, which separated her inordinately spacious bedchamber from the rest of the outside world, suddenly opened without a sound. Someone, also without making a sound, slipped inside. Someone entered, but indecisive on any other action, remained at the doorstep. Frightened, the Khan's Young Khansha, wanted to jump out of bed, but as if frozen, could not even stir. Her hands were listless. Straining to discern the whitish silhouette of the person, who was motionless like a statue in the door's narrow shaft of light, she sought to recognize him. The appearance of this human being in the semi-darkness was vague and vacillating as images of river reptiles under a thick layer of water, in riverbed slime. But now the intruder began to stir. A step forward, then another. Still she could not discern his face.

...O, Allah Almighty, who could this be? It would appear that his image does remind one of someone. At first, his amber-like shining round eyes became discernible. These eyes are looking at the Khan's wife imploringly, mournfully, as if reminding her of some long-standing resentment incurred without any explanations. In these eyes there is this mighty mournfulness, indeed, these eyes are superlative in their sadness. Yes, this look is familiar to her, as if it were something common and routine. But at this point, whose eyes these are, she is unable to recognize. Yet...who could it be who would look at her with such powerful mournfulness—eyes full of hope and hopelessness? O, Almighty One, how could she ever forget this!

After all, with each new encounter with him she would start trembling! Thereafter, in her thoughts she would repeatedly think of him... Who is he?

Eventually she began to realize that he was the one who loved her out of the gloom of hopelessness. She not only recognized these eyes of selfless and humble gaze, but also the swarthy facial features with the profound cheekbones, the straight and lofty nose, and the as-yet-childish mouth with the pouting lips. Indeed, that is the young architect who had erected the azure minaret.

But how was he able to intrude into the Khan's palace, where simply even a fly would be unable to fly into? There are hundreds of guards and servants; they are at every corner. For she had assumed that after that rendezvous with her substitute he had wised up and abandoned his attempts. As it turns out, he didn't. So this means that the sacrifice had been in vain, with all the dressing up and substitution, and in vain did they place the slave girl in royal garments. He was not satisfied with this alone, and he is still unconcerned with saving his own life, but with his thoughts to continue his fatal pursuit of bliss. So he is here, in the palace... What will happen if at this time the harem's old woman supervisor should come? He will not only destroy himself, but he will also place the mark of shame on her name forever.

The Khan's wife wanted to shout, angrily and imperiously, stamp her feet and to chase off this lecherous swamp tomcat, but her

End of the Legend • Abish Kekilbaev

mouth was sealed, she could not emit even the slightest squeak. However, it seemed that the young ustad, the master, noticed the Khan's wife silent anger, stopped and stood in place, looking despondent, almost touching with his knees the bedside of the Khan's wife. His face all distorted as if in pain, eyes blinking in despair, as some child ready to cry. He turned around and walked towards the door. And here is where she felt sorry for him. Sorry for herself. And when he had almost reached the door, she gathered up her strength, and though she still had no voice, she was able to make a sign with her hand: 'Do not leave. Come back. Come quickly to me.'

The uninvited guest hesitated, not knowing what the meaning of this wordless gush of the Khan's wife's commands meant and how to obey them. She reached out her hand to him and without any shadow of doubt signaled to him: 'Come back.' And he came back. They looked into each other's eyes. Suddenly she felt a chill. She thought that if at this time she would chase him off, she will lose him forever. She will lose these innocent and pure eyes. And, reaching out her arms, as lissome as bindweed, discarding all shame, she entwined them around the youth's neck.

She finally realized that this was him; it was for him that she waited all her life in secret passion. From now on she won't let him go free from her embrace. They merged and became a whole coalescence of two bodies. Their blood blended and tumultuously joined a mutual flow. For both, their former separate lives ended together and there was no return.

Her arms, entwined around the firm, strong and aromatic youth's figure, was filled with some wondrous strength, capable of crushing his body. Never before had the Khan's wife experienced such tempestuous ardor of sensuality. It melted the hard substance of their bodies without a trace of residue and turned them into a liquefied continuous flame.

But suddenly the steel grasp of her embrace ceased.

The Khan's wife lay there all debilitated, as a person after an attack of epilepsy. She perceived something damp and cold on her exposed breasts. She opened her eyes and saw the room in the soft diffused illumination of the night lights. There was no one next to her. In the distance, the massive entrance door glimmered with its gilt ornaments.

Aroused by a sudden alarm within her, the Khan's wife raised herself in bed and now became fully aware of her surroundings. Everything was believable and in its place: the round and all the four dark corners of her huge bedchamber.

Thrown over her shoulders, as if it were alive, a light down blanket like a tourniquet is hanging over her breasts. This tourniquet is through and through soaked with nocturnal perspiration and is moving on her body as if it were a cold snake who had reached her breasts in order to seek warmth. With a feeling of loathing, nauseated, the Khan's wife threw the damp blanket off her body.

And here a frenzied fury, perplexing to herself, gripped her, and the destitute result from it spilled out in a flood of sudden tears. The tears soaked her face and breasts, but she did not even bother to wipe them off. In her destitute delirium, she imagined that the more tears were shed the sooner they would extinguish the scorching coals of her unbearable suffering.

The Khan's wife wept for a long time, covering her face with her hands, her bare shoulders shuddering. And, without fail, following the tears a terrifying headache set in. It resounded like the striking of alarm bells in her temples. Now she certainly would not be able to fall asleep.

Before the crack of dawn next morning, the heavy gilt door swung open and the old woman harem keeper showed up in her bedchamber. Right behind her, with silly grimaces, peeking from behind her shoulder, with mischievous grins on their faces, a crowd of bedchamber servant girls and court ladies rushed in. Rushing up to her bedside, they circled the Khan's wife bed in a merry round dance and song. Not comprehending a thing, she lost her head from all their happy voices and their senseless and merry bustle, and she stared in amazement at her usual morning retinue of servants wondering whether they had lost their minds. But in turn, they also looked at her, and ultimately, seeing the look of their mistress, they all became quiet and lowered their heads in embarrassment as if by a command. Indeed, with her frightening appearance the Khan's wife could evoke nothing but fear and pity; confronting them was this pallid dead person, who had limped her way from the cemetery, bluish face, and sunken eyes with huge dark circles beneath them. Her eyes were begging only for one thing: to let her finally have her eternal peace after all her earthly torment. The old harem keeper jerked her head meaningfully for all to leave the bedchamber immediately. After that, being alone with the Khan's wife, she sat next to her and embraced this pallid dead woman, into which person her mistress had thus turned, and she began speaking in her old woman's creaky voice, stroking her hair tenderly and with due care:

- O, Allah…you look awful, my most precious mistress! Don't tell me that the great Amir has said something bad to you? To think of it—for some reason he left your bedchamber in a bad mood. What could have happened?

What is the old woman saying? The Khan's wife was shocked and her eyes grew large and frenzied.

- You said the great Amir…He…has been here?"
- Yes, o Great One… At night. To be sure, he stayed here only briefly, and then he left.

The Khan's wife, just as a bird shot down, dropped on the bed. The old woman bent down to her and saw that she had lost consciousness.

She came to only by noon. She saw sitting at her bedside the old woman, but she did not even begin to question her. The old woman also remained quiet, not possessing the courage to start speaking to her, and she only looked at her mistress with concern, gazing inquisitively into her eyes.

Yes, it so happened that due to her great misfortune she had committed an immense sin against her royal and wedded husband. Yes, this had been an act of adultery, not an actual one but one committed in a loathsome dream. Yet even this sole, delirious, and illusory crime had not been bypassed by the hawkeyed observation of the Arbiter of half of the world. He has caught her in the act at the location of the crime when in her dreams she submitted to copulation with another man, and had offered her passion to another man. For the Lord, wise to life's experiences, it would have been easy enough to figure it all out when looking at her tossing about in her bed, all perspired, and in her most intimate and tumultuous body movements…

Now that she was aware of the fact that her husband, the Khan, had seen everything with his own eyes and had a clear understanding, it had become so difficult for her to go on living and breathing, as if she had been oppressed by the fiercest most merciless of July afternoons. She was even afraid to emit a deep sigh in the presence of her slaves, being afraid even to involuntarily disclose to them that which she would never wish to acknowledge to herself.

Now she lived as if on a borrowed existence, dragging her body devoid of her soul which had died in it some time ago, by forcing herself to go on in life. She could care less even if one would sever her head. Now the most horrible and unforgivable was that of which she had accused herself; that which she had admitted freely herself. Only she was guilty before the great Amir. The young architect was not to blame at all. To be sure, he did fall madly in love with her, but he did not dare to approach her even one step and to transgress the taboo. But in her dream she had surrendered to him on her own free will and with a great deal of desire. Therefore, committing the entire transgression, all the blame for this sin, lies only on her alone. But if one should have asked whether she would have acted likewise had this happened not in her dream but in reality, she could not have provided a definitive answer. And another thing she understood that which she considered her fervent, profound and eternal love of her master, the diamond-crowned monarch, was nothing more than an inherent attraction and yearning of a female towards a powerful male, a woman's desire and her need for an iron fist, a domineering male. This was the longing of a woman and her need for an iron-clad, mighty hand not tolerating resistance to a hand of a warrior, leader and the Lord. And, who knows, had the young architect been able to somewhat steal into the palace and without hindrance reach her bedchamber, would she have acted differently than in her horrific-terrific and ardent dream? The devil, who had been able to seduce her in her nocturnal thoughts and dreams, could he have not mastered this during the day with its evil thereof? Moreover, she is ready in any case to accept any form of punishment for her committed lowly act of adultery against her royal and wedded husband, be this act perpetrated in reality or in a lascivious dream.

If at this moment, rushing into her bedchamber, her enraged husband had been tearing at her hair, had beaten her or had turned her over to the executioners to cut strips off her back or to drive the evil spirits out of her by pouring icy water over her, or simply stamp her with his feet, break all her bones and throw the bloody bagful to the devouring desert jackals—she would have accepted all these as a just punishment. But the Creator did not offer her even such a slave's happiness—to experience the beating of one's husband. In her utter despair she was capable of scratching her face, tear off her hair, and to beat her head against the indifferent stone walls.

Suicidal thoughts had dominated her completely during these days of her tormented solitary life, as if she were a fly, who had flown unto a dry hull of her dead being, weakly buzzing with her tiny wings or sitting-waiting in a dark corner, flapping its tiny paws. She was thinking over numerous ways of ending her life, and all were quite doable, but somehow this was not suitable for its implementation.

For there was no regret concerning loss of her vacillating and temporal life. As she began to hate her spiritual lapse from virtue, she likewise started to hate this life which had doomed her to slavery. Gratefully, she now perceived her dream as a farewell kiss of a vision unfulfilled. And she no longer was ashamed that she has had such a dream. She clearly understood how silly and sinful it would have been to ask the Heavens to have this dream repeated, and yet at the same time she was ready to declare to the Heavens that she does not wish to live a life without this dream of true and great human happiness.

But no matter how empty and senseless one's life would be, she has no right to willfully end it. It was not only by reason, but also by all her vital instincts and profound subconsciousness the Khan's wife realized that one should not commit such an act. Before her a deep abyss of decline had arisen, an abyss into which the fame of the Lord would collapse as a result of the shame incurred by his august wife. People of subsequent generations will no doubt condemn in all sorts of ways this act as one of shame of her royal husband, who had been chosen by God. No! She won't allow this.

As to the royal husband, well, there is still not one word from him. It had become a distressing and painful habit for her to sit, staring at the gilt-decorated door. What of it that her chambers are bright and spacious, and furnished with a fairytale luxury? For her they are worse than the most confined dungeon, more confined than a burial niche, where the dead person is placed wrapped in a shroud. O, how one wishes at times to grab an axe and to shatter this despicable golden door into slivers and to escape to freedom! O, to smash this entire despicable palace, to throw it into a heap of debris of all the oppression and burden of this cursed life, and on top of it to discard the axe!

One day she called for the old woman harem keeper. She ordered her to gather her entire entourage and the bedchamber servant girls, and she took them for a walk in the park. The palace servants and guards they met along the way greeted them with a deep bow. But it appeared to the Khan's wife that on their facial expressions one could no longer observe the former fear and respect; it was more that they were looking at her with compassion, and she also diverted her eyes. However, by some sense of eyesight in the back of one's head she felt the morose looks of her servants. Also, the womenfolk of her entourage marching beside her were walking with a sort of strained and estranged look, as if they just now had discussed among themselves some kind of unseemly matters and secret vice of their mistress.

She decided to avoid the places where earlier, when the Lord would be absent, she spent careless times with her ladies in waiting and her servant girls; the Young Khansha of the Khan headed for the more distant tree-lined walks, which she earlier did not visit too often, but even there she found no secluded quiet and cozy corner. It appeared to her that some illusory unkind eyes were staring at her from all sides; they seemed to appear simply from nowhere. Without getting her desired peace of mind, the Khan's wife hurried back to the palace.

From now on her royal domain would be the ungainly long—like the dragon's innards—and bleak bedchamber and additionally the window through which one espied a small portion of the park path. Finally, the source of her endless anguish ran dry and the spring of her cogitation became exhausted.

The days dragged on in a viscous and drawn-out manner like a twisted strand of rubber. But in comparison the nights, the cursed and sleepless ones, were a hundred fold more torturous. At night she became both Munkar and Nakir, who conduct a severe interrogation of the soul of the deceased person. During these nights she would descend to the very depths of her despair and would hate not only herself, but also everything which formed her life: including the naïve youth, who, unbeknownst to himself, had exhibited to the entire world his insane love, putting to shame and destroying her, the Young Khansha of the Khan, and the azure minaret, which had become an indisputable piece of evidence of their crime, and the misbegotten day when the messenger brought her the case with the valuables, and the arrogant Senior Wife of the Khan, who had become the cause of all of her senseless suicidal actions. And even for her own father and mother, who had discarded her into this, the most sorrowful of all places in the world, she harbored a grievous resentment.

May this pitch black night of witches be cursed, and these days and nights the babbling of all sorts of nonsense by the khauz with their fountains, and this bed and cursed blanket which did not hide but exposed her fatal secret hidden in the deep recess of her soul! Cursed be the heavens, which were calmly observing all the events on earth, and not interfering! Cursed be the very earth that obediently endures all of human perniciousness! Be cursed the world of humanity, bloodthirsty and merciless, perverting all lofty intentions of sincere people, making them in their despair beat their heads against stone walls!

But, though vehemently cursing the entire world, not even stopping mentioning the Creator, the Khan's wife did not place a curse on her husband, the Great Lord.

She was actually herself amazed at such absurdity. If one should reason sensibly, isn't He one of the first who had turned her life into downright hell? More than likely, removing her from his presence, he had prepared a consummate and horrible execution—a slow and agonizing death as result of her repentance and vexation devouring her insides like a beef tapeworm. It is likely that He would displace this evil by submitting her to a public persecution.

But what will he gain, what will all of her incredible suffering bring him? Will not the ruthlessness of an angry mob, beating her, bring forth pain in him? For after all she is his wife. What will the vile accusations of the masses do? Will he stand for all the calumny against her? Will he tolerate the verbal abuse directed at her? Something never heard of before? O, but doesn't he have pity for her, for it had been his doing to place her young life for kindling wood! He had maimed her life and caused her to shed bitter tears. May they fall upon his head!

And at this point the Khan's wife shuddered in horror. What is it that she is ranting in her evil delirium? As if she were the lowest of ordinary females, she had begun to defame the name of her royal spouse with her vile mouth!

How could she ever forget that she is the radiant Khan's wife, and not a lowly slave girl! Should Her Majesty find fault with the Ruler of the country before the masses?

The Khan's wife wrinkled her nose in disgust. She became disgusted with herself. At once she began whispering her prayer, fervently beseeching the Creator: "Almighty Allah, forgive me my words of abuse towards the great Amir; these words were so unworthy of my noble origins. Please forgive me at least this, my transgression, even if You will not forgive me the rest of my sins!"

In her impassioned burst of repentance she was imploring from the Almighty to summon her as soon as possible to the Last Judgment, while she is still of clear mind and unruffled memory, and is still able with the last of her strength to withstand the delusions of Satan, who had the most vile intentions to get her to mix with the lowly people, the street trash. She was humbly asking the Highest Judge to bring her closer to that day when she will be entirely consumed by that cleansing fire which had been built by her committed transgressions.

When the spiritually divine gift of prayer had filled her entire being, as holy water would a vessel, fervent tears of hope and penitence began streaming from her eyes.

END OF THE LEGEND

1

At the river crossing he came out of the covered Khan's carriage and mounted a horse. While their column was being loaded onto the ferries, he rode, accompanied by his nukers towards the ford. The summer had passed its middle point, and the merciless intense heat had weakened its oppressive stifling effect as if it were catching its breath. Born in the glaciers and flowing from its mountainous heights, the river now had entered its usual course and did not have its erosive effect as at the start of summer, having far retreated from its usual rapids.

The ford was crossing a multitude of narrow channels running along the arc-like plain; these channels streamed from the main rapids as if they were many petite braids of a young girl. Traditionally, this ford was used by merchants' caravans, shuttling between the *Mashreq* and the *Maghreb*, the East and West, but such a huge military horde, under whose weight the landmass was virtually sagging, had never before made this river crossing. On the opposite side of the river an immense crowd had gathered, waiting for the crossing by ferries, and they were gazing at this unusual sight in amazement. These were merchants with the caravans, the dehkans on their *arbas* — the wagons drawn by horses or oxen and loaded with fruits, vegetables, watermelons and melons, and baskets full of grapes; there were also residents of the nearby *kishlaks,* the villages, riding donkeys and mules, horses, as well as all sorts of free and idle folk such as market porters, buffalo drivers, and assorted vagrants seeking work.

Making way for and retreating from the fierce and aggressive and spear-carrying warriors of the advance detachment, the people were crowding both sides of the road, pressing against each other, trying to get a closer look at the great Amir, who is surrounded by the spear-carrying, mounted nukers and riding—as if radiating light—a dazzling white argamak, with its black trimmed bangs.

The Lord rode with face aloof, ignoring those who rapturously were devouring him with their eyes; he rode straight as a rod, head high and not diverting his gaze from the distant expanse of the faded autumn plain, vast and boundless spreading itself before him.

The silver pommel of his saddle and the steel stirrups were reflecting the harsh as a blade's edge direct rays of the reflected sun, but their luster did not cover the frigid radiance emitted by the stern face of the Lord.

The thunderous untamed river, coming from its source beyond the clouds from the looming heights of the snow-white mountain range, had not lost its raging might flowing here unto the plain, and it boiled in a whirlpool of the foaming stream as if in a dazzling smile. But when the horses of the military horde had entered the river's waters, in an instant its smile changed and was clouded by murky lees of silt lifted by countless hoofs.

The Lord remained stern, imperturbable and aloof. He seemed oblivious to everything around him. He merely eased his horse's reins in his mighty hand, sensing that his snow-white argamak was beginning to get nervous under him after entering the icy water up to its fetlocks. His superlative horse maneuvered through the ford's numerous channels impeccably, but at the last shallow channel, virtually at the river's bank, all of a sudden it stumbled. Amir's proudly raised head swayed involuntarily forward, he quickly changed hands on the reins, and suddenly felt that from a finger of his hand which held the *kamcha*-whip something slipped off and fell into the turbulent waters. His heart stood still: indeed, his forefinger no longer felt the silver ring with the rare stone mined in Zulu country, with an innate design in the form of a feline eye. Many years ago this ring was passed on to him by his dying, old father-in-law, designating him, the Supreme Amir, in his stead.

The Lord looked in alarm at the pale imprint left by the missing ring on his forefinger. Two of his bodyguards from both sides obligingly rushed to his side, anticipating some form of danger and seeking to prevent it, but the Khan cast a fierce glance at them stopping them; thereafter he straightened himself in the saddle, once again picked up the reins and rode on. The bodyguards averted their eyes and instantly dashed off to a respectable distance.

Nonetheless, the Lord became distraught, for he saw a bad omen in the loss of his ring. He had it for many years on his hand:

when he was in exile, on all his distant campaigns and it had become his talisman. And suddenly here this loss and at the beginning of the campaign!

His irritability, changing into silent rage, engulfed the Lord. He had instituted an absolute rule: when starting a campaign, two days in advance to clear the road of sundry idly straying curious folk. On the road where he would be passing with his army—be it in the Khan's carriage, surrounded by spear-carrying guards or on horseback on a combat horse, heading his entourage—he was not to encounter a single outsider. The preceding avant-garde detachments, changing each other, chased off the people on the road and the encountered caravans. This was done for the reason so that the army, formed by the Amir's orders from among the inhabitants of that particular country, would depart for combat without seeing tears and not hearing the lamentation of the relatives and dear ones left behind. Even when departing from the capital city—accompanied by the mournful howl of the karnay, the long trumpet, and the horrifying din of huge drums—the army did not encounter any of the citizenry, who were strictly forbidden to come out to the streets. So the people were watching through slits in curtains and holes in fences as the armies marched by along the streets.

But here for some reason the patrols blundered (or, perhaps, provoked the situation), by not chasing off these massive crowds at the river crossing. To be concerned with these trivialities simply did not enter his mind, and this is what happened. The Lord shored up an immense rage towards the 'leader of the thousand' [equivalent approximately to a colonel] and head of his primary guard detachment.

Ahead, along both side of the caravan road, a huge and unruly crowd of riffraff awaited them. On their arba wagons, pulled over to the side of the road, there were heaps of watermelons, melons, and grapes in reed baskets, and the korzhun bags were stuffed full with dried raisins and apricots—and all of these were emitting overpowering aromas of the abundant fruits of the earth. Amir, the warrior, had his ire grow ever more because he realized how much these scents of human life, goodness and happiness aggravated and debilitated the hearts of warriors, who were leaving all this behind—perhaps never to return...

Approaching the crowd, Amir, the Fierce One, without turning his head to either side was listening carefully to the noise of the crowd, the roar of the camels and hee-hawing of donkeys of the caravans, and suddenly, as if by some command, the human hum of voices ceased and through the fence he saw that the caravan leaders were in a rush, the dromedaries were made to kneel, and those who comprised the caravan, in foreign garb and multicolored turbans are also on their knees, with hand on chest and obsequiously bowed heads. Beside them, as if these were cut reeds, the citizenry in skullcaps, shaggy sheepskin hats, tall fur hats and white turbans.

But suddenly on this servile plain of bent backs he saw one person standing as if a solitary desiccated tree. Some insolent daredevil remained standing completely amidst the mass of his citizenry prostate and squirming in the dust in front of him. This man was haggard and wiry, and he stood upright on a low cart, as if in a tense expectation, raising his head with face upwards to the sky. In place of his eyes black holes were gaping.

Years of suffering did harm to this man... Back then, the young architect had a powerful and nimble body, now it was desiccated and debilitated. On a thin neck a large and bony Adam's apple was protruding.

Indeed, back then during their first and last meeting, the youth appeared delicate and handsome. And these withered arms of a blind beggar were back then replete with taut muscles.

2

He entered with a meek mien and a deep bow. As everyone else who appeared before the Lord, the face of the one who entered exhibited a profound degree of agitation. But this particular face did not bear the expression of confidence of a person who has some form of high achievements before the Lord, but neither was there any frenetic fear of someone who had committed a transgression against him and was now summoned for an inquest. Not at all, he entered with the humble dignity befitting any master and bowed before the great Khan, dropping to one knee, with profound respect, however devoid of a slavish servility. In his bow he did not bend his back too long; thereafter he straightened, and with an open and calm look gazed at the Lord.

Unintentionally, the Lord gazed at the young architect with admiration, noting for himself the handsome features of his vibrant youth, his excellent manners, soft but powerful and confident movements, which bespoke of his noble and worthy soul. Furthermore, he noticed a rare charm and attraction of this young person, to which no one could remain unresponsive. The Khan was examining him thoroughly as if he were attempting to discover the secret of the unusual attraction of this young architect. The latter, however, to the Khan's amazement, acted in such a fashion as if he knew why he had been summoned, and calmly, in the manner of a doomed man, but without fear and pleading in his eyes, he stood before the Lord awaiting his fate.

The Khan examined the architect at great length, pointblank staring right through him with his piercing and domineering eyes—at this point interrogating him silently. But the youth did not become flustered, did not break down instantly before the fierce ruler, which somewhat amazed the latter. Still kneeling on one knee, he slowly raised his head and met the Khan's gaze. Here is where the Lord became aware of the great attraction and irresistible power hidden in these huge, domineering over his face, sparkling, passionate and bold eyes of this young architect. It was impossible to resist their enchanting attraction, unusually abundant and stunning, as a summer's nocturnal sky, and their youthful nature. His eyes were expressing a naïve plea and amazement: 'Is it really possible that you will let me out of here alive?' They were unable to hide an expression of his guilt, but yet they did not wish to express during this silent interrogation by the Khan any form of treachery and secretiveness, a reptilian evasiveness... These naïve eyes were lost in a nebulous uncertainty whether this was a dream taking place right now before him or this is a reality... And then, seeing in the light of this youthful purity these huge and superlative eyes, and becoming convinced in the eloquent sincerity of the youth's silence, the Great Khan came to understand now without the slightest doubt that all of this is the truth, that which the Khan's senior wife had reported to him in a different way by sending him the red apple with the wormhole... The Khan diverted his eyes from the man whose fatal fate had been decided, even though not one word had been exchanged between the two; he was led away, but before the Khan's inner vision there remained his huge—as huge as tea cups—eyes, which were rejecting everything else in this world, these eyes which are filled with the enchanting light of the unsurpassed magic of tenderness and compassion.

The stern Amir knew that leaving the palace the architect will soon wind up in a deep cell carved out of rock, and more than likely will never see sunlight again. But thinking about this and still envisioning before him the enchanting eyes of the youth—full of extreme hope—the Khan did not experience any sort of compassion for him. With a mute and abstruse irritability he would observe these no longer existing huge eyes, flaming and scorching his soul as much so as the coal made from the saxaul.

Misfortune and shame in this world, at times, commence with the stupendously tender feelings flowing precisely from such enchanting eyes. For frivolous men these could cost their head, while to immoral women this could bring the shame of their loss of honor. If on one's trousers the string is broken, inevitably the trousers shall fall, thus lust and unrestrained behavior will assuredly lead to the loss of honor and chastity. The vital inquiry which was of concern to the Khan at this point had been evoked by no other than the loss of honor and chastity. That is the reason the Khan had established his laws and codes in order to protect the human race from their very own created evil. To be sure, the great Amir has no idea where Ibis and Azazel, the angels of carnal temptation reside, whose evil intrigues are, thus warns us the Sharia, most successful with prodigal sons and daughters. Nonetheless, it is well known to the Lord that the habitation of sin is the human soul.

But the human soul is as weak as a puppy: a most impressive impact on it is the power of opinion and voice. Having these thoughts, the Lord stared at length at the door through which they had led away the young architect, and he envisioned before him the architect's huge, beckoning and annoying eyes, which had gazed at him with a lucid look, though they actually had left after the door had slammed shut after them. The man was no longer, but his gaze remained. The eyes of the one, who had become invisible, remained and were as though suspended in space in front of him, following his every move.

With an odd feeling—the presence of the one who had been absent for quite a while—the Lord looked gloomily about him. There was no one nearby. And then, not daring to turn his back to the door, through which he had expelled the architect, who had not said one word, and to whom he also said nothing, the Khan began to retreat, step by step, towards the babbling stream of water of the fountain. What is this? Are these bothersome eyes going to pursue him for the rest of his life? It is likely that the young wife of the Khan had also experienced the magic charm of these eyes upon her as well. So that if Amir's, a man's, soul has no rest from these eyes, calling within him for some goodness, how then could have a weak, young and tiny woman withstand this delusion? For if a man is seeking to save his honor, sacrificing his own head to be decapitated, then a woman seeks to restore her peace of mind by offering her own body for humiliation.

What then is to be done now? What should fearsome Amir do now, he who has always destroyed without mercy any of his enemies, who dared to stand in his way?

The Lord stopped and straightened out—and it seemed as if he shifted the slackened reins in his hands and then drew them tighter. A rapacious smile flashed across his lips. He shall put an end to him. He shall bury these greedy eyes in sand; these eyes which had coveted the royal property.

But his heart did not rest with this harsh and cruel decision alone. From its depths a licking, frosty doubt had escaped secretly. Is it permissible for the Ruler to cut down with his sabre his own citizen who had come to him with such a clear and open face and lucid eyes? Here they are again confronting him! O, had these been other eyes, those full of rage, threat and hatred! For a warrior they are a present from heaven, when his blood boils within him, and his entire body, as if it were a moistened hirsute lasso, is filled with an extraordinary strength and resilient force. Clenched teeth, blood rushing into his head and the warrior is rushing forward as an irrepressible turbulent, foaming breaker wave. And the enemy is struck down before him, bleeding profusely from his slashed neck, and this blood shall cleanse the warrior's heart of all his fury and cruelty...and his gaze will become calm, once again it will be bright with a radiant light as the mountain range of the Cape Fold Mountains in the early morning when the wind blows away the fog's curtain...

But to use a sword on an obediently offered throat of a humble resident is equally as shameful and dishonorable as it would be to cut the tail of a mangy donkey with the holy and blessed sword, the weapon of many a military victory... And to shed blood of a pitiful commoner is not worthy of a person, and it is just as loathsome as it would be to crush a river toad with one's foot. Moreover, these eyes are beckoning with some unearthly purity and enigma...there is not an inkling of hostility or malice.

This was the first time that the Lord's soul became perturbed and flustered, unable to heed the voice of reason or to relinquish oneself uncontrollably to give oneself to anger. He imagined himself to be the hunter whose borzoi hound is zealously pursuing a hare, and soon coming back and apologetically crawling at the feet of its master... But he somewhere in fact already had seen these befogged, moist and innocent eyes... But where? Whose?

But to categorically say 'innocent eyes'? Why would they be so innocent? Would it not be for the fact that they had coveted the sanctity of the royal bed? Is that the reason they are so 'innocent' that they are willing to look under the lap of a skirt of someone's wife? Impudence is more so offensive than a trick of a treacherous enemy when he furtively sneaks up to your large tent and pierces its canopy with his spear. Allah has seen that I have been insulted not for the offense towards my golden crown, and I have no intentions to punish the offender for the humiliation of my throne—not at all! Even if I were to be the most despicable beggar with a vagabond's staff, in a shabby fur coat and hat—I still should not forgive a man who had the audacity to commit such a vile outrage against my masculine honor! For there is nothing more sacred for a man than to protect the peace in the land of his forefathers, to respect the memory of his honorable and worthy ancestors and to protect the purity of one's sacred marital bonds. Great Allah! How could He have allowed that the honor even of one as lofty as the mountainous peaks, the royal husband, would have to depend on the frisky skirts of an insignificant female with the habits of a butterfly? It appears that in this manner the Creator has thus punished the male gender on earth.

Fired up by his own thoughts, the Lord could not remain still; he jumped on his feet and began pacing up and down along the khauza. 'Innocent eyes' indeed... Why, he would be willing to poke these innocent calf's eyes with his own hands! He would strangle the one who possessed them... With a heavy gait, Amir came up to the window. And here, o Allah! he once again encountered the same incredibly pure and joyous look of the innocent eyes! The azure minaret, lofty above the treetops of the park's trees, presented to him its enchanting and meek smile—as if it had looked at length, waiting for the Lord to deign to look in his direction. So this is where he had seen these innocent and meek eyes, and he was not able to remember this no matter how hard he tried... During the very first day of his visit to the construction site, approaching the tower, he was duly impressed by the sudden discovery that the minaret had been looking at him! It seemed as if it sought his mercy, and at the same time it was ready, it would appear, to accept anything that the Lord would be imparting on it.

At that time the Lord did not pay any mind to this, his first impression, but as it turned out the entire tower as a whole, from its base to the top of its cupola, was saturated with these sentiments: an infinite heavenly love and yearning, a plea for mercy and the readiness to accept a fatal torture for its misdeeds. This architect, with the appearance of a lamb, in actuality was ingeniously inaccessible. In the azure minaret he was able to incorporate his entire horrific and lofty passion, huge as the tower itself, consuming him entirely. And looking through the bedchamber window of the young wife of the Khan, the minaret has revealed to her the feelings of the audacious architect...

Words are the downfall of a man, the eyes that of a woman. Man wants to be master of his own words, the woman to own that to which her eyes are lured. Man is willing to pay with his life for his honor; woman is ready to forgo her honor for the sake of that upon which she had set her eyes. And she will not rest until she is satisfied. It is no wonder that our ancestors had covered their women tightly with a *chador,* a veil, because to open them up to the gaze of outsiders is equivalent to lifting the laps of their skirts.

Now everything became rather clear to the Khan. The Khan's wife was at first enchanted by the magic of the azure minaret. Then she experienced a burning desire to look at that genius who had erected such a majestic structure and had realized her dream. She had ascended the tower and had seen him... And she did not even notice how she became a prisoner of the meek, melancholic and 'innocent' eyes of the young enchanter.

Nothing stopped her; no one restrained her on this fatal move. Neither the dignity of her husband of the diamond crown, who was sharing the sacred bonds of marriage with her, nor crown and throne, shared by both, nor the parental blessing, nor fear from publicity amidst the masses—none were hindrances for her to step onto the fatal path. So that all of this could not serve as better protection than the narrow-as-a-palm net woven from the hairs of a horse's tail and placed in front of the black chador; as one of the most reliable grids, separating the covetous male lust from the wavering shameless female caprice. Granted that there are no ways of restraining a low-caste, lustful female—who is not watched too closely—from sinning with the shaytan, the Devil, but how could this happen in the presence of numerous guards, who are forbidden even to have a fly enter the palace, how could an outsider, a djigit, an audacious man, sneak into the compound? Where were the courtiers, whose duties were not to leave the Khan's wife at any given time, and where had been the harem overseer, the vigilant old woman, whose duties were to never leave her alone?

The Khan spent the entire night without sleep or rest. Impatiently he waited for dawn and decided to summon the harem overseer. She could dispel thousands of his doubts, for it so turned out to be that in palace life he could rely entirely only upon this old hag and perhaps also the chief purser.

During the morning meal he ordered the servant girl to summon the harem overseer. The latter entered as if sailing in, head held high and arrogantly, and approaching so slowly that it almost cut the Khan's breathing from indignation and anger at such a self-complacent shrew, as ugly by appearance as she was insolent in her behavior. She thinks she is the navel of the earth, perhaps even higher—and only because she is serving in a place where the Khan enters alone, on foot and without the crown on his head. The old hag is hardly dragging herself in, trying to show how tired she gets at her job with neither sleep nor rest, and on her wrinkled and sleepy physiognomy there is not a trace of timidity towards her Lord. Finally, she lets it be known that being the guardian of the Khan's marital bed, she commands nigh the entire world, and everything depends on her, including the Lord himself... Silently, he was steaming with rage: does she imagine herself that she is the only one who knows everything, but he is unaware of their activities during his absence?

At long last, the old woman made it across half of the hall and approached the Khan. She folded her hands across her chest and bowed slightly. Then she stuck her grossly powdered face with her bulging eyes out at the Khan, as if asking impatiently: 'Well, what's the problem? You wish to say something? I'm listening.' Unprepared for such insolence even on her behalf, almost choking from anger, the great Lord only caught his breath, not knowing what to say. With great effort he was able to contain his rage, which was ready to burst out in the open; he calmed down and began to conduct the conversation with a deliberately quiet and flat voice. But the hawk-like looks he gave the outrageous old woman were much more expressive than his words. However, the old woman noticed nothing of this and pretended that she was listening with half an ear, absent-mindedly, thinking about some more important matters than his words. All of a sudden, her eyes rimmed by the pink eyelids, with their sparse eyelashes, lit up with the fire of suspicion. She flashed a look of her liquid-swollen eyes towards

End of the Legend • Abish Kekilbaev

the Khan and lowered her gaze, as if listing to see if there is veracity in his words, or if it is a new move in his endless palace games with his subordinates, the loss of such by the latter would be equivalent to a fate of a mouse winding up in the cat's paws. Thereafter, perhaps becoming frightened in earnest or realizing finally where he is leading, the old hag once again assumed her demeanor of an impenetrable wall and hid her gaze under the cover of her mangy swollen eyelids. And she heeded his statements, and became all ears. At a certain time during his speech, the old woman reacted rather strongly, as result of which the five or six long hairs of the old hag's mustache under her hook nose bristled, her withered mouth exhibited a grin, and its corners drooped—all of these unsightly grimaces of her face meant none other than an ironic reptilian smile. Seeing this, the Lord abruptly stopped talking, perceiving a considerable degree of aversion. Guessing why he stopped short in speaking, being an experienced schemer, she instantly terminated her smile, as if she had swallowed it, and bowed before the Lord in a most respectful pose. However, he no longer said a word and only silently stared at her with his hard stare, giving her to understand that he had already made his statement and that it would be her turn to speak.

And so the old woman began to speak. Even after such horrible and unheard of in their intrinsic frankness questions by the Lord, the harem overseer did not falter and retained her composure completely. She began to tell her story in a composed manner. During the course of her narrative, as she spoke in her measured manner and her speech sounded self-assured, it seemed that the Lord himself somehow became increasingly less important in comparison to the ornate presentation of the old woman, and he even decreased in stature considerably. Trying not to disclose the storm of emotions raging within him, the Lord listened as if petrified. In numerous harsh interrogations he had in the past, he sought the whole truth, and presently, as a skilled interrogator, he continued staring at the harem overseer with his tenacious and cold eyes.

When the old woman had expounded everything she had to say, he merely moved his chin sidewise, ordering her: 'Leave!' The harem overseer rendered him a most respectful bow and departed. But she did not leave the hall in a slow gait of a snail, as she had done at arrival, but rather with frisky mincing steps.

The old woman's confessions had the Lord pondering. As it turned out, they had decided to trick the audacious boy-architect and substituted a young and good-looking slave girl for the Khan's wife.

However, the cowardly womenfolk do not comprehend that in order to avoid the Lord's anger, they should have not sought to indulge the lascivious flesh of the vile adulterer, but rather summarily chop off his head with the axe of a henchman, but instead these brainless women have now their headaches. For upon whom had this kafir, dared to raise his wicked and despicable eyes? What did he dare to wish in his filthy intentions? Why just for the mere fact that he dared to glance upon the sacred Khan's wife with his lecherous look, one would need to gouge out his eyes and to fill the bloody gaps with sand! And everything had been set up in such a manner that this wicked architect should believe that he, a simple mortal, had embraced the tender body of the divine Wife of the Khan! Why he just sat confronting the Khan and looking him in the eye and silently admitting this—and with the undeniable willingness to acquiesce for all of this by his death penalty! Well, then so be it! Let him cleanse with his hot blood, pulsating out of his headless body, that pain of this monstrous insult and offense which this worthless plebeian had imparted into the heart of the Lord. No, his head must not remain on his neck and bring about delusions into this world which are contrary to God. And let the living and scarlet blood stream from the blade of the axe and cleanse the shameful mark of the Devil left on the pure marital bed of the great Amir.

Let retribution take place, but in such a way that not a single look of an outsider would be able to penetrate and no one's ears should hear about it... But is that possible at all? People's rumors have thousands upon thousands of mouths and ears. One must send off spies and informers—faceless and soulless people—out on the streets and bazaars, let them listen and report what the masses of rabble and riff-raff are saying.

So that there are no longer any doubts. Reprisal is awaiting the architect. He no longer evokes any obscure pity from the Lord—only an algid fury and a furious hatred.

The soulless informers had reported that the bazaar riff-raff had heard nothing about the architect being summoned to the palace by the Khan. He then sent these soulless people to the mahalla neighborhood, an enclave with self-rule in the city, where the architect of the azure minaret had lived. These informers reported that the landlord of the house where the architect was boarding is bragging about the fact that his tenant had been summoned by the Khan in order to assign him the construction of yet another new mosque. The Lord did not particularly like this gossip, and so after several days he decided to repeat the raid of the bazaar by his spies. By that time the crowd would be aware of the fact that the architect still has not left the palace; this is the point where it will be significant to find out what false rumors surface in the talk among the people.

The humid summer days were slowly passing like languishing beauties strolling unhurriedly in the Khan's park. No worthwhile news was forthcoming, neither good nor bad, from the town squares to the Khan's palace. No messengers came from the Senior Wife. After she found out that the Khan questioned who had been sending him the red apples with the wormholes, the Khan's Senior Wife became apprehensive and assumed a wait-and-see attitude on what would happen now.

A strange feeling overpowered the Khan. It seemed as if his entire surroundings had become apprehensive and quiescent—and are spying on their Lord, following his every move, observing him through unseen cracks. It was disquieting and uncomfortable as if it had not been the Khan who had apprehended the dishonorable architect and sent him off to the underground cell, but rather had incarcerated himself in a zindan, the subterranean cell carved in the rock where he now languishes suffering and in loneliness. For the Khan had become well aware that even he is not able to resolve the fate of the architect of the azure minaret only by his own arbitrariness, without taking into account to what degree the crowd, the masses of rabble and riff-raff would consider his act just and in accordance with the legend created by them. But during the entire time of his rule he had not given any reason for the despicable masses to doubt his lofty and irreproachable decisions. And he preferred to personally create the ending of any legend about himself, rather than to entrust this to a spontaneous crowd. For this to happen, he had to follow up and find what gossip had been spreading amidst these people. This time, however, the crowd was mute.

He tried in every way to unravel the reason for this silence, but he couldn't find a single suitable explanation. He couldn't comprehend why the bazaar folk, as a rule so eager for some unusual gossip, this time are not at all discussing such notable news as the disappearance of the young architect, who had created in the capital of the Khan's empire such a grandiose sight of interest, the azure mosque of magical beauty. Indeed, this was a mystery to the Khan: why are the people, being aware of this, so tight-lipped and silent like deaf-mutes? Or is everybody mortally frightened of this, which they know for some time now, and their Lord had learned and figured out only very recently? What had the insolent architect told the world by means of his azure tower? For, after all, the one that would dare to blurt out even a word about this would instantly lose his head. Such a lethal law had been instituted by the Lord for some time now. However, no matter how often he had punished by his cruel executions the blabbermouths and double-dealers throughout his entire nation, establishing his autocratic order, they were to be found everywhere, ready to relate with foaming mouth the truth which had become known to them. But in this case, amidst the multitude of bazaar folk not a single person could be found who would wish to let the cat out of the bag—the horrible secret... Or could there be another reason and it is not due to fear that the people are silent? If so, what is the reason?

The Lord felt to be poisoned by these cursed issues, as if by blood-sucking mosquitoes and gnats, herded into a swamp devoid of exits, a swamp with gurgling quagmires, where it is impossible to make a single step without being in danger of slithering into the slimy abyss. As if awaiting his salvation, the Khan was sitting in his palace, motionless, staring at the huge door decorated with gold ornaments.

But week after week, this door did not witness a messenger with any reasonable news. Nonetheless, finally the long-awaited hour did come. The door opened quietly and into the hall slithered in a soulless informer. Bending in half, the soulless one crawled up to the Lord, and, waiting for him to say something, froze in place.

- Say it! What did you find, what did you hear?

Looking in alarm at the Khan, the soulless one began to make his report. From this report it became clear that amidst the bazaar folk talk was heard that the great Lord, presumably not wishing to have a similar fairytale minaret to be built anywhere else in the world, with the exception of his capital, had actually caused the architect to be blinded and then sent him off into exile. The Great Amir stared at length with his unblinking eyes at the despicable bazaar spy, as if he did not notice him in his profound thoughts, then, with a nod of his head indicated the door, sending him away. The informer sneaked out of the hall just as quietly as he had entered, as if he were indeed an apparition without a soul.

The Lord jumped instantly off his seat and began to pace alone up and down in the hall. That, which started with the crowds in a hollow mumble, this was indeed the birth of a legend! And its finale is suggested in a most convincing way! Everything here is authentic: could the Great Amir permit for another miraculous tower to be built in this big, wide world of ours? One to equal that of the azure minaret erected by this architect? So that there is nothing amazing if this young architect should share the fate of many a genius master whose creation had become the reason for their horrible fate—and that was due to the zeal of the rulers who did not wish for the master to repeat a similar masterpiece somewhere in a foreign land. Well then, so be it, as the crowing of the ravens of the bazaar masses had suggested! In this world there has not been a single case for such grandiose and superlative structures, such as the azure minaret, to be devoid of their own legends. And so this time also a legend is ripe and worthy of such a wonderful azure tower! So as it turns out to be, there is also some sense in the words of the senseless crowds, words, which would easily and conveniently be stored by every person's ears!

For many days now the Lord had been as a recluse, not even once leaving the premises of his bedchamber. But on that day when this quiet soulless spy had come, the Khan had for the first time in many weeks walked his secluded pathway, and sat on the rock near the softly murmuring spring. The clear waters, coming forth from the inscrutable depths of the earth, in a pleasant sort of way, restrained his troubled spirit, cleansed and cured the wounds of his soul. The pain in his temples had at long last eased; the Khan opened his shirt and bared his open chest to the refreshing wind streams, which penetrated the verdant shrubbery. All around him a serene appeasement reigned, the spring was murmuring, and the trees were whispering to each other by bowing their crowns. Why would anyone in such a wondrous world need to create for oneself and subject others to various horrible misfortunes and suffering? Why would one strangle oneself by the world's invisible anguish and to raise to ecumenical heights the triviality of one's paltry tribulations? To die of spiritual wounds, which no one had inflicted? To wish that which does not exist, and to dream of something truly veritable and real, and not be satisfied with what one has?

An inevitable retribution awaits each and every sensual person, who is a slave of his own unbridled lust. And this architect of the azure minaret shall no longer build other towers and shall be no longer capable of turning anyone's head. For a skillful master-executioner shall cut out his eyes with a sharp knife, these very large, anxious and bewitching eyes, with whose magical help he had initially gained another's heart, from where he carried off her love, which was not intended for him. Yes, these thief's eyes will be cut out with a small steel knife, such as is used to castrate stallions not submitting to bridle and lash. But this is not the end of it: so that the blinded common tramp would not prattle unduly in the bazaars, the Khan shall also order to cut off the tongue of his frivolous enemy down to the very root of it. And then without his eyes and tongue, he shall drag on his pitiful existence amidst the people—now without posing any danger to anyone whatsoever.

Tonight had been the first time in many a night that the Khan could get a good night's sleep. This morning, after proceeding to the throne, he wanted to summon the chief keeper of the zindans, when suddenly the Young Khansha made her appearance at the door.

Stepping across the doorsill, she greeted the Lord with a deep bow, but thereafter she conducted herself in a strange manner. He did not utter a single word as she came up to him shuffling along, swaying mightily from side to side she headed straight towards the Khan and right away dropped to her knees and touched the throne's base with her forehead. Then she lifted her head, turning her pale and exhausted face towards him. From the reflection of the blood-red ruby, sparkling on her forehead, her eyes seemed to be surrounded by a bluish tinge; these eyes gazed at her husband from the deep zindans of despair and fear. It seemed as if her beautiful face was a frozen mask of death. The Khan's wife sat down at the feet of her royal husband, with her face slightly averted, as if embarrassed to display it to him. The Lord was somewhat bewildered; he had not expected her appearance in the throne hall at all. Such event was unheard of: for someone to arrive without being summoned by the ruler. From this unexpected development the Khan did not even know how to conduct himself and what to say to her. A rather lengthy silence ensued. Finally, inundated by a sudden pity for her, he reached out his hand to her. As soon as his hand had reached out to her, the distraught Khan's wife shed endless tears. As she touched his hand with her lips, her head collapsed upon his knees. Her shoulders trembled and she wept uncontrollably like a child. It had been merely yesterday that the Lord could not think of her other than with aversion, as of a most filthy being in this world, but now he looked in bewilderment at the woman at his feet and did not know how he should act. He was in a state of confusion. Pity overwhelmed his harsh heart. Just a few days ago he was seething in anger towards the woman who had gotten to such a worthless and shameful condition, but now seeing how she, his young wife, is weeping at the base of the throne, he lost all of his resolve... He bent down, lifted her with his powerful arms and placed her upright in front of him. Then he moved over and seated her next to him on the throne. As if desirous to keep her from any words or explanations, he folded both of his hands, pressing between them the tender and fervid hand of his wife. Lowering his large head, the Khan gazed over her head somewhere into the distance. The Khan's wife wept a long time and inconsolably. It would appear that she could never weep away her entire grief accumulated within her heart. But the silent tenderness of her husband triumphed in its effect and the young wife slowly began to regain her composure. But when her tears ran dry, the weeping ceased, her breathing quieted, she knew not what to do, what to say. The Lord also was in no hurry to question her. Thus they both sat silently next to each other for a considerable time, and the Khan's Wife, feeling a sense of embarrassment and awkwardness, was getting ready to leave. Getting up, she once again bowed to the Khan, her husband, and turned to the exit. But not having made more than one step, she froze in place, stood indecisively and in thought, inclined her head and asked quietly:

- Great Master! Is it true that you had ordered to incarcerate the master who had built the tower I commissioned?"

For the Khan these words sounded like thunder amidst blue skies. Deeply hurt and offended, he did not, however, show that he had become enraged, and he answered in a calm voice:

- Indeed, it is so.

The cheeks of the Khan's wife flared up. Once again she wanted to throw herself at his feet, but this time he did not let her do it, and with his powerful hand he held her by her elbow.

- He is not guilty at all, my Master... Nothing took place.
- I know.

'Did he tell the truth?' the Khan's wife looked at him quickly, with amazement in her eyes. The Lord's face was impassive and calm. She turned towards the exit and left. He followed her with an intent look. At the doorstep she stopped briefly and looked back—with the appearance of a person who is departing in despair of total nescience. And thus she left, disappointed and depressed, downcast and head hung low.

The Lord, on the other hand, simply could not come to his senses from this unexpected and unannounced visit by the Young Khansha. Up to this time, even the First Wife did not commit anything of this nature. How could one interpret such a flagrant violation of his established palace regulations? Perhaps she had simply been missing his attention, which he had not bestowed upon her for such a lengthy time? And even after a campaign which had lasted numerous years, he had not visited his young wife—even for just a courtesy visit. Why not? This is quite conceivable. Quite likely the rumors have not reached her yet that the old wife had sent him the red apples with the wormholes. Brought to a point of despair, his young wife forgot all fear of him and decided to come and see him first.

Now, more than likely, she has her peace of mind and has returned to her bedchamber. And yet, why had she, without a single word of a courteous greeting, only wept bitter tears and prior to her departure had spoken only of one subject, the young master architect? Could it be possible that she dared to disregard all rules of propriety only for the sake of concern for the fate of this handsome fellow? 'He is not guilty at all.' What did the young wife have in mind? Did she seek to protect him from a bloody retribution? But why did she not ask to show mercy to the young master? Possibly his brief 'I know' she had understood to be a promise of mercy. Yes, indeed, he knows fully well that between these two nothing reprehensible had occurred. But how can he let him live, even be it only for the fact that he dared in his thoughts to encroach upon the honor and dignity of the Lord? Worthless worm, he dared, without fearing a brutal execution, to encroach upon that which is sacred and untouchable for all mortals! Thus, there is no longer any doubt that the one who committed sacrilege must have punishment meted out to him, which had already been predetermined for the master by the bazaar crowds in their calloused, feebleminded imagination.

Yet another unsettled mystery flashed in the last look of the Khan's wife, who had stopped for a moment at the door. Her eyes gazed at him apprehensively, in fearful alarm she looked at him, frozen in a mute question: will he show mercy or his usual ruthless severity? She sought to read the answer on his face. But surely this was not the first time that she had seen his impassive face, which could not exhibit any emotion of weak-willed pity? This would signify that she looked at him with a sense of despair, not trusting his capability for forgiveness and mercy? But could it really be that a street vagabond with filthy feet is so precious to her that she had fallen into despair for his sake? This must not be! Instead of requesting from her royal husband a ferocious public execution for this slave who had the audacity in his filthy thoughts to strive to obtain her body, she bursts with an insane bravery into the presence of her royal husband and almost is voicing her plea to spare the life of the criminal. Why should that be so? Does she really desire for the Lord to let him go free as a bird without punishment? 'Nothing took place between us.' But had it been not her who had, with the help of the old woman, the harem-overseer, substituted in her stead the young and pretty slave girl? The Khan's wife had learned about the criminal solicitation of this wicked man by means of the azure tower, which was day and night jutting out in front of her bedchamber windows. And she—o, shaytan!—herself was not averse to have some fun with his emotions. And perhaps not only fun with his emotions! Why did she deem it fit to send the slave girl in her stead? She was not concerned about her honor, which the crowds are always ready to defame with their filthy language; she is sorry for the fellow who climbs over the wall for the sake of satisfying his lust, and so she sends her servant girl... So that from one aspect, the Khan's wife had the usual female's bent for amusement, and for the other one, the moral duty before the throne. And what had the priority? Not having given herself to her enticer, she nonetheless did not slap him on the wrists.

At this point the Khan's thoughts came to a standstill and became numb, not unlike a bird under the stare of a python. Unable to stir and move ahead—yonder where the ominous black demonic conjecture existed: the Khan's wife was not merely showing compassion due to a feminine vanity, for the love shown by the architect; no, not at all, she herself felt an irresistible penchant for him. The Lord clearly imagined that which he had seen on that night in his wife's bedchamber. The human female who in her dreams had given herself to this male, whom she was squeezing in her embrace, without the shadow of a doubt, had been that scoundrel. Unable to become intimate with him in reality, she did so in her dreams. This clear-eyed young man was so much more precious to her than old and fearsome Amir. Today she had come to sacrifice herself for the sake of saving the young man. Even the Lord of half of the world, with all the wisdom of his state craft, had no understanding of this at all, and his heart had softened when she began to shed her tears. He showed his weakness which has not been characteristic during his entire life. He had obviously forgotten that the tears of a woman are gold in the hands of a magician, it is forged. He, of course, thought that she had a yearning for their marital bed, of which she had been deprived for a long time, but he had been grossly mistaken. This he realized standing over the bed on which the perspiring and flushed Khan's wife was tossing about in an obscene way. That, which she could not fulfill during broad daylight, she had carried out under the diabolical cover of night in her sleep. And there was no desire to protect one's royal dignity in her actions. During her sleep, on their sacred marital bed she was committing a natural ritual of copulation, when she found herself alone in bed with a strange man, she feigned to be repelling his hands, which already for some time had shamelessly been groping along her body all fired up by lust.

In his chest he perceived unbearable pain, as if stabbed by a knife. Never before had Amir experienced such pain. Nothing the likes of this had he experienced, so that the soul of the conqueror of the world had the taste of the most bitter cup of suffering during his entire life. And this mighty man dropped to his knees and grabbed his head in despair.

3

His life for him had lost all its value, and it seemed as if in his soul all desire had vanished. To the soulless informers, who were brought to him several times during the day, he listened without interest. Nor did he rush into an execution of the architect incarcerated in a zindan, not for any particular reason, but rather for the same lack of interest. His ravaging thirst for revenge, which formerly gave him no rest, seemed somehow to have disappeared.

What became oppressive was not the suffering of his soul, but rather the lack of any suffering; so that his days proceeded in a listless sequence as when food is being digested in a long intestine, and such a life denigrated its own name, losing any of its dignity. But neither did he have any desire to sort out the reasons for such a condition of his soul, and the sluggish suffocating waves of a somnolent daze carried him on day after day. It was unbearable for the Khan to overcome this pain of existence so strange to him, and he would have rather preferred to suffer from wounds obtained in combat when a wounded body is spurting blood in streams.

He felt sluggish and stunned as a fish which had knocked its head on a rock. Said to be infinitely wise and sagacious as a prophet, he was now helpless and blind, having suddenly such a stroke of bad luck in his life, something he could have never foreseen. He knew, of course, that the young master will be executed, as any human being even once to dare and oppose him. But any, even a most severe type of torture, and any, a most ferocious execution could not cleanse the offense and abate the pain which this desert tramp has inflicted upon his soul. His blow had in an instant demolished into pieces the entire grandiose monument of the Lord's fame, and all of his greatness, which is higher than the Cape Fold Mountains—all of this had been dumped into the river of existence and floated on it as strewn straw.

The real name of that stifling and depressed condition in which the Lord found himself was sorrow. This condition is endured by a combatant when all around blood is no longer flowing, the ferocious combat malice is not raging, and the one who has suffered defeat, has disappeared from the battlefield and is languishing from being a nonentity and a weakling. The Lord regretted and grieved that similar to the clawed golden eagle, which had captured its prey, the fox, he, the Lord, although he had conquered half of the world's human race, he had been unable to capture only that little woman. And he is inconsolable from such a universal triviality that two human beings, upon uniting, sharing one bed and merging their bodies, will never have their souls coalesce. Thus it had become clear: his Young Khansha and the resentment of her became the reason of the total helplessness experienced by the great Amir.

He got to know great loneliness—all because of her. A hopelessly cold loneliness, which chilled his old bones. The overpowering unhappy thoughts did not help overcome, but rather intensified his curse of loneliness. Looking back at his entire past life, he saw that essentially he never had that simple human happiness which warms the uncomplicated lives of common people. Familial joys, love games with one's darling wife of young years, the children and the incomparable joy of parenthood—all these no longer comprised his happiness. Somehow rather quickly the children from sundry wives were born and became adults. And he became as lonely as God who has no comrades. Overcoming all of his most dangerous enemies, he dreamt of a quiet life, and remembering his mother's precepts, decided to marry a young wife and live the rest of his years with here at his side. He married his Young Khansha not for the amusement of his aging body, but for a spiritual intimacy and sincere warmth. In her he sought his salvation from an encroaching loneliness. And in his prayers he thanked the Almighty One for this wonderful and generous gift. This had taken place when he saw the superlative and wondrous azure minaret and learned that it had been the Junior Khan's Wife who had built this tower in honor of his great fame and dedicated this as a sign of her devotion and love for him. At that time he had been overjoyed as a child. But now this joy, just as the sun with its sparkling rays of warmth, had changed to an ominous luster of an autumn cold cobweb. His sorrow was not only the cry about the inconstancy of feelings of his beloved woman and wife, but it was also the sadness for the phantom treachery of all human life. It is sad that once a person is born into this world, he strives to achieve the resplendent apex of happiness, but when he reaches it and becomes the Mighty One of this world, he suddenly sees himself to be a prisoner of an infinitely dismal loneliness. Is this the unenviable fate of all mortals? Is such loneliness known to those who are accustomed to be content with bare essentials, those who share their humble income equally with all members of their household, and those who live in crowded conditions, and yet who feel no resentment for living in their hearth-sooty hut. Perhaps this is indeed the human happiness on earth? To get by just as humbly and in humility during their brief life—perhaps that is where the great dignity of man is to be found? One can't jump over one's own head, and no other fate had been foreseen for anyone. No matter how attractively and solemnly we name our own ambitious desires, be it dreams, goals in life or an honorable duty—in reality though they're called savage greed, avarice or selfishness. For where it is intertwining with sin, no divine gift is possible.

Here, the great Amir had lived a life leaning on the sun with his elbow, placing the moon under his foot. But had he ever had a good night's sleep without worries and alarm, and stretching his legs in bed in relaxation? Up to his neck in riches, fame and honors, man does not know happiness if he has not experienced that one moment in the life of a poor man, returning after a laborious day back to his peaceful hearth at night.

Perhaps the Young Khansha had these dreams once about such a simple and true happiness, disregarding the crown on her head and piles of gold under her feet? But perhaps all that she needs for happiness is one tiny sixth of a troy ounce of an ordinary human affection?

Perhaps he too should find for himself such a tiny troy ounce of affection? To sit on his throne and to possess all the wealth of this world, surrounded by swarms of his offspring and to feel in the process oneself to be a lonely wanderer in a fatal desert—is this indeed happiness? To steal to one's marital bed at night like a thief, apprehensive to be spotted by the ever-present servants and slaves—

what sort of happiness is that? To be considered the wisest of all rulers of humanity in the entire world, but at that to be afraid of the rumors of the bazaar crowds, which could doom to an eternal shame the name of their fearsome Lord—is that what happiness is? It turns out then that only Allah is able to stand above all of the sinful humanity in this world. And excessive power and fame, wealth and a great talent granted by Him to one person is not happiness, but rather a source of the greatest woes for mankind. What can one then say about this unhappy and pitiful architect, who had at his cost gained fame among the citizenry, if even the ruler of half of the world is unable to escape the fate of a victim of the bazaar crowds? Its verdict is inexorable both for emperors and for the lowliest of slaves. And so it turns out to be that all three of them are the victims of the rabble, and they are deeply unhappy people, and life for them just isn't life at all. They are unable as simple residents to be frank even to one's relative, to weep at his chest, complaining about their unhappy lot, and to tell him about their trials and tribulations. No, for the three of them this is impossible!

If this were to happen to other people, and if these three would come for his judgement, seeking the truth in such a case, would he be able to get to the root of it: who is guilty and deserves punishment, and who is not guilty and should be let free in peace? No, he wouldn't be able, because all three are poor devils and victims of the bazaar crowds, and being one of them he is not able to pass judgement neither upon himself nor on this pitiful pair... All three of them are poor of spirit, since poor people are unable to share with each other and to offer that which they do not have. They all love, all three, but none of them can offer love to the other, because this love does not belong to any of them. Therefore it is expedient to have the trial resolved, without giving it further thought, as the rumors of the cruel bazaar crowds are suggesting. These crowds, as if they were ducks with their loud quacking, inform only of that which is available to their wretched understanding. The real executioner of this young master genius will in effect be the bazaar legend, with its end also suggested by the crowds.

But should he wish to pardon these mad lads gone astray, and would reunite the lovers—what deafening racket would the duck of bazaar rumors raise! What fetid filth they would pour on the Lord and his entire dynasty! During all times of the existence of this world it had been precisely this rabble who would be throwing into disorder and bedlam the town squares, sowing civil strife throughout history, and piling up monstrous intrigues in the legends for posterity. It is precisely the rabble and riff-raff that has beforehand predetermined the verdict of the young architect with the huge, sad and mysterious eyes. May what the people have desired come true.

4

In the zindan one place had been vacated. The huge, sad and mysterious eyes of the young master, which had seen something inaccessible to others in this world, had fizzed out, leaked out, pierced by a red-hot metal rod. The executioner had completed his work by cutting out his tongue. The horrible screams of the victim were choked from the gurgling of his blood. He was struggling in the hands of the executioners until they tied him with a hirsute lasso, thereafter they stuffed his drooping body into a striped sack. At night, two apprentice executioners transported the sack from the prison courtyard and brought it to a distant kishlak, a village, beyond the river.

This was not a singular case of such evil deed committed in the Great City, which had been inflicted upon the great masters of lofty art, those who had extolled the fame of this beautiful capital of the southern hemisphere. But there were also such desperate daredevils who were able to avoid such cruel fate, by forcefully escaping from the executioners' hands and throwing into their mouths gold *dinars*. Some of these lucky persons left town forever, abandoning their art and taking up an entirely different occupation and hiding their past. Others rushed off to the other end of the world and yonder, in a foreign land, erected palaces to a local Lord. Only but a small number of those who had escaped the execution, the bravest, were in hiding in their homeland, waiting for the death of the previous *amin*. When a new ruler turned up on the throne, he granted an amnesty to the master, who then returned to the capital.

Well aware of similar such stories, the Lord decided to be personally present during the process, and after it to ascertain the condition of the prisoner, who, according to the verdict, was to be deprived of sight and speech. Therefore the Khan himself descended to the subterranean torture chamber and demanded to see the contents of the striped bag.

But even after seeing the disfigured face, of the half-dead from suffering, unrecognizable human being, the Khan felt no joy from the accomplished act of revenge. He did not feel himself to be the victorious one who is trampling a defeated enemy with his foot, and the two executioners who were tinkering with the sack, appeared to him as disgusting petty thieves, making their living on dark nights in the back alleys, stuffing and carting off in their sacks, at times, a calf from its tether or some not too cautious chicken. With a repulsive feeling in his soul he commanded to immediately transport the master's maimed body to a distant kishlak.

The following day after this event, the spacious palace seemed empty and desolate for a long time. The soulless spies no longer came to him to spread malicious gossip, being deathly afraid of him, while the chief of all the informers and spies tried to send off to the bazaars more experienced soulless ones under the guise of out-of-town traders and mad divan-dervishes. But even these endeavors of the informer service brought nothing new. The bazaar crowds seemed to have conspired and not a single word was said about the punishment of the architect of the azure minaret. Yet after all, quite recently they themselves suggested what punishment should be meted out. Among the glib traders, it seemed, their eyes knew nothing but to look at the scales weighing their wares, and would have no time to even once gaze at the azure minaret, which protruded literally under their noses. The merchant folk and storehouse keepers, vociferously calling out and inviting repeatedly, with strong handshaking traditions, haggling, as if forgetting that besides their mercenary petty business in this world there are also state matters, and there is also their fearsome Lord! But no matter how intensive a search was established by the chief of the investigative branch, from these twirling mustaches and trimmed beards, tall-turbaned shopkeepers one could not obtain an iota of information. What treacherous dogs are hiding in their souls, what fat conniving flies are flapping their paws in their heads? Thereafter the surveillance was intensified and allocated throughout the city—not only to the bazaars, but also in the streets of the mahallas of the city, near the homes of the merchants innumerable divan-dervishes and crippled beggars appeared. An entire gang of vagabonds sought to burst into the courtyard of the merchant in whose house the young master from Ortyube had lived earlier, but the straw-mattress-like petty merchant did not give in to the spies dressed up as vagabonds and dervishes, and did not reveal anything intelligible about his former tenant.

As in the past, this phrase-monger would only blabber in ecstasy with whom he had arguments and had proficiently cut him down, and what bird would be a sure bet in the quail fights. Only once did he mention with a mysterious mien: "The father of the master who had built the tower, at one time was subject to persecution, but managed to disappear and only for that reason remained among the living. After twenty years, he returned to the Great City and brought with him his son, the ustad—the master and expert—to build the Great Mosque. But the father fell ill and died, for he had a mean case of consumption. Just look, the very same fate has befallen his son! The ustad no longer lives in my house, but he left behind him many a good deed, and someday, my righteous people, he will surely be back!" The soulless chief of the Khan's investigative service had him tailed by his best informers, among whom there had been one unsurpassed windbag and cunning person, but he too had been unable to fish out from the merchant any additional information about the love affair between the Young Khansha, the azure minaret and its young builder.

But what irked the Lord most was actually the ominous silence in the city about this threesome. He disliked the sanctimonious, seemly attitude of the crowd, which doubtlessly had learned about everything that he knew himself. Whatever happened to the talkative crowds, who are now stubbornly holding their tongue? But what had taken place is that the crowd is deathly afraid to say the truth which is known to everyone, of which the azure tower had informed the entire world, and which is threatening with death anyone who would mention it merely with one word—and this will be known to the *Lord.* But what is he to do now? He has spent many a sleepless night, seeking an answer to this tormenting question. During the day, however, from morning until evening, he would spend his time in solitude, pacing up and down the deserted throne hall until his feet would tire from such long walks. He would lower himself onto the throne's seat to rest and look blankly in front of him, as if seeking to count the specks of dust before his eyes suspended in the sun's rays penetrating into the hall. Thereupon, he would jump up—how many times he did so!—running towards the window and staring intensely, eyes aflame, at the azure minaret. The latter would respond with a derisive look as if to taunt him. Is that not the way in which the residents of many mahalla neighborhoods of the city are looking at the tower themselves, seeing in it the Lord, with head hung low and crushed in shame? Do they not point their fingers derisively, from bottom up to the top, at the tower? Aye! This tower for him is a pillory, and it is pointing a mocking finger directly at his face, as well as one of fate, threateningly raised towards the sky! Now one can neither destroy the tower nor raze from the face of the earth with a fierce blow of one's angry fist, lest he should be disgraced, to remain in the aura of ill fame for eternity. For, having destroyed the tower, he would admit to the entire world of despicable slaves and residents, rogues and filthy crooks that all their vague conjectures are being clarified and confirmed down to the last devastating kernel of truth. And his head will lower itself even more so from this weight of shame.

And he gripped his unhappy head with both his hands and fell on his knees near the throne's pedestal. He felt that the shameful reputation is approaching him as would a hired murderer with his dagger. He wanted to take a good look at the eyes of this murderer, and suddenly in front of him appeared the face of the chief of construction. Here is one that knows everything—for certain, verily, everything is known to him in great detail! Here is from whom the spark of the fiercest malicious gossip had its origin! He should have been done away with long ago. And one should shift upon him all the suspicions of the thickly seething masses. This should be accomplished artfully, according to the tastes and expectations of the very same crowds, which are susceptible to bloodthirsty and vocal revelations. It shall be done thusly: to announce that it became known to the Lord that the older master had been jealous and envious of the young master. For any master, another one who surpasses him even the least bit in his talent becomes his bitter enemy. Without this being known to everyone, one can advise the young one to omit placing several bricks into the wall, thus leaving an open breach. The latter, without asking the reason for such action, obediently implements this advice. Thereafter, publicly, before the people, the breach, which had been left in the wall on the side of the Khan's park, becomes a disclosing piece of evidence for the sake of an impudent and dishonest act... To the people it should be announced in such a manner: This older master, who has been fiercely envious of the gifted younger one, who has built almost with his own hands and by rule of thumb this superlative structure, has decided to destroy the young architect. The old master at first sought to slander him before the Lord, and thereafter he had this criminal intent somehow to demolish it, so that a similar one would not exist in this world. However, his intentions were just in time discovered and disclosed, even though, unfortunately, the slandered younger architect by that time had already suffered a cruel punishment. A new verdict follows and in public view of his people the real perpetrator is subjected to his deserved punishment and will be executed. And the azure tower shall remain inviolable for many centuries to the glory of the Great City and to exalt the name of the Lord... While all this is going to take place, all gossip about the Khan's young wife and the young architect will gradually come to naught, and in the public eye only the legend of the fatal rivalry of the two outstanding masters will remain.

All that was needed to be done in order for such a legend to arise, was to assign this task to the chief of the soulless ones, and he will accomplish it quickly and adroitly in a mere two days.

The older expert was dragged in shackled, and the Lord did not even bother to interrogate him. Not an old man as yet, robust and stately, his hair had turned grey overnight and he was crushed; now he was trembling and weeping, while standing on his knees. As he, pitifully sobbing, attempted to say something, the Khan ordered the guard:

"Cut out his vile tongue which had brought him his grief, and throw this slanderer into a zindan. Let him rot there."

Indifferently, somewhat squeamish his gaze followed him when this chief-ustad was led away to the torture chamber. The Lord had his share of suffering greatly during his lifetime from people weak and envious; they were ready more than any others to slander a person and to defame him, but precisely such people he preferred to designate as his assistants and appoint them for his government posts as chiefs. He specifically chose them for such positions where one needed to monitor the skillful craftsmen, goldsmiths, jewelers, architects and the miraculous shop masons and bricklayers. And everywhere to supervise these great masters and skilled craftsmen he placed these preposterous, disingenuous nonentities, and envious bunglers. For the Lord knew that such petty people would not praise good masters, but will try somehow to find fault with them, to denigrate the work of a master, to find in it some insignificant flaws and exaggerate these no end. It had been this chief of construction, who had now been forever put away in a dark dungeon, and was more than likely one of these squinting, with sharp ears, soulless informers rather than a master from among the masons and bricklayers. One of his major construction projects had been a subterranean dungeon with numerous cells, comprised of solitary confinement zindans. When this project—so useful for the state—was completed, the Khan ordered to carve into the rock over the main entrance the following inscription: *Sooner or later you will also find yourself in the ground.* Let him now on his own hide experience the entire bitter truth of these words.

Putting him away in a zindan, the Lord experienced a much greater satisfaction than when he had blinded and thrown out into the world the maimed young master.

5

The news that the chief-ustad had wound up in the zindan stirred up the entire city, but for some reason very quickly all talk about it ceased. As dry grass bursts into flames, blazing with a high flame, it just as quickly burns down to the ground. The soulless informers, who had much work these days, also glowed as if their father had been resurrected and had returned from the Other World. These spies were no longer needed and ceased making their appearance at the palace. News no longer was coming from the court of the Khan's Senior Wife. The ruler looked with an eager hope, as a hungry canine looks at his master, at every person who came to the Khan's headquarters. The Khan waited for certain changes or at least hints of such, and he sought to guess and find the secret signs or machinations on the plates of food he was served or some changes in the clothing brought to him every morning. But nothing in particular or new in the daily life of the Lord could be discovered, and at this point nothing, not even the most negative and vile gossip would have been able to upset the dejection and despair in his everyday existence. These soulless, faceless, specter-like heartless people may have understood the despair tormenting the Lord's soul; therefore they did not report any bad news to him, but rather brought him rosy and innocuous tales as bedtime stories. Any given soulless spy was not inclined for the sake of saving the Lord's life to sacrifice his own soulless existence.

In the meantime, the city had already swallowed and digested the presumed story of the mortal enmity between the two master builders, the soap bubble inflated and burst. The city knew quite well the real reason why under the cupola of the azure minaret the inappropriate hole had not been sealed for such a long time, for which the young architect had been blinded, and why the older builder had been forever incarcerated in the zindan. The city also knew that the Great Khan, after returning from his campaign of many years, had not even once visited the Young Wife in her bedchamber; but the city had an explanation for it as usual on the level of their own homespun wisdom: the Lord, presumably, had passed that age when it is usual for a man, by inhaling the air with his nostrils, to get a whiff of various nooks and crannies of the female body, and to lose one's mind from games of love. In any case, upon his return from his campaign, by no means did he spend his time in sensual embraces of his wife. If he did not appear in public view in the Great City, this was not at all due to a preoccupation in love's delights with her, but rather presumably caused by his shame to face the public in person.

From these various conjectures the Khan felt frightfully unwell, and he left the palace eager to visit his huge park which had become wild. There he rushed about along the deserted pathways like a tiger, feeling much like a live target upon which thousands of unseen hunters' sights were aimed. Having wandered about the park, the Khan would return to the palace. Once again his wandering about in the rooms and halls would begin. A prison without locks, where the prisoner is incarcerated without shackles, without the right for clemency, and to the end of his days... The great Lord knows not simple freedom which is quite available to the common people: their freedom to commit acts, may they be ever so insipid, but pursuant to their own wishes. Not at all! For a Lord it is proper not to commit acts, but feats, which must inevitably stun the human imagination. And if the crowds should suddenly learn that the Lord is merely a simple mortal as they are, heartbroken due to his wife's infidelity, they would ignore him. Unheard of defamation will commence, such filthy profanity will be heard that would make the dead turn in their graves. They will cry out mockingly and they will say that in the past he had as if by magic overthrown foreign thrones, wiped out great dynasties, and now he is bewildered, not knowing how to insert an elastic twig into the pharynx of a she-goat with an early estrus. Instead having a frank male fight with the man who had gotten under his wife's lap of her skirt, he started to settle the score with him in some rather illicit ways. The one, whom they have considered second after Allah, turned out to be a nobody among nonentities! While vilifying their Lord they slap themselves on their thighs and pinch their own cheeks from sheer irrepressible ecstasy. This would be the time to come out of his palatial incarceration and confront them! We will see how they will ingratiate themselves, and how they will squirm before him!

But enough of solitary life, lying around like a bear in its lair! Maybe set up a grandiose festivity? And for what reason? Wouldn't be a bad idea to get these scoundrels, completely drunk and to listen to what they will babble while intoxicated... Indeed, one would need to sever all rotten ropes of suspicion, which tie down his hands and feet, and to stand up to it and face one's subjects...

The following day he summoned the Chief Vizier. That one was hardly able to crawl across the doorstep and he froze in place, bent in a bow, looking with his bulging eyes as a bullfrog, with round eyes staring in front of him, without turning his head, not moving it, but seeing everybody and everything around him. After hearing the Lord's orders, the vizier bowed silently and deeply and withdrew, backing out of the hall. The Khan did not like it at all that this old court fox had seemed to be so frightened, so much so that he hurriedly sought to withdraw, without trying to hide his fright. Is he not perhaps frightened that the Lord may call him to account—right after the chief builder— for giving his permission to build the azure minaret during his, the Lord's, absence? But perhaps that is what he should do? What a pity that the vizier has been freed from his audience, for one could have exhausted him some more! One would need to summon him again on some pretext.

One would need to take a look at some other court dung bugs appearing before him. Also, he had not seen for some time the others who are close to the throne: his children and the emirs close to him... Would be interesting to see if they will confront him by looking at his face directly or will they also drop in their bow and will hide their eyes as this Chief Vizier? If that is so, it would signify that they had, perhaps, heard something and have learned something...

After five days the Khan's hunt was announced. Slim borzois on leads, packs of spotted hounds, wolfhounds on short leashes, hunters with bows and arrows on horseback, the Khan's guards surrounding the Lord in his light and comfortable hunting outfit, numerous mounted nukers, hunting drovers, trumpeters and drummers—the drawn out huge caravan moved from the city in the direction of the mountain range, vaguely visible in blue-white spots through the haze of clouds. After an entire day's crossing, the caravan reached a huge gorge. The court high officials, aristocrats and military leaders, as well as the Khan's relatives set up their large tents along the banks of the thundering mountain river and amidst the undergrowth of the autumn tugai. The following day the hunt was to commence up along the gorge, the groves near the banks as well as the gorge slopes were to be combed and searched.

The opulent and well-equipped caravan, the well-groomed racers of lengthy endurance, quality arms and superlative hunting equipment—all this brought former times to the Lord's mind. In the mountains the sun had a different warmth about it than on the burning hot plain; here it had a caressing warmth about it, while down in the sandy deserts it was virtually knocking one's head with a fiery sledgehammer, as a result of which one's brains resounded with the din of alarm from the heat.

That first evening, when they had first pitched camp on the riverbank, Amir ordered to have the festive dastarkhan tablecloths spread in honor of the hunt. There was no shortage of wine. The repast was lively and joyous. And there was nothing of a suspicious nature which during this festive meal the Lord could observe. All the conversations, which he happened to overhear, were only about the hunt and hunting matters. There were those bragging about their horses and their hunting dogs. Hunting tales were told. Listening to all these cheerful, guttural male voices, the Lord did not know whether to be happy about this or to be chagrined. Again it appeared that there was some sort of a conspiracy surrounding him. A conspiracy of a universal and deliberate silence about matters which were driving him out of his mind... And shortly, the Lord once again became gloomy and sullen. He looked like a man who had been deceived in his best expectations.

That night, in his large tent, he just couldn't fall asleep. The entire camp, though, was emerged in a deep sleep. It was quiet and serene in the natural surroundings. A velvety night enveloped the world of living beings. The fresh breeze was saturated with the herbaceous aromas of the mountains. The hearts of the sleeping hunters were beating in agitated anticipation of the forthcoming hunt—they already had visions of the hunt in their dreams. The Lord, himself an avid hunter, well understood the dreams of the impatient, and with some satisfaction, even with a degree of envy, he listened to the mighty and ever-more increasing snoring of the sleeping hunters.

These nights and this life the Lord loved above everything else! When after the hunt they will all descend from the mountains in order to travel each to his own mahalla neighborhood, every single one of these djigits, who with a spear in his hand is part of his united and mighty detachment, will go back to his place and will change to a common small owl, fluffing his feathers, and possibly even babbling about his Lord. But should the Khan call upon him, the entire detachment is reunited in order to implement his commands, not a

End of the Legend • Abish Kekilbaev

single one of them will even think about saying one word against him. They will all only seek to catch his eye, they look at his mouth to see what he will say, and they will carry out any of his orders. At times it seems to him that all his military *sarbaz* are his children, a branch of his familial roots, the innumerous young tribe grown up under his mighty protection. They have only to move away from their usual peaceful life a short distance and to turn up in a campaign situation; they would altogether and each on his own feel a boundless sense of loyalty for him. In him they see a patronage and a shield for themselves. Now, on this moonlit night in the mountains, surrounded by scraggy cliffs, they had acted like his small grandsons, who had tired of their games and pranks, after a good meal, had surrounded on all sides their huge, warm grandfather and instantly had fallen sound asleep. In rivalry with the mountain river, rolling across the boulders with its rapids, the djigits' snoring is shaking the mountains with their mighty sound. The Lord's keen sense of hearing is able to catch each and every rustle and susurration born in the night and flying about right outside the thin walls of his campaign tent. And nowhere is there in the surroundings any such sound which would pose a threat or which would cause alarm from a hostile uncertainty—each sound in this serene night was compatible and therefore fully explicable. How marvelous and wonderful this night! Yet sleep will not come to him. Somewhere in the darkness the royal borzoi hounds from India are whining: hark! Have they sensed the smell of some animal?

Right outside the threshold of the tent, barely audible, some minute living being is puttering about and tinkering. Perhaps some insect or a mouse is without much ado continuing its life's pursuits. From a distance the trill of night cicadas can be heard. Everything is so simple, and yet at the same time so quaint, mysterious and incomprehensible in nature! This very minute, the dense fog of hopelessness, which had saturated every single fiber of his troubled mind, began to leave it, occasionally obscuring with its dark patches the clear vision of his enlivened soul. He no longer wanted to sleep, for he felt vigorous and refreshed. Alas! if one could only once and for all leave tonight, to dissipate into the night and totally forget the way to the palaces, forget about the throne, the crown, and the golden huge tents with the tall shanrak! Ah, if one could only exist in this world like that minute creature of nature right by the threshold, which crawls along, scratching with its tiny claws, without worries, and in its humble existence there is, yes, there is God's Providence! O, Allah… To slip away like a grass snake now from the tent, from this hunters' camp, and to lose oneself in the dense growth of the tugai near the river! And tomorrow his hunters' caravan would return to the Great City, not finding the Lord in his tent neither alive nor dead, and the entire army of his bodyguards would be marching, hiding their faces in shame, and his mysterious disappearance would give birth to legends, one more improbable than the other. And he would be sitting somewhere on a mountain boulder looking down on the Great City, and with a smile envisioning the boundless sea of human insipidness and vanity.

He was aware of the entire sad unrealizable nature of his aspirations, but from the bottom of his heart he amused himself with this ingenuous game of his mind. At least in this game he was able to leave the iron cordons of his countless guards, which had surrounded his tent with a tight circle and no one would be allowed to enter living or to exit alive, including—ha ha!—him as well, presumably.

Oh, how he did not wish to leave that narrow pathway so unusual for him, the Amir-Lord-Lord, the path of free thought! How one did not wish to part with the abundance of this night of trepidation in the mountains! With that little bug or mouse under the threshold!

But here it seems he had been able to come out onto that path and gradually proceed on it! It led further away, both from the hunting camp and from all that which constituted a regrettable triviality of his existence full of endless confusion. He decided to leave all of this forever and go away without looking back.

Walking along the road, he suddenly discovered that in some manner he had been able to free himself of the cumbersome and heavy royal garments, and the crown on his head was no longer there. Instead of these on his body was the garment of the Hajj—pilgrimage to Mecca—the *ihram,* which consisted of two un-hemmed white sheets. In such clothing the righteous Muslims travel to their Holy City, to the sacred Black Stone of Kaaba. He is walking, with pleasure sinking with his feet in the light road dust. All around him is a terrain heretofore unseen by him and unfamiliar. Amidst the sun-bleached, faded pale-yellow mountains one can see a white city. In its direction, by various roads and from various sides, endless files of people in white pilgrim clothing are moving. At the tail end of one such file he also is plodding along, barely moving his tired feet. He is constantly shouting out words of prayer, and from this his throat is sore. Soon his voice is completely gone, and out of his mouth only a barely audible hissing sound can be heard. In vain did he open his mouth and moved his lips. No one could hear his prayers. Ahead of them on the road a low mountain crest could be seen. All the travelers near him increased their pace. Only after midday did they reach the foot of the mountain slope. Some person wearing a white turban and riding a white dromedary, draped by a rug with a design, ascended the top of the crest. Without dismounting his camel, the man opened a book in front of him and began to read in a singsong voice. His rich resounding voice, at times, broke off as if choking in emotion, and then the pilgrims of the multitudinous crowd, standing and fanning themselves with the white *ihram* hanging from their shoulders, would respond in unison with their ungainly voices:

- Almighty and Merciful! You are the Ruler of the World! We are ready to serve You!

He had heard these words of submissiveness from others, but he had never uttered these words himself, but now, changed, he taught his lips to pronounce them; therefore his voice sounded apart from the other voices, somewhat lagging behind. The pilgrims standing next to him had tears running down their faces. But on his hardened, stern face, constantly facing his enemies, not a single tear was to be seen. Wanting to conceal from the others his insensitivity, he bowed his head low, senselessly moving his lips, pretending that he is praying. The man on the white camel slammed shut the book and raising his hands before him, began to perform the prayer of blessing. People squatted down and drew their open palms together. After this, the entire mass of pilgrims, swooped as a white stream onto the crest of the mountain pass, and thereupon came tumbling down like an avalanche into the valley. And somewhere in this huge avalanche the Lord pilgrim was lost, whirling about and swept up in the torrent. It took away his breath, but trying with all his might not to fall behind the others, he was running along with all the other pilgrims. They had descended from the mountain and had passed its foothills, when all of a sudden whining, clanging, droning music could be heard. Just as sudden night fell. At midday yet, upon ascending the crest, he had seen in the valley a multitude of tall wooden towers, lined up all along the way of the pilgrims' stream. And now flaming signal torches were on these towers. In the sky fiery spheres were exploding. The entire elaborate valley surrounded by the hills brightened by the countless lights of campfires, in the reflection of which in the night thousands of varicolored large tents stood out. Amidst these, in the commotion of a motley night camp, being aware of his prayers, the Lord also awaited dawn.

Once again the Venerable One on his white camel appeared and called for prayer. The pilgrims performed the morning namaz, the prayer, along with him. Then they all moved en masse to the middle of the valley. There stood a tall, black stone pillar, and each pilgrim threw seven small stones the size of a grain of corn at this pillar. Ultimately, the praying crowd came to a wall built of rough black cobblestone. And at it they threw a fistful of seven stones taken out of their pocket. After this, the pilgrims in their white clothing went over to the earthen hearths over which were suspended huge kazan. Near the hearths meat-carvers were busy with their large knives, butchers were bustling around over the carcasses of sacrificed cattle. Between the hearth fires, grimacing and pestering people, a diverse lot of vagrants and dervishes was running about in their ghastly rags; the beggars and the maimed from all over the world were supplicating alms from the foreign and distant pilgrims. Some pilgrims, going aside, shaved their heads with the local barbers, doing their good deed in the name of the Almighty One. In the dexterous hands of the goodwill barbers the sharp razors were flashing and shining. They were shaving off the pilgrims' hair, soaked by the water stream coming from the long nozzle of a *kumgan*-jug; the pilgrims held their heads humbly bent. At a blink of an eye, after shaving their heads, the barbers commenced with trimming their nails on their hands and feet. Then, wrapping the cut hair and trimmed nails into separate scraps of cloth, tying the ends in a knot, the pilgrim would bury this for God in the Holy Ground.

From the earthen hearths they removed the cauldrons. In front of the pilgrims, who sat down on the ground in long rows, they placed trays with boiled meat. After the meal, the white pilgrim crowds went to the Sacred Black Stone of the Kaaba. It was standing there covered with a black Egyptian cloth before the jostling pilgrims. The priest took off the cover from the Stone and began to tear it with a crackling sound into pieces and distributing those to the believers. This was last year's cover from Kaaba, and it had to be torn and given out to the faithful, in order for them to retain the power of the sacred Stone and to bring them success in their lives. In the distance there is the white marble dais of the *minbar* from which the *qadi* delivers his sermon. A small cupola has been erected above the sacred *Zamzam* Well.

Having paid his respects to the grave of Prophet Ibrahim, who had erected the revered Kaaba, he wanted to drink, as the others did, the waters of the sacred Well. But he was unable to even make one swallow, because for him the water of the well had an unthinkable taste and burned his mouth as alkali would. The Lord prayed along with all the others, raising his palms to the mountain, performed the standing and making the seven circuits around the Black Stone of Kaaba, whose front part has been polished to a shine by the touching of hands and lips of the faithful. But when the Lord also sought to make his way to the Stone and kiss it in veneration, the Stone had moved to the side as if it were alive and did not offer him a chance to touch it. Crowded out by other pilgrims, he once again joined the circuitous walk around the Stone and approached it the second time seeking to touch it with his palm and kiss it thereafter, but the Black Kaaba once again, in an illusory way, moved away from his hand and lips. And then, swept to the side by the human flow, he began to jump up and down as the others implementing with their jumps the ritual of the circuit walking around the Kaaba, and in this fashion he made the circuit four times. And each time, once again coming close to it, he sought to kiss it or at least touch it with his hand, but the Stone would adamantly avoid him. Thus he was forced back by the mighty flow of the white-clothed crowds from the Holy Stone, having been very close to it, but being unable to touch it.

After visiting the Kaaba, the pilgrims moved on to the hills of Safa and Marwah, which were there nearby like twins. He also did not lag behind the others, and farther on carried out everything that a righteous Muslim had to do who had gone on a Hajj to the Holy Land. He did not miss a single ablution, performed every namaz; had his nails trimmed short and dyed with henna, anointed his body with incense, which drives off the unclean spirit of Iblis the Devil; for the sacred sacrifice he brought a white camel; but he did not leave out any saints in his prayers at their gravesites in the vicinity of the Kaaba, and at each grave he tied a small knot with his alms. Since that time when he had the ihram hanging from his shoulder he did not shed blood, did not eat sweet fruit, did not look into the mirror, and did not even allow himself thoughts about women and carnal pleasures, far less committing them. He had waited so eagerly for that sacred moment when he finally could be called a Hajj and shall wind a blessed turban around his head. But the Sacred Black Stone did not let him approach it. Why? Why did he deserve such harsh punishment? Did not the saints tell us that all sins are forgiven to those who are able to reach Holy Mecca and, upon entering its terrain, are to fulfill all the required rituals, shall kiss the Black Stone of Kaaba? And why is it that the sacred water of Zamzam, so sweet to others, for him is so unbearably bitter like alkali?

But he continues to run without complaining after the rest of the crowd, and everything is swimming in front of his eyes and the road dust has stuffed his throat and hampered his breathing. And he is constantly confronted by the Black Stone, rough at its base, with a visible sprinkling of crimson coloring, but higher up on the frontal part, polished to a shine by the reverent touch of the faithful. But the Stone definitely endeavors to stay at a distance from him as if it were carried off by the rotation of a huge potter's wheel. And there is no way one can catch up with it now.

They now reached the dale between the Safa and Marwah hills. At one time the wife of Ibrahim had walked around them seven times in search of water for her one and only son Ismail, while his father, Ibrahim, was erecting the sanctuary of Kaaba. The tired Lord reached it as well. He felt that his strength was nearly exhausted, and an involuntary lamentation of despair escaped from the very depths of his soul: "Almighty Creator, Only You alone! I am willing to serve You in every way! Why then are You rejecting me, depriving me of Your good graces with which you so generously reward others?" And sensing that his feeble and exhausted voice does not reach Allah, he strains his numb throat and cries out: "O, Allah! May Your will prevail throughout!"

The Lord woke up, frightened by his own outcry. Sunlight was filtering through the tent's silken cloth. Dawn had broken some time ago. From the outside scarcely audible voices of the awakened hunters were drifting in. The Lord jiggled a small bell, at the entrance a servant appeared, carrying a light hunter's outfit. When he got dressed and walked outside, the sun had already risen to the length of horse fetters. The horses were already saddled. The borzoi-*tazy* hounds, the mighty *boribasar* wolfhounds, the lip-drooping mighty *tobet*, bred to hunt bears, impatiently were tugging on their leashes and standing straight up in the air, barking resonantly. The golden eagles, sitting on the arms of the falconers, hawks, falcons, and the kestrels were screeching, turning their hooded heads, and their screeching carried far into the fresh morning air. The morning was totally cloudless; the snowy mountain peaks were sparkling like polished mirrors. In the mountains, silence and serenity prevailed. And only on the very bottom of the gorge the mountain river thundered monotonously. The chorus of small songbirds resounds, their voices sounding carefree and happy, as if these tiny creatures are aware that there is no danger coming for them from the numerous and fear-invoking hunters, their mighty dogs and birds of prey they use for hunting. As to the larger birds and all the

End of the Legend • Abish Kekilbaev

animals, they all have hidden themselves the best they could. The Lord turned to his aristocrats and military leaders who were all humbly lined up not too far from the Khan's tent. The entire formation bowed as sedge grass would from a gust of wind. With a listless nod their Lord returned their greeting and in a lumbering manner, mounted his horse held by two of his *nuker* guards. He donned his quiver with the arrows, which was handed to him by his professional hunter. His aristocratic entourage also mounted their horses quickly thereafter. At this point the hoarse and screeching voices of the karnay trumpets cut into the silence of the ravine in the mountains. The hunt had begun. The first to move out were the drovers, accompanied by the noise-makers: the drummers, those making rattling sounds, tambourine and karnay trumpet players. Their task was to go deep into the ravines and gorges, the riverside undergrowth and ravines, to frighten away and chase out the game for the marksmen and dogs. On a spacious open area, the Lord and his entire retinue positioned themselves on horseback. In the back, in a wide semi-circle the Khan's guards and individual bodyguards for the various aristocrats were lined up.

In the hunting camp but a few of the servants and watchmen were left behind. These were those who remained behind and were not sent off for the chase of the game. At the cauldrons cooks and firewood preparers were bustling about.

Alienated from everyone, the Lord sat sullen on his horse. His retinue was likewise taciturn and morose as if they were afraid of provoking his anger. Formerly their hunt was quite different; they always sought by some means to bring about his spirited disposition. At present, however, the faces of the aristocrats and military leaders were apprehensive and sullen as if they had been somehow subjected to an insult by the Khan. Or perhaps they are experiencing some form of pity and a secretive disdain towards him? Is it likely that by now they know, having discussed this among themselves, that in the morning, prior to his awakening, he had been crying out in a plaintive voice, in a delirium, words of pleading and seeking forgiveness addressed to Allah? But it was difficult to guess from their facial expressions what their actual thoughts were.

At this point one could hear how in the distance, from the direction of the gorge, there was shouting and the tumultuous barking of dogs; drums were beaten, and the bellowing of karnay trumpets resounded and the flushing out of game had begun. Blending with the tumultuous noise of the river, the thunderous flushing out was increasingly coming closer. And soon everything merged into a chaos of deafening sounds: the cracking sounds of breaking twigs in the dense undergrowth, the beating of hundreds of hoofs, and the crumbling, rumbling rocks. All the aristocrat hunters became alert, leaning forward in their saddles they pulled out their bows from the quivers. Only the Lord did not move. The barking of dogs came closer. His nuker-guards, awaiting his orders, could barely restrain their horses by the bridle. However, as previously, the Lord still remained motionless. Only at the point when the cracking sounds of twigs and the hallooing sounds were almost next to him, he nodded in silence to the chief vizier.

Letting almost all of the aristocrat hunters ahead of him, the Lord galloped off towards the drovers. Purposefully, he restrained his horse, got to be behind all the others who were flying forward, whooping and howling, and galloped in the direction of the open steppe. This is precisely the direction, jumping out of a breakup of the undergrowth of the tugai, from which a herd of deer came flying out. Most of the hunters, quickly bridled their horses, began chasing the deer. Thus, getting rid of his bodyguards, who lost him for a moment in the overall commotion of the horsemen, the Lord rode into the undergrowth along one of the ravines and headed towards the river. Coming to a quiet channel, he stopped and dismounted. Those who managed to notice him, in their indecision bridled their horses, not knowing what to do. The nukers began hurriedly to comb through the riverside dale. Then they froze in place, not daring to approach him. He rested a bit, came up and bent down to the water, scooped up a handful and rinsed his face. Then he took off his shoulders the quiver with the bow, placed it on a boulder and stretched out next to it, facing the sky. He frequently had the occasion to be outside palaces and halls, amidst pristine nature, but he never had the opportunity to experience complete solitude in such surroundings. Now he was almost happy, having finally had the chance to get away from his obtrusive retinue and hide from the watchful eyes of his guards. Let his loquacious aristocrats talk about him whatever they want behind his back, but not to bother him or to obsequiously try to catch his every gaze as if they were dogs. Otherwise, with their repulsive hypocrisy they will simply be the death of him!

All around him was the emerald kingdom of grass. The nocturnal dew was still glistening on the leaves. The jagged mountaintops, seen in the distance beyond the crests of reeds, were exuding such freshness and purity as if they had bathed in streams of nocturnal dew. From the river a cool wind had gathered suddenly gently tugging at the Khan's clothes open at his chest. But this wind is slight and transitory to be able to dissipate the oppressiveness in his heart. He could not forget his predawn strange dream. In front of his eyes now are mountains covered with white ice caps, not at all like the dark brown, like an overcooked liver, hills of Arafat and Muzdalifah, the straw-colored Safa and Marwah hills, which he had seen in his dream, and of which he had only heard from accounts by pilgrims. The real mountains confronting him now, the forests and mountain meadows, upon which now with wild whoops the royal hunt is chasing game, are totally unlike the expanse of deserts, wherein in his dream he had traveled together with the pilgrims. But how steadfast and clear were the dust of the wanderers' roads and the somewhat bitter smell of the sun-scorched earth impregnated in his memory! And how realistic in his dream had been the image of the country, where he had never been! Or had it been the lengthy tales of the Holy Sayed, the spiritual teacher, who had made the Hajj to the Holy Land several times, which were so deeply imbedded in his memory? Why did he have a dream about a country at the other end of the world, where the Muslim holy places are, for which he didn't have the time being so busy with the constant battles in life and war? Or are these his ancestors' spirits who had brought to his consciousness such a dream, and have shown him the way out of this fatal impasse in which his soul has found itself? Indeed, why shouldn't he go on a Hajj to Mecca? There were quite a few kings and Lords in this world who had in the twilight of their life, having kissed the Sacred Black Stone, exchanged their diamond crown for a Hajj turban and, having relinquished their throne, went off to walk the dusty roads in the crowd of dervishes. Isn't it rather clear that these kings had gone through the same spiritual collapse and disappointment in life as he had? But why then in his dream the Black Stone, when he wanted to kiss it, had moved aside not giving him the opportunity to touch it? Or is it that his sins are so immense that they are wholly unforgiveable and surpass in their gravity the sins of the most dreadful criminal who has ever existed in this world? But why is it then that in the Holy Book all the Khans, kings and Lords, enthroned and crowned, come to resemble the golden pillar of a royal tent, which Allah had erected for humanity in this world? Is it possible that the Creator is so severe concerning the pillars of his tent? And why did He select him out of the multitude of humanity and signaled him: this is not your place among those who have come here wearing their ihram? But if one gives this a thought, what then had doomed him, the Lord, to such demeaning, filthy and narrow-minded suffering? Could there possibly be found an abasement more disgraceful than that inflicted by a woman's meager mind? A considerable amount of mundane poison he had to take, many a misfortune he had lived through, numerous times he had been at the brink of death, but he had never suffered in his soul so much as he has now. In all dangerous situations he remained on horseback, and even risking his life, he was able to save his honor. Then, what is his misdeed before the Creator, that He, without any defeat of the Lord in the battle with his enemies, had deprived him of his honor? Is it perhaps his fault that he served faithfully and protected the dignity of the throne, which He Himself had provided him with. Or didn't the Lord root out by fire and sword the tribes of the infidels, planting in their countries the green banner the Prophet? No matter what he has done in the name of the latter, has been implemented thoroughly, vigorously, so that among the despicable rabble, during their times of bestial satiety, doubts should not arise that all of his deeds are in the name of Allah, and the rabble should marvel at him no end, rather than having their doubts. And it isn't his, the Lord's, sin that by the name of Allah and with His help he had done everything better than the others, which for the others was too much. What, then, was his sin in this life? Perhaps in his insatiable lust? Alas! Throughout history lust brought sin to mankind. But take an inordinate love of power or intemperate cruelty—is that not sin? And an excessive virtue, singing its own praises—is that not sin? All—ambition, sensuality, and lust for power—have one progenitor. Similar to the one, where an incorrigible petty thief from the bazaar is no different from a peddling slut, who never makes up her bed in her lair; the omnipotent ruler, who tortures his people without constraints and impetuously in the name of rule, does not differ much from a contemptible, miserable strumpet, who is tempting and taking money for that which females, naturally, provide for free.

This then only means that the limitless rule he now commanded, all his monumental tasks, all his notorious fame—is nothing more than an illusory, cheap tinsel of human existence, the crass rouge on the cheeks of a downright tart or moth-eaten junk fur in the chests of a skinflint.

Nonetheless, why is it then that the Black Stone, which had avoided his lips had slipped away from his hands, albeit permitting the others to come close to it, the others, who possibly, were up to their ears in the sewage of their vile sins? What did the Almighty note in the Lord's soul which was unacceptable for Him? An excessive arrogance towards those like him? Forgetting the fact that he was also given birth by a woman, he came here as a Lord, even though for the sake of appearance he had crawled on his knees at the temple's entrance. Everyone else came to pray their sins away, but you had come in order to show how humbly the great Lord conducts himself in the great holy places. But if that is so, why does he want, following the example of many Lords, to take into his hand a beggar's staff, hang a sack on his neck, and to walk the roads amidst the crowds of dervishes in their torn rags? Perhaps behind this desire in his heart lies not so much his concern about his soul, inherent to all the rest, but rather a profound fear to become in old age, when one's strength will be gone, a pitiful laughingstock for the bazaar crowds?

Is this the mere mortal, as they say, who is the one always jealously determining whether you are loftier or lower in comparison to him? Should you be loftier, then he will prostrate himself at your feet, kiss the edge of your robe and answer to all that you are saying only one thing: "It shall be done, master!" But should you descend below his level, he will say: "What poor fellow! What a stage he has reached! This unfortunate one!" And the most important matter would be not to be placed on a par with this 'mere mortal' or to become the same as he, an ordinary scoundrel. And, being apprehensive of this, many Lords with renowned names had preferred in old age to exchange their golden scepter for a wooden staff. To renounce their crown, to go on the Hajj, take into one's hands the staff of a wise man, to hang on one's neck the beggar's bag and to withdraw oneself into a blessed solitary life—isn't this the true path of deliverance from evil intrigues of the abhorrent rabble? Perhaps only when you are in a short sheepskin coat full of holes, which does not evoke envy in anyone, the rabble then will forgive you, and their hatred which they held for years towards you, the inaccessible Lord, one fine day they will change to a peaceful reconciliation with you. And in the irreconcilably hostile eyes of the rabble there suddenly will appear the shadow of compassion. And for you by now it will no longer be unendurably painful from the fact that some slug was able to punish you by besmirching your male honor. Then it is doubtful that anyone will think of verifying what shaytan had made such a smoking fire in your soul!

Indeed, the Lord had a fervent desire to change his destiny in a radical manner and to start a simple and inconspicuous life as most people live in this world. To be lost in obscurity! His pre-dawn dream manifested itself as direct instructions from his ancient *aruakh*, who wanted to save and protect him. At this time he remembered that the coming month was that of *Zulhijja*—the time for the righteous Muslims to go on their Hadjj to the Holy Land.

The Lord wanted to see his Holy Seer in order to discuss with him the significance of his early morning dream. So that he decided to end this unnecessary hunt and to return to the Great City immediately. After a short time he will leave this river valley and will order his signalman to blow his horn announcing the end of the hunt.

He got up from the boulder and felt that his side was rather numb after lying on the hard rock. At this point he heard that something huge and heavy was making its way through the undergrowth, breaking up the reed with its feet. The Khan gave a start and became alert, and is if perceiving his alarm, that someone making his way through the reeds, also stopped and became quiet. The Lord began to look around, standing at his full height. Here is when he saw in the slightly verdant undergrowth of reeds something striped and fiery orange-colored. That instant, as if he no longer wished to hide, this orange-colored, striped monster moved the reeds and came into view from the undergrowth. A tiger… The huge Indian tiger began to creep in his direction, looking at him constantly with fiery eyes. Everything happened so fast that the Lord did not even have time to become frightened, and only his back had become instantly frozen and then just as quickly was covered with perspiration. His hand did not even have enough time to reach over to the quiver with its bow, which was next to him on the boulder.

In his head a thought flashed: so that is why he had that pre-dawn dream! That is why the Black Stone had been evading him, predicting an imminent unnatural death. So that is what it is all about: his lot must not be the same as everyone else's, the Lord, whose life had been different from all the others!

The tiger was coming closer. Almost impatiently did the Lord await this rapid and honorable death, which Allah, having heard his prayers and seeing his suffering, had sent upon him, saving him from his endless grief, which had smitten his chest like a noose. Forever, without leaving a trace, the unkind, hateful and viscid looks of the crowds directed at his restless soul. Subsequent to his death, the crowd will award him posthumously with a magnificent legend, which throughout the centuries will only build up its magnificence.

The tiger came very close and flattened its ears. Its spine curved in a convulsive wave, its tail swung from one side to the other, and then the beast crouched to the ground. 'He's going to jump now,' the Lord thought. These crooked, sharp claws will thrust into his neck. The huge fangs will penetrate his head and crush his skull. But suddenly the beast made a strange jerking movement and, turning its head, looked to its right.

From that direction, a nuker came forth and, suddenly spying the beast so close, was taken aback, and froze in place. But right away he regained his senses, grabbed his bow and began to place an arrow on it. In this instant the Lord also reached out for his bow.

The nuker saw how the striped, fire-orange deadly beast hurled itself through the air at him—but something happened to it… Mortally wounded, the tiger dropped to the ground. Shaken by this event, the djigit lowered his bow. And here he saw that the Lord calmly and business-like was shouldering the bow.

The Khan came up to the dead animal. The arrow had found exactly the tiger's heart and the beast perished in flight, not yet hitting the ground. Life was departing from it with the heavy, convulsive movements of its mighty paws. The Khan sighed profoundly—perhaps from his post-traumatic experience, or from regret that instead of dying a heroic death himself, it had been the Lord of animals killed by his arrow. And then, not knowing why, he laughed briefly. Possibly he was pleased that the tiger had not been killed by the nuker. Otherwise there would have been so much praise, pounding of fists on chests, so many legends about how a common nuker had saved the Lord himself from certain death at the hunt.

The Lord came out of the river flood plain. The horse keepers, already notified, were hurrying to the reeds area in order to skin the tiger. That first day the only conversations held were how the Lord had killed the tiger. And the following day, when the Lord, unexpectedly for everyone, announced the end of the hunt, the entire caravan during their return to the city spoke only of this event.

As to the Lord, he was taciturn as usual, immersed in his unhappy thoughts. By evening the royal hunt entered the city. The night was sleepless for the Khan, and he tossed and turned without sleep until the hours of the morning. The unusually clairvoyant, long dream he had that morning before the hunt, and the tiger, killed by him during the hunt, had added another dimension to his life, something even more mysterious and inexplicable.

But no matter what it had been, life was coming to the point for him to make a decision for further actions. Based on the fact that the Almighty One had saved him from death in the tiger's claws, some very significant and courageous action was to be expected on behalf of the Khan. But what would it be? To act as in his dream, to remove the crown from his head and wrap a turban around his head? But one thing was clear, to continue living in his magnificent palace as a timorous apparition was more than he could bear. One needed to see his Holy Seer as soon as possible and tell him about his dream, let the prophet explain it to him. The Khan had not seen his spiritual teacher for some time now. Hopefully the holy venerable old man bore no hard feelings for this inattention.

Next day, during the early cool of the morning he traveled in his carriage. The road led through gloomy, bare hills located south of the Great City. Unexpectedly, he caught himself having the impression that these places were strikingly similar to those holy places he had seen in his dream. The brown hills in the morning semidarkness reminded him likewise of an overcooked liver. Here was also an odor of earth baked in the July heat.

In the middle of a high hill with a pointed peak, formed by tons of quaint huge boulders, overgrown by furry moss and crests of broken shale towered a cliff with a tiny cave, reminding one of a perched *Samuryk-Simurgh* on the slope. The cave's entrance was towards the *qiblah,* the direction of the Kaaba to which the righteous turn in prayer. At the entrance of the cave there was something whitish. It was the holy venerable old man sitting in his white turban under the overhang of the black cliff. From the height of the hill, he had surely noticed the approaching royal carriage, but he continued sitting there, without stirring, in the same manner facing in the direction of the qiblah. As has been his custom in the past, the Lord left his nukers down below, and ascended alone to the abode of the holy hermit. No matter how distant his travels or long campaigns in his quest for foreign thrones and crowns that the Lord-warrior would be conducting, prior to these ventures he would always travel to his spiritual teacher, the holy hermit, and he would ascend on the barely noticeable, pathway winding between boulders, in order to receive the blessing and to touch the grey small beard of the holy venerable old man sitting under the cliff, as if he were a red-footed falcon with its ruffled feathers. After the visit, the Lord would travel to the largest mosque in the Great City in order to perform a namaz. Only after all of these actions did he consider it feasible to commence with his campaign.

On this occasion, the minute, jug-sized, little old man seemed to ignore the person clambering the steep path to his place. He sat, with a blank look in the direction of the qiblah. His smallish head had a turban wrapped around it. Gusts of wind were blowing about in his sparse small beard, and it seemed that the bony diminutive face was shuddering from some inner anxiety. The Lord, finally, had reached the small platform in front of the cave on the cliff, and stopping before the old man, clearing his throat, sought to attract the latter's attention. But the hermit sat, eyes closed, not moving. The Lord could only wait humbly and look him over. The bottom of the worn and faded chapan, the overcoat, of the hermit was torn by thorny branches, and the wide trousers, which hung down to his bare feet, had holes in many places. The soles of his feet were cracked, scarred and had fresh scabs. Holding his staff with both hands, which he had placed on his lap, his wrists were covered with knotty blue veins. The old Seer was immersed in a profound inner contemplation.

The old man opened his eyes only after the Lord had lowered himself on his knees in front of him, raising his hands in prayer and bowing his head low. As if awakened, the hermit quickly raised his head, opened his eyes and looked at the newcomer for the first time. Reserved and in a low voice he uttered the customary greeting. He asked the Lord what brought him here. And the Lord humbly and in detail told him of all his concerns. The Seer listened, sitting as motionless as a stake which had been driven into the ground. He had an absent-minded expression on his face. But on several occasions his thin lips pursed in a hardly noticeable smirk. Seeing this, the Lord would be embarrassed and fall silent, but then with some effort forced himself to continue speaking. The venerable old man would suddenly open his eyes, bleary and swollen with the tears of old age, and sought to look into the eyes of the newcomer. The Lord related to him his recent dream and the episode with the tiger, which he had killed during the hunt, albeit his desire had been just the opposite: to be killed by this animal. At long last the Khan fell silent, expecting some replies from his teacher, the *Saiyid*.

The Saiyid sat there for a long time in thought. Several times he would quickly glance at the Khan, as if in doubt whether it would be fitting for him to provide an answer of any kind. But sitting there in his state of misgiving, he still began to talk:

"All the forces of the mountain, and the Almighty Creator Himself, and the saints, and the ancestor spirits, never express themselves directly and frankly on things they wish to impart on their sinful wards. But if for reasons of compassion towards him they wish to provide direct instructions or a prophetic knowledge, then it looks simple and straight as this staff. It must be that you have greatly angered the spirit of ancestors and turned away from your person the good graces of your guarding angels. Think about it and try to recall!" That was the only thing that the old hermit said and fell silent, once again dropping off into his state of oblivion.

After this he didn't utter a single word. He took up his staff from his lap, and he stuck it with all his might into the ground in front of him, and stretching his thin neck, he continued to gaze into the direction of the qiblah. The Lord understood immediately that on this note their meeting has ended, and the remaining decisions were his alone. The venerable old man had always been laconic and stern, at times frankly bilious, callous and unsociable. However, this is the first time that the Lord had seen him as unfriendly as he had been today. Every movement, the changing facial expressions, each spoken word— all were scratching just as those thorny shrubs, which were tearing on the holy venerable old man his hermit's tatters. But holding back his involuntary indignation, the Lord humbly bowed in a *ruku,* bending over by putting one's hands on one's knees, and turning around, he headed for the steep goat path by which he had ascended to the cave of the holy man. The Saiyid continued sitting there like a statue. It is not that he would not say a few parting words, but he didn't even bless the Lord who came to him begging for advice. While in the past, when the Khan was younger, the holy Saiyid would meet him in a friendly manner, blessing him, gently stroking his head and permitting the Lord to respond by touching his beard. But this time, just harshness, unapproachable attitude and an old age irreconcilability remained frozen on his face.

While already sitting in his carriage, the Lord looked back at the stony hill. At the cliff's overhang, below which just a bit earlier one could have seen the hermit in white, there was nothing there now, and therefore it seemed that the cliff had turned its back. With bitterness in his heart, the Lord returned to his palace.

During his entire conscious life of a warrior he had adhered to this rule: 'Do not place yourself into a dead end from which there is no exit. Just in case, always leave yourself a loophole.' But at this point this rule had been violated. He is in a trap, while a loophole of rescue out of it, it seems, can't be foreseen. Now he, a ruler with a crown of diamonds, crushing under his throne the entire world, he now sits alone and downtrodden in his palace on a crudely made rug with a harsh pile piercing his palm as the bristles of a hedgehog. And he feels as an unfaithful wife would when caught with her lover or a petty thief whose hand had been grabbed during his act. There is no one nearby from whom one could seek advice, who could simply listen to him with sympathy and understanding.

And a merciless and frightful thought came to his mind. The youth, whom he had blinded and maimed, living his remaining life somewhere in a forsaken kishlak, and the chief builder-architect, rotting alive in a zindan, without seeing daylight, and the Young Khansha of the Khan, according to his cruel will is doomed to spend the rest of her days within the four walls of the harem—all of them, nonetheless, have a more dignified and humane fate than his. If only because each one of them has the opportunity and hope to meet someone and tell that someone everything, to complain and to give the name of the evildoer who had doomed them to this torment. But he, the Great Lord, whom could he name as his tormentor? Whom could he accuse that he is plagued by torment, huge and weighty, like the Cape Fold Mountains? Could a Lord of a golden crown, complain about Allah Himself? There is no one else left. But who is to listen to his complaints, if even the old morel at his cave did not wish to deal with him? He didn't even look at him, as if he is so great that with his rotten staff he is actually propping up the blue sky. Is there possibly a more dreadful humiliation than servility before those in power? He experienced this on himself: better to be an outcast with head raised with pride, than to be a slave in his homeland. However, hating servitude at heart, did he try to get to be like the one who stood servile before him on his knees? The heads of the proud ones he sacrificed for the sake of his unbridled rage, and at the heads of the despicable ones who were crawling before him on their stomachs, embracing his feet, he looked with a squeamish pity. The reason for his executions and beheadings had not been a lack of his kindness and mercy, but it had been only due to necessity to retain the severity of his rule and the high dignity of his royal title. Respect is not friends with squalor, and when the rich give alms to the trembling poor and cripples, this is not manifestation of kindness, but rather a desire to rid oneself as soon as possible from the sight of these gone-to- seed, foul-smelling and disgusting people. Could it be that this obstinate hermit had acted with him impertinently, almost rudely, in order to teach one who had never known mercy towards the weak? Could it be that he wanted to warn that for every atrocity there will always be an even greater atrocity? But couldn't the old man have made the reprimand in a different way, without an obvious alienation and an impatient disdain? How everything had been different previously: regardless how difficult the matter would have been with which the Lord would come to see the *Saiyid,* the venerable old man would speak with him in the language of genuine clarity and lofty sanctity evoking reverence. He had waited for some time for someone from this world of humanity who would have the courage, at times at least, to remove the mask of hypocrisy and to appear before him with their true face, expressing rejection, condemnation and undisguised hatred towards him. Now he had seen such a face—and whose has it been? This was the face of the old *Saiyid,* whom he had considered the sole person holding similar views after Allah. That major rejection, which this world of slaves had harbored within itself, his holy hermit had expressed directly, without beating around the bush. He had virtually nailed the Khan with this horrible accusation: 'You have greatly angered the spirit of ancestors…' How did you anger them? Perhaps by the fact that you had concealed the original sin of your Young Khansha, a female possessed by the lust of no other than Azazel? And instead of removing with fire and sword any trace of the hoofs of Iblis from his marital bed, he is seeking to cover with his palms these traces so loathsome to God in a most shameful manner? To divorce the Young Khansha, exclaiming thrice in public the word *talaq*? But then in all of the legends of humanity he would be the first *Lord* who voluntarily had taken upon himself such shame. Moreover, how could he admit before the entire world that some black-footed desert tramp had seduced his crowned wife? No, the obstinate Saiyid could not have had this in mind in his unspoken accusations.

Why, after all, in this case the Lord should nail to the pillar of shame not his lecherous wife, not her lover, but rather himself. Does it mean then that the holy hermit did not deign to determine the punishment for the real sinners, but believes to commit to condemnation the Lord himself? It would have been quite likely to expect such impulsive actions on the part of the Senior Wife of the Khan, who even in her dreams is seeking ways of getting rid of the Young Khansha of the Khan, and to this end she would be willing to commit to shame even her crowned husband. But how could the Holy Saiyid ever think in terms of animosity, he, who has known the Lord since childhood, and remembers his father? How could he, with the white turban of the Hajj, with the name of Allah on his lips, think on the same lines as the old Wife of the Khan gone mad with jealousy? And thus the Lord can assume only one thing: the Holy Saiyid had been drawn into the network of court intrigues and is unable to disentangle himself. Alas! the serpent's smile which is accompanying the secretive baseness of the courtiers, could have been only adopted by the old man from them! This means that the sorcerers and witches, accompanying the Senior Wife and her entourage everywhere, have also placed the holy hermit at their mercy! Sorcery and witchcraft turned out to be more powerful than the prayers of the holy man, which were addressed directly to Allah!

A bitter sneer flashed across the Lord's face. He began to pity the old and god-fearing Saiyid, who also turned out to be helpless before the diabolic Sabbath of witches and sorceresses at the court of the Senior Wife of the Khan. Here not only a frail little old man, who is hanging on to dear life, is unable to withstand the onslaught, but even the Creator of the World, if He were not sitting in his mountainous heights, but would come down to earth and would mingle with the crowds of sinners, why, even the Almighty One would be bewildered and entangled in the intrigues and insidious temptations in the court of the Older Wife of the Khan. And it wouldn't be a surprise if the human race, which had originated from temptation, will perish from temptation as well.

If any given passion is temptation, and temptation is a sin, then the passion of ambition and passion of a spiritual love of power ae essentially also temptations. And therefore the old Saiyid, accustomed to the fact that people come from afar to visit him, to fall at his feet and to stroke his beard to be cleansed of sins, is himself committing the sin of ambition. He is seized by haughtiness from the fact that the Lord comes to see him in person to worship him and prostrates himself before him. Thus it would seem that both, the Lord and his spiritual teacher have a common sin of boundless ambition. He, the Lord, loves the power of rule, and gives free rein to his stern temper, and exactly the same holds for the Saiyid, who does not fall behind him an iota, despite his wisdom. And the fact that he had exhibited arrogance towards a man, who is noted by the special attention of Allah—all is a muddy swamp of sacrilege in which particularly vain people have become mired up to their waist. In response to the call by the demon and tempter Azazel, the people who respond to it had been for some time and hopelessly lost in the fog of mundane trivialities, and knowing this, the old hermit should have not shared the values, devoid of spirituality, of the court of the Senior Wife and her entourage. However, the Saiyid, is well informed about the fact that the successor to the throne will become someone among the sons of the Baybishe, the

Senior Wife, and is considering not only his current situation, but is also thinking about his future!

Not seeing a log of sinfulness in his eye, he seeks to point out a speck of sin in the eye of the Lord. For after all, it is stated in the Quran: "Man must know: Allah is One, no associates and partners has He...He neither begets nor is born, nor is there any equal to Him. He is but One on His throne, He has neither co-rulers nor descendants to His Kingdom. He is the One who had been before the beginning of time, and the One who shall be after its end... He rules over everything in heaven and on earth, on land and on water, He is the sole Master, and there are no other rulers and intercessors for Him. All human fate is in His hands: He is the only One who brings illness and who cures, who imparts life and who takes it away. But weak and insignificant are His creations—be they angels, prophets or animal creatures. Only He is the Almighty Power, and He is omniscient, all-knowing, and comprehending all that is hidden. And He alone is eternal and unfathomable."

Now if the Creator Himself has created this world erratic and unequal, with flaws and errors, what can be said about him, the Lord, and impute as sin his lack of perfection during his reign? If the Creator Himself, for all of the eighteen thousand worlds would not leave His rule, had created imperfectly, with faults and weaknesses, each living creature from each world, and as result of this imperfection of the creatures His own perfection achieves superiority over everyone and is ruling, why then is it forbidden for the Lord to rule over his empire, using the weaknesses of his subjects? Why condemn a human being for that when he is merely repeating errors made by the Creator? And if even Allah in Heaven must be wary of His downfall and the betrayal from some of His highest creations, how then could He not be wary of fomenters [of civil strife] and traitors here on earth? Or God's highest Providence is relevant amidst people only of separate exclusively chosen ones, rejecting all the other sons and daughters of mankind? The right to perform *miracles*, show great mercy, to send down punishment from Heaven—the Pantocrator reserved for Himself, and He is keeping a strict watch so that no one would encroach upon His deeds or would think of something that is known only to Him.

For the human race doubting the Creator's omnipotence and assuming some possible weakness of His, the Shariat promises an impending coming end of the world. And if it will come, what significance will all this have of which the small, holy old man accuses the Khan, and also whether this abhorrent azure minaret will remain protruding into the sky or will it be razed to the ground by the Lord, by this acknowledging himself to be a cuckold? What ravings, pitiful absurdity, trivial paltry passions!

No, neither Allah nor the aruakhs nor the holy ones or the prophets were able to help him—be it in deeds, revelations or prophetic words. That dream he had seen on the hunt turned to be prophetic. The Holy Black Stone, which had shunned his hands, was a sign that the Lord will not find a solution for his troubles. He wound up in a trap and there were no loopholes for his salvation. If the Pantocrator would now level the Great City to the ground, the capital of his empire, which he had built up throughout his life, cherished and decorated, the Lord would not have any regrets. Let the city's ruins sink in the waters of a new world-wide flood along with all the filthy gossip about him, and he would go down with them as well. It is only infinitely sad that the Great Allah, always favorably disposed towards him and rescuing him from all misfortunes, this time for some reason had definitively turned away from him.

This was the first time in his life that he regretted that due to his fate and the will of the Almighty One, he had become the great and proprietary Lord the world had ever known. In all the nearby and distant bounds no worthy enemies remained who could come and conquer the Great City of sin, weakened and rotted internally from verbiage and debauchery. Now even the narrow-eyed ones from the East, who sit behind their stone walls, will not dare to come. They sit silently and have frenzied dreams about the boundless western lands. But for some reason they have not been heard of for a very long period now, wouldn't it be time to go over there ourselves?

This thought about the distant eastern neighbors, insidious and mighty, had suddenly and totally seized the Lord. He had nurtured this plan of conquest and seizure of this great country for a long time, and now time had come to implement it. Enough of breaking up from one's own weakness, one needs to move forward immediately on a campaign. One needs to have a good blood bath in order to properly shake up the ignorant masses, who have fed themselves and gotten fat, lazy and due to their over-satiation have accumulated foul-smelling winds from their bellies, and one needs to give them the opportunity to rid themselves of such. That bloody harvest which neither Allah nor the enemy did not accomplish, he shall organize himself. This innumerous stinking rabble, which one can't slaughter one-by-one, he will induce to go with him to this carnage, and then he'll return after decimating it by the thousands in the war. And those who survived and remained alive will not be capable of gossip. On the contrary, for the fact that they survived, they will be thankful not to the Creator, but to their own great military leader, Amir, and they shall deify him.

The Lord decided to begin his campaign immediately.

6

They left the river behind them. The crowds, lining the riverbank along the caravan road and staring at the passing army, began to thin evermore. Soon all the people were left behind. The army stepped upon their unknown road of fate. Gradually, the brown autumn steppe changed to a grey and sandy desert. Above the desert the scorching air was swaying and a suffocating, baking and intense heat prevailed. The cavalry proceeded, with their horses' ankles sinking in the blistering sand. The sun at its zenith had shortened the horsemen's shadows to such an extent that each shadow was nearly invisible, and it seemed that the desert had swallowed all shadows and is now getting ready to do likewise to the very horsemen as well. The torrid wind intensified. Without hesitation, the fiery wind penetrated the Khan's carriage. Breathing became a task which was more than one could bear. Seeking to get even a mere gulp of fresh air, the Lord pulled back the carriage's window curtain and stuck his head outside. His eyes were confronted by a monotonous grey and blinding desert. Groups of flat dunes were spread out along it, as if they were liquid molten lead. It seemed as if the horses were floating in the quivering air and running unsteadily. Some tiny bird which had strayed from its flock flew, skipping along with the Khan's carriage, seeking shelter in its short shadow.

The Lord cocked his hawk's eyes, looking curiously at the little bird. And all of a sudden he perceived that no one in this world was more close to him than this orphaned tiny bird. What a bitter strange thing could be seen in the attempts of this small bird to survive in this horrid hell of the desert! Its diminutive beak is wide open, petite tongue protruding, and its chest is pulsing alarmingly, tremoring. It is cheeping and chirping, terrified and trying to save itself from the fire-spewing dragon of the desert. Throughout this, nature's elements of living there is no other reason than this pitiful, desperate desire to save oneself, to survive, to hang on to life to the very last moment. Everything else beyond that is excess, coming from the wily shaytan. The more excesses, the closer one is brought to shaytan. Strange as it may seem, the initial source of the hellish desert wind is the gentle and cool breeze, the zephyr, of the mountain wind, is it not so? Chaste and pure like an angel, the clear wind swoops down into the valley in order to cleanse the world of the dust and debris, of the dry leaves and blades of grass, but soon after, continuing to fill with the stormy strength of the swirls of the steppe, unnoticed, had turned into a fire-spewing dragon, flying across the desert, scorching everything along its path to ashes... Here, with the orphaned bird, the dragon had already singed its little wings, scalded and blistered its tiny feet, and was preparing to rob it of its last breath. Unable to watch the small bird about to perish, writhing and fluttering its wings, the tiny bird, the sole living being close to him, the Khan drew the window shade shut and leaned back into his seat.

The fiery sun, which was scorching the desert, as if it were a carcass of a slaughtered wild sheep, reached the body of the Lord, as well. He became so steaming hot in his clothes that he almost suffocated and could not even move, as if an entire gang of henchmen was sitting on top of him, seeking to choke him to death right here in his carriage. In his delirious state he imagined that hundreds of angels of death had surrounded him in a heavenly circle dance and chorus singing, demanding that he open his mortal vessel's chest and present them with his soul. So, this must be why his favorite ring had slipped off his finger at the river crossing! A signal had been given to him that he would not return alive from this campaign... But the most dreadful inevitable omen had been that at the very beginning of the campaign he had met that man, whom he least of all wanted to meet in his life.

...Before the Lord's eyes remained the persistent face of the eyeless blind man. Instead of his eyes—two black holes. But it had been the familiar, unforgettable large receding forehead and the sharp cheekbones of the man of the steppes...

It had been at the ford by the river that this man was standing on a small two-wheeled cart, squeezed in between the *arba*-wagons at the edge of the road, but suddenly he appeared in the Khan's carriage facing him now.

Since that time when he had lost his huge, mysterious eyes, in their stead were now two horrible black holes, and his face had forever lost its kind, humane radiance. Nothing remained of his former enchanting youth, natural beauty or spirituality. All of it had vanished without a trace, and in his empty eye sockets appeared to be the Demon of Death himself, looking out at him. The man was a frightful sight, his neck was repugnantly elongated raising the blind man's chin up high, his nostrils were turned inside out inhaling the air and probing the space before him… Here he bent forward as if wishing to approach the Lord as close as possible. But not one muscle moved on the paralyzed face of the eyeless man, which resembled a stone mask. Now he neither feared the thousands of soldiers of the Lord, nor the threatening hordes of his guards. And he no longer shall have fear and trepidation when the name of the Lord is mentioned, which in all the languages of his infinitely huge empire sounds like a threatening clang of steel blades. The bony hands with bent fingers of the blind man reached forward, ready to close in on the Lord's throat.

"Have no fear," a hoarse voice sounded. "Sooner or later you will wind up under the ground anyway."

The Lord was not frightened, he was shocked. How could this be? The young man had had his tongue cut out! The Khan had been present when the executioner, in whose hand a knife was shining, threw down on the floor of the cell that piece of bloody human flesh. So how and from where could this horrifying voice be coming from? Or had it been the power of Providence returning to the architect his voice? But is it likely that this voice is the voice of the Lord himself, which sounds within his suffocating, like the desert, infinite loneliness?

His eyes bulged, his mouth opened wide—he was falling flat on his back, and he was able to see yet how on the face of the disfigured blind man a harsh and venomous smile froze. The Lord perceived how under him a shifting quagmire was forming, which was engulfing his body, pulling it somewhere into a broiling liquid abyss. He began to grope the air with his hands, as if he wanted to paddle with them and swim. His strength left him, his legs and arms had become numb, filled with an ominous heaviness.

He regained consciousness and opened his eyes. He was slowly recovering his sense of reality. Inside the carriage the air was as hot as a scorching frying pan. As he had fallen into his unconscious state, he had buried himself deeply in a down blanket, from which heat was being emitted. With great effort, the Khan raised his head, inside the carriage he was once again alone, no blind man with a head disfigured by executioners was visible anywhere. Only now did the Amir realize that this had been a nightmarish delirium, and that the murderous desert heat, merging with a feeling of a hopeless loneliness in his soul, had brought forth an abnormal vision of an eyeless apparition. For all of this—the blinded architect from the crossing, and the boiling hellish kettles, and the sinister devil incarnate—all these were neither messengers nor Angels of Death, but rather the delusion of his fears and suffering, the morose fruits of his sick imagination. But with a clear mind and a sober realization, he now understood to what an irreparable misfortune and inescapable guilt his life was doomed, for this would become the reason for his ruination.

The unbearable, intense heat was making him dizzy and leading him into a state of semi-consciousness. The apparition in front of him is the very same infinite desert. The humpbacked sand dunes, lying down for their eternal rest, marked up with enigmatic *vyaz* of mysterious characters. Squinting in the sun, straining his waning eyesight, he attempts to decipher the sandy vyaz swept in by the wind. And, at long last, the meaning of these elaborate inscriptions had finally become clear to him: *Traveler! Your road will end underground, anyway.*

Once again, he opened his eyes wide. In front of him, something blurry and dark appeared, with large clumps hanging from it. Yet now he is no longer able to determine his location – is he resting in the tent of his gilded Khan's carriage, or is he laying down, thrown to the ground in one of the solitary confinement cells, in the damp and confining zindan, which had once been built in accordance with his wishes...

GLOSSARY OF KAZAKH WORDS

Adyraspan – *Peganum harmala* plant, also known as Wild Rue.

Arba – A type of cart.

Argamak – A breed of horses indigenous to Central Asia.

Aruakh – Mythical ancestral spirits.

Askehr – Turkic soldiers.

Aul – Village.

Bahsi – Traditional spiritual medic; shaman.

Batyr – Men of courage, war hero.

Baybishe – The main, older wife.

Beks – Emir, Prince.

Bey – Local chief

Chador – A large piece of cloth that is wrapped around the head and upper body, leaving only the face exposed.

Chapan – A coat worn over clothes, usually during the winter.

Chetki-Tazbikh – Prayer-beads.

Dastarkhan – A traditional space where food is eaten, "great spread".

Dauilpaz – Kazakh national drum, stretched on both sides with leather.

Dekhan – A peasant.

Dermene – *Artemisia Cina* plant.

Djigit – A skillful or brave man, oftentimes an equestrian.

Dinar – A type of currency, coin.

Divan – State Council.

Dutar – A traditional Central Asian long-necked two-string lute.

Duval – A fence made of clay and straw.

Dzhugary – Grain of the Durra plant.

Giaour – Ethnic slur used by Muslims to denote those of Non-Muslim origin.

Hazret – An honorific Arabic title, literally meaning "Presence".

Houriss – Lovely, doe-eyed women.

Inshallah – God-Willing

Kafir – Non-Muslim settlers of Nuristan Region.

Kamcha – A type of short whip.

Karnay – A traditional trumpet that is very long and thin.

Kazi – an Islamic legal scholar or judge.

Khansha – The wife of a Khan.

Khanzada – Son of Khan, prince.

Khauz – Water-basin, pool of water, sometimes with a fountain.

Korzhun – A traditional bag used for transporting goods.

Khazret – High-Priest of the court.

Kishlak – Rural settlement of semi-nomadic peoples; "wintering place".

Koumiss – A fermented dairy product made from mare's milk.

Kumgan – A ceramic or metal vessel for water.

Kurgan – A hill, oftentimes also functioning as a burial mound.

Kylkobyz – Ancient Kazakh string instrument, owned by shamans and Bahshi.

Madrasah – College for Islamic Instruction.

Mahallah – Sub-division of a city, self-ruled.

Minaret – The tower of a Mosque.

Minbar – A set of steps used as a platform by a preacher in a Mosque.

Muezzin – A man who call Muslims to prayer from the Minaret.

Naizager – Master spear-bearer.

Namaz – Muslim prayer.

Nuker – A type of soldier, personal guard.

Qadi – A magistrate or judge in a Sharia court.

Padishah – A superlative royal title, literally "Great King".

Parandja – A traditional Central Asian robe for women, which shrouds
the entire head and body.

Ruku – Bowing down while in a standing position, during recitation
of the Qu'ran.

Salwar – Loose pants, a component of the traditional outfit.

Samovar – Heated metal container used to boil water.

Samsa – A type of meat-filled pastry.

Samuryk-Simurgh – A benevolent mythical flying creature.

Sarbaz – Imperial guards.

Saukele – A traditional, tall, heavily ornamented headdress of a bride.

Saxaul – A type of tree that grows in the desert.

Shanrak – A type of circular metallic structure that is located at the top
of a yurt to let sunlight in, allows smoke to escape; also a
family reliquary, represents continuation of a bloodline,
much like a family crest.

Shaytan – The Devil, Satan.

Shelpek – Traditional Kazakh flatbread.

Sirnay – The Kazakh national reed wind musical instrument.

Surah – A passage from the Qu'ran.

Surpa – A broth made from lamb.

Taksir – A Lord.

Talaq – A phrase meaning "I divorce you", reconciliation is possible
after the first two times it is uttered by the husband, yet once it

is uttered a third time, the divorce is final.

Tandyr – A traditional oven used to bake bread and other food.

Tobet – Central-Asian shepherd dog.

Tokal – Younger wife.

Toy – A festive celebration.

Tugai – Riparian forest or woodland.

Tulpar – Winged horse of Tatar-Mongol mythology, akin to Pegasus.

Tumen – Nomadic soldiers.

Ustad – Honorific title used for teachers, masters and artists.

Vyaz – Cyrillic calligraphy.

Yurt – A portable round tent covered with skins or felt, used by Nomads in Central-Asian steppes.

Zam Zam – A well located in Mecca, 20 miles east of the Kaaba.

Zhenge – The wife of the eldest brother.

Zindan – An underground dungeon.

Zulhijja – The 12th month in the Islamic calendar.

End of the Legend •Abish Kekılbaev